THE
THRONE
OF FIRE

Books by Rick Riordan

The Percy Jackson series:
PERCY JACKSON AND THE LIGHTNING THIEF
PERCY JACKSON AND THE SEA OF MONSTERS
PERCY JACKSON AND THE TITAN'S CURSE
PERCY JACKSON AND THE BATTLE OF THE LABYRINTH
PERCY JACKSON AND THE LAST OLYMPIAN
PERCY JACKSON: THE DEMIGOD FILES

The Heroes of Olympus series:
THE LOST HERO

The Kane Chronicles series:
THE RED PYRAMID
THE THRONE OF FIRE

RICK RIORDAN

THE
THRONE
OF FIRE

PUFFIN

PUFFIN BOOKS

Published by the Penguin Group
Penguin Books Ltd, 80 Strand, London WC2R 0RL, England
Penguin Group (USA) Inc., 375 Hudson Street, New York, New York 10014, USA
Penguin Group (Canada), 90 Eglinton Avenue East, Suite 700, Toronto, Ontario, Canada M4P 2Y3
(a division of Pearson Penguin Canada Inc.)
Penguin Ireland, 25 St Stephen's Green, Dublin 2, Ireland (a division of Penguin Books Ltd)
Penguin Group (Australia), 250 Camberwell Road, Camberwell, Victoria 3124, Australia
(a division of Pearson Australia Group Pty Ltd)
Penguin Books India Pvt Ltd, 11 Community Centre, Panchsheel Park, New Delhi – 110 017, India
Penguin Group (NZ), 67 Apollo Drive, Rosedale, Auckland 0632, New Zealand
(a division of Pearson New Zealand Ltd)
Penguin Books (South Africa) (Pty) Ltd, 24 Sturdee Avenue, Rosebank,
Johannesburg 2196, South Africa

Penguin Books Ltd, Registered Offices: 80 Strand, London WC2R 0RL, England

puffinbooks.com

First published in the USA by Hyperion Books for Children, an imprint of Disney Book Group, 2011
Published simultaneously in Great Britain in Puffin Books 2011
001 – 10 9 8 7 6 5 4 3 2 1

Text copyright © Rick Riordan, 2011
Hieroglyph art by Michelle Gengaro-Kokmen
Composition by Brad Walrod
All rights reserved

The moral right of the author and illustrator has been asserted

Set in Goudy Old Style
Printed in Great Britain by Clays Ltd, St Ives plc

British Library Cataloguing in Publication Data
A CIP catalogue record for this book is available from the British Library

HARDBACK
ISBN: 978-0-141-33565-0

TRADE PAPERBACK
ISBN: 978-0-141-33566-7

www.greenpenguin.co.uk

*For Conner and Maggie, the Riordan
family's great brother-sister team*

Contents

CONTENTS

WARNING

This is a transcript of an audio recording. Carter and Sadie Kane first made themselves known in a recording I received last year, which I transcribed as The Red Pyramid. *This second audio file arrived at my residence shortly after that book was published, so I can only assume the Kanes trust me enough to continue relaying their story. If this second recording is a truthful account, the turn of events can only be described as alarming. For the sake of the Kanes, and for the world, I hope what follows is fiction. Otherwise we are all in very serious trouble.*

1. Fun with Spontaneous Combustion

Look, we don't have time for long introductions. I need to tell this story quickly, or we're all going to die.

If you didn't listen to our first recording, well...pleased to meet you: the Egyptian gods are running around loose in the modern world; a bunch of magicians called the House of Life is trying to stop them; everyone hates Sadie and me; and a big snake is about to swallow the sun and destroy the world.

[Ow! What was that for?]

Sadie just punched me. She says I'm going to scare you too much. I should back up, calm down and start at the beginning.

Fine. But, personally, I think you *should* be scared.

The point of this recording is to let you know what's really happening and how things went wrong. You're going to hear a lot of people talking trash about us, but we didn't cause those deaths. As for the snake, that wasn't our fault either.

1

Well…not exactly. All the magicians in the world *have* to come together. It's our only chance.

So here's the story. Decide for yourself. It started when we set Brooklyn on fire.

The job was supposed to be simple: sneak into the Brooklyn Museum, borrow a particular Egyptian artefact and leave without getting caught.

No, it wasn't robbery. We would have returned the artefact eventually. But I guess we did look suspicious: four kids in black ninja clothes on the roof of the museum. Oh, and a baboon, also dressed like a ninja. *Definitely* suspicious.

The first thing we did was send our trainees Jaz and Walt to open the side window, while Khufu, Sadie and I examined the big glass dome in the middle of the roof, which was supposed to be our exit strategy.

Our exit strategy wasn't looking too good.

It was well after dark, and the museum was supposed to be closed. Instead, the glass dome glowed with light. Inside, forty feet below, hundreds of people in tuxedos and evening gowns mingled and danced in a ballroom the size of an airplane hangar. An orchestra played, but with the wind howling in my ears and my teeth chattering I couldn't hear the music. I was freezing in my linen pyjamas.

Magicians are supposed to wear linen because it doesn't interfere with magic, which is probably a great tradition in the Egyptian desert, where it's hardly ever cold and rainy. In Brooklyn, in March – not so much.

My sister, Sadie, didn't seem bothered by the cold. She

was undoing the locks on the dome while humming along to something on her iPod. I mean, seriously – who brings their own tunes to a museum break-in?

She was dressed in clothes like mine except she wore combat boots. Her dyed blonde hair was streaked with red highlights – very subtle for a stealth mission. With her blue eyes and her light complexion, she looks absolutely nothing like me, which we both agree is fine. It's always nice to have the option of denying that the crazy girl next to me is my sister.

'You said the museum would be empty,' I complained.

Sadie didn't hear me until I pulled out her earbuds and repeated myself.

'Well, it was *supposed* to be empty.' She'll deny this, but after living in the States for the last three months she was starting to lose her British accent. 'The website said it closed at five. How was I to know there'd be a wedding?'

A wedding? I looked down and saw that Sadie was right. Some of the ladies wore peach-coloured bridesmaid dresses. One of the tables had a massive tiered white cake. Two separate mobs of guests had lifted the bride and groom on chairs and were carrying them through the room while their friends swirled around them, dancing and clapping. The whole thing looked like a head-on furniture collision waiting to happen.

Khufu tapped on the glass. Even in his black clothes, it was hard for him to blend into the shadows with his golden fur, not to mention his rainbow-coloured nose and rear end.

'*Agh!*' he grunted.

Since he was a baboon, that could've meant anything from

Look, there's food down there to *This glass is dirty* to *Hey, those people are doing stupid things with chairs.*

'Khufu's right,' Sadie interpreted. 'We'll have a hard time sneaking out through the party. Perhaps if we pretend we're a maintenance crew –'

'Sure,' I said. '"Excuse us. Four kids coming through with a three-ton statue. Just going to float it up through the roof. Don't mind us."'

Sadie rolled her eyes. She pulled out her wand – a curved length of ivory carved with pictures of monsters – and pointed it at the base of the dome. A golden hieroglyph blazed, and the last padlock popped open.

'Well, if we're not going to use this as an exit,' she said, 'why am I opening it? Couldn't we just come out the way we're going in – through the side window?'

'I told you. The statue is *huge.* It won't fit through the side window. Plus, the traps –'

'Try again tomorrow night, then?' she asked.

I shook my head. 'Tomorrow the whole exhibit is being boxed up and shipped off on tour.'

She raised her eyebrows in that annoying way she has. 'Perhaps if someone had given us more *notice* that we needed to steal this statue –'

'Forget it.' I could tell where this conversation was going, and it wasn't going to help if Sadie and I argued on the roof all night. She was right, of course. I hadn't given her much notice. But, hey – my sources weren't exactly reliable. After weeks of asking for help, I'd finally got a tip from my buddy the falcon war god Horus, speaking in my dreams: *Oh, by the way, that artefact you wanted? The one that might hold the key to saving the planet? It's been sitting down the street in the Brooklyn Museum for the last thirty years, but tomorrow it leaves for Europe, so you'd better hurry! You'll have five days to figure out how to use it, or we're all doomed. Good luck!*

I could've screamed at him for not telling me sooner, but it wouldn't have made any difference. Gods only talk when they're ready, and they don't have a good sense of mortal time. I knew this because Horus had shared space in my head a few months ago. I still had some of his antisocial habits – like the occasional urge to hunt small furry rodents or challenge people to the death.

'Let's just stick to the plan,' Sadie said. 'Go in through the side window, find the statue and float it out through the ballroom. We'll figure out how to deal with the wedding party when we get that far. Maybe create a diversion.'

I frowned. 'A diversion?'

'Carter, you worry too much,' she said. 'It'll be brilliant. Unless you have another idea?'

The problem was – I didn't.

You'd think magic would make things easier. In fact, it usually made things more complicated. There were always a million reasons why this or that spell wouldn't work in certain situations. Or there'd be other magic thwarting you – like the protective spells on this museum.

We weren't sure who had cast them. Maybe one of the museum staff was an undercover magician, which wouldn't have been uncommon. Our own dad had used his PhD in Egyptology as a cover to gain access to artefacts. Plus, the

Brooklyn Museum has the largest collection of Egyptian magic scrolls in the world. That's why our uncle Amos had located his headquarters in Brooklyn. A lot of magicians might have reasons to guard or booby-trap the museum's treasures.

Whatever the case, the doors and windows had some pretty nasty curses on them. We couldn't open a magic portal into the exhibit, nor could we use our retrieval *shabti* – the magical clay statues that served us in our library – to bring us the artefact we needed.

We'd have to get in and get out the hard way; and if we made a mistake there was no telling what sort of curse we'd unleash: monster guardians, plagues, fires, exploding donkeys (don't laugh; they're bad news).

The only exit that wasn't booby-trapped was the dome at the top of the ballroom. Apparently the museum's guardians hadn't been worried about thieves levitating artefacts out of an opening forty feet in the air. Or maybe the dome *was* trapped, and it was just too well hidden for us to see.

Either way, we had to try. We only had tonight to steal – sorry, *borrow* – the artefact. Then we had five days to figure out how to use it. I just love deadlines.

'So we push on and improvise?' Sadie asked.

I looked down at the wedding party, hoping we weren't about to ruin their special night. 'Guess so.'

'Lovely,' Sadie said. 'Khufu, stay here and keep watch. Open the dome when you see us coming up, yeah?'

'*Agh!*' said the baboon.

The back of my neck tingled. I had a feeling this heist was *not* going to be lovely.

'Come on,' I told Sadie. 'Let's see how Jaz and Walt are doing.'

We dropped to the ledge outside the third floor, which housed the Egyptian collection.

Jaz and Walt had done their work perfectly. They'd duct-taped four Sons of Horus statues around the edges of the window and painted hieroglyphs on the glass to counteract the curses and the mortal alarm system.

As Sadie and I landed next to them, they seemed to be in the middle of a serious conversation. Jaz was holding Walt's hands. That surprised me, but it surprised Sadie even more. She made a squeaking sound like a mouse getting stepped on.

[Oh yes, you did. I was *there*.]

Why would Sadie care? Okay, right after New Year's, when Sadie and I sent out our *djed* amulet beacon to attract kids with magic potential to our headquarters, Jaz and Walt had been the first to respond. They'd been training with us for seven weeks, longer than any of the other kids, so we'd got to know them pretty well.

Jaz was a cheerleader from Nashville. Her name was short for Jasmine, but don't ever call her that unless you want to get turned into a shrub. She was pretty in a blonde cheerleader kind of way – not really my type – but you couldn't help liking her because she was nice to everyone and always ready to help. She had a talent for healing magic, too, so she was a great person to bring along in case something went wrong, which happened with Sadie and me about ninety-nine percent of the time.

Tonight she'd covered her hair in a black bandanna. Slung

7

across her shoulder was her magician's bag, marked with the symbol of the lion goddess Sekhmet.

She was just telling Walt, 'We'll figure it out,' when Sadie and I dropped down next to them.

Walt looked embarrassed.

He was...well, how do I describe Walt?

[No thanks, Sadie. I'm not going to describe him as *hot*. Wait your turn.]

Walt was fourteen, same as me, but he was tall enough to play basketball. He had the right build for it – lean and muscular – and the dude's feet were huge. His skin was coffee-bean brown, a little darker than mine, and his hair was buzz cut so that it looked like a shadow on his scalp. Despite the cold, he was dressed in a black sleeveless tee and workout shorts – not standard magician clothes – but nobody argued with Walt. He'd been our first trainee to arrive – all the way from Seattle – and the guy was a natural *sau* – a charm maker. He wore a bunch of gold neck chains with magic amulets he'd made himself.

Anyway, I was pretty sure Sadie was jealous of Jaz and liked Walt, though she'd never admit it because she'd spent the last few months moping about another guy – actually a god – she had a crush on.

[Yeah, fine, Sadie. I'll drop it for now. But I notice you're not denying it.]

When we interrupted their conversation, Walt let go of Jaz's hands real quick and stepped away. Sadie's eyes moved back and forth between them, trying to figure out what was going on.

Walt cleared his throat. 'Window's ready.'

'Brilliant.' Sadie looked at Jaz. 'What did you mean, "We'll figure it out"?'

Jaz flapped her mouth like a fish trying to breathe.

Walt answered for her: 'You know. The Book of Ra. We'll figure it out.'

'Yes!' Jaz said. 'The Book of Ra.'

I could tell they were lying, but I figured it was none of my business if they liked each other. We didn't have time for drama.

'Okay,' I said before Sadie could demand a better explanation. 'Let's start the fun.'

The window swung open easily. No magic explosions. No alarms. I breathed a sigh of relief and stepped into the Egyptian wing, wondering if maybe we had a shot at pulling this off, after all.

The Egyptian artefacts brought back all kinds of memories. Until last year, I'd spent most of my life travelling around the world with my dad as he went from museum to museum, lecturing on Ancient Egypt. That was before I knew he was a magician – before he unleashed a bunch of gods, and our lives got complicated.

Now I couldn't look at Egyptian artwork without feeling a personal connection. I shuddered when we passed a statue of Horus – the falcon-headed god who'd inhabited my body last Christmas. We walked by a sarcophagus, and I remembered how the evil god Set had imprisoned our father in a golden coffin at the British Museum. Everywhere there were pictures of Osiris, the blue-skinned god of the dead, and I thought about how Dad had sacrificed himself to become Osiris's new host. Right now, somewhere in the magic realm of the Duat, our dad was the king of the underworld. I can't even describe how weird it felt seeing a five-thousand-year-old painting of some blue Egyptian god and thinking, 'Yep, that's my dad.'

All the artefacts seemed like family mementos: a wand just like Sadie's; a picture of the serpent leopards that had once attacked us; a page from the Book of the Dead showing demons we'd met in person. Then there were the *shabti*, magical figurines that were supposed to come to life when summoned. A few months ago, I'd fallen for a girl named Zia Rashid, who'd turned out to be a *shabti*.

Falling in love for the first time had been hard enough. But when the girl you like turns out to be ceramic and cracks to pieces before your eyes – well, it gives 'breaking your heart' a new meaning.

We made our way through the first room, passing under a big Egyptian-style zodiac mural on the ceiling. I could hear the celebration going on in the grand ballroom down the hallway to our right. Music and laughter echoed through the building.

In the second Egyptian room, we stopped in front of a stone frieze the size of a garage door. Chiselled into the rock was a picture of a monster trampling some humans.

'Is that a griffin?' Jaz asked.

I nodded. 'The Egyptian version, yeah.'

The animal had a lion's body and the head of a falcon,

but its wings weren't like most griffin pictures you see. Instead of bird wings, the monster's wings ran across the top of its back – long, horizontal and bristly like a pair of upside-down steel brushes. If the monster could've flown with those things at all, I figured they must've moved like a butterfly's wings. The frieze had once been painted. I could make out flecks of red and gold on the creature's hide, but even without colour the griffin looked eerily lifelike. Its beady eyes seemed to follow me.

'Griffins were protectors,' I said, remembering something my dad had once told me. 'They guarded treasures and stuff.'

'Fab,' Sadie said. 'So you mean they attacked...oh, *thieves*, for instance, breaking into museums and stealing artefacts?'

'It's just a frieze,' I said. But I doubt that made anyone feel better. Egyptian magic was all about turning words and pictures into reality.

'There.' Walt pointed across the room. 'That's it, right?'

We made a wide arc around the griffin and walked over to a statue in the centre of the room.

The god stood about eight feet tall. He was carved from black stone and dressed in typical Egyptian style: bare-chested, with a kilt and sandals. He had the face of a ram and horns that had partially broken off over the centuries. On his head was a frisbee-shaped crown – a sun disc, braided with serpents. In front of him stood a much smaller human figure. The god was holding his hands over the little dude's head, as though giving him a blessing.

Sadie squinted at the hieroglyphic inscription. Ever since

she'd hosted the spirit of Isis, goddess of magic, Sadie had had an uncanny ability to read hieroglyphs.

'KNM,' she read. 'That'd be pronounced *Khnum*, I suppose. Rhymes with *ka-boom?*'

'Yeah,' I agreed. 'This is the statue we need. Horus told me it holds the secret to finding the Book of Ra.'

Unfortunately, Horus hadn't been very specific. Now that we'd found the statue, I had absolutely no idea how it was supposed to help us. I scanned the hieroglyphs, hoping for a clue.

'Who's the little guy in front?' Walt asked. 'A child?'

Jaz snapped her fingers. 'No, I remember this! Khnum made humans on a potter's wheel. That's what he's doing here, I bet – forming a human out of clay.'

She looked at me for confirmation. The truth was I'd forgotten that story myself. Sadie and I were supposed to be the teachers, but Jaz often remembered more details than I did.

'Yeah, good,' I said. 'Man out of clay. Exactly.'

Sadie frowned up at Khnum's ram head. 'Looks a bit like that old cartoon... Bullwinkle, is it? Could be the moose god.'

'He's not the moose god,' I said.

'But if we're looking for the Book of Ra,' she said, 'and Ra's the *sun* god, then why are we searching a moose?'

Sadie can be annoying. Did I mention that?

'Khnum was one aspect of the sun god,' I said. 'Ra had three different personalities. He was Khepri the scarab god in the morning; Ra during the day; and Khnum, the ram-headed god, at sunset, when he went into the underworld.'

"That's confusing,' Jaz said.

'Not really,' Sadie said. 'Carter has different personalities. He goes from zombie in the morning to slug in the afternoon to –'

'Sadie,' I said, 'shut up.'

Walt scratched his chin. 'I think Sadie's right. It's a moose.'

'*Thank* you,' Sadie said.

Walt gave her a grudging smile, but he still looked preoccupied, like something was bothering him. I caught Jaz studying him with a worried expression, and I wondered what they'd been talking about earlier.

'Enough with the moose,' I said. 'We've got to get this statue back to Brooklyn House. It holds some sort of clue –'

'But how do we find it?' Walt asked. 'And you still haven't told us why we need this Book of Ra so badly.'

I hesitated. There were a lot of things we hadn't told our trainees yet, not even Walt and Jaz – like how the world might end in five days. That kind of thing can distract you from your training.

'I'll explain when we get back,' I promised. 'Right now, let's figure out how to move the statue.'

Jaz knitted her eyebrows. 'I don't think it's going to fit in my bag.'

'Oh, such worrying,' Sadie said. 'Look, we cast a levitation spell on the statue. We create some big diversion to clear the ballroom –'

'Hold up.' Walt leaned forward and examined the smaller human figure. The little dude was smiling, like being fashioned out of clay was awesome fun. 'He's wearing an amulet. A scarab.'

'It's a common symbol,' I said.

'Yeah...' Walt fingered his own collection of amulets. 'But the scarab is a symbol of Ra's rebirth, right? And this statue shows Khnum creating a new life. Maybe we don't need the entire statue. Maybe the clue is –'

'Ah!' Sadie pulled out her wand. 'Brilliant.'

I was about to say, 'Sadie, no!' but of course that would've been pointless. Sadie never listens to me.

She tapped the little dude's amulet. Khnum's hands glowed. The smaller statue's head peeled open in four sections like the top of a missile silo, and sticking out of its neck was a yellowed papyrus scroll.

'*Voila*,' Sadie said proudly.

She slipped her wand into her bag and grabbed the scroll just as I shouted, 'It might be trapped!'

Like I said, she never listens.

As soon as she plucked the scroll from the statue, the entire room rumbled. Cracks appeared in the glass display cases.

Sadie yelped as the scroll in her hand burst into flames. They didn't seem to consume the papyrus or hurt Sadie, but when she tried to shake out the fire ghostly white flames leaped to the nearest display case and raced around the room as if following a trail of gasoline. The fire touched the windows and white hieroglyphs ignited on the glass, probably triggering a ton of protective wards and curses. Then the ghost fire rippled across the big frieze at the entrance of the room. The stone slab shook violently. I couldn't see the carvings on the other side, but I heard a raspy scream – like a really large, really angry parrot.

Walt slipped his staff off his back. Sadie waved the flaming scroll as if it were stuck to her hand. 'Get this thing off me! This is *so* not my fault!'

'*Um* . . .' Jaz pulled her wand. 'What was that sound?'

My heart sank.

'I think,' I said, 'Sadie just found her big diversion.'

2. We Tame a Seven-thousand-pound Hummingbird

A FEW MONTHS AGO, things would've been different. Sadie could've spoken a single word and caused a military-grade explosion. I could've encased myself in a magical combat avatar, and almost nothing would've been able to defeat me.

But that was when we were fully merged with the gods – Horus for me, Isis for Sadie. We'd given up that power because it was simply too dangerous. Until we had better control of our own abilities, embodying Egyptian gods could make us go crazy or literally burn us up.

Now all we had was our own limited magic. That made it harder to do important stuff – like survive when a monster came to life and wanted to kill us.

The griffin stepped into full view. It was twice the size of a regular lion, its reddish-gold fur coated with limestone dust. Its tail was studded with spiky feathers that looked as hard and sharp as daggers. With a single flick, it pulverized the stone slab it had come from. Its bristly wings were now straight up on its back. When the griffin moved, they fluttered so fast, they blurred and buzzed like the wings of the world's largest, most vicious hummingbird.

The griffin fixed its hungry eyes on Sadie. White flames still engulfed her hand and the scroll, and the griffin seemed to take that as some kind of challenge. I'd heard a lot of falcon cries – hey, I'd *been* a falcon once or twice – but when this thing opened its beak it let loose a screech that rattled the windows and set my hair on end.

'Sadie,' I said, 'drop the scroll.'

'Hello? It's stuck to my hand!' she protested. 'And I'm on fire! Did I mention that?'

Patches of ghost fire were burning across all the windows and artefacts now. The scroll seemed to have triggered every reservoir of Egyptian magic in the room, and I was pretty sure that was bad. Walt and Jaz stood frozen in shock. I suppose I couldn't blame them. This was their first real monster.

The griffin took a step towards my sister.

I stood shoulder to shoulder with her and did the one magic trick I still had down. I reached into the Duat and pulled my sword out of thin air – an Egyptian *khopesh* with a wickedly sharp hook-shaped blade.

Sadie looked pretty silly with her hand and scroll on fire, like an overenthusiastic Statue of Liberty, but with her free hand she managed to summon her main offensive weapon – a five-foot-long staff carved with hieroglyphs.

Sadie asked, 'Any hints on fighting griffins?'

'Avoid the sharp parts?' I guessed.

'Brilliant. Thanks for that.'

'Walt,' I called. 'Check those windows. See if you can open them.'

'B-but they're cursed.'

'Yes,' I said. 'And if we try to exit through the ballroom, the griffin will eat us before we get there.'

'I'll check the windows.'

'Jaz,' I said, 'help Walt.'

'Those markings on the glass,' Jaz muttered. 'I – I've seen them before –'

'Just do it!' I said.

The griffin lunged, its wings buzzing like chain saws. Sadie threw her staff, and it morphed into a tiger in midair, slamming into the griffin with its claws unsheathed.

The griffin was not impressed. It knocked the tiger aside, then lashed out with unnatural speed, opening its beak impossibly wide. SNAP. The griffin gulped and burped, and the tiger was gone.

'That was my favourite staff!' Sadie cried.

The griffin turned its eyes on me.

I gripped my sword tight. The blade began to glow. I wished I still had Horus's voice inside my head, egging me on. Having a personal war god makes it easier to do stupidly brave things.

'Walt!' I called. 'How's it coming with that window?'

'Trying it now,' he said.

'H-hold on,' Jaz said nervously. 'Those are symbols of Sekhmet. Walt, stop!'

Then a lot of things happened at once. Walt opened the window, and a wave of white fire roared over him, knocking him to the floor.

Jaz ran to his side. The griffin immediately lost interest in me. Like any good predator, it focused on the moving target – Jaz – and lunged at her.

I charged after it. But instead of snapping up our friends the griffin soared straight over Walt and Jaz and slammed into the window. Jaz pulled Walt out of the way while the griffin went crazy, thrashing and biting at the white flames.

It was trying to *attack* the fire. The griffin snapped at the air. It spun, knocking over a display case of *shabti*. Its tail smashed a sarcophagus to pieces.

I'm not sure what possessed me, but I yelled, 'Stop it!'

The griffin froze. It turned towards me, cawing in irritation. A curtain of white fire raced away and burned in the corner of the room, almost like it was regrouping. Then I noticed other fires coming together, forming burning shapes that were vaguely human. One looked right at me, and I sensed an unmistakable aura of malice.

'Carter, keep its attention.' Sadie apparently hadn't noticed the fiery shapes. Her eyes were still fixed on the griffin as she pulled a length of magic twine from her pocket. 'If I can just get close enough –'

'Sadie, wait.' I tried to process what was going on. Walt was flat on his back, shivering. His eyes were glowing white, as if the fire had got inside him. Jaz knelt over him, muttering a healing spell.

'*RAAAWK!*' The griffin croaked plaintively as if asking permission – as if it was *obeying* my order to stop, but didn't like it.

The fiery shapes were getting brighter, more solid. I counted seven blazing figures, slowly forming legs and arms.

Seven figures . . . Jaz had said something about the symbols of Sekhmet. Dread settled over me as I realized what kind of curse was really protecting the museum. The griffin's release had just been accidental. It wasn't the real problem.

Sadie threw her twine.

'Wait!' I yelled, but it was too late. The magic twine whipped through the air, elongating into a rope as it raced towards the griffin.

The griffin squawked indignantly and leaped after the fiery shapes. The fire creatures scattered, and a game of total-annihilation tag was on.

The griffin buzzed around the room, its wings humming. Display cases shattered. Mortal alarms blared. I yelled at the griffin to stop, but this time it did no good.

Out of the corner of my eye, I saw Jaz collapse, maybe from the strain of her healing spell.

'Sadie!' I yelled. 'Help her!'

Sadie ran to Jaz's side. I chased the griffin. I probably looked like a total fool in my black pyjamas with my glowing sword, tripping over broken artefacts and screaming orders at a giant hummingbird-cat.

Just when I thought things couldn't get any worse, half a dozen party guests came round the corner to see what the noise was about. Their mouths fell open. A lady in a peach-coloured dress screamed.

The seven white fire creatures shot straight through the wedding guests, who instantly collapsed. The fires kept going, whipping round the corner towards the ballroom. The griffin flew after them.

I glanced back at Sadie, who was kneeling over Jaz and Walt. 'How are they?'

'Walt is coming around,' she said, 'but Jaz is out cold.'

'Follow me when you can. I think I can control the griffin.'

'Carter, are you *mad*? Our friends are hurt and I've got a flaming scroll stuck to my hand. The window's open. Help me get Jaz and Walt out of here!'

She had a point. This might be our only chance to get our friends out alive. But I also knew what those seven fires were now, and I knew that if I didn't go after them a lot of innocent people were going to get hurt.

I muttered an Egyptian curse – the cussing kind, not the magic kind – and ran to join the wedding party.

The main ballroom was in chaos. Guests were running everywhere, screaming and knocking over tables. A guy in a tuxedo had fallen into the wedding cake and was crawling around with a plastic bride-and-groom decoration stuck to his rear. A musician was trying to run away with a snare drum on his foot.

The white fires had solidified enough so that I could make out their forms – somewhere between canine and human, with elongated arms and crooked legs. They glowed like superheated gas as they raced through the ballroom, circling the pillars that surrounded the dance floor. One passed straight through a bridesmaid. The lady's eyes turned milky white, and she crumpled to the floor, shivering and coughing.

I felt like curling into a ball myself. I didn't know any spells that could fight these things, and if one of them touched me . . .

Suddenly the griffin swooped down out of nowhere, followed closely by Sadie's magic rope, which was still trying to bind it. The griffin snapped up one of the fire creatures in a single gulp and kept flying. Wisps of smoke came out of its nostrils, but, otherwise, eating the white fire didn't seem to bother it.

'Hey!' I yelled.

Too late, I realized my mistake.

The griffin turned towards me, which slowed it down just enough for Sadie's magic rope to wrap round its back legs.

'SQUAWWWWK!' The griffin crashed into a buffet table. The rope grew longer, winding round the monster's body while its high-speed wings shredded the table, the floor and plates of sandwiches like an out-of-control wood chipper.

Wedding guests began clearing the ballroom. Most ran for the elevators, but dozens were unconscious or shaking in fits, their eyes glowing white. Others were stuck under piles of debris. Alarms were blaring, and the white fires – six of them now – were still completely out of control.

I ran towards the griffin, which was rolling around, trying in vain to bite at the rope. 'Calm down!' I yelled. 'Let me help you, stupid!'

'FREEEEK!' The griffin's tail swept over my head and just missed decapitating me.

I took a deep breath. I was mostly a combat magician. I'd never been good at hieroglyph spells, but I pointed my sword at the monster and said: 'Ha-tep.'

A green hieroglyph – the symbol for *Be at peace* – burned in the air, right at the tip of my blade:

The griffin stopped thrashing. The buzzing of its wings slowed. Chaos and screaming still filled the ballroom, but I tried to stay calm as I approached the monster.

'You recognize me, don't you?' I held out my hand, and another symbol blazed above my palm – a symbol I could always summon, the Eye of Horus:

'You're a sacred animal of Horus, aren't you? That's why you obey me.'

The griffin blinked at the war god's mark. It ruffled its neck feathers and squawked in complaint, squirming under the rope that was slowly wrapping round its body.

'Yeah, I know,' I said. 'My sister's a loser. Just hang on. I'll untie you.'

Somewhere behind me, Sadie yelled, 'Carter!'

I turned and saw her and Walt stumbling towards me, half-carrying Jaz between them. Sadie was still doing her Statue of Liberty impression, holding the flaming scroll in one hand. Walt was on his feet and his eyes weren't glowing any more, but Jaz was slumped over like all the bones in her body had turned to jelly.

They dodged a fiery spirit and a few crazy wedding guests and somehow made it across the ballroom.

Walt stared the griffin. 'How did you calm it down?'

'Griffins are servants of Horus,' I said. 'They pulled his chariot in battle. I think it recognized my connection to him.'

The griffin shrieked impatiently and thrashed its tail, knocking over a stone column.

'Not very calm,' Sadie noticed. She glanced up at the glass dome, forty feet above, where the tiny figure of Khufu was waving at us frantically. 'We need to get Jaz out of here *now*,' she said.

'I'm fine,' Jaz muttered.

'No, you're not,' Walt said. 'Carter, she got that spirit out of me, but it almost killed her. It's some kind of sickness demon –'

'A *bau*,' I said. 'An evil spirit. These seven are called –'

'The Arrows of Sekhmet,' Jaz said, confirming my fears. 'They're plague spirits, born from the goddess. I can stop them.'

'You can *rest*,' Sadie said.

'Right,' I said. 'Sadie, get this rope off the griffin and –'

'There's no time.' Jaz pointed. The *bau* were getting larger and brighter. More wedding guests were falling as the spirits whipped around the room unchallenged.

'They'll die if I don't stop the *bau*,' Jaz said. 'I can channel the power of Sekhmet and force them back to the Duat. It's what I've been training for.'

I hesitated. Jaz had never tried such a large spell. She was already weak from healing Walt. But she *was* trained for this. It might seem strange that healers studied the path of Sekhmet, but since Sekhmet was the goddess of destruction, plagues and famine, it made sense that healers would learn how to control her forces – including *bau*.

Besides, even if I freed the griffin, I wasn't one hundred percent sure I could control it. There was a decent chance it would get excited and gobble us up rather than the spirits.

Outside, police sirens were getting louder. We were running out of time.

'We've got no choice,' Jaz insisted.

She pulled her wand and then – much to my sister's shock – gave Walt a kiss on the cheek. 'It'll be okay, Walt. Don't give up.'

Jaz took something else from her magician's bag – a wax figurine – and pressed it into my sister's free hand. 'You'll need this soon, Sadie. I'm sorry I can't help you more. You'll know what to do when the time comes.'

I don't think I'd ever seen Sadie at such a loss for words.

Jaz ran to the centre of the ballroom and touched her wand to the floor, drawing a circle of protection around her feet. From her bag she produced a small statue of Sekhmet, her patron goddess, and held it aloft.

She began to chant. Red light glowed around her. Tendrils of energy spread out from the circle, filling the room like the branches of a tree. The tendrils began to swirl, slowly at first, then picking up speed until the magic current tugged at the *bau*, forcing them to fly in the same direction, drawing them towards the centre. The spirits howled, trying to fight the spell. Jaz staggered, but she kept chanting, her face beaded with sweat.

'Can't we help her?' Walt asked.

'*RAWWWWK!*' the griffin cried, which probably meant, *Helloooo! I'm still here!*

The sirens sounded like they were right outside the building now. Down the hall near the elevators, someone was shouting into a megaphone, ordering the last wave of wedding guests to exit the building – like they needed encouragement. The police had arrived, and if we got arrested this situation was going to be difficult to explain.

'Sadie,' I said, 'get ready to dispel the rope on the griffin. Walt, you still got your boat amulet?'

'My –? Yeah. But there's no water.'

'Just summon the boat!' I dug through my pockets and found my own magic twine. I spoke a charm and was suddenly holding a rope about twenty feet long. I made a loose slipknot in the middle, like a huge necktie, and carefully approached the griffin.

'I'm just going to put this round your neck,' I said. 'Don't freak.'

'*FREEEEK!*' the griffin said.

I stepped closer, conscious of how fast that beak could snap me up if it wanted to, but I managed to loop the rope round the griffin's neck.

Then something went wrong. Time slowed down. The red swirling tendrils of Jaz's spell moved sluggishly, like the air had turned to syrup. The screams and sirens faded to a distant roar.

You won't succeed, a voice hissed.

26

I turned and found myself face to face with a *bau*.

It hovered in the air a few inches away, its fiery white features almost coming into focus. It seemed to smile, and I could swear I'd seen its face before.

Chaos is too powerful, boy, it said. *The world spins beyond your control. Give up your quest!*

'Shut up,' I murmured, but my heart was pounding.

You'll never find her, the spirit taunted. *She sleeps in the Place of Red Sand, but she will die there if you follow your pointless quest.*

I felt like a tarantula was crawling down my back. The spirit was talking about Zia Rashid – the *real* Zia, who I'd been searching for since Christmas.

'No,' I said. 'You're a demon, a deceiver.'

You know better, boy. We've met before.

'Shut up!' I summoned the Eye of Horus, and the spirit hissed. Time sped up again. The red tendrils of Jaz's spell wrapped round the *bau* and pulled it screaming into the vortex.

No one else seemed to have noticed what just happened.

Sadie was playing defence, swatting at *bau* with her flaming scroll whenever they got close. Walt set his boat amulet on the ground and spoke the command word. In a matter of seconds, like one of those crazy expand-in-water sponge toys, the amulet grew into a full-size Egyptian reed boat, lying across the ruins of the buffet table.

With shaking hands, I took the two ends of the griffin's new necktie and tied one end to the boat's prow and one to the stern.

'Carter, look!' Sadie called.

I turned in time to see a flash of blinding red light. The entire vortex collapsed inward, sucking all six *bau* into Jaz's circle. The light died. Jaz fainted, her wand and the Sekhmet statue both crumbling to dust in her hands.

We ran to her. Her clothes were steaming. I couldn't tell if she was breathing.

'Get her into the boat,' I said. 'We have to get out of here.'

I heard a tiny grunt from far above. Khufu had opened the dome. He gestured urgently as searchlights swept the sky above him. The museum was probably surrounded by emergency vehicles.

All around the ballroom, afflicted guests were starting to regain consciousness. Jaz had saved them, but at what cost? We carried her to the boat and climbed in.

'Hold on tight,' I warned. 'This thing is *not* balanced. If it flips –'

'Hey!' a deep male voice yelled behind us. 'What are you – Hey! Stop!'

'Sadie, rope, now!' I said.

She snapped her fingers, and the rope entangling the griffin dissolved.

'GO!' I shouted. 'UP!'

'FREEEEK!' The griffin revved its wings. We lurched into the air, the boat rocking crazily, and shot straight for the open dome. The griffin barely seemed to notice our extra weight. It ascended so fast, Khufu had to make a flying leap to get on board. I pulled him into the boat, and we held on desperately, trying not to capsize.

'*Agh!*' Khufu complained.

'Yeah,' I agreed. 'So much for an easy job.'

Then again, we were the Kane family. This was the easiest day we were going to have for quite a while.

Somehow, our griffin knew the right way to go. He screamed in triumph and soared into the cold rainy night. As we flew towards home, Sadie's scroll burned brighter. When I looked down, ghostly white fires were blazing across every rooftop in Brooklyn.

I began to wonder exactly what we'd stolen – if it was even the right object, or if it would make our problems worse. Either way, I had a feeling we'd finally pushed our luck too far.

3. The Ice-cream Man
Plots Our Death

ODD HOW EASILY YOU CAN FORGET your hand is on fire.

Oh, sorry. Sadie, here. You didn't think I'd let my brother prattle on forever, did you? Please, no one deserves a curse *that* horrible.

We arrived back at Brooklyn House, and everyone swarmed me because my hand was stuck to a flaming scroll.

'I'm fine!' I insisted. 'Take care of Jaz!'

Honestly, I appreciate a bit of attention now and then, but I was hardly the most interesting thing happening. We'd landed on the roof of the mansion, which itself is an odd attraction – a five-storey limestone-and-steel cube, like a cross between an Egyptian temple and an art museum, perched atop an abandoned warehouse on the Brooklyn waterfront. Not to mention that the mansion shimmers with magic and is invisible to regular mortals.

Below us, the whole of Brooklyn was on fire. My annoying magic scroll had painted a wide swathe of ghostly flames over the borough as we'd flown from the museum. Nothing was actually burning, and the flames weren't hot, but we'd still caused quite a panic. Sirens wailed. People clogged the streets, gawking up at the blazing rooftops. Helicopters circled with searchlights.

If that wasn't exciting enough, my brother was wrangling a griffin, trying to untie a fishing boat from round its neck and keep the beast from eating our trainees.

Then there was Jaz, our real cause for concern. We'd determined she was still breathing, but she seemed to be in some sort of coma. When we opened her eyes, they were glowing white – typically *not* a good sign.

During the boat ride, Khufu had attempted some of his famous baboon magic on her – patting her forehead, making rude noises and trying to insert jelly beans into her mouth. I'm sure he thought he was being helpful, but it hadn't done much to improve her condition.

Now Walt was taking care of her. He picked her up gently and put her on a stretcher, covering her with blankets and stroking her hair as our other trainees gathered round. And that was fine. Completely fine.

I wasn't at all interested in how handsome his face looked in the moonlight, or his muscular arms in that sleeveless tee, or the fact that he'd been holding hands with Jaz, or . . .

Sorry. Lost my train of thought.

I plopped down at the far corner of the roof, feeling absolutely knackered. My right hand itched from holding the papyrus scroll so long. The magic flames tickled my fingers.

I felt around in my left pocket and brought out the little

wax figure Jaz had given me. It was one of her healing statues, used to expel sickness or curses. Generally speaking, wax figures don't look like anyone in particular, but Jaz had taken her time with this one. It was clearly meant to heal one specific person, which meant it would have more power and would most likely be saved for a life-and-death situation. I recognized the figurine's curly hair, its facial features, the sword pressed into its hands. Jaz had even written its name in hieroglyphs on its chest: CARTER.

You'll need this soon, she'd told me.

As far as I knew, Jaz was not a diviner. She couldn't tell the future. So what had she meant? How was I supposed to I know when to use the figurine? Staring at the mini-Carter, I had a horrible feeling that my brother's life had been quite literally placed in my hands.

'Are you all right?' asked a woman's voice.

I quickly put away the figurine.

My old friend Bast stood over me. With her slight smile and glinting yellow eyes, she might've been concerned or amused. It's hard to tell with a cat goddess. Her black hair was pulled back in a ponytail. She wore her usual leopard-skin leotard, as if she were about to perform a backflip. For all I knew, she might. As I said, you never can tell with cats.

'I'm fine,' I lied. 'Just...' I waved my flaming hand about helplessly.

'Mmm.' The scroll seemed to make Bast uncomfortable. 'Let me see what I can do.'

She knelt next to me and began to chant.

I pondered how odd it was having my former pet cast a spell

on me. For years, Bast had posed as my cat, Muffin. I hadn't even realized I had a goddess sleeping on my pillow at night. Then, after our dad unleashed a slew of gods at the British Museum, Bast had made herself known.

She'd been watching over me for six years, she'd told us, ever since our parents released her from a cell in the Duat, where she'd been sent to fight the chaos snake Apophis forever.

Long story, but my mum had foreseen that Apophis would eventually escape his prison, which would basically amount to Doomsday. If Bast continued to fight him alone, she'd be destroyed. However, if Bast were freed, my mum believed she could play an important role in the coming battle with Chaos. So my parents freed the goddess before Apophis could overwhelm her. My mother had died opening, then quickly closing, Apophis's prison, so naturally Bast felt indebted to our parents. Bast had become my guardian.

Now she was also our chaperone, travel companion and sometime personal chef (hint: if she offers you the Friskies du Jour, say no).

But I still missed Muffin. At times I had to resist the urge to scratch Bast behind the ears and feed her crunchy treats, although I was glad she no longer tried to sleep on my pillow at night. That would've been a bit strange.

She finished her chant, and the scroll's flames sputtered out. My hand unclenched. The papyrus dropped into my lap.

'God, thank you,' I said.

'Goddess,' Bast corrected. 'You're quite welcome. We can't have the power of Ra lighting up the city, can we?'

I looked out across the borough. The fires were gone. The

Brooklyn night skyline was back to normal, except for the emergency lights and crowds of screaming mortals in the streets. Come to think of it, I suppose that *was* fairly normal.

'The power of Ra?' I asked. 'I thought the scroll was a clue. Is this the actual Book of Ra?'

Bast's ponytail puffed up as it does when she's nervous. I'd come to realize she kept her hair in a ponytail so that her entire head wouldn't explode into a sea-urchin shape each time she got startled.

'The scroll is...part of the book,' she said. 'And I *did* warn you. Ra's power is almost impossible to control. If you insist on trying to wake him, the next fires you set off might not be so harmless.'

'But isn't he your pharaoh?' I asked. 'Don't you want him awakened?'

She dropped her gaze. I realized how foolish my comment was. Ra was Bast's lord and master. Aeons ago, he'd chosen her to be his champion. But he was also the one who'd sent her into that prison to keep his arch-enemy Apophis occupied for eternity, so Ra could retire with a clear conscience. Quite selfish, if you ask me.

Thanks to my parents, Bast had escaped her imprisonment; but that also meant she'd abandoned her post fighting Apophis. No wonder she had mixed feelings about seeing her old boss again.

'It's better we talk in the morning,' Bast said. 'You need rest, and that scroll should only be opened in the daylight, when the power of Ra is easier to control.'

I stared at my lap. The papyrus was still steaming. 'Easier to control … as in, it won't set me on fire?'

'It's safe to touch now,' Bast assured me. 'After being trapped in darkness for a few millennia, it was just very sensitive, reacting to any sort of energy – magical, electrical, emotional. I've, ah, dialled down the sensitivity so it won't burst into flames again.'

I took the scroll. Thankfully, Bast was right. It didn't stick to my hand or set the city on fire.

Bast helped me to my feet. 'Get some sleep. I'll let Carter know you're all right. Besides …' She managed a smile. 'You've got a big day tomorrow.'

Right, I thought miserably. *One person remembers, and it's my cat.*

I looked over at my brother, who was still trying to control the griffin. It had Carter's shoelaces in its beak and didn't seem inclined to let go.

Most of our twenty trainees were surrounding Jaz, trying to wake her up. Walt hadn't left her side. He glanced up at me briefly, uneasily, then turned his attention back to Jaz.

'Maybe you're right,' I grumbled to Bast. 'I'm not needed up here.'

My room was a lovely place to sulk. The last six years I'd lived in an attic in Gran and Gramps's flat in London, and although I missed my old life, my mates Liz and Emma, and almost everything about England, I couldn't deny that my room in Brooklyn was much more posh.

My private balcony overlooked the East River. I had an enormous comfy bed, my own bathroom and a walk-in closet with endless new outfits that magically appeared and cleaned themselves as needed. The chest of drawers featured a built-in refrigerator with my favourite Ribena drinks, imported from the UK, and chilled chocolates (well, a girl does have to treat herself). The sound system was absolutely bleeding edge, and the walls were magically soundproofed so I could play my music as loud as I wanted without worrying about my stick-in-the-mud brother next door. Sitting on the dresser was one of the only things I'd brought from my room in London: a beaten-up cassette recorder my grandparents had given me ages ago. It was hopelessly old-fashioned, yes, but I kept it around for sentimental reasons. Carter and I had recorded our adventures at the Red Pyramid on it, after all.

I docked my iPod and scrolled through my playlists. I chose an older mix labelled SAD, as that's how I felt.

Adele's 19 began playing. God, I hadn't heard that album since . . .

Quite unexpectedly I began to tear up. I'd been listening to this mix on Christmas Eve when Dad and Carter picked me up for our trip to the British Museum – the night our lives changed forever.

Adele sang as if someone were ripping her heart out. She went on about the boy she fancied, wondering what she must do to make him want her properly. I could relate to that. But last Christmas, the song had made me think of my family as well: my mum, who'd died when I was quite small, and my father and Carter, who travelled the world together, left me in London with my grandparents and didn't seem to need me in their lives.

Of course I knew it was more complicated than that. There'd been a nasty custody battle involving lawyers and spatula attacks, and Dad had wanted to keep Carter and me apart so we didn't agitate each other's magic before we could handle the power. And, yes, we'd all grown closer since then. My father was back in my life a bit more, even if he was the god of the underworld now. As for my mother... well, I'd met her ghost. I suppose that counted for something.

Still, the music brought back all the pain and anger I'd felt at Christmas. I suppose I hadn't got rid of it as completely as I'd thought.

My finger hovered over the fast-forward icon, but I decided to let the song play. I tossed my stuff on the dresser – the papyrus scroll, the wax mini-Carter, my magic bag, my wand. I reached for my staff, then remembered I didn't have it any more. The griffin had eaten it.

'Manky birdbrain,' I muttered.

I started changing for bed. I'd plastered the inside of my closet door with photos, mostly of my mates and me from school last year. There was one of Liz, Emma and me making faces in a photo booth in Piccadilly. We looked so young and ridiculous.

I couldn't believe I might be seeing them tomorrow for the first time in months. Gran and Gramps had invited me to visit, and I had plans to go out with just my mates – at least, that *had* been the plan before Carter dropped his 'five-days-to-save-the-world' bombshell. Now who knew what would happen?

Only two non-Liz-and-Emma pictures decorated my closet door. One showed Carter and me with Uncle Amos the day Amos left for Egypt on his ... hmm, what do you call it when someone goes for healing after being possessed by an evil god? Not a holiday, I suppose.

The last picture was a painting of Anubis. Perhaps you've seen him: the fellow with the jackal's head, god of funerals, death and so on. He's everywhere in Egyptian art – leading deceased souls into the Hall of Judgement, kneeling at the cosmic scales, weighing a heart against the feather of truth.

Why did I have his picture?

[Fine, Carter. I'll admit it, if only to shut you up.]

I had a bit of a crush on Anubis. I know how ridiculous that sounds, a modern girl getting moony-eyed over a five-thousand-year-old dog-headed boy, but that's *not* what I saw when I looked at his picture. I remembered Anubis as he'd appeared in New Orleans when we'd met face to face – a boy of about sixteen, in black leather and denim, with tousled dark hair and gorgeous, sad, melted-chocolate eyes. Very much *not* a dog-headed boy.

Still ridiculous, I know. He was a god. We had absolutely nothing in common. I hadn't heard from him once since our adventure with the Red Pyramid, and that shouldn't have surprised me. Even though he'd seemed interested in me at the time and possibly even dropped some hints ... No, surely I'd been imagining it.

The past seven weeks, since Walt Stone had arrived at Brooklyn House, I'd thought I might be able to get over Anubis. Of course, Walt was my trainee, and I wasn't supposed to think of him as a possible boyfriend, but I was fairly sure there'd been a spark between us the first time we saw each other. Now, though, Walt seemed to be pulling away. He was acting so secretive, always looking so guilty and talking to Jaz.

My life was rubbish.

I pulled on my nightclothes while Adele kept singing. Were *all* her songs about not being noticed by boys? Suddenly I found that quite annoying.

I turned off the music and flopped into bed.

Sadly, once I fell asleep my night only got worse.

At Brooklyn House, we sleep with all sorts of magic charms to protect us against malicious dreams, invading spirits and the occasional urge our souls might get to wander off. I even have a magic pillow to make sure my soul – or *ba*, if you want to get Egyptian about it – stays anchored to my body.

It isn't a perfect system, though. Every so often I can sense some outside force tugging on my mind, trying to get my attention. Or my soul will let me know it has some other place to go, some important scene it needs to show me.

I got one of those sensations immediately when I fell asleep. Think of it as an incoming call, with my brain giving me the option to accept or decline. Most of the time, it's best to decline, especially when my brain is reporting an unknown number.

But sometimes those calls are important. And my birthday

was tomorrow. Perhaps Dad and Mum were trying to reach me from the underworld. I imagined them in the Hall of Judgement, my father sitting on his throne as the blue-skinned god Osiris, my mum in her ghostly white robes. They might be wearing paper party hats and singing 'Happy Birthday' while Ammit the Devourer, their extremely tiny pet monster, jumped up and down, yapping.

Or it could be, just maybe, Anubis calling. *Hi, um, thought you might want to go to a funeral or something?*

Well... it was possible.

So I accepted the call. I let my spirit go where it wanted to take me, and my *ba* floated above my body.

If you've never tried *ba* travel, I wouldn't recommend it – unless of course you fancy turning into a phantom chicken and rafting uncontrollably through the currents of the Duat.

The *ba* is usually invisible to others, which is good, as it takes the form of a giant bird with your normal head attached. Once upon a time, I'd been able to manipulate my *ba*'s form into something less embarrassing, but since Isis vacated my head I didn't have that ability. Now when I lifted off I was stuck in default poultry mode.

The doors of the balcony swung open. A magical breeze swept me into the night. The lights of New York blurred and faded, and I found myself in a familiar underground chamber: the Hall of Ages, in the House of Life's main headquarters under Cairo.

The room was so long, it could've hosted a marathon. Down the middle was a blue carpet that glittered like a river. Between the columns on either side, curtains of light shimmered – holographic images from Egypt's long history. The light changed colour to reflect different eras, from the white glow of the Age of the Gods all the way to the crimson light of modern times.

The roof was even higher than the ballroom at the Brooklyn Museum, the vast space lit by glowing orbs of energy and floating hieroglyphic symbols. It looked as if someone had detonated a few kilos of children's cereal in zero gravity, all the colourful sugary bits drifting and colliding in slow motion.

I floated to the end of the room, just above the dais with the pharaoh's throne. It was an honorary seat, empty since the fall of Egypt, but on the step below it sat the Chief Lector, master of the First Nome, leader of the House of Life, and my least favourite magician: Michel Desjardins.

I hadn't seen Monsieur Delightful since our attack on the Red Pyramid, and I was surprised how much he'd aged. He'd only become Chief Lector a few months ago, but his slick black hair and forked beard were now streaked with grey. He leaned wearily on his staff, as if the Chief Lector's leopard-skin cape across his shoulders was as heavy as lead.

I can't say I felt sorry for him. We hadn't parted as friends. We'd combined forces (more or less) to defeat the god Set, but he still considered us dangerous rogue magicians. He'd warned us that if we continued studying the path of the gods (which we had) he would destroy us the next time we met. That hadn't given us much incentive to invite him over for tea.

His face was gaunt, but his eyes still glittered evilly. He studied the blood-red images in the curtains of light as if he were waiting for something.

'*Est-il allé?*' he asked, which my grammar-school French led me to believe meant either 'Is he gone?' or possibly 'Have you repaired the island?'

Fine . . . it was probably the first one.

For a moment I was afraid he was talking to me. Then from behind the throne, a raspy voice answered, 'Yes, my lord.'

A man stepped out of the shadows. He was dressed completely in white – suit, scarf, even white reflective sunglasses. My first thought was: *My god, he's an evil ice-cream vendor.*

He had a pleasant smile and a chubby face framed in curly grey hair. I might've mistaken him as harmless, even friendly – until he took off his glasses.

His eyes were ruined.

I'll admit I'm squeamish about eyes. A video of retinal surgery? I'll run out of the room. Even the idea of contact lenses makes me cringe.

But the man in white looked as if his eyes had been splashed with acid, then repeatedly clawed by cats. His eyelids were masses of scar tissue that didn't close properly. His eyebrows were burned away and raked with deep grooves. The skin above his cheekbones was a mask of red welts, and the eyes themselves were such a horrible combination of blood red and milky white that I couldn't believe he was able to see.

He inhaled, wheezing so badly the sound made my chest hurt. Glittering against his shirt was a silver pendant with a snake-shaped amulet.

'He used the portal moments ago, my lord,' the man rasped. 'Finally, he has gone.'

That voice was as horrible as his eyes. If he *had* been

splashed with acid, some of it must have got into his lungs. Yet the man kept smiling, looking calm and happy in his crisp white suit as if he couldn't wait to sell ice cream to the good little children.

He approached Desjardins, who was still staring at the curtains of light. The ice-cream man followed his gaze. I did the same and realized what the Chief Lector was looking at. At the last pillar, just next to the throne, the light was changing. The reddish tint of the modern age was darkening to a deep purple, the colour of bruises. On my first visit to the Hall of Ages, I'd been told that the room grew longer as the years passed, and now I could actually see it happening. The floor and walls rippled like a mirage, expanding ever so slowly, and the sliver of purple light widened.

'Ah,' said the ice-cream man. 'It's much clearer now.'

'A new age,' Desjardins murmured. 'A darker age. The colour of the light has not changed for a thousand years, Vladimir.'

An evil ice-cream man named Vladimir? All right, then.

'It is the Kanes, of course,' said Vladimir. 'You should've killed the elder one while he was in our power.'

My *ba* feathers ruffled. I realized he was talking about Uncle Amos.

'No,' Desjardins said. 'He was under our protection. All who seek healing must be given sanctuary – even Kane.'

Vladimir took a deep breath, which sounded like a clogged vacuum cleaner. 'But surely now that he has left we must act. You heard the news from Brooklyn, my lord. The children have found the first scroll. If they find the other two –'

'I know, Vladimir.'

'They humiliated the House of Life in Arizona. They made peace with Set rather than destroy him. And now they seek the Book of Ra. If you would allow me to deal with them –'

The top of Desjardins's staff erupted in purple fire. 'Who is Chief Lector?' he demanded.

Vladimir's pleasant expression faltered. 'You are, my lord.'

'And I will deal with the Kanes in due time, but Apophis is our greatest threat. We must divert all our power to keeping down the Serpent. If there is any chance the Kanes can help us restore order –'

'But, Chief Lector,' Vladimir interrupted. His tone had a new intensity – an almost magical force to it. 'The Kanes are part of the problem. They have upset the balance of Ma'at by awakening the gods. They are teaching forbidden magic. Now they would restore Ra, who has not ruled since the beginning of Egypt! They will throw the world into disarray. This will only help Chaos.'

Desjardins blinked, as if confused. 'Perhaps you're right. I…I must think on this.'

Vladimir bowed. 'As you wish, my lord. I will gather our forces and await your orders to destroy Brooklyn House.'

'Destroy…' Desjardins frowned. 'Yes, you will await my orders. I will choose the time to attack, Vladimir.'

'Very good, my lord. And if the Kane children seek the other two scrolls to awaken Ra? One is beyond their reach, of course, but the other –'

'I will leave that to you. Guard it as you think best.'

Vladimir's eyes were even more horrible when he got

excited – slimy and glistening behind those ruined eyelids. They reminded me of Gramps's favourite breakfast: soft-boiled eggs with Tabasco sauce.

[Well, I'm sorry if it's disgusting, Carter. You shouldn't try to eat while I'm narrating, anyway!]

'My lord is wise,' Vladimir said. 'The children *will* seek the scrolls, my lord. They have no choice. If they leave their stronghold and come into my territory –'

'Didn't I just say we will dispose of them?' Desjardins said flatly. 'Now, leave me. I must think.'

Vladimir retreated into the shadows. For someone dressed in white, he managed to disappear quite well.

Desjardins returned his attention to the shimmering curtain of light. 'A new age...' he mused. 'An age of darkness...'

My *ba* swirled into the currents of the Duat, racing back to my sleeping form.

'Sadie?' a voice said.

I sat up in bed, my heart pounding. Grey morning light filled the windows. Sitting at the foot of my bed was...

'U–Uncle Amos?' I stammered.

He smiled. 'Happy birthday, my dear. I'm sorry if I scared you. You didn't answer your door. I was concerned.'

He looked back to full health and as fashionably dressed as ever. He wore wire-rimmed glasses, a porkpie hat and a black wool Italian suit that made him seem a bit less short and stout. His long hair was braided in cornrows decorated with pieces of glittering black stone – obsidian, perhaps. He might've passed for a jazz musician (which he was) or an African American Al Capone (which he wasn't).

I started to ask, 'How –?' Then my vision from the Hall of Ages – the implications of what I'd seen – sank in.

'It's all right,' Amos said. 'I've just returned from Egypt.'

I tried to swallow, my breath almost as laboured as that ghastly man Vladimir's. 'So have I, Amos. And it's *not* all right. They're coming to destroy us.'

4. A Birthday Invitation to Armageddon

AFTER EXPLAINING MY HORRIBLE VISION, only one thing would do: a proper breakfast.

Amos looked shaken, but he insisted we wait to discuss matters until we'd assembled the entire Twenty-first Nome (as our branch of the House of Life was called). He promised to meet me on the veranda in twenty minutes.

After he'd gone, I showered and considered what to wear. Normally, I would teach Sympathetic Magic on Mondays, which would require proper magician's linen. However, my birthday was *supposed* to be a day off.

Given the circumstances, I doubted Amos, Carter and Bast would let me go to London, but I decided to think positive. I put on some ripped jeans, my combat boots, a tank top and my leather jacket – not good for magic, but I was feeling rebellious.

I stuffed my wand and the mini-Carter figure into my magic supply bag. I was about to sling it over my shoulder when I thought – No, I'll not be lugging this about on my birthday.

I took a deep breath and concentrated on opening a space in the Duat. I hate to admit it, but I'm *rubbish* at this trick. It's simply not fair that Carter can pull things out of thin air at a moment's notice, but I normally need five or ten minutes of absolute focus, and even then the effort makes me nauseous. Most of the time, it's simpler just to keep my bag over my shoulder. If I went out with my mates, however, I didn't want to be burdened with it, and I didn't want to leave it behind completely.

At last the air shimmered as the Duat bent to my will. I tossed my bag in front of me, and it disappeared. Excellent – assuming I could figure out how to get it back again later.

I picked up the scroll we'd stolen from Bullwinkle the night before and headed downstairs.

With everyone at breakfast, the mansion was strangely silent. Five levels of balconies faced the Great Room, so normally the place was bustling with noise and activity; but I remembered how empty it had felt when Carter and I first arrived last Christmas.

The Great Room still had many of the same touches: the massive statue of Thoth in the middle, Amos's collection of weapons and jazz instruments along the wall, the snakeskin rug in front of the garage-size fireplace. But you could tell that twenty young magicians lived here now as well. An assortment of remote controls, wands, iPads, snack-food wrappers and *shabti* figurines littered the coffee table. Someone with big feet – probably Julian – had left his muddy trainers on the stairs. And one of our hoodlums – I assumed Felix – had magically converted the fireplace into an Antarctic wonderland, complete with snow and a live penguin. Felix does love penguins.

Magical mops and brooms sped about the house, trying to clean up. I had to duck to avoid getting dusted. For some reason, the dusters think my hair is a maintenance issue.

[No comments from you, Carter.]

As I expected, everyone was gathered on the veranda, which served as our dining area and albino-crocodile habitat. Philip of Macedonia splashed around happily in his pool, jumping for bacon strips whenever a trainee tossed him one. The morning was cold and rainy, but the fire in the terrace's magic braziers kept us toasty.

I grabbed a *pain au chocolat* and a cup of tea from the buffet table and sat down. Then I realized the others weren't eating. They were staring at me.

At the head of the table, Amos and Bast both looked grim. Across from me, Carter hadn't touched his plate of waffles, which was *very* unlike him. To my right, Jaz's chair was empty. (Amos had told me she was still in the infirmary, no change.) To my left sat Walt, looking quite good as usual, but I did my best to ignore him.

The other trainees seemed to be in various states of shock. They were a motley assortment of all ages from all over the world. A handful were older than Carter and me – old enough for university, in fact – which was nice for chaperoning the younger ones, but always made me feel a bit uncomfortable when I tried to act as their teacher. The others were mostly between ten and fifteen. Felix was just nine. There was Julian from Boston, Alyssa from Carolina, Sean from Dublin and

Cleo from Rio de Janeiro (yes, I know, Cleo from Rio, but I'm not making it up!). The thing we all had in common: the blood of the pharaohs. All of us were descended from Egypt's royal lines, which gave us a natural capacity for magic and hosting the power of the gods.

The only one who didn't seem affected by the grim mood was Khufu. For reasons we never quite understood, our baboon eats only foods that end in -o. Recently he had discovered Jell-O, which he regarded as a miracle substance. I suppose the capital O made everything taste better. Now he would eat almost anything encased in gelatin – fruit, nuts, bugs, small animals. At the moment he had his face buried in a quivering red mountain of breakfast and was making rude noises as he excavated for grapes.

Everyone else watched me, as if waiting for an explanation.

'Morning,' I muttered. 'Lovely day. Penguin in the fireplace, if anyone's interested.'

'Sadie,' Amos said gently, 'tell everyone what you told me.'

I sipped some tea to settle my nerves. Then I tried not to sound terrified as I described my visit to the Hall of Ages.

When I was done, the only sounds were the fires crackling in the braziers and Philip of Macedonia splashing in his pool.

Finally nine-year-old Felix asked what was on everyone's mind: 'So we're all going to die, then?'

'No.' Amos sat forward. 'Absolutely not. Children, I know I've just arrived. I've hardly met most of you, but I promise we'll do everything we can to keep you safe. This house is layered with magic protection. You have a major goddess on your side –' he gestured to Bast, who was opening a can of Fancy Feast Tuna Supreme with her fingernails – 'and the Kane family to protect you. Carter and Sadie are more powerful than you might realize, and I've battled Michel Desjardins before, if it comes to that.'

Given all the trouble we'd had last Christmas, Amos's speech seemed a tad optimistic, but the trainees looked relieved.

'*If* it comes to that?' Alyssa asked. 'It sounds pretty certain they'll attack us.'

Amos knitted his brow. 'Perhaps, but it troubles me that Desjardins would agree to such a foolish move. Apophis is the real enemy, and Desjardins knows it. He should realize he needs all the help he can get. Unless...' He didn't finish the sentence. Whatever he was thinking, it apparently troubled him greatly. 'At any rate, if Desjardins decides to come after us, he will plan carefully. He knows this mansion will not fall easily. He can't afford to be embarrassed by the Kane family again. He'll study the problem, consider his options and gather his forces. It would take several days for him to prepare – time he should be using to stop Apophis.'

Walt raised an index finger. I don't know what it is about him, but he has a sort of gravity that draws the group's attention when he's about to speak. Even Khufu looked up from his Jell-O.

'If Desjardins *does* attack us,' Walt said, 'he'll be well prepared, with magicians who are a lot more experienced than we are. Can he get through our defences?'

Amos gazed at the sliding glass doors, possibly remembering the last time our defences had been breached. The results hadn't been good.

'We must make sure it doesn't come to that,' he said. 'Desjardins knows what we're attempting, and that we only have five days – well, four days, now. According to Sadie's vision, Desjardins is aware of our plan and will try to prevent it out of some misguided belief that we are working for the forces of Chaos. But, if we succeed, we'll have bargaining power to make Desjardins back off.'

Cleo raised her hand. '*Um . . . We* don't know the plan. Four days to do what?'

Amos gestured at Carter, inviting him to explain. That was fine with me. Honestly, I found the plan a bit crazy.

My brother sat up. I must give him credit. Over the last few months, he'd made progress at resembling a normal teenager. After six years of home-schooling and travelling with Dad, Carter had been hopelessly out of touch. He'd dressed like a junior executive, in crisp white shirts and slacks. Now at least he'd learned to wear jeans and T-shirts and the occasional hoodie. He'd let his hair grow out in a curly mess – which looked *much* better. If he kept on improving, the boy might even get a date some day.

[What? Don't poke me. It was a compliment!]

'We're going to wake the god Ra,' Carter said, as if it was as easy as getting a snack from the fridge.

The trainees glanced at one another. Carter wasn't known for his sense of humour, but they must've wondered if he were joking.

'You mean the sun god,' Felix said. 'The old king of the gods.'

Carter nodded. 'You all know the story. Thousands of years ago, Ra got senile and retreated into the heavens, leaving Osiris in charge. Then Osiris got overthrown by Set. Then Horus defeated Set and became pharaoh. Then –'

I coughed. 'Short version, please.'

Carter gave me a cross look. 'The point is, Ra was the first and most powerful king of the gods. We believe Ra is still alive. He's just asleep somewhere deep in the Duat. If we can wake him –'

'But if he retired because he was senile,' Walt said, 'wouldn't that mean he's really, *really* senile now?'

I'd asked the same thing when Carter first told me his idea. The last thing we needed was an all-powerful god who couldn't remember his own name, smelled like old people and drooled in his sleep. And how could an immortal being get senile in the first place? No one had given me a satisfactory answer.

Amos and Carter looked at Bast, which made sense, as she was the only Egyptian god present.

She frowned at her uneaten Fancy Feast. 'Ra is the god of the sun. In olden times, he aged as the day aged, then sailed through the Duat on his boat each night and was reborn with the sunrise each morning.'

'But the sun isn't reborn,' I put in. 'It's just the rotation of the earth –'

'Sadie,' Bast warned.

Right, right. Myth and science were both true – simply

different versions of the same reality, blah, blah. I'd heard that lecture a hundred times, and I didn't want to hear it again.

Bast pointed at the scroll, which I'd set next to my teacup. 'When Ra stopped making his nightly journey, the cycle was broken, and Ra faded into permanent twilight – at least, so we think. He meant to sleep forever. But if you could find him in the Duat – and that's a big *if* – it's possible he might be brought back and reborn with the right magic. The Book of Ra describes how this might be done. Ra's priests created the book in ancient times and kept it secret, dividing it into three parts, to be used only if the world was ending.'

'If...the world was ending?' Cleo asked. 'You mean Apophis is really going to...to swallow the sun?'

Walt looked at me. 'Is that possible? In your story about the Red Pyramid, you said Apophis was behind Set's plan to destroy North America. He was trying to cause so much chaos that he could break out of his prison.'

I shivered, remembering the apparition that had appeared in the sky over Washington, DC – a writhing giant snake.

'Apophis is the *real* problem,' I agreed. 'We stopped him once, but his prison is weakening. If he manages to escape –'

'He will,' Carter said. 'In four days. Unless we stop him. And then he'll destroy civilization – everything humans have built since the dawn of Egypt.'

That put a chill over breakfast table.

Carter and I had talked privately about the four-day deadline, of course. Horus and Isis had both discussed it with us. But it had seemed like a horrible possibility rather than absolute certainty. Now, Carter sounded sure. I studied his face and realized he'd seen something during the night – possibly a vision even worse than mine. His expression said, *Not here. I'll tell you later.*

Bast was digging her claws into the dining table. Whatever the secret was, she must be in on it.

At the far end of the table, Felix counted on his fingers. 'Why four days? What's so special about...*um*, March twenty-first?'

'The spring equinox,' Bast explained. 'A powerful time for magic. The hours of day and night are exactly balanced, meaning the forces of Chaos and Ma'at can be easily tipped one way or the other. It's the perfect time to awaken Ra. In fact, it's our *only* chance until the autumn equinox, six months from now. But we can't wait that long.'

'Because unfortunately,' Amos added, 'the equinox is also the perfect time for Apophis to escape his prison and invade the mortal world. You can be sure he has minions working on that right now. According to our sources among the gods, Apophis will succeed, which is why we have to awaken Ra first.'

I'd heard all this before, but discussing it in the open, in front of all our trainees, and seeing the devastated looks on their faces, it all seemed much more frightening and real.

I cleared my throat. 'Right...so *when* Apophis breaks out, he'll try to destroy Ma'at, the order of the universe. He'll swallow the sun, plunge the earth into eternal darkness, and otherwise make us have a very bad day.'

'Which is why we need Ra.' Amos modulated his tone, making it calm and reassuring for our trainees. He projected such composure that even I felt a little less terrified. I wondered if this was a kind of magic, or if he was just better at explaining Armageddon than I was.

'Ra was Apophis's arch-enemy,' he continued. 'Ra is the Lord of Order, whereas Apophis is the Lord of Chaos. Since the beginning of time, these two forces have been in a perpetual battle to destroy one another. If Apophis returns, we have to make sure we have Ra on our side to counteract him. Then we stand a chance.'

'A chance,' Walt said. 'Assuming we can find Ra and wake him, and the rest of the House of Life doesn't destroy us first.'

Amos nodded. 'But if we can awaken Ra, that would be a feat more difficult than any magician has ever accomplished. It would make Desjardins think twice. The Chief Lector...well, it would seem he's not thinking clearly, but he's no fool. He recognizes the danger of Apophis rising. We must convince him that we're on the same side, that the path of the gods is the only way to defeat Apophis. I would rather do this than fight him.'

Personally, I wanted to punch Desjardins in the face and set his beard on fire, but I supposed Amos had a point.

Cleo, poor thing, had gone as green as a frog. She'd come all the way from Brazil to Brooklyn to study the path of Thoth, god of knowledge, and we'd already pegged her as our future librarian, but when the dangers were real, and not just in the pages of books...well, she had a tender stomach. I hoped she could make it to the edge of the terrace if she needed to.

'The – the scroll,' she managed, 'you said there are two other parts?'

I took the scroll. In the daylight it looked more fragile – brittle and yellow and likely to crumble. My fingers trembled. I could feel magic humming in the papyrus like a low-voltage current. I felt an overwhelming desire to open it.

I began to unroll the cylinder. Carter tensed.

Amos said, 'Sadie...'

No doubt they expected Brooklyn to catch fire again, but nothing happened. I spread out the scroll and found it was written in gibberish – not hieroglyphics, not any language I could recognize. The end of the papyrus was a jagged line, as if it had been ripped.

'I imagine the pieces graft together,' I said. 'It will be readable only when all three sections are combined.'

Carter looked impressed. But honestly, I do know *some* things. During our last adventure I'd read a scroll to banish Set, and it had worked much the same way.

Khufu looked up from his Jell-O. '*Agh!*' He put three slimy grapes on the table.

'Exactly,' Bast agreed. 'As Khufu says, the three sections of the book represent the three aspects of Ra – morning, noon and night. That scroll there is the spell of Khnum. You'll need to find the other two now.'

How Khufu fitted all of that into a single grunt, I didn't know, but I wished I could take all my classes from baboon teachers. I'd have middle school and high school finished in a week.

'So the other two grapes,' I said, 'I mean, scrolls... according to my vision last night, they won't be easy to find.'

Amos nodded. 'The first section was lost aeons ago. The

middle section is in the possession of the House of Life. It has been moved many times, and is always kept under tight security. Judging from your vision, I'd say the scroll is now in the hands of Vladimir Menshikov.'

'The ice-cream man,' I guessed. 'Who is he?'

Amos traced something on the table – perhaps a protective hieroglyph. 'The third most powerful magician in the world. He's also one of Desjardins's strongest supporters. He runs the Eighteenth Nome, in Russia.'

Bast hissed. Being a cat, she was quite good at that. 'Vlad the Inhaler. He's got an evil reputation.'

I remembered his ruined eyes and wheezing voice. 'What happened to his face?'

Bast was about to answer, but Amos cut her off.

'Just realize that he's quite dangerous,' he warned. 'Vlad's main talent is silencing rogue magicians.'

'You mean he's an assassin?' I asked. 'Wonderful. And Desjardins just gave him permission to hunt Carter and me if we leave Brooklyn.'

'Which you'll *have* to do,' Bast said, 'if you want to seek the other sections of the Book of Ra. You have only four days.'

'Yes,' I muttered, 'you may have mentioned that. You'll be coming with us, won't you?'

Bast looked down at her Fancy Feast.

'Sadie...' She sounded miserable. 'Carter and I were talking and...well, someone has to check on Apophis's prison. We have to know what's going on, how close it is to breaking and if there's a way to stop it. That requires a first-hand look.'

I couldn't believe I was hearing this. 'You're going *back* there? After all my parents did to free you?'

'I'll only approach the prison from the outside,' she promised. 'I'll be careful. I am a creature of stealth, after all. Besides, I'm the only one who knows how to find his cell, and that part of the Duat would be lethal to a mortal. I – I must do this.'

Her voice trembled. She'd once told me that cats weren't brave, but going back to her old prison seemed like quite a courageous thing to do.

'I won't leave you undefended,' she promised. 'I have a . . . a friend. He should arrive from the Duat by tomorrow. I've asked him to find you and protect you.'

'A friend?' I asked.

Bast squirmed. 'Well . . . sort of.'

That didn't sound encouraging.

I looked down at my street clothes. A sour taste filled my mouth. Carter and I had a quest to undertake, and it was unlikely we would come back alive. Another responsibility on my shoulders, another unreasonable demand for me to sacrifice my life for the greater good. Happy birthday to me.

Khufu belched and pushed away his empty plate. He bared his Jell-O-stained fangs as if to say *Well, that's settled! Good breakfast!*

'I'll get packed,' Carter said. 'We can leave in an hour.'

'No,' I said. I'm not sure who was more surprised – me or my brother.

'No?' Carter asked.

'It's my birthday,' I said, which probably made me sound like a seven-year-old brat – but at the moment I didn't care.

The trainees looked astonished. Several mumbled their good wishes. Khufu offered me his empty Jell-O bowl as a present. Felix half-heartedly started singing 'Happy Birthday', but no one joined him, so he gave up.

'Bast said her friend won't arrive until tomorrow,' I continued. 'Amos said it would take Desjardins some time to prepare any sort of attack. Besides, I've been planning my trip to London for ages. I think I have time for *one* day off before the world ends.'

The others stared at me. Was I selfish? All right, yes. Irresponsible? Perhaps. So why did I feel so strongly about putting my foot down?

This may come as a shock to you, but I don't like feeling controlled. Carter was dictating what we would do, but as usual he hadn't told me everything. He'd obviously consulted Amos and Bast already and made a game plan. The three of them had decided what was best without bothering to ask me. My one constant companion, Bast, was leaving me to embark on a horribly dangerous mission. And I'd be stuck with my brother on my birthday, tracking down another magical scroll that might set me on fire or worse.

Sorry. No thanks. If I was going to die, then it could wait until tomorrow morning.

Carter's expression was part anger, part disbelief. Normally, we tried to keep things civil in front of our trainees. Now I was embarrassing him. He'd always complained how I rushed into things without thinking. Last night he'd been irritated with me for grabbing that scroll, and I suspected in the back of his mind he blamed me for things going wrong – for Jaz's getting hurt. No doubt he saw this as another example of my reckless nature.

I was quite prepared for a knockdown fight, but Amos interceded.

'Sadie, a visit to London is dangerous.' He held up his hand before I could protest. 'However, if you must...' He took a deep breath, as if he didn't like what he was about to say. '...then at least promise you'll be careful. I doubt Vlad Menshikov will be ready to move against us so quickly. You should be all right as long as you use no magic, do nothing to attract attention.'

'Amos!' Carter protested.

Amos cut him off with a stern look. 'While Sadie is gone, we can begin planning. Tomorrow morning, the two of you can begin your quest. I will take over your teaching duties with our trainees and oversee the defence of Brooklyn House.'

I could see in Amos's eyes he didn't want me to go. It was foolish, dangerous and rash – in other words, rather typical of me. But I could also sense his sympathy for my predicament. I remembered how fragile Amos had looked after Set took over his body last Christmas. When he'd gone to the First Nome for healing, I knew he'd felt guilty about leaving us alone. Still, it had been the right choice for his sanity. Amos, of all people, knew what it was like to need to get away. If I stayed here, if I left on a quest straight away without even time to breathe, I felt I would explode.

Besides, I felt better knowing Amos would be covering for us at Brooklyn House. I was relieved to give up my teaching duties for a while. Truth be told, I'm a *horrid* teacher. I simply have no patience for it.

[Oh, be quiet, Carter. You weren't supposed to *agree* with me.]

'Thank you, Amos,' I managed.

He stood, clearly indicating that the meeting was over.

'I think that's enough for one morning,' he said. 'The main thing is for all of you to continue your training, and don't despair. We'll need you in top shape to defend Brooklyn House. We *will* prevail. With the gods on our side, Ma'at will overcome Chaos, as it always has before.'

The trainees still looked uneasy, but they stood and began to clear their dishes. Carter gave me one more angry look, then stormed inside.

That was *his* problem. I was determined not to feel guilty. I would not have my birthday ruined. Still, as I stared down at my cold tea and uneaten *pain au chocolat*, I had a horrible feeling I might never sit at this table again.

An hour later I was ready for London.

I'd chosen a new staff from the arsenal and stowed it in the Duat along with my other supplies. I left the magic Bullwinkle scroll with Carter, who wouldn't even talk to me, then checked on Jaz in the infirmary and found her still in a coma. An enchanted washcloth kept her forehead cool. Healing hieroglyphs floated around her bed, but she still looked so frail. Without her usual smile, she seemed like a different person.

I sat next to her and held her hand. My heart felt as heavy

as a bowling ball. Jaz had risked her life to protect us. She'd gone up against a mob of *bau* with only a few weeks of training. She'd tapped into the energy of her patron goddess, Sekhmet, just as we'd taught her, and the effort had almost destroyed her.

What had I sacrificed lately? I'd thrown a tantrum because I might miss my birthday party.

'I'm so sorry, Jaz.' I knew she couldn't hear me, but my voice quavered. 'I just . . . I'll go mad if I don't get away. We've already had to save the world once, and now I have to do it again . . .'

I imagined what Jaz would say – something reassuring, no doubt: *It's not your fault, Sadie. You deserve a few hours.*

That just made me feel worse. I should never have allowed Jaz to put herself in danger. Six years ago, my mother had died channelling too much magic. She'd burned up closing the gate to Apophis's prison. I'd known that, and yet I'd allowed Jaz, who had much less experience, to risk her life to save ours.

As I said . . . I'm a horrid teacher.

Finally I couldn't stand it any more. I squeezed Jaz's hand, told her to get better soon, and left the infirmary. I climbed to the roof, where we kept our relic for opening portals – a stone sphinx from the ruins of Heliopolis.

I tensed when I noticed Carter at the other end of the roof, feeding a pile of roasted turkeys to the griffin. Since last night, he'd constructed quite a nice stable for the monster, so I guessed it would be staying with us. At least that would keep the pigeons off the roof.

I almost hoped Carter would ignore me. I wasn't in the mood for another argument. But when he saw me he scowled, wiped the turkey grease off his hands and walked over.

I braced myself for a scolding.

Instead he grumbled, 'Be careful. I got you a birthday gift, but I'll wait until...you come back.'

He didn't add the word *alive*, but I thought I heard it in his tone.

'Look, Carter –'

'Just go,' he said. 'It's not going to help us to argue.'

I wasn't sure whether to feel guilty or angry, but I supposed he had a point. We didn't have a very good history with birthdays. One of my earliest memories was fighting with Carter on my sixth birthday, and my cake exploding from the magical energy we stirred up. Perhaps, considering that, I should've left well enough alone. But I couldn't quite do it.

'I'm sorry,' I blurted out. 'I know you blame me for picking up the scroll last night, and for Jaz's getting hurt, but I feel as if I'm falling apart –'

'You're not the only one,' he said.

A lump formed in my throat. I'd been so worried about Carter being angry with me, I hadn't paid attention to his tone. He sounded absolutely miserable.

'What is it?' I asked. 'What happened?'

He wiped his greasy hands on his trousers. 'Yesterday at the museum...one of those spirits – one of them talked to me.'

He told me about his odd encounter with the flaming *bau*, how time had seemed to slow down and the *bau* had warned Carter our quest would fail.

'He said...' Carter's voice broke. 'He said Zia was asleep at the Place of Red Sands, whatever that is. He said if I didn't give up the quest and rescue her, she would die.'

'Carter,' I said carefully, 'did this spirit mention Zia by name?'

'Well, no . . .'

'Could he have meant something else?'

'No, I'm sure. He meant Zia.'

I tried to bite my tongue. Honestly, I did. But the subject of Zia Rashid had become an unhealthy obsession for my brother.

'Carter, not to be unkind,' I said, 'but the last few months you've been seeing messages about Zia *everywhere*. Two weeks ago, you thought she was sending you a distress call in your mashed potatoes.'

'It was a *l*! Carved right in the potatoes!'

I held up my hands. 'Fine. And your dream last night?'

His shoulders tensed. 'What do you mean?'

'Oh, come on. At breakfast, you said Apophis would escape from his prison on the equinox. You sounded completely certain, as if you'd seen proof. You'd already talked to Bast and convinced her to check Apophis's prison. Whatever you saw . . . it must've been bad.'

'I . . . I don't know. I'm not sure.'

'I see.' My irritation rose. So Carter didn't want to tell me. We were back to keeping secrets from each other? Fine.

'We'll continue this later, then,' I said. 'See you tonight.'

'You don't believe me,' he said. 'About Zia.'

'And you don't trust me. So we're even.'

We glared at each other. Then Carter turned and stomped off towards the griffin.

I almost called him back. I hadn't meant to be so cross with him. On the other hand, apologizing is not my strong suit, and he *was* rather impossible.

I turned to the sphinx and summoned a gateway. I'd got rather good at it, if I do say so myself. Instantly a swirling funnel of sand appeared in front of me, and I jumped through.

A heartbeat later, I tumbled out at Cleopatra's Needle on the bank of the River Thames.

Six years before, my mother had died here; it wasn't my favourite Egyptian monument. But the Needle was the closest magic portal to Gran and Gramps's flat.

Fortunately, the weather was miserable and there was no one about, so I brushed the sand off my clothes and headed for the Underground station.

Thirty minutes later, I stood on the steps of my grandparents' flat. It seemed so odd to be...home? I wasn't even sure I could call it that any more. For months I'd been longing for London – the familiar city streets, my favourite shops, my mates, my old room. I'd even been homesick for the dreary weather. But now everything seemed so different, so *foreign*.

Nervously, I knocked on the door.

No answer. I was sure they were expecting me. I knocked again.

Perhaps they were hiding, waiting for me to come in. I imagined my grandparents, Liz and Emma crouching behind the furniture, ready to jump out and yell, 'Surprise!'

Hmm...Gran and Gramps crouching and jumping. Not likely.

I fished out my key and unlocked the door.

The living room was dark and empty. The stairwell light was off, which Gran would never allow. She was mortally afraid of falling down stairs. Even Gramps's television was switched off, which wasn't right. Gramps always kept the rugby matches on, even if he wasn't watching.

I sniffed the air. Six in the evening London time, yet no smell of burning biscuits from the kitchen. Gran should've burned at least one tray of biscuits for teatime. It was a tradition.

I got out my phone to call Liz and Emma, but the phone was dead. I *knew* I'd charged the battery.

My mind was just beginning to process a thought – *I am in danger* – when the front door slammed shut behind me. I spun, grabbing for my wand, which I didn't have.

Above me, at the top of the dark stairwell, a voice that was *definitely* not human hissed, 'Welcome home, Sadie Kane.'

C
A
R
T
E
R

5. I Learn to Really Hate Dung Beetles

THANKS A LOT, SADIE.

Hand me the mic right when you get to a good part.

So yeah, Sadie left on her birthday trip to London. The world was ending in four days, we had a quest to complete and she goes off to party with her friends. Really had her priorities straight, huh? Not that I was bitter, or anything.

On the bright side, Brooklyn House was pretty quiet once she left, at least until the three-headed snake showed up. But first I should tell you about my vision.

Sadie thought I was hiding something from her at breakfast, right? Well, that was sort of true. Honestly, though, what I saw during the night terrified me so badly I didn't want to talk about it, especially on her birthday. I'd experienced some bizarre stuff since I started learning magic, but this took the Nobel Prize for Weird.

After our trip to the Brooklyn Museum, I had a tough time getting to sleep. When I finally managed, I awoke in a different body.

It wasn't soul travel or a dream. I was Horus the Avenger.

When I'd shared a body with Horus before, he'd been in my head for almost a week at Christmas, whispering suggestions and otherwise being annoying. During the fight at the Red Pyramid, I'd even experienced a perfect melding of his thoughts and mine. I'd become what Egyptians called the 'Eye' of the god – all of his power at my command, our memories mixing together, human and god working as one. But I'd still been in my own body.

This time, things were reversed. I was a guest in Horus's body, standing at the prow of a boat on the magical river that wound through the Duat. My eyesight was as sharp as a falcon's. Through the fog, I could see shapes moving in the water – scaly reptilian backs and monstrous fins. I saw ghosts of the dead drifting along either shore. Far above, the cavern ceiling glistened red, as if we were sailing down the throat of a living beast.

My arms were bronze and muscular, circled with bands of gold and lapis lazuli. I was dressed for battle in leather armour, a javelin in one hand and a *khopesh* in the other. I felt strong and powerful like ... well, a god.

Hello, Carter, said Horus, which felt like talking to myself.

'Horus, what's up?' I didn't tell him I was irritated by his intrusion into my sleep. I didn't need to. I was sharing his mind.

I answered your questions, Horus said. *I told you where to find the first scroll. Now you must do something for me. There is something I wish to show you.*

The boat lurched forward. I grabbed the railing of the navigator's platform. Looking back, I could see the boat was a pharaoh's barque, about sixty feet long and shaped like a massive canoe. In the middle, a tattered pavilion covered an empty dais where a throne might once have sat. A single mast held a square sail that had once been decorated, but was now faded and hanging in shreds. Port and starboard, sets of broken oars dangled uselessly.

The boat must've been abandoned for centuries. The rigging was covered in cobwebs. The lines were rotten. The planks of the hull groaned and creaked as the boat picked up speed.

It is old, like Ra, Horus said. *Do you really want to put this boat back into service? Let me show you the threat you face.*

The rudder turned us into the current. Suddenly we were racing downstream. I'd sailed on the River of Night before, but this time we seemed to be much deeper in the Duat. The air was colder, the rapids faster. We jumped a cataract and went airborne. When we splashed down again, monsters began attacking. Horrible faces rose up – a sea dragon with feline eyes, a crocodile with porcupine bristles, a serpent with the head of a mummified man. Each time one rose up, I raised my sword and cut it down, or speared it with my javelin to keep it away from the boat. But they just kept coming, changing forms, and I knew that if I hadn't been Horus the Avenger – if I had just been Carter Kane trying to deal with these horrors – I would go crazy, or die, or both.

Every night, this was the journey, Horus said. *It was not Ra who fended off the creatures of Chaos. We other gods kept him safe. We held back Apophis and his minions.*

We plunged over another waterfall and crashed headlong into a whirlpool. Somehow, we managed not to capsize. The boat spun out of the current and floated towards the shore.

The riverbank here was a field of glistening black stones – or so I thought. As we got closer, I realized they were bug shells – millions and millions of dried-up beetle carapaces, stretching into the gloom as far as I could see. A few living scarabs moved sluggishly among the empty shells, so it seemed like the whole landscape was crawling. I'm not even going to try to describe the smell of several million dead dung beetles.

The Serpent's prison, Horus said.

I scanned the darkness for a jail cell, chains, a pit or something. All I saw was an endless expanse of dead beetles.

'Where?' I asked.

I am showing you this place in a way you can understand, Horus said. *If you were here in person, you would burn to ashes. If you saw this place as it really is, your limited mortal senses would melt.*

'Great,' I muttered. 'I just love having my senses melted.'

The boat scraped against the shore, stirring up a few live scarabs. The whole beach seemed to squirm and writhe.

Once, all these scarabs were alive, Horus said, *the symbol of Ra's daily rebirth, holding back the enemy. Now only a few remain. The Serpent slowly devours his way out.*

'Wait,' I said. 'You mean...'

In front of me, the shoreline swelled as something

underneath pushed upward – a vast shape straining to break free.

I gripped my sword and javelin, but, even with all the strength and courage of Horus, I found myself trembling. Red light glowed beneath the scarab shells. They crackled and shifted as the thing below surged towards the surface. Through the thinning layer of dead bugs, a ten-foot-wide red circle stared up at me – a serpent's eye, full of hatred and hunger. Even in my godly form, I felt the power of Chaos washing over me like lethal radiation, cooking me from the inside out, eating into my soul – and I believed what Horus had said. If I were here in the flesh, I would be burned to ashes.

'It's breaking free.' My throat started closing up with panic. 'Horus, it's getting out –'

Yes, he said. *Soon . . .*

Horus guided my arm. I raised my spear and thrust it into the Serpent's eye. Apophis howled with rage. The riverbank trembled. Then Apophis sank beneath the dead scarab shells, and the red glow faded.

But not today, Horus said. *On the equinox, the bonds will weaken enough for the Serpent to break free at last. Become my avatar again, Carter. Help me lead the gods into battle. Together we may be able to stop the rise of Apophis. But if you awaken Ra and he takes back the throne, will he have the strength to rule? Is this boat in any shape to sail the Duat again?*

'Why did you help me find the scroll, then?' I asked. 'If you don't want Ra awakened –'

It must be your choice, Horus said. *I believe in you, Carter Kane. Whatever you decide, I will support you. But many of the other gods do not feel the same. They think our chances would be better with me as their king and general, leading them into battle against the Serpent. They see your plan to awaken Ra as foolish and dangerous. It is all I can do to prevent open rebellion. I may not be able to stop them from attacking you and trying to prevent you.*

'Just what we need,' I said. 'More enemies.'

It does not have to be that way, Horus said. *Now you have seen the enemy. Who do you think has the best chance to stand against the Lord of Chaos – Ra or Horus?*

The boat pushed away from the dark shore. Horus released my *ba*, and my consciousness floated back to the mortal world like a helium balloon. The rest of the night, I dreamed about a landscape of dead scarabs and a red eye glaring from the depths of a weakening prison.

If I acted a little shaken up the next morning, now you know the reason.

I spent a lot of time wondering why Horus had showed me that vision. The obvious answer: Horus was now king of the gods. He didn't want Ra coming back to challenge his authority. Gods tend to be selfish. Even when they're helpful, they always have their own motives. That's why you have to be careful about trusting them.

On the other hand, Horus had a point. Ra had been old five thousand years ago. No one knew what kind of shape he was in now. Even if we managed to wake him, there was no guarantee he would help. If he looked as bad as his boat, I didn't see how Ra could defeat Apophis.

Horus had asked me who stood the best chance against the Lord of Chaos. Scary truth: when I searched my heart, the answer was none of us. Not the gods. Not the magicians. Not even all of us working together. Horus wanted to be the king and lead the gods into battle, but this enemy was more powerful than anything he'd ever faced. Apophis was as ancient as the universe and he only feared one enemy: Ra.

Bringing Ra back might not work, but my instincts told me it was our only shot. And, frankly, the fact that everyone kept telling me it was a bad idea – Bast, Horus, even Sadie – made me more certain it was the right thing to do. I'm kind of stubborn that way.

The right choice is hardly ever the easy choice, my dad had often told me.

Dad had defied the entire House of Life. He'd sacrificed his own life to unleash the gods because he was sure it was the only way to save the world. Now it was time for me to make the difficult choice.

Fast-forward past breakfast and my argument with Sadie. After she jumped through the portal, I stayed on the roof with no company but my new friend the psychotic griffin.

He screamed '*FREEEEK!*' so much that I decided to call him Freak – plus, it fitted his personality. I'd expected him to disappear overnight – to either fly away or return to the Duat – but he seemed happy in his new roost. I'd feathered it with a stack of morning newspapers, all of them featuring headlines about the bizarre sewer-gas eruption that had swept through Brooklyn the night before. According to the reports, the gas had ignited ghostly fires across the borough, caused extensive damage at the museum and overwhelmed some people with nausea, dizziness and even hallucinations of rhinoceros-size hummingbirds. Stupid sewer gas.

I was tossing Freak more roasted turkeys (jeez, he had an appetite) when Bast appeared next to me.

'Normally, I enjoy birds,' she said. 'But that thing is disturbing.'

'FREEEEK!' said Freak. He and Bast regarded each other as if each were wondering what the other would taste like for lunch.

Bast sniffed. 'You're not going to keep it, are you?'

'Well, he's not tied up or anything,' I said. 'He could leave if he wanted to. I think he likes it here.'

'Wonderful,' Bast muttered. 'One more thing that might kill you while I'm gone.'

Personally, I thought Freak and I were getting along pretty well, but I figured nothing I said would reassure Bast.

She was dressed for travel. Over her usual leopard-skin bodysuit she wore a long black coat embroidered with protective hieroglyphs. When she moved, the fabric shimmered, making her fade in and out of sight.

'Be careful,' I told her.

She smiled. 'I'm a cat, Carter. I can look after myself. I'm more worried about you and Sadie while I'm gone. If your vision is accurate and Apophis's prison is close to breaking . . . Well, I'll be back as soon as I can.'

There wasn't much I could say to that. If my vision was accurate, we were all in deep trouble.

'I may be out of touch for a couple of days,' she continued. 'My friend should get here before you and Sadie leave on your quest tomorrow. He'll make sure you two stay alive.'

'Can't you at least tell me his name?'

Bast gave me a look that was either amused or nervous – possibly both. 'He's a little hard to explain. I'd better let him introduce himself.'

With that, Bast kissed me on the forehead. 'Take care, my kit.'

I was too stunned to respond. I thought of Bast as Sadie's protector. I was just kind of an add-on. But her voice held such affection I probably blushed. She ran to the edge of the roof and jumped.

I wasn't worried about her, though. I was pretty sure she'd land on her feet.

I wanted to keep things as normal as possible for the trainees, so I led my usual morning class. I called it Magic Problem-Solving 101. The trainees called it Whatever Works.

I gave the trainees a problem. They could solve it any way they wanted. As soon as they succeeded, they could go.

I guess this wasn't much like real school, where you have to stay until the end of the day even if you're just doing busywork; but I'd never *been* to a real school. All those years of home-schooling with my dad, I'd learned at my own pace. When I finished my assignments to my dad's satisfaction, the school day was over. The system worked for me, and the trainees seemed to like it, too.

I also thought Zia Rashid would approve. The first time Sadie and I trained with Zia, she'd told us that magic couldn't be learned from classrooms and textbooks. You had to learn by doing. So for Magic Problem-Solving 101, we headed to the training room and blew stuff up.

Today I had four students. The rest of the trainees would be off researching their own paths of magic, practising enchantments or doing regular schoolwork under the supervision of our college-age initiates. As our main adult chaperone while Amos was gone, Bast had insisted we keep everyone up to speed on the regular subjects like math and reading, although she did sometimes add her own elective courses, such as Advanced Cat Grooming or Napping. There was a waiting list to get into Napping.

Anyway, the training room took up most of the second floor. It was about the size of a basketball court, which is what we used it for in the evenings. It had a hardwood floor, god statues lining the walls and a vaulted ceiling with pictures of Ancient Egyptians rocking that sideways walk they always do. On the baseline walls, we'd stuck falcon-headed statues of Ra perpendicular to the floor, ten feet up, and hollowed out their sun-disc crowns so we could use them as basketball hoops. Probably blasphemous – but, hey, if Ra didn't have a sense of humour, that was his problem.

Walt was waiting for me, along with Julian, Felix and Alyssa. Jaz almost always showed up for these sessions, but of course Jaz was still in a coma... and that was a problem none of us knew how to solve.

I attempted to put on my confident teacher-face. 'Okay, guys. Today we'll try some combat simulations. We'll start simple.'

I pulled four *shabti* figurines from my bag and placed them in different corners of the room. I stationed one trainee in front of each. Then I spoke a command word. The four statuettes grew into full-size Egyptian warriors armed with swords and shields. They weren't super-realistic. Their skin looked like glazed ceramic, and they moved slower than real humans, but they'd be good enough for starters.

'Felix?' I called. 'No penguins.'

'Aw, c'mon!'

Felix believed that the answer to every problem involved penguins, but it wasn't fair to the birds, and I was getting tired of teleporting them back home. Somewhere in Antarctica, a whole flock of Magellanic penguins was undergoing psychotherapy.

'Begin!' I yelled, and the *shabti* attacked.

Julian, a big seventh-grader who'd already decided on the path of Horus, went straight into battle. He hadn't quite mastered summoning a combat avatar, but he encased his fist in golden energy like a wrecking ball and punched the *shabti*. It flew backwards into the wall, cracking to pieces. One down.

Alyssa had been studying the path of Geb, the earth god. Nobody at Brooklyn House was an expert in earth magic, but Alyssa rarely needed help. She'd grown up in a family of potters in North Carolina and had been working with clay since she was a little girl.

She dodged the *shabti*'s clumsy swing and touched it on the back. A hieroglyph glowed against its clay armour:

Nothing seemed to happen to the warrior, but when it turned to strike, Alyssa just stood there. I was about to yell at her to duck, but the *shabti* missed her completely. Its blade hit the floor, and the warrior stumbled. It attacked again, swinging half a dozen times, but its blade never got close to Alyssa. Finally the warrior turned in confusion and staggered to the corner of the room, where it banged its head against the wall and shuddered to a stop.

Alyssa grinned at me. '*Sa-per*,' she explained. 'Hieroglyph for *Miss*.'

'Nice one,' I said.

Meanwhile, Felix found a non-penguin solution. I had no idea what type of magic he might eventually specialize in, but today he went for simple and violent. He grabbed a basketball from the bench, waited for the *shabti* to take a step, then bounced the ball off its head. His timing was perfect. The *shabti* lost its balance and fell over, its sword arm cracking off. Felix walked over and stomped on the *shabti* until it broke to pieces.

He looked at me with satisfaction. 'You didn't say we had to use magic.'

'Fair enough.' I made a mental note never to play basketball with Felix.

Walt was the most interesting to watch. He was a *sau*, a charm maker, so he tended to fight with whatever magic items he had on hand. I never knew what he was going to do.

As for his path, Walt hadn't decided which god's magic to study. He was a good researcher like Thoth, the god of knowledge. He could use scrolls and potions almost as well as Sadie, so he could've chosen the path of Isis. He might have even chosen Osiris, because Walt was a natural at bringing inanimate things to life.

Today he was taking his time, fingering his amulets and considering his options. As the *shabti* approached, Walt retreated. If Walt had a weakness, it was his cautiousness. He liked to think a long time before he acted. In other words, he was Sadie's exact opposite.

[Don't punch me, Sadie. It's true!]

'C'mon, Walt,' Julian called. 'Kill it already.'

'You've got this,' Alyssa said.

Walt reached for one of his rings. Then he stepped backwards and stumbled over the shards of Felix's broken *shabti*.

I shouted, 'Look out!'

But Walt slipped and fell hard. His *shabti* opponent rushed forward, slashing down with its sword.

I raced to help, but I was too far away. Walt's hand was already rising instinctively to block the strike. The enchanted ceramic blade was almost as sharp as real metal. It should've hurt Walt pretty badly, but he grabbed it, and the *shabti* froze. Under Walt's fingers, the blade turned grey and became webbed with cracks. The grey spread like frost over the entire warrior, and the *shabti* crumbled into a pile of dust.

Walt looked stunned. He opened his hand, which was perfectly fine.

'That was cool!' Felix said. 'What amulet was that?'

Walt gave me a nervous glance, and I knew the answer. It wasn't an amulet. Walt had no idea how he'd done it.

That would have been enough excitement for one day. Seriously. But the weirdness was just beginning.

Before either of us could say anything, the floor shook. I thought maybe Walt's magic was spreading into the building, which wouldn't have been good. Or maybe someone below us was experimenting with exploding donkey curses again.

Alyssa yelped. 'Guys…'

She pointed to the statue of Ra jutting out from the wall, ten feet above us. Our godly basketball hoop was crumbling.

At first I wasn't sure what I was seeing. The Ra statue wasn't turning to dust like the *shabti*. It was breaking apart, falling to the floor in pieces. Then my stomach clenched. The pieces weren't stone. The statue was turning into scarab shells.

The last of the statue crumbled away, and the pile of dung-beetle husks began to move. Three serpent heads rose from the centre.

I don't mind telling you: I panicked. I thought my vision of Apophis was coming true right then and there. I stumbled back so quickly I ran into Alyssa. The only reason I didn't bolt from the room was because four trainees were looking to me for reassurance.

It can't be Apophis, I told myself.

The snakes emerged, and I realized they weren't three different animals. It was one massive cobra with three heads. Even weirder, it unfurled a pair of hawklike wings. The thing's trunk was as thick as my leg. It stood as tall as me, but it wasn't nearly big enough to be Apophis. Its eyes weren't glowing red. They were regular creepy green snake eyes.

Still... with all three heads staring right at me, I can't say I relaxed.

'Carter?' Felix asked uneasily. 'Is this part of the lesson?'

The serpent hissed in three-part harmony. Its voice seemed to speak inside my head – and it sounded exactly like the *bau* in the Brooklyn Museum.

Your last warning, Carter Kane, it said. *Give me the scroll.*

My heart skipped a beat. The scroll – Sadie had given it to me after breakfast. Stupid me – I should've locked it up, put it in one of our secure cubbyholes in the library, but it was still in the bag on my shoulder.

What are you? I asked the snake.

'Carter.' Julian drew his sword. 'Do we attack?'

My trainees gave no indication that they'd heard either the snake or me speak.

Alyssa raised her hands like she was ready to catch a dodgeball. Walt positioned himself between the snake and Felix, and Felix leaned sideways to see around him.

Give it to me. The serpent coiled to strike, crushing dead beetle shells under its body. Its wings spread so wide they could've wrapped round us all. *Give up your quest, or I will destroy the girl you seek, just as I destroyed her village.*

I tried to draw my sword, but my arms wouldn't move. I

felt paralysed, as if those three sets of eyes had put me into a trance.

Her village, I thought. *Zia's village.*

Snakes can't laugh, but this thing's hiss sounded amused. *You'll have to make a choice, Carter Kane – the girl or the god. Abandon your foolish quest, or soon you'll be just another dry husk like Ra's scarabs.*

My anger saved me. I shook off the paralysis and yelled, 'Kill it!' just as the serpent opened its mouths, blasting out three columns of flames.

I raised a green shield of magic to deflect the fire. Julian chucked his sword like a throwing-axe. Alyssa gestured with her hand and three stone statues leaped off their pedestals, flying at the serpent. Walt fired a bolt of grey light from his wand. And Felix took off his left shoe and lobbed it at the monster.

Right about then, it sucked to be the serpent. Julian's sword sliced off one of its heads. Felix's shoe bounced off another. The blast from Walt's wand turned the third to dust. Then Alyssa's statues slammed into it, smashing the monster under a ton of stone.

What was left of the serpent's body dissolved into sand.

The room was suddenly quiet. My four trainees looked at me. I reached down and picked up one of the scarab shells.

'Carter, that was part of the lesson, right?' Felix asked. 'Tell me that was part of the lesson.'

I thought about the serpent's voice – the same voice as the *bau's* in the Brooklyn Museum. I realized why it sounded so familiar. I'd heard it before during the battle at the Red Pyramid.

'Carter?' Felix looked like he was about to cry. He was such a troublemaker I sometimes forgot he was only nine years old.

'Yes, just a test,' I lied. I looked at Walt, and we came to a silent agreement: *We need to talk about this later.* But first I had someone else to question. 'Class dismissed.'

I ran to find Amos.

6. A Birdbath Almost Kills Me

AMOS TURNED THE SCARAB SHELL in his fingers. 'A three-headed snake, you say.'

I felt guilty dumping this on him. He'd been through so much since Christmas. Then he finally got healed and came home, and *boom* – a monster invades our practice room. But I didn't know who else to talk to. I was kind of sorry Sadie wasn't around.

[All right, Sadie, don't gloat. I wasn't *that* sorry.]

'Yeah,' I said, 'with wings and flamethrower breath. Ever seen something like that before?'

Amos put the scarab shell on the table. He nudged it, as if expecting it to come to life. We had the library to ourselves, which was unusual. Often, the big round chamber was filled with trainees hunting through rows of cubbyholes for scrolls, or sending retrieval *shabti* across the world for artefacts, books or pizza. Painted on the floor was a picture of Geb the earth god, his body dotted with trees and rivers. Above us, the starry-skinned sky goddess Nut stretched across the ceiling. I usually felt safe in this room, sheltered between two gods who'd been friendly to us in the past. But now I kept glancing at the retrieval *shabti* stationed around the library and wondering if they would dissolve into scarab shells or decide to attack us.

Finally Amos spoke a command word: 'A'max.'

Burn.

A small red hieroglyph blazed over the scarab:

The shell burst into flames and crumbled to a tiny mound of ash.

'I seem to recall a painting,' Amos said, 'in the tomb of Thuthmose III. It showed a three-headed winged snake like the one you described. But what it means…' He shook his head. 'Snakes can be good *or* bad in Egyptian legend. They can be the enemies of Ra, or his protectors.'

'This wasn't a protector,' I said. 'It wanted the scroll.'

'And yet it had three heads, which might symbolize the three aspects of Ra. And it was born from the rubble of Ra's statue.'

'It wasn't from Ra,' I insisted. 'Why would Ra want to stop us from finding him? Besides, I recognized the snake's voice. It was the voice of your –' I bit my tongue. 'I mean, it was the voice of Set's minion from the Red Pyramid – the one who was possessed by Apophis.'

Amos's eyes became unfocused.

'Face of Horror,' he remembered. 'You think Apophis was speaking to you through this serpent?'

I nodded. 'I think he set those traps at the Brooklyn Museum. He spoke to me through that *bau*. If he's so powerful that he can infiltrate this mansion –'

'No, Carter. Even if you're right, it wasn't Apophis himself. If he'd broken out of his prison, it would cause ripples through the Duat so powerful that every magician would feel them. But possessing the minds of minions, even sending them into protected places to deliver a message – that's much easier. I don't think the snake could've done you much harm. It would've been quite weak after breaching our defences. It was mostly sent to warn you, and scare you.'

'It worked,' I said.

I didn't ask Amos how he knew so much about possession and the ways of Chaos. Having had his body taken over by Set, the god of evil, had given him an intensive crash course in stuff like that. Now he seemed back to normal, but I knew from my own experience of sharing a mind with Horus: once you hosted a god – whether it was voluntary or not – you were never quite the same. You retained the memories, even some traces of the god's power. I couldn't help noticing that the colour of Amos's magic had changed. It used to be blue. Now when he summoned hieroglyphs, they glowed red – the colour of Set.

'I'll strengthen the charms around the house,' he promised. 'It's high time I upgraded our security. I'll make sure Apophis can't send messengers through again.'

I nodded, but his promise didn't make me feel much better. Tomorrow, *if* Sadie came back safely, we'd be off on a quest to find the other two scrolls for the Book of Ra.

Sure, we'd survived our last adventure fighting Set, but Apophis was in a totally different league. And we weren't hosting gods any more. We were just kids, facing evil magicians, demons, monsters, spirits and the eternal Lord of Chaos. In the plus column, I had a cranky sister, a sword, a baboon and a griffin with a personality disorder. I wasn't liking those odds.

'Amos,' I said, 'what if we're wrong? What if awakening Ra doesn't work?'

It had been a long time since I'd seen my uncle smile. He didn't look much like my father, but when he smiled he got the same crinkles around his eyes.

'My boy, look what you've accomplished. You and Sadie have rediscovered a way of magic that hasn't been practised in millennia. You've taken your trainees further in two months than most First Nome initiates would get in two years. You've battled gods. You've accomplished more than any living magician has – even me, even Michel Desjardins. Trust your instincts. If I were a betting man, my money would be on you and your sister every time.'

A lump formed in my throat. I hadn't had a pep talk like that since my dad was still alive, and I guess I hadn't realized how much I needed one.

Unfortunately, hearing Desjardins's name reminded me that we had other problems besides Apophis. As soon as we started our quest, a magical Russian ice-cream salesman named Vlad the Inhaler was going to try to assassinate us.

And if Vlad was the third most powerful magician in the world . . .

'Who's second?' I asked.

Amos frowned. 'What do you mean?'

'You said this Russian guy, Vlad Menshikov, is the third most powerful magician alive. Desjardins is the most powerful. So who's second? I want to know if we have another enemy to look out for.'

The idea seemed to amuse Amos. 'Don't worry about that. And, despite your past dealings with Desjardins, I would not say he's truly an enemy.'

'Tell *him* that,' I muttered.

'I did, Carter. We talked several times while I was at the First Nome. I think what you and Sadie accomplished at the Red Pyramid shook him deeply. He knows he could not have defeated Set without you. He still opposes you, but if we had more time I might be able to convince him . . .'

That sounded about as likely as Apophis and Ra becoming Facebook buddies, but I decided not to say anything.

Amos passed his hand over the tabletop and spoke a spell. A red holograph of Ra appeared – a miniature replica of the statue in the practice room. The sun god looked like Horus: a falcon-headed man. But, unlike Horus, Ra wore the sun disc as a crown and held a shepherd's crook and a war flail – the two symbols of the pharaoh. He was dressed in robes rather than armour, sitting calmly and regally on his throne, as if he were happy to watch others do the fighting. The god's image looked strange in red, glowing with the colour of Chaos.

'Something else you must consider,' Amos warned. 'I don't

say this to discourage you, but you asked why Ra might want to stop you from waking him. The Book of Ra was divided for a reason. It was made intentionally difficult to find, so only the worthy would succeed. You should expect challenges and obstacles on your quest. The other two scrolls will be *at least* as well protected as the first. And you should ask yourself: what happens if you wake a god who does not want to be awakened?'

The doors of the library banged open, and I almost jumped out of my chair. Cleo and three other girls came in, chatting and laughing with their arms full of scrolls.

'Here's my research class.' Amos flicked his hand, and the holograph of Ra disappeared. 'We'll speak again, Carter, perhaps after lunch.'

I nodded, though even then I had a suspicion we'd never get to finish our conversation. When I looked back from the door of the library, Amos was greeting his students, casually wiping the ashes of the scarab shell off the table.

I got to my room and found Khufu crashed on the bed, surfing the sports channels. He was wearing his favourite Lakers jersey and had a bowl of Cheetos on his stomach. Ever since our trainees moved in, the Great Room had got too noisy for Khufu to watch TV in peace, so he'd decided to become my roommate.

I guess it was a compliment, but sharing space with a baboon wasn't easy. You think dogs and cats shed? Try getting monkey hair off your clothes.

'What's up?' I asked.

'*Agh!*'

That's pretty much what he always said.

'Great,' I told him. 'I'll be on the balcony.'

It was still cold and rainy outside. The wind off the East River would've made Felix's penguins shiver, but I didn't mind. For first time that day, I could finally be alone.

Since our trainees had come to Brooklyn House, I felt like I was always onstage. I had to act confident even when I had doubts. I couldn't lose my temper with anybody (well, except Sadie once in a while) and, when things went wrong, I couldn't complain too loudly. The other kids had come long distances to train with us. Many of them had fought monsters or magicians on the way. I couldn't admit I had no idea what I was doing, or wonder aloud whether this path-of-the-gods thing was going to get us all killed. I couldn't say, *Now that you're here, maybe this wasn't such a good idea.*

But there were plenty of times when that was how I felt. With Khufu occupying my room, the balcony was the only place I could be depressed in solitude.

I looked across the river to Manhattan. It was a great view. When Sadie and I had first arrived at Brooklyn House, Amos had told us that magicians tried to stay out of Manhattan. He said Manhattan had other problems – whatever that meant. And sometimes when I looked across the water, I could swear I was seeing things. Sadie laughed about it, but once I thought I saw a flying horse. Probably just the mansion's magic barriers causing optical illusions, but, still, it was weird.

I turned to the only piece of furniture on the balcony: my scrying bowl. It looked like a birdbath – just a bronze saucer on a stone pedestal – but it was my favourite magic item. Walt had made it for me right after he had arrived.

One day, I'd mentioned how nice it would be to know what was going on in the other nomes, and he'd made me this bowl.

I'd seen initiates use them in the First Nome, but they'd always seemed pretty difficult to master. Fortunately, Walt was an expert with enchantments. If my scrying bowl had been a car, it would have been a Cadillac, with power steering, automatic transmission and a butt warmer. All I had to do was fill it with clean olive oil and speak the command word. The bowl would show me anything, as long as I could visualize it and it wasn't shielded by magic. Places I'd never been to were hard to see. People or places that I'd seen personally or that meant a lot to me – *those* were usually easy.

I'd searched for Zia a hundred times with no luck. All I knew was that her old mentor, Iskandar, had put her into a magical sleep and hidden her somewhere, replacing her with a *shabti* to keep her safe, but I had no idea where the real Zia was sleeping.

I tried something new. I passed my hand over the saucer and imagined the Place of Red Sands. Nothing happened. I'd never been there, had no idea what it looked like apart from possibly being red and sandy. The oil showed me only my own reflection.

Okay, so I couldn't see Zia. I did the next best thing. I concentrated on her secret room in the First Nome. I'd been there only once, but I remembered every detail. It was the first place where I'd felt close to Zia. The surface of the oil rippled and became a magical video feed.

Nothing had changed in the room. Magic candles still burned on the little table. The walls were covered with Zia's photographs – pictures of her family village on the Nile, her mother and father, Zia as a small child.

Zia had told me the story of how her father had unearthed an Egyptian relic and accidentally unleashed a monster on their village. Magicians came to defeat the monster, but not before the entire town was destroyed. Only Zia, hidden by her parents, had survived. Iskandar, the old Chief Lector, had taken her to the First Nome and trained her. He'd been like a father to her.

Then, last Christmas, the gods had been unleashed at the British Museum. One of them – Nephthys – had chosen Zia as a host. Being a 'godling' was punishable by death in the First Nome, whether you meant to host the god's spirit or not, so Iskandar had hidden Zia away. He'd probably meant to bring her back after he sorted things out, but he had died before that could happen.

So the Zia I'd known was a replica, but I had to believe the *shabti* and the real Zia had shared thoughts. Wherever the real Zia was, she would remember me when she woke up. She'd know that we shared a connection – maybe the start of a great relationship. I couldn't accept that I'd fallen in love with nothing but a piece of pottery. And I definitely couldn't accept that Zia was beyond my power to rescue.

I concentrated on the image in the oil. I zoomed in on a photograph of Zia riding on her father's shoulders. She was young in the photo, but you could tell she was going to be beautiful when she grew up. Her glossy black hair was cut in a short wedge, as it had been when I knew her. Her eyes were brilliant amber. The photographer had caught her mid-laugh, trying to cover her dad's eyes with her hands. Her smile radiated playful mischief.

I will destroy the girl you seek, the three-headed snake had said, *just as I destroyed her village.*

I was sure he meant Zia's village. But what did that attack six years ago have to do with Apophis's rising now? If it hadn't been just a random accident – if Apophis had *meant* to destroy Zia's home – then why?

I had to find Zia. It wasn't just personal any more. She was connected somehow to the coming battle with Apophis. And if the snake's warning was true – if I had to choose between finding the Book of Ra and saving Zia? Well, I'd already lost my mom, my dad and my old life for the sake of stopping Apophis. I wasn't going to lose Zia, too.

I was contemplating how hard Sadie would kick me if she heard me say that, when somebody knocked on the balcony's glass door.

'Hey.' Walt stood in the doorway, holding Khufu's hand. '*Um*, hope you don't mind. Khufu let me in.'

'*Agh!*' Khufu confirmed. He led Walt outside, then jumped on the railing, disregarding the hundred-foot drop to the river below.

'No problem,' I said. Not like I had a choice. Khufu loved Walt, probably because he played basketball better than I did.

Walt nodded at the scrying bowl. 'How's that working for you?'

The image of Zia's room still shimmered in the oil. I waved my hand over the bowl and changed it to something else. Since I'd been thinking about Sadie, I picked Gran and Gramps's living room.

'Working fine.' I turned back to Walt. 'How are you feeling?'

For some reason, his whole body tensed. He looked at me like I was trying to corner him. 'What do you mean?'

'The training-room incident. The three-headed snake. What did you think I meant?'

The tendons in his neck relaxed. 'Right...sorry, just a weird morning. Did Amos have an explanation?'

I wondered what I'd said to upset him, but I decided to let it pass. I filled him in on my conversation with Amos. Walt was usually pretty calm about stuff. He was a good listener. But he still seemed guarded, on edge.

When I was done talking, he stepped over to the railing where Khufu was perched. 'Apophis let that thing loose in the house? If we hadn't stopped it –'

'Amos thinks the serpent didn't have much power. It was just here to deliver a message and scare us.'

Walt shook his head in dismay. 'Well...now it knows our abilities, I guess. It knows Felix throws a mean shoe.'

I couldn't help but smile. 'Yeah. Except that wasn't the ability I was thinking of. That grey light you blasted the snake with...and the way you handled the *shabti* practice dummy, turning it to dust –'

'How did I do it?' Walt shrugged helplessly. 'Honest, Carter, I don't know. I've been thinking about it ever since, and...it was just instinctive. At first I thought maybe the *shabti* had some kind of self-destruct spell built into it, and I'd accidentally triggered it. Sometimes I can do that with magic items – cause them to activate or shut down.'

'But that wouldn't explain how you did it again with the serpent.'

'No,' he agreed. He seemed even more distracted by the incident than I was. Khufu started grooming Walt's hair, looking for bugs, and Walt didn't even try to stop him.

'Walt...' I hesitated, not wanting to push him. 'This new ability, turning things to dust – it wouldn't have anything to do with...you know, whatever you were telling Jaz?'

There it was again: that caged-animal look.

'I know,' I said quickly, 'it's none of my business. But you've been acting upset lately. If there's anything I can do...'

He stared down at the river. He looked so depressed Khufu grunted and patted him on the shoulder.

'Sometimes I wonder why I came here,' Walt said.

'Are you kidding?' I asked. 'You're *great* at magic. One of the best! You've got a future here.'

He pulled something out of his pocket – one of the dried-up scarabs from the practice room. 'Thanks. But the timing...it's like a bad joke. Things are complicated for me, Carter. And the future...I don't know.'

I got the feeling he was talking about more than our four-day deadline to save the world.

'Look, if there's a problem...' I said. 'If it's something about the way Sadie and I are teaching –'

'Of course not. You've been great. And Sadie –'

'She likes you a lot,' I said. 'I know she can come on a little strong. If you want her to back off...'

[Okay, Sadie. Maybe I shouldn't have said that. But you aren't exactly subtle when you like somebody. I figured it might be making the guy uncomfortable.]

Walt actually laughed. 'No, it's nothing about Sadie. I like her, too. I'm just –'

'*Agh!*' Khufu barked so loudly, it made me jump. He bared his fangs. I turned and realized that he was snarling at the scrying bowl.

The scene was still Gran and Gramps's living room. But as I studied it more closely I realized something was wrong. The lights and TV were off. The sofa had been tipped over.

I got a metallic taste in my mouth.

I concentrated on shifting the image until I could see the front door. It had been smashed to pieces.

'What's wrong?' Walt came up next to me. 'What is it?'

'Sadie...' I focused all my willpower on finding her. I knew her so well that I could usually locate her instantly, but this time the oil turned black. A sharp pain stabbed behind my eyes, and the surface of the oil erupted in flames.

Walt pulled me back before my face could get burned. Khufu barked in alarm and tipped the bronze saucer over the railing, sending it hurtling towards the East River.

'What happened?' Walt asked. 'I've never seen a bowl do –'

'Portal to London.' I coughed, my nostrils stinging with burned olive oil. 'Nearest one. Now!'

Walt seemed to understand. His expression hardened with resolve. 'Our portal's still on cool-down. We'll need to go back to the Brooklyn Museum.'

'The griffin,' I said.

'Yeah. I'm coming too.'

I turned to Khufu. 'Go tell Amos we're leaving. Sadie's in trouble. No time to explain.'

Khufu barked and leaped straight over the side of the balcony – taking the express elevator down.

Walt and I bolted from my room, racing up the stairs to the roof.

7. A Gift from the Dog-headed Boy

WELL, YOU TALKED LONG ENOUGH, brother dear.

As you've been babbling on, everyone's been imagining me frozen in the doorway of Gran and Gramps's flat, screaming 'AAHHHHH!'

And the fact that you and Walt bolted off to London, assuming I needed to be rescued – men!

Yes, fair enough. I *did* need help. But that's not the point.

Back to the story: I'd just heard a voice hissing from upstairs: 'Welcome home, Sadie Kane.'

Of course, I knew this was bad news. My hands tingled as if I'd stuck my fingers in a light socket. I tried to summon my staff and wand, but, as I may have mentioned, I'm rubbish at retrieving things from the Duat on short notice. I cursed myself for not coming prepared – but, really, I couldn't have been expected to wear linen pyjamas and lug around a magic duffel bag for a night on the town with my mates.

I considered fleeing, but Gran and Gramps might be in danger. I couldn't leave without knowing that they were safe.

The stairwell creaked. At the top, the hem of a black dress appeared, along with sandalled feet that weren't quite human. The toes were gnarled and leathery, with overgrown nails like a bird's talons. As the woman descended into full view, I made a very undignified whimpering noise.

She looked a hundred years old, hunched over and emaciated. Her face, earlobes and neck sagged with folds of wrinkly pink skin, as if she'd melted under a sunlamp. Her nose was a drooping beak. Her eyes gleamed in their cavernous sockets, and she was almost bald – just a few greasy black tufts like weeds pushing through her craggy scalp.

Her dress, however, was absolutely lush. It was midnight black, fluffy and huge like a fur coat six sizes too big. As she stepped towards me, the material shifted, and I realized that it wasn't fur. The dress was made from black feathers.

Her hands appeared from her sleeves – clawlike fingers beckoning me forward. Her smile revealed teeth like broken bits of glass. And did I mention the smell? Not just old person smell – old *dead* person smell.

'I've been waiting for you,' said the hag. 'Fortunately, I'm very patient.'

I grasped the air for my wand. Of course, I had no luck. Without Isis in my head, I couldn't simply speak words of power any more. I had to have my tools. My only chance was to stall for time and hope I could collect my thoughts enough to access the Duat.

'Who are you?' I asked. 'Where are my grandparents?'

The hag reached the foot of the stairs. From two metres away, her feathery dress appeared to be covered with bits of ... Egad, was that meat?

'Don't you recognize me, dear?' Her image flickered. Her dress turned into a flowered housecoat. Her sandals became fuzzy green slippers. She had curly grey hair, watery blue eyes and the expression of a startled rabbit. It was Gran's face.

'Sadie?' Her voice sounded weak and confused.

'Gran!'

Her image changed back to the black-feathered hag, her horrible melted face grinning maliciously. 'Yes, dear. Your family is blood of the pharaohs, after all – perfect hosts for the gods. Don't make me strain myself, though. Your grandmother's heart isn't what it used to be.'

My whole body began to shake. I'd seen possession before, and it was always hideous. But *this* – the idea of some Egyptian hag taking over my poor old gran – this was horrifying. If I had any blood of the pharaohs, it was turning to ice.

'Leave her alone!' I meant to shout, but I'm afraid my voice was more of a terrified squeak. 'Get out of her!'

The hag cackled. 'Oh, I can't do that. You see, Sadie Kane, some of us doubt your strength.'

'Some of who – the gods?'

Her face rippled, momentarily changing into a horrible bird's head, bald and scaly pink with a long sharp beak. Then she morphed back into the grinning hag. I really wished she would make up her mind.

'I don't bother the strong, Sadie Kane. In the old days, I even protected the pharaoh if he proved himself worthy. But the weak…Ah, once they fall under the shadow of my wings, I never let them go. I wait for them to die. I wait to feed. And I think, my dear, that you will be my next meal.'

I pressed my back to the door.

'I know you,' I lied. Frantically, I ran down my mental list of Egyptian gods, trying to place the old hag. I still wasn't half as good as Carter at remembering all those odd names. [And no, Carter. That's not a compliment. It simply means you're a bigger nerd.] But after weeks of teaching our trainees, I'd got better.

Names held power. If I could figure out my enemy's name, that was a good first step to defeating her. A grisly black bird …A bird that feeds on the dead…

To my amazement, I actually remembered something.

'You're the vulture goddess,' I said triumphantly. 'Neckbutt, is it?'

The old hag snarled. 'Nekhbet!'

All right, so I was close.

'But you're supposed to be a *good* goddess!' I protested.

The goddess spread her arms. They turned into wings – black, matted plumage buzzing with flies and smelling of death. 'Vultures are *very* good, Sadie Kane. We remove the sickly and weak. We circle them until they die, then feed on their carcasses, cleaning the world of their stench. You, on the other hand, would bring back Ra, that wizened old carcass of a sun god. You would place a weak pharaoh on the throne of the gods. It goes against nature! Only the strong should live. The dead should be eaten.'

Her breath smelled like roadkill.

Despicable creatures, vultures: without a doubt the most disgusting birds ever. I supposed they served their purpose, but did they have to be so greasy and ugly? Couldn't we have cute fuzzy rabbits that cleaned up roadkill instead?

'Right,' I said. 'First, get *out* of my gran. Then, if you're a good vulture, I'll buy you some breath mints.'

This must've been a sore subject for Nekhbet. She lunged at me. I dived sideways, clambering over the couch and tipping it in the process. Nekhbet swept Gran's china collection off the sideboard.

'You will die, Sadie Kane!' she said. 'I will pick clean your bones. Then the other gods will see you were not worthy!'

I waited for another attack, but she just glared at me from the other side of the sofa. It occurred to me that vultures don't usually kill. They wait for their prey to die.

Nekhbet's wings filled the room. Her shadow fell over me, wrapping me in darkness. I began to feel trapped, helpless, like a small sickly animal.

If I hadn't tested my will against gods before, I might not have recognized this as magic – this insistent nagging in the back of my mind, urging me to give up in despair. But I'd stood against any number of horrid gods from the underworld. I could handle a greasy old bird.

'Nice try,' I said. 'But I'm not going to lie down and die.'

Nekhbet's eyes glittered. 'Perhaps it will take some time, my dear, but, as I told you, I'm patient. If you won't succumb, your mortal friends will be here soon. What are their names – Liz and Emma?'

'Leave them out of this!'

'Ah, they'll make lovely appetizers. And you haven't even said hello to dear old Gramps yet.'

Blood roared in my ears. 'Where is he?' I demanded.

Nekhbet glanced at the ceiling. 'Oh, he'll be along shortly. We vultures like to follow a nice big predator around, you know, and wait for it to do the killing.'

From upstairs came a muffled crash – as if a large piece of furniture had been thrown out a window.

Gramps shouted, 'No! No-o-o-o!' Then his voice changed into the roar of a mad animal. 'NOOOOOOAHHH!'

The last of my courage melted into my combat boots. 'Wh-what –'

'Yes,' Nekhbet said. 'Babi is waking.'

'B-bobby? You've got a god named Bobby?'

'B-A-B-I,' the vulture goddess snarled. 'You really are quite dense, aren't you, dear?'

The ceiling plaster cracked under the weight of heavy footsteps. Something was tromping towards the stairwell.

'Babi will take good care of you,' Nehkbet promised. 'And there will be plenty left over for me.'

'Goodbye,' I said, and I bolted for the door.

Nekhbet didn't try to stop me. She shrieked behind me, 'A hunt! Excellent!'

I made it across the street when our front door exploded. Glancing back, I saw something emerge from the ruins and dust – a dark hairy shape much too big to be my grandfather.

I didn't wait for a better look.

I raced round the corner of South Colonnade and ploughed straight into Liz and Emma.

'Sadie!' Liz yelped, dropping a birthday present. 'What's wrong?'

'No time!' I said. 'Come on!'

'Nice to see you, too,' Emma grumbled. 'Where are you rushing off –'

The creature behind me bellowed, quite close.now.

'Explain later,' I said. 'Unless you'd like to be ripped apart by a god named Bobby, follow me!'

Looking back, I can appreciate just what a *miserable* birthday I was having, but at the time I was too panicked to feel properly sorry for myself.

We ran down South Colonnade, the roaring behind us almost drowned out by Liz and Emma's complaining.

'Sadie!' Emma said. 'Is this one of your jokes?'

She'd got a bit taller, but still looked much the same, with her oversize, glittery glasses and short spiky hair. She wore a black leather miniskirt, a fuzzy pink jumper and ridiculous platform shoes that she could barely walk in, much less run. Who's that flamboyant rock 'n' roll chap from the 70s – Elton John? If he had an Indian daughter, she might look like Emma.

'It's no joke,' I promised. 'And for god's sake, lose those shoes!'

Emma looked appalled. 'You know how much these cost?'

'Honestly, Sadie,' Liz put in. 'Where are you dragging us to?'

She was dressed more sensibly in jeans and trainers, a

white top and denim jacket, but she looked just as winded as Emma. Tucked under her arm, my birthday present was getting a bit squashed. Liz was a redhead with lots of freckles, and when she got embarrassed or overexerted herself, her pale face became so flushed, her freckles disappeared. Under normal circumstances Emma and I would've teased her about this, but not today.

Behind us, the creature roared again. I looked back, which was a mistake. I faltered to a stop, and my mates ran into me.

For a brief moment, I thought, *My god, it's Khufu.*

But Khufu wasn't the size of a grizzly bear. He didn't have glittering silver fur, fangs like scimitars or a look of bloodlust in his eyes. The baboon ravaging Canary Wharf looked like he would eat *anything*, not just foods ending with an -o, and would have no difficulty ripping me limb from limb.

The only good news: the activity on the street had momentarily distracted him. Cars swerved to avoid the beast. Pedestrians screamed and ran. The baboon began overturning taxis, smashing shop windows and causing a general riot. As he got closer to us, I saw a bit of red cloth hanging from his left arm – the remains of Gramps's favourite cardigan. Stuck on his forehead were Gramps's glasses.

Until that moment, the shock hadn't fully hit me. That thing was my *grandfather*, who had never used magic, never done anything to annoy the Egyptian gods.

There were times I didn't like my grandparents, especially when they'd said bad things about my dad, or ignored Carter, or when they'd let Amos take me away last Christmas without a fight. But, still, they'd raised me for six years. Gramps had put

me on his lap and read me his dusty old Enid Blyton stories
when I was small. He'd watched after me at the park and taken
me to the zoo countless times. He'd bought me sweets even
though Gran disapproved. He may have had a temper, but he
was a reasonably harmless old pensioner. He certainly didn't
deserve to have his body taken over like this.

The baboon ripped the door off a pub and sniffed inside.
Panicked patrons smashed through a window and ran
off down the street, still holding their pints. A policeman
ran towards the commotion, saw the baboon, then turned
and ran the other way, yelling into his radio for reinforce-
ments.

When faced with magical events, mortal eyes tended
to short-circuit, sending the brain only images it could
understand. I had no idea what these people *thought* they were
seeing – possibly an escaped zoo animal or an enraged gunman
– but they knew enough to flee. I wondered what the London
security cameras would make of the scene later.

'Sadie,' Liz said in a very small voice, 'what *is* that?'

'Babi,' I said, 'the angry god of baboons. He's taken over
my granddad. And he wants to kill us.'

'Excuse me,' Emma said. 'Did you just say a baboon god
wants to kill us?'

The baboon roared, blinking and squinting as if he had
forgotten what he was doing. Maybe he'd inherited Gramps's
absentmindedness and bad eyesight. Maybe he didn't realize
his glasses were on his head. He sniffed the ground, then
bellowed in frustration and smashed the window of a bakery.

I almost believed we'd got a bit of good luck. Perhaps

we could sneak away. Then a dark shape glided overhead, spreading its black wings and crying, 'Here! Here!'

Wonderful. The baboon had air support.

'Two gods, actually,' I told my friends. 'Now, unless there are any more questions – run!'

This time Liz and Emma needed no encouragement. Emma kicked off her shoes, Liz tossed aside my present – pity, that – and we raced one another down the street.

We zigzagged through alleyways, hugging walls for cover whenever the vulture goddess swooped overhead. I heard Babi roaring along behind us, ruining people's evenings and smashing up the neighbourhood, but he seemed to have lost our scent for the moment.

We paused at a T in the road while I considered which way to run. In front of us stood a little church, the sort of ancient building you often find in London – a sombre bit of medieval stone wedged between a Caffè Nero and a pharmacy with neon signs offering selected hair products 3 for £1. The church had a tiny graveyard enclosed with a rusty fence, but I wouldn't have paid it much attention if a voice inside the yard hadn't whispered, 'Sadie.'

It's a miracle my heart didn't jump out of my throat. I turned and found myself face to face with Anubis. He was in his mortal form as a teen boy with dark, windblown hair and warm brown eyes. He wore a black Dead Weather T-shirt and black jeans that fitted him extremely well.

Liz and Emma are not known for being smooth around

good-looking boys. In fact, their brains more or less cease to function.

Liz gasped in single syllables that sounded like Lamaze breathing, 'Oh – ah – hi – who – what –?'

Emma lost control of her legs and stumbled into me.

I shot both of them a harsh look, then turned to Anubis.

'It's about time someone friendly showed up,' I complained. 'There's a baboon and a vulture trying to kill us. Would you *please* sort them out?'

Anubis pursed his lips, and I got the feeling that he wasn't there to bring me good news. 'Come into my territory,' he said, opening the graveyard gate. 'We need to talk, and there isn't much time.'

Emma stumbled into me again. 'Your, *um*, territory?'

Liz gulped. 'Who – ah –?'

'Shhh,' I told them, trying to stay composed, as if I met hot guys in graveyards every day. I glanced down the street and saw no sign of Babi or Nekhbet, but I could still hear them – the baboon god roaring, the vulture goddess shrieking, 'This way! This way!' in my gran's voice (if Gran had been eating gravel and taking steroids).

'Wait here,' I told my friends, and I stepped inside the gate.

Immediately, the air turned colder. Mist rose from the soggy ground. The gravestones shimmered, and everything outside the fence went slightly out of focus. Anubis made me feel unbalanced in many ways, of course, but I recognized this effect. We were slipping into the Duat – experiencing the graveyard on two levels at once: Anubis's world and mine.

He led me to a crumbling stone sarcophagus and bowed to it respectfully. 'Beatrice, do you mind if we sit?'

Nothing happened. The inscription on the sarcophagus had worn away centuries ago, but I supposed this was Beatrice's final resting place.

'Thank you.' Anubis gestured for me to sit. 'She doesn't mind.'

'What happens if she *does* mind?' I sat down a bit apprehensively.

'The Eighteenth Nome,' Anubis said.

'Excuse me?'

'That's where you must go. Vlad Menshikov has the second section of the Book of Ra in the top drawer of his desk, in his headquarters in St Petersburg. It's a trap, of course. He's hoping to bait you. But if want the scroll, you've got no choice. You should go tonight, before he has time to strengthen his defences even further. And, Sadie, if the other gods found out I was telling you this, I would be in big trouble.'

I stared at him. Sometimes he acted so much like a teenager, it was hard to believe he was thousands of years old. I suppose that came from living a sheltered life in the Land of the Dead, unaffected by the passage of time. The boy really needed to get out more.

'You're worried about getting into trouble?' I asked. 'Anubis, not that I'm ungrateful, but I've got bigger problems at the moment. Two gods have possessed my grandparents. If you want to lend a hand –'

'Sadie, I can't intervene.' He turned up his palms in frustration. 'I told you when we first met, this isn't an actual physical body.'

'Shame,' I mumbled.

'What?'

'Nothing. Go on.'

'I can manifest in places of death, like this churchyard, but there is very little I can do outside my territory. Now, if you were already dead and you wanted a nice funeral, I could help you, but –'

'Oh, thanks!'

Somewhere nearby, the baboon god roared. Glass shattered, and bricks crumbled. My friends called to me, but the sounds were distorted and muffled, as if I were hearing them from underwater.

'If I go on without my friends,' I asked Anubis, 'will the gods leave them alone?'

Anubis shook his head. 'Nekhbet preys on the weak. She knows that hurting your friends will weaken you. That's why she targeted your grandparents. The only way to stop her is by facing her down. As for Babi, he represents the darkest qualities of you primates: murderous rage, uncontrolled strength –'

'We primates?' I said. 'Sorry, did you just call me a baboon?'

Anubis studied me with a kind of confused awe. 'I'd forgotten how irritating you are. My point was that he will kill you just for the sake of killing.'

'And you can't help me.'

He gave me a mournful look with those gorgeous brown eyes. 'I told you about St Petersburg.'

Lord, he was good-looking, and *so* annoying.

'Well, then, god of pretty much nothing useful,' I said, 'anything else before I get myself killed?'

He held up his hand. A strange sort of knife materialized in his grasp. It was shaped like a Sweeney Todd razor: long, curvy and wickedly sharp along one edge, made from black metal.

'Take this,' Anubis said. 'It will help.'

'Have you seen the *size* of the baboon? Am I supposed to give him a shave?'

'This is not to fight Babi or Nekhbet,' he said, 'but you will need it soon for something even more important. It's a *netjeri* blade, made from meteoric iron. It's used for a ceremony I once told you about – the opening of the mouth.'

'Yes, well, if I survive the night, I'll be sure to take this razor and open someone's mouth. Thanks ever so much.'

Liz screamed, 'Sadie!' Through the mist of the graveyard, I saw Babi a few blocks away, lumbering towards the church. He'd spotted us.

'Take the Underground,' Anubis suggested, pulling me to my feet. 'There's a station half a block south. They won't be able to track you very well below the earth. Running water is also good. Creatures of the Duat are weakened by crossing a river. If you must battle them, find a bridge over the Thames. Oh, and I told your driver to come get you.'

'My driver?'

'Yes. He wasn't planning to meet you until tomorrow, but –'

A red Royal Mail box hurtled through the air and smashed

into the building next door. My friends screamed at me to hurry.

'Go,' Anubis said. 'I'm sorry I can't do more. But happy birthday, Sadie.'

He leaned forward and kissed me on the lips. Then he melted into mist and disappeared. The graveyard became normal again – part of the regular, unshimmery world.

I should've been very cross with Anubis. Kissing me without permission – the nerve! But I stood there, paralysed, staring at Beatrice's crumbling sarcophagus, until Emma yelled, 'Sadie, come on!'

My friends grabbed my arms, and I remembered how to run.

We bolted for the Canary Wharf tube station. The baboon roared and smashed through traffic behind us. Overhead, Nekhbet shrieked, 'There they go! Kill them!'

'Who was that boy?' Emma demanded as we plunged into the station. 'God, he was hot.'

'A god,' I muttered. 'Yes.'

I slipped the black razor into my pocket and clambered down the escalator, my lips still tingling from my first kiss.

And if I was humming 'Happy Birthday' and smiling stupidly as I fled for my life – well, that was nobody's business, was it?

S
A
D
I
E

8. Major Delays at Waterloo Station (We Apologize for the Giant Baboon)

THE LONDON UNDERGROUND has lovely acoustics. Sound echoed through the tunnels, so as we descended I could hear the rush of the trains, the musicians playing for coins and of course the killer baboon god roaring for blood as he pulverized the turnstiles behind us.

What with terrorism threats and stepped-up security, one might've expected a few police to be on hand, but sadly not this time of evening, not at such a relatively small station. Sirens wailed from the street above, but we'd be dead or long gone by the time mortal help arrived. And if the police *did* try to shoot Babi while he possessed Gramps's body – no. I forced myself not to think about that.

Anubis had suggested travelling underground. And if I had to fight, I should find a bridge. I had to stick with that plan.

There wasn't much choice of trains at Canary Wharf. Thankfully, the Jubilee Line was running on time. We made it to the platform, jumped aboard the last carriage as the doors were closing and collapsed on a bench.

The train lurched away into the dark tunnel. Behind us, I saw no sign of Babi or Nekhbet chasing us.

'Sadie Kane,' Emma gasped. 'Will you *please* tell us what's going on?'

My poor friends. I'd *never* got them into this much trouble, not even when we got shut in the boys' changing room at school. (Long story, which involved a five-quid bet, Dylan Quinn's knickers and a squirrel. Perhaps I'll tell you later.)

Emma's feet were cut and bruised from running barefoot. Her pink jumper looked like mangled poodle fur, and her glasses had lost several rhinestones.

Liz's face was red as a valentine. She'd taken off her denim jacket, which she *never* does, as she's always cold. Her white top was blotted with sweat. Her arms were so freckly, they reminded me of Nut the sky goddess's constellation skin.

Of the two, Emma looked more annoyed, waiting for my explanation. Liz looked horrified, her mouth moving as if she wanted to speak but had lost her vocal cords. I thought she'd make some comment about the bloodthirsty gods chasing us, but when she finally found her voice she said, 'That boy kissed you!'

Leave it to Liz to have her priorities straight.

'I *will* explain,' I promised. 'I know I'm a horrible friend for dragging you both into this. But, please, give me a moment. I need to concentrate.'

'Concentrate on what?' Emma demanded.

'Emma, hush!' Liz chided. 'She said to let her concentrate.'

I closed my eyes, trying to calm my nerves.

It wasn't easy, especially with an audience. Without my supplies, however, I was defenceless, and I wasn't likely to get another chance to retrieve them. I thought: *You can do this, Sadie. It's only reaching into another dimension. Only ripping a tear in the fabric of reality.*

I reached out. Nothing happened. I tried again, and my hand disappeared into the Duat. Liz shrieked. Fortunately, I didn't lose my concentration (or my hand). My fingers closed round the strap of my magic bag, and I pulled it free.

Emma's eyes widened. 'That's brilliant. How did you do that?'

I was wondering the same thing, actually. Given the circumstances, I couldn't believe I'd managed it on just my second try.

'It's, *um* . . . magic,' I said.

My mates stared at me, mystified and scared, and the enormity of my problems suddenly came crashing down on me.

A year ago, Liz, Emma and I would've been riding this train to Funland or the cinema. We would've been laughing at the ridiculous ring tones on Liz's phone or Emma's Photoshopped pictures of the girls we hated at school. The most dangerous things in my life had been Gran's cooking and Gramps's temper when he saw my marks for the term.

Now Gramps was a giant baboon. Gran was an evil vulture. My friends were regarding me as if I'd dropped from another planet, which wasn't far from the truth.

Even with my magic supplies in hand, I had no idea what I was going to do. I didn't have the full power of Isis at my command any more. If I tried to fight Babi and Nekhbet, I might injure my own grandparents and would likely get myself killed. But if I didn't stop them who would? Godly possession would eventually burn out a human host. That had almost happened to Uncle Amos, who was a full-fledged magician and knew how to defend himself. Gran and Gramps were old, frail and quite unmagical. They didn't have much time.

Despair – much worse than the vulture goddess's wings – overwhelmed me.

I didn't realize I was crying until Liz put her hand on my shoulder. 'Sadie, dear, we're sorry. It's just a bit...strange, you know? Tell us what's the matter. Let us help.'

I took a shaky breath. I'd missed my mates so much. I'd always thought them a bit odd, but now they seemed blissfully *normal* – part of a world that wasn't mine any more. They were both trying to act brave, but I could tell they were terrified inside. I wished I could leave them behind, hide them, keep them out of harm's way, but I remembered what Nekhbet had said: *They'll make lovely appetizers.* Anubis had warned that the vulture goddess would hunt down my friends and hurt them just to hurt me. At least if they were with me I could try to protect them. I didn't want to up-end their lives the way mine had been, but I owed them the truth.

'This will sound absolutely mad,' I warned.

I gave them the shortest version possible – why I'd left London, how the Egyptian gods had escaped into the world, how I'd discovered my ancestry as a magician. I told them about our fight with Set, the rise of Apophis and our insane idea to awaken the god Ra.

Two stations passed, but it felt so good to tell my friends the story that I rather lost track of time.

When I was done, Liz and Emma looked at one another, no doubt wondering how to gently tell me I was bonkers.

'I know it seems impossible,' I said, 'but –'

'Sadie, we believe you,' Emma said.

I blinked. 'You do?'

'Course we do.' Liz's face was flushed, the way she got after several roller coaster rides. 'I've never heard you talk so seriously about anything. You – you've changed.'

'It's just I'm a magician now, and . . . and I can't believe how *stupid* that sounds.'

'It's more than that.' Emma studied my face as if I were turning into something quite frightening. 'You seem older. More mature.'

Her voice was tinged with sadness, and I realized my mates and I were growing apart. It was as if we stood on opposite sides of a widening chasm. And I knew with gloomy certainty the breach was already too wide for me to jump back across.

'Your boyfriend is amazing,' Liz added, probably to cheer me up.

'He's not my . . .' I stopped. There was no winning that argument with Liz. Besides, I was so mixed up about that damn jackal Anubis that I didn't know where to begin.

The train slowed. I saw the signs for Waterloo Station.

'Oh, god,' I said. 'I meant to get off at London Bridge. I need a bridge.'

'Can't we backtrack?' Liz asked.

A roar from the tunnel behind us answered that question. Looking back, I saw a large shape with glittering silver fur loping along the tracks. Its foot touched the third rail, and sparks flew, but the baboon god lumbered on, unfazed. As the train braked, Babi started to gain on us.

'No going back,' I said. 'That baboon's too big for Hungerford Bridge. We'll have to try Waterloo Bridge.'

'That's half a mile from the station!' Liz protested. 'What if it catches us?'

I rummaged through my bag and pulled out my new staff. Instantly it expanded to full length, the lion-carved tip blazing with golden light. 'Then I suppose we'll have to fight.'

Should I describe Waterloo Station as it was before or after we destroyed it? The main concourse was massive. It had a polished stone floor, loads of shops and kiosks, and a glass-and-girder ceiling high enough so that a helicopter could fly about inside comfortably.

Rivers of people flowed in and out, mixing, separating and occasionally colliding as they made their way to various escalators and platforms.

When I was small, the station building had rather frightened me. I worried that the giant Victorian clock hanging from the ceiling might fall and crush me. The announcers' voices were much too loud. (I prefer to be the noisiest thing in my environment, thank you very much.) The masses of commuters

119

standing mesmerized under the departure boards, watching for their trains, reminded me of a mob in a zombie movie – which, granted, I shouldn't have watched as a young child, but I was always rather precocious.

At any rate, my mates and I were racing through the main station, pushing our way towards the nearest exit, when a stairwell behind us exploded.

Crowds scattered as Babi climbed from the rubble. Businessmen screamed, dropping their briefcases and sprinting for their lives. Liz, Emma and I pressed against the side of the Paperchase kiosk to avoid getting trampled by a group of tourists yelling in Italian.

Babi howled. His fur was covered with grime and soot from his run through the tunnels. Gramps's cardigan was ripped to shreds on his arm, but, miraculously, his glasses were still on his head.

He sniffed the air, probably trying to catch my scent. Then a dark shadow passed overhead.

'Where are you going, Sadie Kane?' Nekhbet shrieked. She soared through the terminal, swooping down on the already panicked crowds. 'Would you fight by running away? You are not worthy!'

An announcer's calm voice echoed through the terminal: 'The 20:02 train for Basingstoke will arrive on platform three.'

'ROOOAR!' Babi swatted a bronze statue of some poor famous bloke and knocked his head clean off. Liz and Emma both screamed.

I'd never seen so many people clear out of a terminal so

quickly. I considered following them, but decided it would be too dangerous. I couldn't have these insane gods killing loads of innocent people just because I was in their midst and if we tried to join the exodus we'd only get stuck or crushed in a stampede.

'Sadie, look!' Liz pointed up, and Emma yelped.

Nekhbet sailed into the ceiling girders and perched there with the pigeons. She glared down at us and cried to Babi, 'Here she is, my dear! Here!'

'I wish she'd shut up,' I muttered.

'Isis was foolish to choose you!' Nekhbet yelled. 'I will feed on your entrails!'

'ROOOOAR!' said Babi, in hearty agreement.

'The 20:14 train for Brighton is delayed,' said the announcer. 'We apologize for the inconvenience.'

Babi had seen us now. His eyes smouldered with primal rage, but I also saw something of Gramps in his expression. The way he furrowed his brow and jutted out his chin – just as Gramps did when he got angry at the telly and yelled at the rugby players. Seeing that expression on the baboon god almost made me lose my nerve.

I wasn't going to die here. I wasn't going to let these two repulsive gods hurt my friends or burn up my grandparents.

Babi lumbered towards us. Now that he'd found us, he didn't seem in any hurry to kill us. He lifted his head and made a deep barking sound to the left and right, as if calling out, summoning friends for dinner. Emma's fingers dug into my arm. Liz whimpered, 'Sadie...?'

The crowds had mostly cleared out now. No other police

were in sight. Perhaps they'd fled, or perhaps they were all on their way to Canary Wharf, not realizing the problem was now here.

'We're not going to die,' I promised my mates. 'Emma, hold my staff.'

'Your – Oh, right.' She took the staff gingerly as if I'd handed her a rocket launcher, which I suppose it could've been with the proper spell.

'Liz,' I ordered, 'watch the baboon.'

'Watching the baboon,' she said. 'Rather hard to miss the baboon.'

I rummaged through my magic bag, desperately taking inventory. Wand... good for defence, but against two gods at once I needed more. Sons of Horus, magic chalk – this wasn't the place to draw a protective circle. I had to get to the bridge. I needed to buy time to get out of this terminal.

'Sadie...' Liz warned.

Babi had jumped onto the roof of the Body Shop. He roared, and smaller baboons began to appear from every direction – climbing over the heads of fleeing commuters, swinging down from the girders, popping out of the stairwells and shops. There were dozens of them, all wearing black-and-silver basketball jerseys. Was basketball some sort of international baboon sport?

Until today, I'd been rather fond of baboons. The ones I'd met before, like Khufu and his sociable friends, were the sacred animals of Thoth, god of knowledge. They were generally wise and helpful. I suspected, however, that Babi's troop of baboons was a different sort altogether. They had blood-red fur, wild eyes, and fangs that would've made a sabre-toothed tiger feel inadequate.

They began to close in, snarling as they prepared to pounce.

I pulled a block of wax from my bag – no time to fashion a *shabti*. Two *tyet* amulets, the sacred mark of Isis – ah, those might be helpful. Then I found a corked glass vial I'd quite forgotten about. Inside was some murky sludge: my first attempt at a potion. It had been sitting at the bottom of my bag for ages because I'd never been desperate enough to test it.

I shook the potion. The liquid glowed with a sickly green light. Bits of gunk swirled inside. I uncorked it. The stuff smelled worse than Nekhbet.

'What *is* that?' Liz asked.

'Disgusting,' I said. 'Animation scroll blended with oil, water and a few secret ingredients. Came out a bit chunky, I'm afraid.'

'Animation?' Emma asked. 'You're going to summon cartoons?'

'That would be brilliant,' I admitted. 'But this is more dangerous. If I do it right, I can ingest a great deal of magic without burning myself up.'

'And if you do it wrong?' Liz asked.

I handed them each an amulet of Isis. 'Hold on to these. When I say Go, run for the taxi stands. Don't stop.'

'Sadie,' Emma protested, 'what on earth –'

Before I could lose my nerve, I gagged down the potion.

Above us, Nekhbet cackled. 'Give up! You cannot oppose us!' The shadow of her wings seemed to spread over the entire concourse, making the last of the commuters flee in panic and weighing me down with fear. I knew it was only a spell, but, still, the temptation to accept a quick death was almost overwhelming.

A few of the baboons got distracted by the smell of food and raided McDonald's. Several others were chasing a train conductor, beating him with rolled-up fashion magazines.

Sadly, most of the baboons were still focused on us. They made a loose ring round the Paperchase kiosk. From his command station atop the Body Shop, Babi howled – a clear command to attack.

Then the potion hit my gut. Magic coursed through my body. My mouth tasted like I'd swallowed a dead toad, but now I understood why potions were so popular with ancient magicians.

The animation spell, which had taken me days to write and would normally take at least an hour to cast, was now tingling in my bloodstream. Power surged into my fingertips. My only problem was channelling the magic, making sure it didn't burn me to a crisp.

I called on Isis as best I could, tapping her power to help me shape the enchantment. I envisioned what I wanted, and the right word of power popped into my head: *Protect. N'dah.* I released the magic. A gold hieroglyph burned in front of me:

A wave of golden light rippled through the concourse. The troop of baboons hesitated. Babi stumbled on the Body Shop roof. Even Nekhbet squawked and faltered on the ceiling girders.

All around the station, inanimate objects began to move. Backpacks and briefcases suddenly learned to fly. Magazine racks, gum, sweets and assorted cold drinks exploded out of the shops and attacked the baboon troop. The decapitated bronze head from the statue shot out of nowhere and slammed into Babi's chest, knocking him backwards through the roof of the Body Shop. A tornado of pink *Financial Times* newspapers swirled towards the ceiling. They engulfed Nekhbet, who stumbled blindly and fell shrieking from her perch in a flurry of pink and black.

'Go!' I told my friends. We ran for the exit, weaving around baboons who were much too busy to stop us. One was being pummelled by a half-dozen bottles of sparkling water. Another was fending off a briefcase and several kamikaze BlackBerrys.

Babi tried to rise, but a maelstrom of Body Shop products surged around him – lotions, loofah sponges and shampoos all battering him, squirting in his eyes and trying to give him an extreme makeover. He bellowed in irritation, slipped and fell back into the ruined shop. I doubted my spell would do the gods any permanent damage, but with luck it would keep them occupied for a few minutes.

Liz, Emma and I made it out of the building. With the entire station evacuated, I didn't really expect any cabs to be in the taxi queue, and indeed the kerb was empty. I resigned myself to running all the way to Waterloo Bridge, though Emma had no shoes, and the potion had made me queasy.

'Look!' Liz said.

'Oh, well done, Sadie,' Emma said.

'What?' I asked. 'What did I do?'

Then I noticed the chauffeur – an extremely short, scruffy man standing at the end of the drive in a black suit, holding a placard that read KANE.

I suppose my friends thought I'd summoned him by magic. Before I could tell them differently, Emma said, 'Come on!' and they sprinted towards the little man. I had no choice but to follow. I remembered what Anubis had said about sending my 'driver' to meet me. I supposed this must be him, but the closer we got, the less eager I was to meet him.

He was shorter than me by half, stouter than my Uncle Amos and uglier than anyone else on the planet. His facial features were positively Neanderthal. Under his thick furry mono-brow, one eye was bigger than the other. His beard looked as if it had been used to scrape greasy pots. His skin was poxy with red welts, and his hair looked like a bird's nest that had been set on fire then stomped out.

When he saw me, he scowled, which did nothing to help his appearance.

'About time!' His accent was American. He belched into his fist, and the smell of curry nearly knocked me over. 'Bast's friend? Sadie Kane?'

'Um... possibly.' I decided to have a serious talk with Bast about her choice of friends. 'Just by the way, we have two gods trying to kill us.'

The warty little man smacked his lips, clearly unimpressed. 'Guess you'll want a bridge, then.'

He turned towards the kerb and yelled, 'BOO!'

A black Mercedes limousine appeared out of nowhere, as if it had been scared into existence.

The chauffeur glanced back at me and arched his brow. 'Well? Get in!'

I'd never been in a limousine before. I hope most are nicer than the one we took. The back seat was littered with takeaway curry containers, old fish-and-chip paper, crisps bags and various dirty socks. Despite this, Emma, Liz and I crammed together in the back, because none of us dared ride up front.

You may think I was mad to get in a car with a strange man. You're right, of course. But Bast had promised us help, and Anubis had told me to expect a driver. The fact that our promised help was a little man with bad hygiene and a magical limousine did not particularly surprise me. I'd seen stranger things.

Also, I didn't have much choice. The potion had worn off, and the strain of releasing so much magic had made me lightheaded and wobbly-legged. I wasn't sure I could've walked to Waterloo Bridge without passing out.

The chauffeur floored the accelerator and barrelled out of the station. The police had cordoned it off, but our limo swerved round the barricades, past a cluster of BBC news vans and a mob of spectators, and no one paid us any attention.

The chauffeur started whistling a tune that sounded like 'Short People'. His head barely reached the headrest. All I could see of him was a grubby nest of hair and a set of furry hands on the wheel.

Stuck in the sun visor was an identification card with his picture – sort of. It had been taken at point-blank range, showing only an out-of-focus nose and a hideous mouth, as if he'd been trying to eat the camera. The card read: *Your Driver is BES.*

'You're Bes, I guess?' I said.

'Yes,' he said.

'Your car's a mess,' Liz muttered.

'If one more person rhymes,' Emma grumbled, 'I'll throw up.'

'Is it Mr Bes?' I asked, trying to place his name from Egyptian mythology. I was fairly sure they hadn't had a god of chauffeurs. 'Lord Bes? Bes the Extremely Short?'

'Just Bes,' he grunted. 'One *s*. And, no, it's NOT a girl's name. Call me Bessie, and I'll have to kill you. As for being short, I'm the dwarf god, so what do you expect? Oh, there's bottled water for you back there if you're thirsty.'

I looked down. Rolling about at my feet were two partially empty bottles of water. One had lipstick on the cap. The other looked as if it had been chewed on.

'Not thirsty,' I decided.

Liz and Emma murmured agreement. I was surprised they weren't absolutely catatonic after the evening's events, but then again they were *my* mates. I didn't hang out with weak-willed girls, did I? Even before I discovered magic, it took a strong constitution and a fair amount of adaptability to be my friend. [And no comment from you, Carter.]

Police vehicles were blocking Waterloo Bridge, but Bes

swerved round them, jumped the pavement and kept driving. The police didn't even blink.

'Are we invisible?' I asked.

'To most mortals.' Bes belched. 'They're pretty dense, aren't they? Present company excepted, et cetera.'

'You're really a god?' Liz asked.

'Huge,' Bes said. 'I'm *huge* in the world of gods.'

'A huge god of dwarves,' Emma marvelled. 'You mean as in Snow White, or –'

'All dwarves.' Bes waved his hands expansively, which made me a bit nervous as he took both of them off the wheel. 'Egyptians were smart. They honoured people who were born unusual. Dwarves were considered extremely magical. So, yeah, I'm the god of dwarves.'

Liz cleared her throat. 'Isn't there a more polite term we're supposed to use nowadays? Like...little person, or vertically challenged, or –'

'I'm not going to call myself the god of vertically challenged people,' Bes grumbled. 'I'm a dwarf! Now, here we are, just in time.'

He spun the car to a stop in the middle of the bridge. Looking behind us, I almost lost the contents of my stomach. A winged black shape was circling over the riverbank. At the end of the bridge, Babi was taking care of the barricade in his own fashion. He was throwing police cars into the River Thames while the officers scattered and fired their weapons, though the bullets seemed to have no effect on the baboon god's steely fur.

'Why are we stopping?' Emma asked.

Bes stood on his seat and stretched, which he could do quite easily. 'It's a river,' he said. 'Good place to fight gods, if I do say so myself. All that force of nature flowing underneath our feet makes it hard to stay anchored in the mortal world.'

Looking at him more closely, I could see what he meant. His face was shimmering like a mirage.

A lump formed in my throat. This was the moment of truth. I felt sick from the potion and from fear. I wasn't at all sure I had enough magic to combat those two gods. But I had no choice.

'Liz, Emma,' I said. 'We're getting out.'

'Getting...out?' Liz whimpered.

Emma swallowed. 'Are you sure –'

'I know you're scared,' I said, 'but you'll need to do exactly as I say.'

They nodded hesitantly and opened the car doors. The poor things. Again I wished I'd left them behind, but, honestly, after seeing my grandparents possessed, I couldn't stand the idea of letting my friends out of my sight.

Bes stifled a yawn. 'Need my help?'

'Um...'

Babi was lumbering towards us. Nekhbet circled over him, shrieking orders. If the river were affecting them at all, they didn't show it.

I didn't see how a dwarf god could stand against those two, but I said, 'Yes. I need help.'

'Right.' Bes cracked his knuckles. 'So get out.'

'What?'

'I can't change clothes with you in the car, can I? I have to put on my ugly outfit.'

'Ugly outfit?'

'Go!' the dwarf commanded. 'I'll be out in a minute.'

It didn't take much encouragement. None of us wanted to see any more of Bes than we had to. We got out, and Bes locked the doors behind us. The windows were heavily tinted, so I couldn't see in. For all I knew Bes would be relaxing, listening to music while we got slaughtered. I certainly didn't have much hope that a wardrobe change was going to defeat Nekhbet and Babi.

I looked at my frightened mates, then at the two gods charging towards us.

'We'll make our last stand here.'

'Oh, no, no,' Liz said. 'I really don't like the term "last stand".'

I rummaged through my bag and took out a piece of chalk and the four sons of Horus. 'Liz, put these statues at the cardinal points – north, south and so on. Emma, take the chalk. Draw a circle connecting the statues. We only have a few seconds.'

I traded her the chalk for my staff, then had a horrible flash of déjà vu. I'd just ordered my friends into action exactly as Zia Rashid had bossed me the first time we'd faced an enemy god together.

I didn't want to be like Zia. On the other hand, I realized for the first time just how much courage she must've had to stand up to a goddess while protecting two complete novices.

I hate to say it, but it gave me a newfound respect for her. I wished I had her bravery.

I raised my staff and wand and tried to focus. Time seemed to slow down. I reached out with my senses until I was aware of everything around me – Emma scrawling with chalk to finish the circle, Liz's heart beating too fast, Babi's massive feet pounding on the bridge as he ran towards us, the Thames flowing under the bridge and the currents of the Duat flowing around me just as powerfully.

Bast once told me the Duat was like an ocean of magic under the surface of the mortal world. If that was true, then this place – a bridge over moving water – was like a jet stream. Magic flowed more strongly here. It could drown the unwary. Even gods might be swept away.

I tried to anchor myself by concentrating on the landscape around me. London was *my* city. From here I could see everything – the Houses of Parliament, the London Eye, even Cleopatra's Needle on the Victoria Embankment, where my mother had died. If I failed now, so close to where my mother had worked her last magic – No. I couldn't let it come to that.

Babi was only a metre away when Emma finished the circle. I touched my staff to the chalk, and golden light flared up.

The baboon god slammed into my protective force field like it was a metal wall. He staggered backwards. Nekhbet swerved away at the last second and flew around us, cawing in frustration.

Unfortunately, the circle's light began to flicker. My mum had taught me at a very young age: for every action there is an equal and opposite reaction. That applied to magic as well as

132

science. The force of Babi's assault left me seeing black spots. If he attacked again, I wasn't sure I could hold the circle.

I wondered if I should step outside it, make myself the target. If I channelled energy into the circle first, it might maintain itself for a while, even if I died. At least, my friends would live.

Zia Rashid had probably been thinking the same thing last Christmas when she stepped outside her circle to protect Carter and me. She really had been annoyingly brave.

'Whatever happens to me,' I told my friends, 'stay inside the circle.'

'Sadie,' Emma said, 'I know that tone of voice. Whatever you're planning, don't.'

'You can't leave us,' Liz pleaded. Then she shouted at Babi in a squeaky voice: 'G-go away, you horrible foamy ape! My friend here doesn't want to destroy you, but – but she will!'

Babi snarled. He *was* rather foamy, thanks to the Body Shop attack, and he smelled wonderful. Several different colours of shampoo foam and bath beads were matted in his silver fur.

Nekhbet hadn't fared so well. She perched atop a nearby lamp-post, looking as if she'd been assaulted by the entire contents of the West Cornwall Pasty Company. Bits of ham, cheese and potato splattered her feathery cloak, giving testament to the brave enchanted meat-pies that had given their brief lives to delay her. Her hair was decorated with plastic forks, napkins and bits of pink newsprint. She looked quite keen to tear me to shreds.

The only good news: Babi's minions evidently hadn't made

it out of the train station. I imagined a troop of pasty-splattered baboons shoved against police cars and handcuffed. It lifted my spirits somewhat.

Nekhbet snarled. 'You surprised us at the station, Sadie Kane. I'll admit that was well done. And bringing us to this bridge – a good try. But we are not so weak. You don't have the strength to fight us any longer. If you cannot defeat us, you have no business raising Ra.'

'You lot should be helping me,' I said. 'Not trying to stop me.'

'*Uhh!*' Babi barked.

'Indeed,' agreed the vulture goddess. 'The strong survive without help. The weak must be killed and eaten. Which are you, child? Be honest.'

The truth? I was about to drop. The bridge seemed to be spinning beneath me. Sirens wailed on both banks of the river. More police had arrived at the barricades, but for now they made no effort to advance.

Babi bared his fangs. He was so close I could smell his shampooed fur and his horrid breath. Then I looked at Gramps's glasses still stuck on his head, and all my anger came back.

'Try me,' I said. 'I follow the path of Isis. Cross me, and I'll destroy you.'

I managed to light my staff. Babi stepped back. Nekhbet fluttered on her lamp-post. Their forms shimmered briefly. The river *was* weakening them, loosening their connection to the mortal world like interference on a mobile-phone line. But it wasn't enough.

Nekhbet must've seen the desperation in my face. She was a vulture. She specialized in knowing when her prey was finished.

'A good last effort, child,' she said, almost with appreciation, 'but you have nothing left. Babi, attack!'

The baboon god reared up on his back legs. I got ready to charge and deliver one final burst of energy – to tap into my own life source and hopefully vaporize the gods. I had to make sure Liz and Emma survived.

Then the limo's door opened behind me. Bes announced: 'No one is attacking anyone! Except me, of course.'

Nekhbet shrieked in alarm. I turned to see what was going on. Immediately, I wished I could burn my eyes out of my head.

Liz made a gagging sound. 'Lord, no! That's *wrong*!'

'*Agh!*' Emma shouted, in perfect baboon-speak. 'Make him stop!'

Bes had indeed put on his ugly outfit. He climbed onto the roof of the limo and stood there, legs planted, arms akimbo, like Superman – except with only the underwear.

For those faint of heart, I won't go into great detail, but Bes, all of a metre tall, was showing off his disgusting physique – his pot belly, hairy limbs, awful feet, gross flabby bits – and wearing only a blue Speedo. Imagine the worst-looking person you've ever seen on a public beach – the person for whom swimwear should be illegal. Bes looked worse than that.

I wasn't sure what to say except: 'Put on some clothes!'

Bes laughed – the sort of guffaw that says, *Ha-ha! I'm amazing!*

'Not until they leave,' he said. 'Or I'll be forced to scare them back to the Duat.'

'This is not your affair, dwarf god!' Nekhbet snarled, averting her eyes from his horribleness. 'Go away!'

'These children are under my protection,' Bes insisted.

'I don't know you,' I said. 'I never met you before today.'

'Nonsense. You expressly asked for my protection.'

'I didn't ask for the Speedo Patrol!'

Bes leaped off the limo and landed in front of my circle, placing himself between Babi and me. The dwarf was even more horrible from behind. His back was so hairy it looked like a mink coat. And on the back of his Speedo was printed DWARF PRIDE.

Bes and Babi circled each other like wrestlers. The baboon god swiped at Bes, but the dwarf was agile. He scrambled up Babi's chest and head-butted him in the nose. Babi staggered backwards as the dwarf continued pounding away, using his face as a deadly weapon.

'Don't hurt him!' I yelled. 'It's my Gramps in there!'

Babi slumped against the railing. He blinked, trying to regain his bearings, but Bes breathed on him, and the smell of curry must've been too much. The baboon's knees buckled. His body shimmered and began to shrink. He crumpled on the pavement and melted into a stocky grey-haired pensioner in a tattered cardigan.

'Gramps!' I couldn't stand it. I left the protective circle and ran to his side.

'He'll be fine,' Bes promised. Then he turned towards the vulture goddess. 'Now it's your turn, Nekhbet. *Leave.*'

136

'I stole this body fair and square!' she wailed. 'I like it in here!'

'You asked for it.' Bes rubbed his hands, took a deep breath and did something I will never be able to erase from my memory.

If I simply said he made a face and yelled, 'BOO,' that would be technically correct, but it wouldn't begin to convey the horror.

His head swelled. His jaw unhinged until his mouth was four times too big. His eyes bulged like grapefruits. His hair stuck straight up like Bast's. He shook his face and waggled his slimy green tongue and roared, 'BOOOO!' so loudly the sound rolled across the Thames like a cannon shot. This blast of pure ugly blew the feathers off Nekhbet's cloak and drained all the colour from her face. It ripped away the essence of the goddess like tissue paper in a storm. The only thing left was a dazed old woman in a flower-print dress, squatting on the lamp-post.

'Oh, dear...' Gran fainted.

Bes jumped up and caught her before she could topple into the river. The dwarf's face went back to normal – well, normally *ugly*, at least – as he eased Gran onto the pavement next to Gramps.

'Thank you,' I told Bes. 'Now, will you please put on some clothes?'

He gave me a toothy grin, which I could have lived without. 'You're all right, Sadie Kane. I see why Bast likes you.'

'Sadie?' my grandfather groaned, his eyelids fluttering open.

'I'm here, Gramps.' I stroked his forehead. 'How do you feel?'

'Strange craving for mangoes.' He went cross-eyed. 'And possibly insects. You...you saved us?'

'Not really,' I admitted. 'My friend here –'

'Certainly she saved you,' Bes said. 'Brave girl you have here. Quite a magician.'

Gramps focused on Bes and scowled. 'Blimmin' Egyptian gods in their blimmin' revealing swimwear. This is why we *don't* do magic.'

I sighed with relief. Once Gramps started complaining, I knew he was going to be all right. Gran was still passed out, but her breathing seemed steady. The colour was coming back into her cheeks.

'We should go,' Bes said. 'The mortals are ready to storm the bridge.'

I glanced towards the barricades and saw what he meant. An assault team was gathering – heavily armoured men with rifles, grenade launchers and probably many other fun toys that could kill us.

'Liz, Emma!' I called. 'Help me with my grandparents.'

My friends ran over and started to help Gramps sit up, but Bes said, 'They can't come.'

'What?' I demanded. 'But you just said –'

'They're mortals,' Bes said. 'They don't belong on your quest. If we're going to get the second scroll from Vlad Menshikov, we need to leave *now*.'

'You know about that?' Then I remembered that he'd spoken with Anubis.

'Your grandparents and friends are in less danger here,' Bes said. 'The police will question them, but they won't see old people and children as a threat.'

'We're not children,' Emma grumbled.

'Vultures...' Gran whispered in her sleep. 'Meat pies...'

Gramps coughed. 'The dwarf is right, Sadie. Go. I'll be tiptop in a moment, though it's a pity that baboon chap couldn't leave me some of his power. Haven't felt that strong in ages.'

I looked at my bedraggled grandparents and friends. My heart felt like it was being stretched in more directions than Bes's face. I realized the dwarf was right: they'd be safer here facing an assault team than going with us. And I realized, too, that they didn't belong on a magic quest. My grandparents had chosen long ago not to use their ancestral abilities. And my friends were just mortals – brave, mad, ridiculous, wonderful mortals. But they couldn't go where I had to go.

'Sadie, it's fine.' Emma adjusted her broken glasses and tried for a smile. 'We can handle the police. Won't be the first time we've had to do some quick talking, eh?'

'We'll take care of your gran and gramps,' Liz promised.

'Don't need taking care of,' Gramps complained. Then he broke down in a fit of coughing. 'Just go, my dear. That baboon god was in my head. I can tell you – he means to destroy you. Finish your quest before he comes after you again. I couldn't even stop him. I couldn't...' He looked resentfully at his shaky old hands. 'I never would've forgiven myself. Now, off with you!'

'I'm sorry,' I told them all. 'I didn't mean –'

'Sorry?' Emma demanded. 'Sadie Kane, that was the most *brilliant* birthday party ever! Now, go!'

She and Liz both hugged me, and before I could start crying Bes shepherded me into the Mercedes.

We drove north towards Victoria Embankment. We were almost to the barricades when Bes slowed down.

'What's wrong?' I asked. 'Can't we go past invisibly?'

'It's not the mortals I'm worried about.' He pointed.

All the police, reporters and spectators around the barricades had fallen asleep. Several military types in body armour were curled on the pavement, cuddling their assault rifles like teddy bears.

Standing in front of the barricades, blocking our car, were Carter and Walt. They were dishevelled and breathing heavily, as if they'd run here all the way from Brooklyn. They both had wands at the ready. Carter stepped forward, pointing his sword at the windshield.

'Let her go!' he yelled at Bes. 'Or I'll destroy you!'

Bes glanced back at me. 'Should I frighten him?'

'No!' I said. That was something I *didn't* need to see again. 'I'll handle it.'

I stepped out of the limo. 'Hello, boys. Brilliant timing.'

Walt and Carter frowned.

'You're not in danger?' Walt asked me.

'Not any more.'

Carter lowered his sword reluctantly. 'You mean the ugly guy –'

'Is a friend,' I said. 'Bast's friend. He's also our driver.'

Carter looked equal parts confused, annoyed and uneasy, which made a satisfying ending to my birthday party.

'Driver to where?' he asked.

'Russia, of course,' I said. 'Hop in.'

9. We Get a Vertically Challenged Tour of Russia

As usual, Sadie left out some important details, like how Walt and I nearly killed ourselves trying to find her.

It wasn't fun, flying to the Brooklyn Museum. We had to hang from a rope under the griffin's belly like a couple of Tarzans, dodging policemen, emergency workers, city officials and several old ladies who chased after us with umbrellas screaming, 'There's the hummingbird! Kill it!'

Once we managed to open a portal, I wanted to take Freak through with us, but the gate of swirling sand kind of... well, freaked him out, so we had to leave him behind.

When we got to London, television monitors in the storefronts were showing footage of Waterloo Station – something about a strange disturbance inside the terminal with escaped animals and windstorms. Gee, wonder who that could have been? We used Walt's amulet for Shu the air god to summon a burst of wind and jump to Waterloo Bridge. Of course, we landed right in the middle of a heavily armed riot squad. Just luck that I remembered the sleep spell.

Then, *finally*, we were ready to charge in and save Sadie, and she rides up in a limousine driven by an ugly dwarf in a swimsuit, and she accuses *us* of being late.

So when she told us the dwarf was driving us to Russia, I was like, 'Whatever.' And I got into the car.

The limousine drove through Westminster while Sadie, Walt and I traded stories.

After hearing what Sadie had been through, I didn't feel so bad about my day. A dream of Apophis and a three-headed snake in the training room didn't seem nearly as scary as gods taking over our grandparents. I'd never liked Gran and Gramps that much, but still – yikes.

I also couldn't believe our chauffeur was Bes. Dad and I used to laugh about his pictures in museums – his bulging eyes, wagging tongue and general lack of clothing. Supposedly, he could scare away almost anything – spirits, demons, even other gods – which is why the Egyptian commoners had loved him. Bes looked out for the little guy … *um*, which wasn't meant as a dwarf joke. In the flesh, he looked *exactly* like his pictures, only in full colour, with full smell.

'We owe you,' I told him. 'So you're a friend of Bast's?'

His ears turned red. 'Yeah … sure. She asks me for a favour once in a while. I try to help out.'

I got the feeling there was some history there he didn't want to go into.

'When Horus spoke to me,' I said, 'he warned that some

of the gods might try to stop us from waking Ra. Now I guess we know who.'

Sadie exhaled. 'If they didn't like our plan, an angry text message would've done. Nekhbet and Babi almost tore me apart!'

Her face was a little green. Her combat boots were splattered with shampoo and mud, and her favourite leather jacket had a stain on the shoulder that looked suspiciously like vulture poop. Still, I was impressed that she was conscious. Potions are hard to make and even harder to use. There's always a price for channelling that much magic.

'You did great,' I told her.

Sadie looked resentfully at the black knife in her lap – the ceremonial blade Anubis had given her. 'I'd be dead if not for Bes.'

'Nah,' Bes said. 'Well, okay, you probably would be. But you would've gone down in style.'

Sadie turned the strange black knife over as if she might find instructions written on it.

'It's a *netjeri*,' I said. 'A *serpent* blade. Priests used it for –'

'The opening-of-the-mouth ceremony,' she said. 'But how does that help us?'

'Don't know,' I admitted. 'Bes?'

'Death rituals. I try to avoid them.'

I looked at Walt. Magic items were his speciality, but he didn't seem to be paying attention. Ever since Sadie had told us about her talk with Anubis, Walt had been awfully quiet. He sat next to her, fidgeting with his rings.

'You okay?' I asked him.

'Yeah…just thinking.' He glanced at Sadie. 'About *netjeri* blades, I mean.'

Sadie tugged at her hair, like she was trying to make a curtain between her and Walt. The tension between them was so thick I doubted even a magic knife could cut through it.

'Stupid Anubis,' she muttered. 'I could have died, for all he cared.'

We drove in silence for a while after that. Finally, Bes turned onto Westminster Bridge and doubled back over the Thames.

Sadie frowned. 'Where are we going? We need a portal. All the best artefacts are at the British Museum.'

'Yeah,' Bes said. 'And the other magicians know that.'

'Other magicians?' I asked.

'Kid, the House of Life has branches all over the world. London is the Ninth Nome. With that stunt at Waterloo, Miss Sadie just sent up a big flare telling Desjardins's followers, *Here I am!* You can bet they're going to be hunting you now. They'll be covering the museum in case you make a run for it. Fortunately, I know a different place we can open a portal.'

Schooled by a dwarf. It should've occurred to me that London had other magicians. The House of Life was everywhere. Outside the security of Brooklyn House, there wasn't a single continent where we'd be safe.

We rode through south London. The scene along Camberwell Road was almost as depressing as my thoughts. Rows of grubby brick apartments and low-rent shops lined the street. An old woman scowled at us from a bus stop. In the doorway of an Asda grocery store, a couple of young tough guys eyed the Mercedes as if they wanted to steal it. I wondered if they were gods or magicians in disguise, because most people didn't notice the car.

I couldn't imagine where Bes was taking us. It didn't seem like the kind of neighbourhood where you'd find a lot of Egyptian artefacts.

Finally a big park opened up on our left: misty green fields, tree-lined paths and a few ruined walls like aqueducts, covered in vines. The land sloped upward to a hilltop with a radio tower.

Bes jumped the kerb and drove straight over the grass, knocking down a sign that said KEEP TO THE PATH. The evening was grey and rainy, so there weren't many people around. A couple of joggers on the nearby path didn't even look at us, as if they saw Mercedes limos four-wheeling across the park every day.

'Where are we going?' I asked.

'Watch and learn, kid,' Bes said.

Being called 'kid' by a guy shorter than me was a little annoying, but I kept my mouth shut. Bes drove straight up the hill. Close to the top was a stone staircase maybe thirty feet wide, built into the hillside. It seemed to lead nowhere. Bes slammed on the brakes and we swerved to a stop. The hill was higher than I'd realized. Spread out below us was the whole of London.

Then I looked more closely at the staircase. Two sphinxes made of weathered stone lay on either side of the stairs, watching over the city. Each was about ten feet long with the typical lion's body and pharaoh's head, but they seemed totally out of place in a London park.

'Those aren't real,' I said.

Bes snorted. 'Of course they're real.'

'I mean they aren't from Ancient Egypt. They're not old enough.'

'Picky, picky,' Bes said. 'These are the stairs to the Crystal Palace. Big glass-and-steel exhibit hall the size of a cathedral used to sit right here on this hill.'

Sadie frowned. 'I read about that in school. Queen Victoria had a party there or something.'

'A party or something?' Bes grunted. 'It was the Grand Exhibition in 1851. Showcase of British Imperial might, et cetera. They had good candied apples.'

'You were there?' I asked.

Bes shrugged. 'The palace burned down in the 1930s, thanks to some stupid magicians – but that's another story. All that's left now are a few relics, like these stairs and the sphinxes.'

'A stairway to nowhere,' I said.

'Not nowhere,' Bes corrected. 'Tonight it'll take us to St Petersburg.'

Walt sat forward. His interest in the statues had apparently shaken him out of his gloom.

'But if the sphinxes aren't really Egyptian,' he said, 'how can they open a portal?'

Bes gave him a toothy grin. 'Depends on what you mean by *really Egyptian*, kid. Every great empire is a wannabe Egypt. Having Egyptian stuff around makes them feel important.

That's why you've got "new" Egyptian artefacts in Rome, Paris, London – you name it. That obelisk in Washington –'

'Don't mention that one, please,' Sadie said.

'Anyway,' Bes continued, 'these are still Egyptian sphinxes. They were built to play up the connection between the British Empire and the Egyptian Empire. So, yeah, they can channel magic. Especially if *I'm* driving. And now...' He looked at Walt. 'It's probably time for you to get out.'

I was too surprised to say anything, but Walt stared at his lap as if he'd been expecting this.

'Hang on,' Sadie said. 'Why can't Walt come with us? He's a magician. He can help.'

Bes's expression turned serious. 'Walt, you haven't told them?'

'Told us what?' Sadie demanded.

Walt clutched his amulets, as if there might be one that would help him avoid this conversation. 'It's nothing. Really. It's just...I should help out at Brooklyn House. And Jaz thought –'

He faltered, probably realizing that he shouldn't have brought up her name.

'Yes?' Sadie's tone was dangerously calm. 'How's Jaz doing?'

'She's – she's still in a coma,' Walt said. 'Amos says she'll probably make it, but that's not what I –'

'Good,' Sadie said. 'Glad she'll get better. So you need to get back, then. That's brilliant. Off you go. Anubis said we should hurry.'

Not very subtle, the way she threw his name out there. Walt looked like she'd kicked him in the chest.

I knew Sadie wasn't being fair to him. From my conversation with Walt back at Brooklyn House, I knew he liked Sadie. Whatever was bothering him wasn't any kind of romantic thing with Jaz. On the other hand, if I tried to take his side, Sadie would just tell me to butt out. I might even make things worse between Sadie and him.

'It's not that I want to go back,' he managed.

'But you can't go with us,' Bes said firmly. I thought I heard concern in his voice, even pity. 'Go on, kid. It's fine.'

Walt fished something out of his pocket. 'Sadie, about your birthday...you, *um*, probably don't want any more presents. It's not a magic knife, but I made this for you.'

He poured a gold necklace into her hand. It had a small Egyptian symbol:

'That's the basketball hoop on Ra's head,' I said.

Walt and Sadie both frowned at me, and I realized I probably wasn't making the moment more magical for them. 'I mean it's the symbol that surrounds Ra's sun crown,' I said. 'A never-ending loop, the symbol of eternity, right?'

Sadie swallowed as if the magic potion was still bubbling in her stomach. 'Eternity?'

Walt shot me a look that clearly meant *Please stop helping.*

'Yeah,' he said, '*um*, it's called *shen*. I just thought, you know, you're looking for Ra. And good things, important things, should be eternal. So maybe it'll bring you luck. I meant to give it to you this morning, but...I kind of lost my nerve.'

Sadie stared the talisman glittering in her palm. 'Walt, I don't – I mean . . . thank you, but –'

'Just remember I didn't want to leave,' he said. 'If you need help, I'll be there for you.' He glanced at me and corrected himself: 'I mean both of you, of course.'

'But now,' Bes said, 'you need to go.'

'Happy birthday, Sadie,' Walt said. 'And good luck.'

He got out of the car and trudged down the hill. We watched until he was just a tiny figure in the gloom. Then he vanished into the woods.

'Two farewell gifts,' Sadie muttered, 'from two gorgeous guys. I hate my life.'

She latched the gold necklace round her throat and touched the *shen* symbol.

Bes gazed down at the trees where Walt had disappeared. 'Poor kid. Born unusual, all right. It isn't fair.'

'What do you mean?' I asked. 'Why were you so anxious for Walt to leave?'

The dwarf rubbed his scraggly beard. 'Not my place to explain. Right now we've got work to do. The more time we give Menshikov to prepare his defences, the harder this is going to get.'

I wasn't ready to drop it, but Bes stared at me stubbornly, and I knew I wasn't going to get any more answers from him. Nobody can look stubborn like a dwarf.

'So, Russia,' I said. 'By driving up an empty staircase.'

'Exactly.' Bes floored the accelerator. The Mercedes churned grass and mud and barrelled up the stairs. I was sure we'd reach the top and get nothing but a broken axle, but at the last second a portal of swirling sand opened in front of us. Our wheels left the ground, and the black limousine flew headlong into the vortex.

We slammed into pavement on the other side, scattering a group of surprised teenagers. Sadie groaned and prised her head off the headrest.

'Can't we go anywhere *gently*?' she asked.

Bes hit the wipers and scraped the sand off our windshield. Outside it was dark and snowy. Eighteenth-century stone buildings lined a frozen river lit with street lamps. Beyond the river glowed more fairy-tale buildings: golden church domes, white palaces and ornate mansions painted Easter-egg green and blue. I might have believed we'd travelled back in time three hundred years – except for the cars, the electric lights and of course the teenagers with body piercings, dyed hair and black leather clothes screaming at us in Russian and pounding on the hood of the Mercedes because we'd almost run them over.

'They can see us?' Sadie asked.

'Russians,' Bes said with a kind of grudging admiration. 'Very superstitious people. They tend to see magic for what it is. We'll have to be careful here.'

'You've been here before?' I asked.

He gave me a *duh* look, then pointed to either side of the car. We'd landed between two stone sphinxes standing on pedestals. They looked like a lot of sphinxes I'd seen – with crowned human heads on lion bodies – but I'd never seen sphinxes covered in snow.

'Are those authentic?' I asked.

'Furthest-north Egyptian artefacts in the world,' Bes said. 'Pillaged from Thebes and brought up here to decorate Russia's new imperial city, St Petersburg. Like I said, every new empire wants a piece of Egypt.'

The kids outside were still shouting and banging on the car. One smashed a bottle against our windshield.

'*Um*,' Sadie said, 'should we move?'

'Nah,' Bes said. 'Russian kids always hang out by the sphinxes. Been doing it for hundreds of years.'

'But it's like midnight here,' I said. 'And it's snowing.'

'Did I mention they're Russian?' Bes said. 'Don't worry. I'll take care of it.'

He opened his door. Glacier-cold wind swept into the Mercedes, but Bes stepped out wearing nothing but his Speedo. The kids backed up quickly. I couldn't blame them. Bes said something in Russian, then roared like a lion. The kids screamed and ran.

Bes's form seemed to ripple. When he got back into the car, he was wearing a warm winter coat, a fur-lined hat and fuzzy mittens.

'See?' he said. 'Superstitious. They know enough to run from a god.'

'A small hairy god in a Speedo, yes,' Sadie said. 'So what do we do now?'

Bes pointed across the river at a glowing palace of white-and-gold stone. 'That's the Hermitage.'

'Hermits live there?' Sadie asked.

'No,' I said. 'I've heard of that place. It was the tsar's palace. Now it's a museum. Best Egyptian collection in Russia.'

'Dad took you there, I suppose?' Sadie asked. I thought we were over the whole jealous-about-travelling-the-world-with-Dad thing, but every once in a while it cropped up again.

'We never went.' I tried not to sound defensive. 'He got an invitation to speak there once, but he declined.'

Bes chuckled. 'Your dad was smart. Russian magicians don't exactly welcome outsiders. They protect their territory fiercely.'

Sadie stared across the river. 'You mean the headquarters of the Eighteenth Nome is *inside* the museum?'

'Somewhere,' Bes agreed, 'but it's hidden with magic, because I've never found the entrance. That part you're looking at is the Winter Palace, the old home of the tsar. There's a whole complex of other mansions behind it. I've heard it would take eleven days just to see everything in all the Hermitage collections.'

'But unless we wake Ra the world ends in four days,' I said.

'Three days now,' Sadie corrected, 'if it's after midnight.'

I winced. 'Thanks for the reminder.'

'So take the abbreviated tour,' Bes said. 'Start with the Egyptian section. Ground floor, main museum.'

'Aren't you coming with us?' I asked.

'He can't, can he?' Sadie guessed. 'Like Bast couldn't enter Desjardins's house in Paris. The magicians charm their headquarters against the gods. Isn't that right?'

Bes made an even uglier face. 'I'll walk you down to the bridge, but I can't go any further. If I cross the River Neva too close to the Hermitage, I'll set off all kinds of alarms. You'll have to sneak inside somehow –'

'Breaking into a museum at night,' Sadie muttered. 'We've had such good luck with that.'

'– and find the entrance to the Eighteenth Nome. And don't get captured alive.'

'What do you mean?' I asked. 'It's better to be captured dead?'

The look in his eyes was grim. 'Just trust me. You don't want to be Menshikov's prisoner.'

Bes snapped his fingers, and suddenly we were wearing fleece parkas, ski pants and winter boots.

'Come on, *malyshi*,' he said. 'I'll walk you to the Dvortsovaya Bridge.'

The bridge was only a few hundred yards away, but it seemed farther. March obviously wasn't springtime in St Petersburg. The dark, the wind and the snow made it feel more like January in Alaska. Personally, I would've preferred a sweltering day in the Egyptian desert. Even with the warm clothes Bes had summoned for us, my teeth couldn't stop chattering.

Bes wasn't in a hurry. He kept slowing down and giving us the guided tour until I thought my nose would fall off from frostbite. He told us we were on Vasilevsky Island, across the Neva River from the centre of St Petersburg. He pointed out the different church spires and monuments, and when he got excited, he started slipping into Russian.

'You've spent a lot of time here,' I said.

He walked in silence for a few paces. 'Most of that was long ago. It wasn't –'

He stopped so abruptly I stumbled into him. He stared

across the street at a big palace with canary-yellow walls and a green gabled roof. Lit up in the night through a swirl of snow, it looked unreal, like one of the ghostly images in the First Nome's Hall of Ages.

'Prince Menshikov's palace,' Bes muttered.

His voice was full of loathing. I almost thought he was going to yell 'BOO' at the building, but he just gritted his teeth.

Sadie looked at me for an explanation, but I wasn't a walking Wikipedia like she seemed to think. I knew stuff about Egypt, but Russia? Not so much.

'You mean Menshikov as in Vlad the Inhaler?' I asked.

'He's a descendant.' Bes curled his lip with distaste. He said a Russian word I was willing to bet was a pretty bad insult. 'Back in the 1700s, Prince Menshikov threw a party for Peter the Great – the tsar who built this city. Peter loved dwarves. He was a lot like the Egyptians that way. He thought we were good luck, so he always kept some of us in his court. Anyway, Menshikov wanted to entertain the tsar, so he thought it would be funny to stage a dwarf wedding. He forced them... he forced *us* to dress up, pretend to get married and dance around. All the big folk were laughing, jeering...'

His voice trailed off.

Bes described the party like it was yesterday. Then I remembered that this weird little guy was a god. He'd been around for aeons.

Sadie put her hand on his shoulder. 'I'm sorry, Bes. Must have been awful.'

He scowled. 'Russian magicians... they love capturing

gods, using us. I can still hear that wedding music and the tsar laughing...'

'How'd you get away?' I asked.

Bes glared at me. Obviously, I'd asked a bad question.

'Enough of this.' Bes turned up his collar. 'We're wasting time.'

He forged ahead, but I got the feeling he wasn't really leaving Menshikov's palace behind. Suddenly its cheery yellow walls and brightly lit windows looked sinister.

Another hundred yards through the bitter wind, and we reached the bridge. On the other side, the Winter Palace shimmered.

'I'll take the Mercedes the long way round,' Bes said. 'Down to the next bridge and circle south of the Hermitage. Less likely to alert the magicians that I'm here.'

Now I realized why he was so paranoid about setting off alarms. Magicians had snared him in St Petersburg once before. I remembered what he'd told us in the car: *Don't get captured alive.*

'How do we find you if we succeed?' Sadie asked.

'*When* you succeed,' Bes said. 'Think positive, girl, or the world ends.'

'Right.' Sadie shivered in her new parka. 'Positive.'

'I'll meet you on the Nevsky Prospekt, the main street with all the shops, just south of the Hermitage. I'll be at the Chocolate Museum.'

'The *what* now?' I asked.

'Well, it's not really a museum. More of a shop – closed this time of night, but the owner always opens up for me. They've got chocolate *everything* – chess sets, lions, Vladimir Lenin heads –'

'The communist guy?' I asked.

'Yes, Professor Brilliant,' Bes said. 'The communist guy, in *chocolate.*'

'So let me get this straight,' Sadie said. 'We break into a heavily guarded Russian national museum, find the magicians' secret headquarters, find a dangerous scroll and escape. Meanwhile, you will be eating chocolate.'

Bes nodded solemnly. 'It's a good plan. It might work. If something happens and I can't meet you at the Chocolate Museum, our exit point is the Egyptian Bridge, to the south at the Fontanka River. Just turn on the –'

'Enough,' Sadie said. 'You *will* meet us at the chocolate shop. And you *will* provide me with a takeaway bag. That is final. Now, go!'

Bes gave her a lopsided smile. 'You're okay, girl.'

He trudged back towards the Mercedes.

I looked across the half-frozen river to the Winter Palace. Somehow, London didn't seem as dreary or dangerous any more.

'Are we in as much trouble as I think?' I asked Sadie.

'More,' she said. 'Let's go crash the tsar's palace, shall we?'

10. An Old Red Friend Comes to Visit

GETTING INSIDE THE HERMITAGE wasn't a problem.

State-of-the-art security doesn't protect against magic. Sadie and I had to combine forces to get past the perimeter, but with a little concentration, ink and papyrus, and some tapped energy from our godly friends Isis and Horus, we managed to pull off a short stroll through the Duat.

One minute we were standing in the abandoned Palace Square. Then everything went grey and misty. My stomach tingled like I was in free fall. We slipped out of sync with the mortal world and passed through the iron gates and solid stone into the museum.

The Egyptian room was on the ground floor, just as Bes had said. We re-entered the mortal realm and found ourselves in the middle of the collection: sarcophagi in glass cases, hieroglyphic scrolls, statues of gods and pharaohs. It wasn't much different from a hundred other Egyptian collections I'd seen, but the setting was pretty impressive. A vaulted ceiling

157

soared overhead. The polished marble floor was done in a white-and-grey diamond pattern, which made walking on it kind of like walking on an optical illusion. I wondered how many rooms there were like this in the tsar's palace, and if it really took eleven days to see them all. I hoped Bes was right about the secret entrance to the nome being somewhere in this room. We didn't have eleven days to search. In less than seventy-two hours, Apophis would break free. I remembered that glowing red eye beneath the scarab shells – a force of chaos so powerful it could melt human senses. Three days, and that *thing* would be unleashed on the world.

Sadie summoned her staff and pointed it at the nearest security camera. The lens cracked and made a sound like a bug zapper. Even in the best of situations, technology and magic don't get along. One of the easiest spells in the world is to make electronics malfunction. I just have to look at a cell phone funny to make it blow up. And computers? Forget about it. I imagined Sadie had just sent a magical pulse through the security system that would fry every camera and sensor in the network.

Still, there were other kinds of surveillance – *magical* kinds. I pulled a piece of black linen and a pair of crude wax *shabti* out of my bag. I wrapped the *shabti* in the cloth and spoke a command word: 'I'*mun*.'

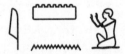

The hieroglyph for *Hide* glowed briefly over the cloth. A mass of darkness bloomed from the package, like a squid's ink cloud. It expanded until it covered both Sadie and me in a gauzy bubble of shadows. We could see through it, but hopefully nothing could see in. The cloud would be invisible to anyone outside.

'You got it right this time!' Sadie said. 'When did you master the spell?'

I probably blushed. I'd been obsessed with figuring out the invisibility spell for months, ever since I'd seen Zia use it in the First Nome.

'Actually I'm still –' A gold spark shot out of the cloud like a miniature fireworks rocket. 'I'm still working on it.'

Sadie sighed. 'Well...better than last time. The cloud looked like a lava lamp. And the time before, when it smelled like rotten eggs –'

'Could we just get going?' I asked. 'Where should we start?'

Her eyes locked on one of the displays. She drifted towards it in a trance.

'Sadie?' I followed her to a limestone grave marker – a stele – about two feet by three feet. The description next to it was in Russian and English.

'"From the tomb of the scribe Ipi,"' I read aloud. '"Worked in the court of King Tut." Why are you interested...Oh.'

Stupid me. The picture on the gravestone showed the deceased scribe honouring Anubis. After talking with Anubis in person, Sadie must've found it strange to see him in a three-thousand-year-old tomb painting, especially when he was pictured with the head of a jackal, wearing a skirt.

'Walt likes you.'

I have no idea why I blurted that out. This wasn't the time

159

or the place. I knew I wasn't doing Walt any favours by taking his side. But I'd started to feel bad for him after Bes kicked him out of the limo. The guy had come all the way to London to help me save Sadie, and we'd dumped him in Crystal Palace Park like an unwanted hitchhiker.

I was kind of angry at Sadie for giving him the cold shoulder and crushing so hard on Anubis, who was five thousand years too old for her and not even human. Plus, the way she snubbed Walt reminded me too much of the way Zia had treated me at first. And maybe, if I was honest with myself, I was also irritated with Sadie because she'd solved her own problems in London without needing our help.

Wow. That sounded really selfish. But I suppose it was true. Amazing how many different ways a younger sister can annoy you at once.

Sadie didn't take her eyes off the stele. 'Carter, you have no idea what you're talking about.'

'You're not giving the guy a chance,' I insisted. 'Whatever's going on with him, it's got nothing to do with you.'

'Very reassuring, but that's not –'

'Besides, Anubis is a *god*. You don't honestly think –'

'Carter!' she snapped. My cloaking spell must've been sensitive to emotion, because another gold spark whistled and popped from our not-so-invisible cloud. 'I wasn't looking at this stone because of Anubis.'

'You weren't?'

'No. And I'm certainly not having an argument with you about *Walt*. Contrary to what you might think, I don't spend every waking hour thinking about boys.'

'Just most waking hours?'

She rolled her eyes. 'Look at the gravestone, birdbrain. It's got a border round it, like a window frame or –'

'A door,' I said. 'It's a false door. Lots of tombs had those. It was like a symbolic gateway for the dead person's *ba*, so it could go back and forth from the Duat.'

Sadie pulled her wand and traced the edges of the stele. 'This bloke Ipi was a scribe, which was another word for magician. He could've been one of us.'

'So?'

'So maybe that's why the stone is *glowing*, Carter. What if this false door's not false?'

I looked at the stele more closely, but I didn't see any glow. I thought maybe Sadie was hallucinating from exhaustion or too much potion in her system. Then she touched her wand to the centre of the stele and spoke the first command word we'd ever learned: '*W'peh.*'

Open. A golden hieroglyph burned on the stone:

The grave marker shot out a beam of light like a movie projector. Suddenly, a full-size doorway shimmered in front of us – a rectangular portal showing the hazy image of another room.

I looked at Sadie in amazement. 'How did you do that?' I asked. 'You've never been able to do that before.'

She shrugged as if it were no big deal. 'I wasn't thirteen before. Maybe that's it.'

'But I'm fourteen!' I protested. 'And I *still* can't do that.'

'Girls mature earlier.'

I gritted my teeth. I hated the spring months – March, April, May – because until my birthday rolled around in June, Sadie could claim to be only a year younger than me. She always got an attitude after her birthday, as if she'd catch up to me somehow and become my *big* sister. Talk about a nightmare.

She gestured at the glowing doorway. 'After you, brother, dear. You're the one with the sparkly invisibility cloud.'

Before I could lose my cool, I stepped through the portal.

I almost fell and broke my face. The other side of the portal was a mirror hanging five feet off the floor. I'd stepped onto a fireplace mantel. I caught Sadie as she came through, just in time to keep her from toppling off the ledge.

'Ta,' she whispered. 'Someone's been reading too much *Alice Through the Looking Glass*.'

I'd thought the Egyptian room was impressive, but it was nothing compared to this ballroom. Coppery geometric designs glittered on the ceiling. The walls were lined with dark green columns and gilded doors. White and gold inlaid marble made a huge octagonal pattern on the floor. With a blazing chandelier above, the golden filigree and green and white polished stone gleamed so brightly they hurt my eyes.

Then I realized most of the light wasn't coming from the chandelier. It was coming from the magician casting a spell at the other end of the room. His back was turned, but I could tell it was Vlad Menshikov. Just as Sadie had described, he was a pudgy little man with curly grey hair and a white suit. He stood in a protective circle that pulsed with emerald light. He raised his staff, and the tip burned like a welding torch. To his right, just outside the circle, stood a green vase the size of a grown man. To his left, writhing in glowing chains, was a creature I recognized as a demon. It had a hairy humanoid body with purplish skin, but instead of a head a giant corkscrew sprouted between its shoulders.

'Mercy!' it screamed in a watery, metallic voice. Don't ask me how a demon could scream with a corkscrew head – but the sound resonated up the screw like it was a massive tuning fork.

Vlad Menshikov kept chanting. The green vase throbbed with light.

Sadie nudged me and whispered, 'Look.'

'Yeah,' I whispered back. 'Some kind of summoning ritual.'

'No,' she hissed. 'Look *there*.'

She pointed to our right. In the corner of the room, twenty feet from the fireplace mantel, was an old-fashioned mahogany desk.

Sadie had told me about Anubis's instructions: we were supposed to find Menshikov's desk. The next section of the Book of Ra would be in the middle drawer. Could that really be the desk? It seemed too easy. As quietly as we could, Sadie and I climbed off the mantel and crept along the wall. I prayed the invisibility shroud wouldn't send up any more fireworks.

We were about halfway to the desk when Vlad Menshikov finished his chant. He slammed his staff against the floor, and it stuck there straight up, the tip still burning at a million degrees.

He turned his head slightly, and I caught the glint of his white sunglasses. He rummaged in his coat pockets while the big green vase glowed and the demon screamed in his chains.

'Don't fuss, Death-to-Corks,' Menshikov chided. His voice was even rougher than Sadie had described – like a heavy smoker talking through the blades of a fan. 'You know I need a sacrifice to summon such a major god. It's nothing personal.'

Sadie frowned at me and mouthed, *Major god?*

I shook my head, baffled. The House of Life didn't allow mortals to summon gods. It was the main reason Desjardins hated us. Menshikov was supposedly his best bud. So what was he doing, breaking the rules?

'Hurts!' the poor demon wailed. 'Served you for fifty years, master. Please!'

'Now, now,' Menshikov said without a trace of sympathy. 'I *have* to use execration. Only the most painful form of banishment will generate enough energy.'

From his suit coat pocket, Menshikov pulled a regular corkscrew and a shard of pottery covered with red hieroglyphics.

He held up both items and began to chant again: 'I name you Death-to-Corks, Servant of Vladimir, He Who Turns in the Night.'

As the demon's names were spoken, the magical chains steamed and tightened round his body. Menshikov held the corkscrew over the flame of his staff. The demon thrashed and wailed. As the smaller corkscrew turned red hot, the demon's body began to smoke.

I watched in horror. I knew about sympathetic magic, of course. The idea was to make something small affect something large by binding them together. The more alike the items were – like the corkscrew and the demon – the easier they were to bind. Voodoo dolls worked on the same theory.

But execration was serious stuff. It meant destroying a creature utterly – erasing its physical form and even its name from existence. It took some serious magic to pull off that kind of spell. If done wrong, it could destroy the caster. But, if done right, most victims didn't stand a chance. Regular mortals, magicians, ghosts, even demons could be wiped off the face of the earth. Execration might not destroy major powers like gods, but it would still be like detonating a nuclear bomb in their face. They'd be blasted so deep into the Duat, they might never come back.

Vlad Menshikov worked the spell as if he did it every day. He kept chanting as the corkscrew began to melt, and the demon melted with it. Menshikov dropped the pottery shard on the floor – the red hieroglyphs that spelled all the demon's various names. With one final word of power, Menshikov stepped on the shard and crushed it to bits. Death-to-Corks dissolved, chains and all.

Usually I don't feel sorry for creatures of the underworld, but I couldn't help getting a lump in my throat. I couldn't believe the casual way Menshikov had snuffed out his servant just to power a larger spell.

As soon as the demon was gone, the fire on Menshikov's staff died. Hieroglyphs burned around the summoning circle. The big green jar trembled and a voice from deep inside boomed, 'Hello, Vladimir. Long time.'

Sadie inhaled sharply. I had to cover her mouth to keep

her from screaming. We both knew that voice. I remembered it all too well from the Red Pyramid.

'Set.' Menshikov didn't even look tired from the summoning. He sounded awfully calm for someone addressing the god of evil. 'We need to talk.'

Sadie pushed my hand away and whispered, 'Is he mad?'

'Desk,' I said. 'Scroll. Out of here. *Now.*'

For once, she gave me no argument. She began fishing supplies out of her bag.

Meanwhile the big green jar wobbled as if Set were trying to tip it over.

'A malachite vase?' The god sounded annoyed. 'Really, Vladimir. I thought we were on friendlier terms than that.'

Menshikov's laugh sounded like someone choking a cat. 'Excellent at constraining evil spirits, isn't it? And this room has more malachite than any other place on earth. Empress Alexandra was quite wise to have it built for her drawing room.'

The jar plinked. 'But it smells like old pennies in here, and it's much too cold. Have you ever been stuck in a malachite jar, Vlad? I'm not a genie. I'd be so much more talkative if we could sit face to face, perhaps over tea.'

'I'm afraid not,' said Menshikov. 'Now, you'll answer my questions.'

'Oh, very well,' Set said. 'I like Brazil for the World Cup. I'd advise investing in platinum and small-cap funds. And your lucky numbers this week are two, thirteen –'

'Not those questions!' Menshikov snapped.

Sadie pulled a lump of wax from her bag and worked

furiously, fashioning some kind of animal shape. I knew she was going to test the desk for magic defences. She was better at that kind of spell than I was, but I wasn't sure how she'd do it. Egyptian magic is pretty open-ended. There are always a thousand different ways to accomplish a task. The trick is being creative with your supplies and picking a way that won't get you killed.

'You will tell me what I need to know,' Menshikov demanded, 'or that jar will become even more uncomfortable.'

'My dear Vladimir.' Set's voice was full of evil amusement. 'What you *need* to know may be very different from what you *want* to know. Didn't your unfortunate accident teach you that?'

Menshikov touched his sunglasses, as if making sure they hadn't fallen off.

'You will tell me the binding for Apophis,' he said in a steely tone. 'Then you will tell me how to neutralize the enchantments on Brooklyn House. You know Kane's defences better than anyone. Once I destroy him, I will have no opposition.'

As the meaning of Menshikov's words sank in, a wave of rage nearly knocked me off my feet. This time, Sadie had to clamp *my* mouth shut.

'Calm!' she whispered. 'You're going to start the invisibility shield popping again!'

I pushed her hand away and hissed, 'But he wants to free Apophis!'

'I know.'

'And attack Amos –'

167

'I know! So help me get the scroll and let's get out of here!'
She put her wax animal on the desk – a dog, I thought – and
began writing hieroglyphs on its back with a stylus.

I took a shaky breath. Sadie was right, but still – Menshikov
was talking about freeing Apophis and killing our uncle. What
kind of magician makes deals with Set? Except for Sadie and
me. That was different.

Set's laugh echoed inside the green vase. 'So: the binding
for Apophis and the secrets of Brooklyn House. Is that all,
Vladimir? I wonder what your master Desjardins would think
if he found out your real plan, and the sort of friends you keep.'

Menshikov snatched up his staff. The carved-serpent tip
flared again. 'Be careful with your threats, *Evil Day*.'

The jar trembled. Throughout the room, glass cases
shivered. The chandelier jangled like a three-ton wind chime.

I gave Sadie a panicked look. 'Did he just –'

'Set's secret name,' she confirmed, still writing on her wax
dog.

'How –'

'I don't know, Carter. Now, shh!'

A god's secret name had all kinds of power. It was supposed
to be almost impossible to get. To truly learn it, you couldn't
just hear it repeated by some random person. You had to hear
it straight from the god himself, or from the person closest to
his heart. Once you had it, it gave you serious magical leverage
over that god. Sadie had learned Set's secret name during our
quest last Christmas, but how had Menshikov got it?

Inside the jar, Set growled with annoyance. 'I really *hate*
that name. Why couldn't it have been Glorious Day? Or the

Rockin' Red Reaper? That's rather nice. Bad enough when you were the only one who knew it, Vlad. Now I've got the Kane girl to worry about –'

'Serve us,' Menshikov said, 'and the Kanes will be destroyed. You will be the honoured lieutenant of Apophis. You can raise another temple, even grander than the Red Pyramid.'

'Uh-huh,' Set said. 'Maybe you haven't noticed, but I don't do well with the whole second-in-command concept. As for Apophis, he's not one to suffer other gods getting attention.'

'We will free Apophis with or without your help,' Menshikov warned. 'By the equinox, he *will* rise. But if you help us make that happen sooner you will be rewarded. Your other option is execration. Oh, I know it won't destroy you completely, but with your secret name I can send you into the abyss for aeons, and it will be very, very painful. I'll give you thirty seconds to decide?'

I nudged Sadie. 'Hurry.'

She tapped the wax dog, and it came to life. It started sniffing around the desk, looking for magic traps.

Inside the jar, Set sighed. 'Well, Vladimir, you do know how to make an appealing offer. The binding for Apophis, you say? Yes, I was there when Ra cast the Serpent into that prison of scarabs. I suppose I could remember the ingredients he used for the binding. Quite a day that was! I was wearing red, I think. At the victory feast they served the most delicious honey-baked locusts –'

'You have ten seconds,' Menshikov said.

'Oh, I'll cooperate! I hope you have a pen and paper handy. It's a rather long list of ingredients. Let's see . . . what did Ra use for a base? Bat dung? Then there were the dried toads, of course. And then...'

Set began rattling off ingredients, while Sadie's wax dog sniffed around the desk. Finally it lay down on the blotter and went to sleep.

Sadie frowned at me. 'No traps.'

'That's too easy,' I whispered back.

She opened the top drawer. There was the papyrus scroll, just like the one we'd found in Brooklyn. She slipped it into her bag.

We were halfway back to the fireplace when Set caught us by surprise.

He was going on with his list of ridiculous ingredients: 'And snakeskins. Yes, three large ones, with a sprinkling of hot sauce –' Then he stopped abruptly, like he'd had a revelation. He spoke in a much louder voice, calling across the room. 'And a sacrificial victim would be good! Maybe a young idiot magician who can't do a proper invisibility spell, like CARTER KANE over there!'

I froze. Vladimir Menshikov turned, and my panic became too much for the invisibility shroud.

Half a dozen golden sparks shot up with a loud happy WHEEEEE! The cloud of darkness dissolved.

Menshikov stared right at me. 'My, my... how kind of you to deliver yourselves. Well done, Set.'

'Hmm?' Set asked innocently. 'Do we have visitors?'

'Set!' Sadie growled. 'I'll kick you in the *ba* for that, so help me!'

The voice in the jar gasped. 'Sadie Kane? How exciting! Too bad I'm stuck in *this jar* and no one will *let me out*.'

The hint wasn't too subtle, but surely he couldn't believe we'd free him after he'd blown our cover.

Sadie faced Menshikov, her wand and staff ready. 'You're working with Apophis. You're on the wrong side.'

Menshikov removed his glasses. His eyes were ruined pits of scar tissue, burned skin and glistening corneas. Believe me, that's the *least* gross way I can describe them.

'The wrong side?' Menshikov asked. 'Girl, you have no idea the powers that are in play. Five thousand years ago, Egyptian priests prophesied how the world would end. Ra would grow old and tired, and Apophis would swallow him and plunge the world into darkness. Chaos would rule forever. Now the time is here! You can't stop it. You can only choose whether you'll be destroyed, or whether you'll bow to the power of Chaos and survive.'

'Right,' Set chimed in. 'It's too bad I'm stuck in *this jar*. Otherwise I might have to *take sides and help someone*.'

'Shut up, Set,' Menshikov snapped. 'No one is crazy enough to trust you. And as for you, children, you are clearly not the threat I imagined.'

'Great,' I said. 'So we can go?'

Menshikov laughed. 'Would you run to Desjardins and tell him what you've heard? He wouldn't believe you. He'd put you on trial, then execute you. But I'll spare you that embarrassment. I'll kill you right now.'

'How fun!' Set said. 'Wish I could see it, but I'm stuck in *this jar*.'

I tried to think. Menshikov was still inside a protective circle, which meant he had a big defensive advantage. I wasn't sure I could bust through it, even if I could summon a combat avatar. Meanwhile, Menshikov could take his time trying out different ways to destroy us. Would he blast us with elemental magic? Change us into bugs?

He threw his staff to the ground, and I cursed.

Throwing down your staff may sound like a sign of surrender, but in Egyptian magic it's bad news. It usually means *Hey, I'm going to summon a big nasty thing to kill you while I stand safely inside my circle and laugh!*

Sure enough, Menshikov's staff began to writhe and grow.

Great, I thought. *Another serpent.*

But something was wrong with this one. Instead of a tail, it had a head on both ends. At first I thought we'd caught some luck, and Menshikov had summoned a monster with a rare genetic birth defect. Then the thing sprouted four dragon legs. Its body grew until it was the size of a draught horse, curved like a U, with mottled red and green scales and a rattlesnake head on either side. It reminded me of that two-headed animal from *Doctor Dolittle*. You know – the pushmi-pullyu? Except Doctor Dolittle would never have wanted to talk to *this* thing, and, if he had, it would probably have said just *Hello, I'm going to eat you.*

Both heads turned towards us and hissed.

'I've really had enough snakes for one week,' I muttered.

Menshikov smiled. 'Ah, but serpents are my speciality, Carter Kane!' He touched a silver pendant hanging over his necktie – an amulet shaped like a snake. 'And this particular creature is my favourite: the *tjesu heru*. Two hungry mouths to feed. Two troublesome children. Perfect!'

Sadie and I looked at each other. We had one of those moments where we could read each other's expressions perfectly.

We both knew we couldn't defeat Menshikov. He'd let the pushmi-pullyu snake wear us down, and if we survived that he'd just blast us with something else. The guy was a pro. We would either die or get captured, and Bes had warned us about not getting taken alive. After seeing what had happened to that demon Death-to-Corks, I took Bes's warning seriously.

To survive, we'd have to do something crazy – something so suicidal Menshikov would never expect it. We had to get help *immediately*.

'Should I?' Sadie asked.

'Do it,' I agreed.

The *tjesu heru* bared its dripping fangs. You wouldn't think a creature with no back end could move so fast, but it bent both heads towards us like a giant horseshoe and charged.

I pulled my sword. Sadie was faster.

She pointed her staff at Set's malachite jar and yelled her favourite command word: '*Ha-di!*'

I was afraid it wouldn't work. She hadn't tried the destruction spell since she separated herself from Isis. But just before the monster reached me the green jar shattered.

Menshikov screamed, '*Nyet!*'

A sandstorm exploded through the room. Hot winds pushed Sadie and me against the fireplace. A wall of red sand slammed into the *tjesu heru* and sent it flying sideways into a malachite column. Vlad Menshikov was blasted right out of his protective circle and banged his head on a table. He crumpled to the ground, red sand swirling over him until he was completely buried.

When the storm cleared, a man in a red silk suit stood in front of us. He had skin the colour of cherry Kool-Aid, a shaved head, a dark goatee and glittering black eyes lined with kohl. He looked like an Egyptian devil ready for a night on the town.

He grinned and spread his hands in a *ta-da* gesture. 'That's better! Thank you, Sadie Kane!'

To our left, the *tjesu heru* hissed and flailed, trying to get back on its feet. The pile of red sand covering Vlad Menshikov started to move.

'Do something, Evil Day!' Sadie commanded. 'Get rid of them!'

Set winced. 'No need to get personal with the names.'

'Maybe you'd prefer Rockin' Red Reaper?' I asked.

Set made a picture frame with his fingers, as if imagining that name on his driver's license. 'Yes... that *is* nice, isn't it?'

The *tjesu heru* staggered to its feet. It shook both heads and glared at us, but it seemed to ignore Set, even though he was the one who'd slammed it against the wall.

'It has beautiful colouration, doesn't it?' Set asked. 'A gorgeous specimen.'

'Just kill it!' I yelled.

Set looked shocked. 'Oh, I couldn't do that! I'm much too fond of snakes. Besides, GETM would have my hide.'

'Get 'em?' I asked.

'Gods for the Ethical Treatment of Monsters.'

'You're making that up!' I yelled.

Set grinned. 'Still…I'm afraid you'll have to deal with the *tjesu heru* on your own.'

The monster hissed at us, which probably meant, *Sweet!* I raised my sword to keep it at bay.

The pile of red sand shifted. Menshikov's dazed face rose from the top. Set snapped his fingers, and a large ceramic pot appeared in the air, shattering on the magician's head. Menshikov slipped back into the sand.

'I'll stay here and entertain Vladimir,' Set said.

'Can't you execrate him, or something?' Sadie demanded.

'Oh, I wish! Unfortunately, I'm rather limited when someone holds my secret name, especially when they've given me specific orders not to kill them.' He stared accusingly at Sadie. 'At any rate, I may be able to buy you a few minutes, but Vlad is going to be quite mad when he comes around, so I'd hurry, if I were you. Good luck surviving! And good luck eating them, *tjesu heru!*'

I wanted to strangle Set, but we had bigger problems. As if encouraged by Set's pep talk, the *tjesu heru* lunged at us. Sadie and I sprinted for the nearest door.

We ran through the Winter Palace with Set's laughter echoing behind us.

11. Carter Does Something Incredibly Stupid (and No One Is Surprised)

I UNDERSTAND, CARTER. I do.

Have me narrate the most painful part. Of course, I can't blame you. What happened was awful enough for me, but for you – well, I wouldn't want to talk about it either.

There we were in the Winter Palace, racing down polished marble hallways that were *not* designed for running. Behind us, the two-headed *tjesu heru* skidded and slammed into walls as it tried to turn corners, much like Muffin used to do whenever Gran mopped the floor. That's the only reason the monster didn't catch us immediately.

Since we'd teleported into the Malachite Room, I had no idea where the nearest exit was. I wasn't even sure if we were actually *in* the Winter Palace, or if Menshikov's office was some clever facsimile that existed only in the Duat. I was beginning to think we'd never get out when we rounded a corner, scrambled down a staircase and spotted a set of glass-and-iron doors leading out to Palace Square.

The *tjesu heru* was right behind us. It slipped and rolled down the staircase, demolishing a plaster statue of some unfortunate tsar.

We were ten metres from the exit when I saw the chains across the doors.

'Carter,' I gasped, waving helplessly at the padlock.

I hate to admit just how weak I felt. I didn't have the strength for another spell. Cracking Set's vase in the Malachite Room had been my last hurrah, which is a good example of why you shouldn't use magic to solve all your problems. Summoning a Divine Word to break the vase had taken so much energy, I felt as if I'd been digging holes in the hot sun. It would've been much easier just to throw a rock. If I lived through the night, I decided to add some rocks to my tool bag.

We were three metres away when Carter thrust his fist towards the doors. The Eye of Horus burned against the padlock, and the doors burst open as if they'd been hit by a giant fist. I hadn't seen Carter do anything like that since our fight at the Red Pyramid, but I didn't have time to be amazed. We bolted outside into the wintry night, the *tjesu heru* roaring behind us.

You'll think I was mad, but my first thought was: *That was too easy.*

Despite the monster chasing us and the business with Set (whom I would strangle at the first opportunity – that backstabbing git!), I couldn't help feeling we'd breached Menshikov's inner sanctum and snatched the scroll without nearly enough trouble. Where were the traps? The alarms? The exploding-donkey curses? I was certain we'd stolen the authentic scroll. I'd felt the same tingle in my fingers as when I'd taken the one from the Brooklyn Museum (without the fire, thankfully). So why hadn't the scroll been better protected?

I was so tired that I fell a few steps behind Carter, which probably saved my life. I felt a crawling sensation across my scalp. I sensed darkness above me – a feeling that reminded me too much of the shadow of Nekhbet's wings. I looked up and saw the *tjesu heru* sailing over our heads like a massive bullfrog, timing its pounce so it would land –

'Carter, stop!' I yelled.

Easier said than done on icy pavement. I skidded to a halt, but Carter was going too fast. He fell on his bum and slid, his sword skittering to one side.

The *tjesu heru* landed right on top of him. If it hadn't been ∪-shaped, Carter would've been crushed, but it curved round him like an enormous pair of headphones, one head glaring down at him from either side.

How could something so large have leaped so far? Too late, I realized we should have stayed inside where it was harder for the monster to move. Out here, we had no chance of outrunning it.

'Carter,' I said. 'Stay perfectly still.'

He froze in crab-walk position. The monster's two heads dripped venom that hissed and steamed on the icy stones.

'Oi!' I yelled. Not having any rocks, I picked up a chunk of broken ice and threw it at the *tjesu heru*. Naturally, I hit Carter in the back instead. Nevertheless, I got the *tjesu heru*'s attention.

SADIE

Both heads turned towards me, twin tongues flickering. First step done: distract the monster.

Second step: find some clever way to draw it away from Carter. That part was giving me a bit more trouble.

I'd used my only potion. Most of my magic supplies were gone. My staff and wand wouldn't do me much good with my magical reserves drained. The knife from Anubis? Somehow I doubted this was the right situation to open someone's mouth.

The amulet from Walt? I had not the slightest idea how to use it.

For the millionth time, I regretted having given up the spirit of Isis. I could really have used the full magic arsenal of a goddess. But, of course, that was exactly why I'd *had* to separate from her. That sort of power is intoxicating, dangerously addictive. It can quickly destroy your life.

But what if I could form a limited bond? In the Malachite Room, I'd managed the *ha-di* spell for the first time in months. And, while it had been difficult, it hadn't been impossible.

Right, Isis, I thought. *Here's what I need –*

Don't think, Sadie, her voice whispered back almost immediately, which was quite a shock. *Divine magic has to be involuntary, like breathing.*

You mean . . . I stopped myself. *Don't think.* Well, that shouldn't be too hard. I held up my staff, and a golden hieroglyph blazed in the air. A one-metre-tall *tyet* lit up the courtyard like a Christmas-tree star.

The *tjesu heru* snarled, its yellow eyes fixed on the hieroglyph.

'Don't like that, eh?' I called. 'Symbol of Isis, you big ugly mutt. Now, get away from my brother!'

It was a complete bluff, of course. I doubted the glowing sign could do anything useful. But I hoped the snake creature wasn't smart enough to know that.

Slowly, Carter edged backwards. He looked for his sword, but it was ten metres away – much too far to reach.

I kept my eyes on the monster. I used the butt of my staff to trace a magic circle in the snow around me. It wouldn't provide much protection, but it was better than nothing.

'Carter,' I called, 'when I say go, run back here.'

'That thing's too fast!' he said.

'I'll try to detonate the hieroglyph and blind it.'

I still maintain that the plan would've worked, but I didn't get the chance to try it. Somewhere off to my left, boots crunched on ice. The monster turned towards the sound.

A young man ran into the light of the hieroglyph. He was dressed in a heavy wool coat and a policeman's hat, with a rifle in his hands, but he couldn't have been much older than me. He was fairly drowning in his uniform. When he saw the monster, his eyes widened. He stumbled backwards, almost dropping his weapon.

He yelled something at me in Russian, probably, 'Why is there a two-headed snake monster with no bum?'

The monster hissed at both of us – which it could do, having two heads.

'That's a monster,' I told the guard. I was fairly sure he couldn't understand, but I tried to keep my tone steady. 'Stay calm and don't shoot. I'm trying to save my brother.'

The guard swallowed. His large ears were the only things holding up his hat. He glanced from the monster to Carter to the *tyet* glowing above my head. Then he did something I wasn't expecting.

He said a word in Ancient Egyptian: '*Heqat*' – the command I always used to summon my staff. His rifle changed to a two-metre oaken rod with the carved head of a falcon.

Wonderful, I thought. *The security guards are secretly magicians.*

He addressed me in Russian – some sort of warning. I recognized the name *Menshikov*.

'Let me guess,' I said. 'You want to take me to your leader.'

The *tjesu heru* snapped its jaws. It was rapidly losing its fear of my glowing *tyet*. Carter wasn't far enough away to make a run for it.

'Look,' I told the guard, 'your boss Menshikov is a traitor. He summoned this thing to kill us so we wouldn't blab about his plans to free Apophis. Savvy the word *Apophis*? Bad snake. Very bad snake! Now, either help me kill this monster or stay out of my way!'

The magician-guard hesitated. He pointed at me nervously. 'Kane.' It wasn't a question.

'Yes,' I agreed. 'Kane.'

His expression was a jumble of emotions – fear, disbelief, possibly even awe. I didn't know what he'd heard about us, but before he could decide whether to help us or fight us the situation spun out of control.

The *tjesu heru* charged. My ridiculous brother – instead of rolling out of the way – tackled the monster.

He locked his arms round the creature's right neck and tried to climb its back, but the *tjesu heru* simply turned its other head to strike.

What was my brother thinking? Perhaps he thought he could ride the beast. Perhaps he was trying to buy me a few seconds to cast a spell. If you ask him about it now, he'll claim he doesn't remember the incident at all. But, if you ask me, the thickheaded fool was trying to save me, even if it meant sacrificing himself. The nerve!

[Oh, yes, *now* you try to explain yourself, Carter. I thought you didn't remember this bit! Just be quiet and let me tell the story.]

As I was saying, the *tjesu heru* struck at Carter, and everything seemed to slow down. I remember screaming, lowering my staff at the monster. The soldier-magician yelled something in Russian. The creature sank its fangs into Carter's left shoulder, and he dropped to the ground.

I forgot about my makeshift circle. I ran towards him, and my staff glowed. I don't know how I managed the power. As Isis said, I didn't think. I simply channelled all my rage and shock into my staff.

Seeing Carter hurt was the final insult. My grandparents had been possessed, my friends had been attacked and my birthday ruined. But my brother was off-limits. No one was allowed to hurt my brother.

I unleashed a beam of golden light that hit the monster with the force of a sandblaster. The *tjesu heru* crumbled to bits, until there was nothing left but a streak of sand steaming in the snow and a few splinters of Menshikov's shattered staff.

I ran to Carter's side. He was shivering, his eyes rolled back in his head. Two puncture wounds in his coat were smoking.

'Kane,' the young Russian said with a tone of awe.

I snatched up a splinter of wood and held it for him to see. 'Your boss Menshikov did this. He's working for Apophis. Menshikov: Apophis. Now, GET OUT!'

The magician may not have understood my words, but he got the message. He turned and ran.

I cradled Carter's head. I couldn't carry him by myself, but I had to get him out of here. We were in enemy territory. I needed to find Bes.

I struggled to get him to his feet. Then someone took Carter's other arm and helped us up. I found Set grinning at me, still in his ridiculous red disco suit, dusted with malachite rubble. Menshikov's broken white sunglasses were propped on his head.

'You,' I said, too filled with loathing to issue a proper death threat.

'Me,' Set agreed cheerily. 'Let's get your brother out of here, shall we? Vladimir is *not* in a good mood.'

The Nevsky Prospekt would've been a lovely place to shop if it hadn't been the wee hours of the morning during a snowstorm, and if I hadn't been carrying my poisoned, comatose brother. The street had wide pavements, perfect for strolling, lined with a dazzling assortment of high-end boutiques, cafés, churches and mansions. With all the signs in Russian, I didn't see how I was going to find the chocolate shop. I couldn't spot Bes's black Mercedes anywhere.

Set volunteered to carry Carter, but I wasn't about to let the god of chaos take full charge of my brother, so we dragged him between us. Set chatted amiably about *tjesu heru* poison: 'Completely incurable! Fatal in about twelve hours. It's amazing stuff!' And his tussle with Menshikov: 'Six vases broken over his head, and he still survives! I envy his thick skull.' And my prospects of living long enough to find Bes: 'Oh, you're toast, my dear! A dozen senior magicians were rallying to Menshikov when I made my, *er*, strategic retreat. They'll be after you shortly. I could've destroyed them all, of course, but I couldn't risk Vladimir using my secret name again. Maybe he'll get amnesia and forget it. Then if you die – that would be both problems solved. Oh, I'm sorry, I suppose that sounded insensitive. Come along!'

Carter's head lolled. His breathing sounded almost as bad as Vlad the Inhaler's.

Now, please don't think I was dense. Of course I remembered the wax mini-Carter figurine Jaz had given me. I recognized that this was just the sort of emergency where it might come in handy. How Jaz had predicted Carter would need healing, I had no idea. But it was possible the figurine could draw the poison out of him, despite what Set said about it being incurable. What does a god of evil know about healing, anyway?

There were problems, however. First, I knew very little about healing magic. I needed time to figure out the proper casting and, since I had only one wax statue, I couldn't afford to get it wrong. Second, I couldn't very well do that while being chased by Menshikov and his squad of magical Russian goons, nor did I want to let my guard down with Set anywhere near me. I didn't know why he'd decided to be helpful all of a sudden, but the sooner I could lose him the better. I needed to find Bes and retreat to somewhere safe – if there was such a place.

Set kept chatting about all the exciting ways the magicians might kill me once they caught up. Finally I spotted a bridge up ahead over a frozen canal. Parked in the middle was the black Mercedes. Bes leaned against the hood, eating pieces off a chocolate chessboard. Next to him sat a large plastic bag – hopefully with more chocolate for me.

I yelled to him, but he was so engrossed in eating chocolate (which I suppose I could understand) that he didn't notice us until we were a few metres away. Then he looked up and saw Set.

I started to say, 'Bes, don't –'

Too late. Like a skunk, the dwarf god activated his default defence. His eyes bulged out. His mouth opened impossibly wide. He yelled, 'BOO!' so loudly that my hair parted and icicles rained down from the bridge's street lamps.

Set didn't look the least bit fazed.

'Hello, Bes,' he said. 'Really, you're not so scary with chocolate smeared on your face.'

Bes glared at me. 'What's *he* doing here?'

'Not my idea!' I promised. I gave him the abbreviated story of our encounter with Menshikov.

'And so Carter's been hurt,' I summed up, which seemed rather obvious. 'We have to get him out of here.'

'But first,' Set interrupted, pointing at the Chocolate

Museum bag next to Bes, 'I can't stand surprises. What's in there? A gift for me?'

Bes frowned. 'Sadie wanted a souvenir. I brought her Lenin's head.'

Set slapped his thigh with delight. 'Bes, how evil! There's hope for you yet.'

'Not his *real* head,' Bes said. 'It's chocolate.'

'Oh . . . shame. Can I have part of your chessboard, then? I simply love eating pawns.'

'Get out of here, Set!' Bes said.

'Well, I could do that, but since our friends are on their way I thought perhaps we should make a deal.'

Set snapped his fingers, and a globe of red light appeared in front of him. In it, the holographic images of six men in security uniforms piled into two white sports cars. Their headlights blazed to life. The cars swerved across a car park, then passed straight through a stone wall as if it were made of smoke.

'I'd say you have about two minutes.' Set smiled, and the globe of light faded. 'You remember Menshikov's minions, Bes. Are you sure you want to meet them again?'

The dwarf god's face darkened. He crushed a white-chocolate chess piece in his hand. 'You lying, scheming, murdering –'

'Stop!' I said.

Carter groaned in his poisoned daze. Either he was getting heavier, or I was getting tired of holding him up.

'We don't have time to argue,' I said. 'Set, are you offering to stop the magicians?'

He laughed. 'No, no. I'm still hoping they'll kill you, you see. But I was going to offer you the location of the last scroll in the Book of Ra. That *is* what you're after, isn't it?'

I assumed he was lying. He usually was – but if he was serious...

I looked at Bes. 'Is it possible he knows the location?'

Bes grunted. 'More than possible. The priests of Ra *gave* him the scroll for safekeeping.'

'Why on earth would they do that?'

Set tried to look modest. 'Come now, Sadie. I was a loyal lieutenant of Ra. If you were Ra, and you didn't want to be bothered by any old magician trying to wake you, wouldn't you trust the key to your location with your most fearsome servant?'

He had a point. 'Where's the scroll, then?'

'Not so fast. I'll give you the location if *you* give me back my secret name.'

'Not likely!'

'It's quite simple. Just say "I give you back your name". You'll forget the proper way to say it –'

'And then I'll have no power over you! You'll kill me!'

'You'd have my word that I won't.'

'Right. That's worth a lot. What if I used your secret name to *force* you to tell me?'

Set shrugged. 'With a few days to research the correct spell, you might manage that. Unfortunately...' He cupped his ear to his hand. In the distance, tyres squealed – two cars, travelling fast, getting closer. 'You don't have a few days.'

Bes cursed in Egyptian. 'Don't do it, girl. He can't be trusted.'

'Can we find the scroll without him?'

'Well . . . maybe. Probably not. No.'

The headlights of two cars swerved onto the Nevsky Prospekt, roughly half a mile away. We were out of time. I had to get Carter away from here, but if Set really was our only way of finding the scroll I couldn't just let him go.

'All right, Set. But I'll give you one last order.'

Bes sighed. 'I can't bear to watch this. Give me your brother. I'll put him in the car.'

The dwarf took Carter and stuffed him into the back seat of the Mercedes.

I kept my eyes on Set, trying to think of the *least* terrible way to make this deal. I couldn't simply tell him to *never* hurt my family. A magical pact needed to be carefully worded, with clear limits and an expiration date, or the whole spell would unravel. '*Evil Day*, you are not to harm the Kane family. You'll maintain a truce with us at least until – until Ra has been awakened.'

'Or until you try and *fail* to awaken him?' Set asked innocently.

'If that happens,' I said, 'the world is going to end. So why not? I will do what you ask concerning your name. In exchange, you will tell me the location of the last part of the Book of Ra, without trickery or deception. Then you'll depart for the Duat.'

Set considered the offer. The two white sports cars were only a few blocks away now. Bes shut Carter's door and ran back over.

'We have a deal,' Set agreed. 'You'll find the scroll at Bahariya. Bes knows the place I mean.'

Bes didn't look happy. 'That place is heavily protected. We'll have to use the Alexandria portal.'

'Yes.' Set grinned. 'Should be interesting! How long can you hold your breath, Sadie Kane?'

'What do you mean?'

'Never mind, never mind. Now, I believe you owe me a secret name.'

'I give you back your name,' I said. Just like that, I felt the magic leave me. I still knew Set's name: Evil Day. But somehow I couldn't remember exactly how I used to say it, or how it worked in a spell. The memory had been erased.

To my surprise, Set didn't kill me on the spot. He just smiled and tossed me Vlad Menshikov's sunglasses. 'I hope you live, after all, Sadie Kane. You're quite amusing. But, if they do kill you, at least enjoy the experience!'

'Gosh, thanks.'

'And, just because I like you so much, I have a free piece of information for your brother. Tell him Zia Rashid's village was called al-Hamrah Makan.'

'Why is that –'

'Happy travels!' Set disappeared in a cloud of blood-coloured mist. A block away, the two white sports cars barrelled towards us. A magician stuck his head out of the sunroof of the lead car and pointed his staff in our direction.

'Time to leave,' Bes said. 'Get in!'

I will say this for Bes: he drove like a maniac. And I mean that in the best possible way. Icy streets didn't bother him at all. Neither did traffic signals, pedestrian pavements or canals, which he twice jumped without bothering to find a bridge. Fortunately, the city was mostly empty that time of morning, or I'm sure we would have mowed down any number of Russians.

We wove through central St Petersburg while the two white sports cars closed behind us. I tried to hold Carter steady next to me on the back seat. His eyes were half open, his corneas the most awful shade of green. Despite the cold, he was burning with fever. I managed to tug off his winter coat and found his shirt soaked with sweat. On his shoulder, the puncture wounds were oozing like ... Well, it's probably best I don't describe that part.

I glanced behind us. The magician in the sunroof aimed his staff – not an easy task in a high-speed car chase – and a glowing white javelin shot from the tip, hurtling towards us like a homing missile.

'Duck!' I yelled, and pushed Carter against the seat.

The javelin broke the rear window and flew straight through the windshield. If Bes had been normal height, he would have got a free head piercing. As it was, the projectile missed him completely.

'I'm a dwarf,' he grumbled. 'I don't duck!'

He swerved to the right. Behind us, a shopfront exploded. Looking back, I saw the entire wall dissolve into a pile of living snakes. Our pursuers were still closing.

'Bes, get us out of here!' I yelled.

'I'm trying, kid. Egyptian Bridge is coming up. It was originally built in the 1800s, but –'

'I don't care! Just drive!'

Truly, it's amazing how many Egyptian bits and bobs there are in St Petersburg, and how *little* I cared about them. Being chased by evil magicians throwing javelins and snake bombs does tend to clarify one's priorities.

Suffice it to say: yes, there really is an Egyptian Bridge over the Fontanka River, leading south out of central St Petersburg. Why? No idea. Don't care. As we raced towards it, I saw black stone sphinxes on either side – lady sphinxes with gilded pharaoh crowns – but the only thing that mattered to me was that they could summon a portal.

Bes barked something in Egyptian. At the top of the bridge, blue light flashed. A swirling sand vortex appeared.

'What did Set mean,' I asked, 'about holding my breath?'

'Hopefully won't be for long,' Bes said. 'We'll only be thirty feet under.'

'Thirty feet under *water?*'

BANG! The Mercedes careened sideways. Only later did I realize another javelin must have hit our back tyre. We spun across the ice and flipped, sliding upside down into the vortex.

My head slammed against something. I opened my eyes, fighting for consciousness, but either I was blind or we were in complete darkness. I heard water trickling through the javelin-shattered glass, and the roof of the Mercedes crumpling like an aluminum can.

I had time to think: *A teenager for less than a day, and I'm going to drown.*

Then I blacked out.

12. I Master the Fine Art of Name-calling

IT'S DISTURBING TO WAKE UP as a chicken.

My *ba* floated through dark water. My glowing wings flapped as I tried to figure out which way was up. I assumed my body was somewhere close by, possibly already drowned in the back of the Mercedes, but I couldn't figure out how to return to it.

Why on earth had Bes driven us through an underwater portal? I hoped poor Carter had somehow survived; perhaps Bes was able to pull him free. But dying from poison rather than drowning didn't seem much of an improvement.

A current caught me and whisked me into the Duat. The water changed into cold fog. Wailing and growling filled the darkness. My acceleration slowed, and when the mist dissipated I was back in Brooklyn House, floating just outside the infirmary door. On a bench against the wall, sitting together like old friends, were Anubis and Walt Stone. They looked like they were waiting for bad news. Walt's hands were folded in his lap. His shoulders slumped. He'd changed clothes

192

– a new sleeveless tee, a new pair of running shorts – but he looked as if he hadn't slept since returning from London.

Anubis talked to him in soothing tones, as if trying to ease his grief. I'd never seen Anubis in traditional Egyptian clothes before: bare-chested with a gold and ruby collar round his neck, a simple black kilt wrapped round his waist. It wasn't a look I'd recommend for most guys, but Anubis pulled it off. I'd always imagined he would look rather skinny with his shirt off (not that I imagined that a lot, mind you) but he was in excellent shape. They must've had quite a good gym in the underworld, bench-pressing tombstones and whatnot.

At any rate, after the shock of seeing them together, my first thought was that something terrible must've happened to Jaz.

'What is it?' I asked, not sure if they could hear me. 'What's happened?'

Walt didn't react, but Anubis looked up. As usual my heart did a little happy dance quite without my permission. His eyes were so mesmerizing, I completely forgot how to use my brain.

I said, '*Um*.'

I know, Liz would've been proud.

'Sadie,' Anubis said, 'you shouldn't be here. Carter is dying.'

That jarred me back to my senses. 'I know that, jackal boy! I didn't *ask* to be – Wait, why *am* I here?'

Anubis pointed at the door of the infirmary. 'I suspect Jaz's spirit called to you.'

'Is she dead? Am *I* dead?'

'Neither,' Anubis said. 'But you are both on death's doorstep, which means your souls can speak to each other quite easily. Just don't stay long.'

Walt still hadn't acknowledged me. He muttered: 'Couldn't tell her. Why couldn't I tell her?' He opened his hands. Cradled in his palms was a golden *shen* amulet exactly like the one he'd given me.

'Anubis, what's wrong with him?' I asked. 'Can't he hear me?'

Anubis put his hand on Walt's shoulder. 'He can't see either of us, though I think he can sense my presence. He called to me for guidance. That's why I'm here.'

'Guidance from you? Why?'

I suppose it sounded harsher than I intended, but, of all the gods Walt might've called, Anubis seemed the least likely choice.

Anubis looked up at me, his eyes even more melancholy than usual.

'You should pass on now, Sadie,' he said. 'You have very little time. I promise I'll do my best to ease Walt's pain.'

'His pain?' I asked. 'Hang on –'

But the infirmary door swung open, and the currents of the Duat pulled me inside.

The infirmary was the nicest medical facility I'd ever been in, but that wasn't saying much. I hated hospitals. My father used to joke that I was born screaming and didn't stop until they got me out of the maternity ward. I was mortally afraid of needles, pills and above all the smell of *sick* people. Dead

people and cemeteries? Those didn't bother me. But sickness
... well, I'm sorry, but does it have to smell so *sick*?

My first visit to Jaz in the infirmary had taken all my
courage. This second time, even in *ba* form, wasn't any easier.

The room was about the size of my bedroom. The walls were
rough-hewn limestone. Large windows let in the nighttime
glow of New York. Cedar cabinets were carefully labelled with
medicines, first aid supplies, magical charms and potions. In
one corner stood a fountain with a life-size statue of the lion
goddess Sekhmet, patron of healers. I'd heard that the water
pouring through Sekhmet's hands could cure a cold or flu
instantly, and provide most of one's daily vitamins and iron,
but I'd never had the courage to take a drink.

The gurgle of the fountain was peaceful enough. Instead of
antiseptic, the air smelled of charmed vanilla-scented candles
that floated around the room. But, still, the place made me
jumpy.

I knew the candles monitored the patients' conditions.
Their flames changed colour to indicate problems. At the
moment, they all hovered around the only occupied bed –
Jaz's. Their flames were dark orange.

Jaz's hands were folded on her chest. Her blonde hair was
combed across her pillow. She smiled faintly as if she were
having a pleasant dream.

And sitting at the foot of Jaz's bed was ... Jaz, or at least
a shimmering green image of my friend. It wasn't a *ba*. The
form was fully human. I wondered if she'd died after all, and
this was her ghost.

'Jaz…' A wave of fresh guilt washed over me. Everything that had gone wrong the past two days had started with Jaz's sacrifice, which was my fault. 'Are you –'

'Dead? No, Sadie. This is my *ren*.'

Her transparent body flickered. When I looked more closely, I saw it was composed of images, like a 3-D video of Jaz's life. Toddler Jaz sat in a high chair, painting her face with baby food. Twelve-year-old Jaz cartwheeled across a gymnasium floor, trying out for her first cheerleading squad. Present-day Jaz opened her school locker and found a glowing *djed* amulet – our magical calling card that had led her to Brooklyn.

'Your *ren*,' I said. 'Another part of your soul?'

The glowing green image nodded. 'Egyptians believed there were five different parts of the soul. The *ba* is the personality. The *ren* is –'

'Your name,' I remembered. 'But how can *that* be your name?'

'My name is my identity,' she said. 'The sum of my experiences. As long as my name is remembered, I still exist, even if I die. Do you understand?'

I didn't, even remotely. But I understood she might die, and that it was my fault.

'I'm so sorry.' I tried not to break into tears. 'If I hadn't grabbed that stupid scroll –'

'Sadie, don't be sorry. I'm glad you've come.'

'But –'

'Everything happens for a reason, Sadie, even bad things.'

'That's not true!' I said. 'It's completely unfair!'

How could Jaz be so calm and nice, even when she was

in a coma? I didn't want to hear that bad things happened as part of some grand plan. I *hated* it when people said that. I'd lost my mother. I'd lost my dad. My life had been turned upside down, and I'd almost died countless times. Now, as far as I knew, I *was* dead or dying. My brother was poisoned and drowning, and I couldn't help him.

'No reason is worth all this,' I said. 'Life is random. It's harsh. It's – it's –'

Jaz was still smiling, looking a bit amused.

'Oh,' I said. 'You wanted to make me mad, didn't you?'

'That's the Sadie we all love. Grief really isn't productive. You do better when you're angry.'

'Humph.' I supposed she was right, but I didn't have to like it. 'So why did you bring me here?'

'Two things,' she said. 'First, you're not dead. When you wake up, you'll only have a few minutes to heal Carter. You'll have to act quickly.'

'Using the wax statue,' I said. 'Yes, I figured that out. But I don't know *how*. I'm no good at healing.'

'There is only one more ingredient that matters. You know what it is.'

'But I don't!'

Jaz raised an eyebrow like I was just being stubborn. 'You're so close to understanding, Sadie. Think about Isis. Think about how you channelled her power in St Petersburg. The answer will come to you.'

'But –'

'We must hurry. The second thing: you're going to need Walt's help. I know it's risky. I know Bes warned against it. But use the amulet to call Walt back to you. It's what he wants. Some risks are worth taking, even if it means losing a life.'

'Losing *whose* life? His?'

The infirmary scene began to dissolve, turning into a blurry watercolour.

'Think about Isis,' Jaz repeated. 'And, Sadie...there *is* a purpose. You taught us that. We choose to believe in Ma'at. We create order out of chaos, beauty and meaning out of ugly randomness. That's what Egypt is all about. That's why its name, its *ren*, has endured for millennia. Don't despair. Otherwise Chaos wins.'

I remembered saying something like that in one of our classes, but even then I hadn't believed it.

'I'll let you in on a secret,' I said. 'I'm a rubbish teacher.'

Jaz's form, all her collected memories, slowly melted into mist. 'I'll let *you* in on a secret,' she said, her voice fading. 'You were an excellent teacher. Now, visit Isis, and see how it began.'

The infirmary evaporated. Suddenly I was on a royal barge, floating down the Nile. The sun blazed overhead. Lush green marsh grass and palm trees lined the riverbanks. Beyond that the desert spread to the horizon – barren red hills so dry and forbidding, they might as well have been on Mars.

The boat was like the one Carter had described from his vision with Horus, though in better condition. Its crisp white sail was emblazoned with the image of the sun disc, glittering in red and gold. Orbs of multicoloured light zipped around the deck, manning the oars and pulling the lines. How they did this without hands, I don't know, but it wasn't the first time I'd seen such a magical crew.

The hull was inlaid with precious metals – copper, silver and gold designs showing pictures of the boat's journey through the Duat, and hieroglyphs invoking the power of the sun.

In the middle of the boat, a blue-and-gold canopy shaded the sun god's throne, which was without a doubt the most impressive and uncomfortable-looking chair I'd ever seen. At first I thought it was molten gold. Then I realized it was fashioned out of living fire – yellow flames that had somehow been sculpted into the shape of a throne. Etched into its legs and armrests, white-hot hieroglyphs glowed so brightly they seared my eyes.

The throne's occupant wasn't quite so impressive. Ra was an old leathery man bent over in the shape of a question mark, his bald scalp cratered with liver spots and his face so saggy and wrinkled it looked like a mask. Only his kohl-lined eyes gave any indication he was alive, because they were full of pain and weariness. He wore a kilt and collar, which did not suit him *nearly* as well as it had Anubis. Until now, the most ancient person I'd ever seen was Iskandar, the former Chief Lector, who'd been two thousand years old. But Iskandar had never looked this bad, even when he was about to die. To make matters worse, Ra's left leg was wrapped in bandages and swollen to twice its proper size.

He groaned and propped his leg on a pile of cushions. Two puncture wounds oozed through the bandages on his shin – very much like the fang marks on Carter's shoulder. As Ra kneaded his leg, green venom spread up the veins of his thigh. Just looking at it made my *ba* feathers shiver with revulsion.

Ra looked to the heavens. His eyes turned molten yellow like his throne.

'Isis!' he cried. 'Very well! I relent!'

A shadow rippled under the canopy. A woman appeared, and knelt before the throne. I recognized her, of course. She had long, dark hair cut Cleopatra-style and a white gossamer dress that complemented her graceful figure. Her luminous rainbow wings shimmered like the northern lights.

With her head bowed and her palms raised in supplication, she looked like the picture of humility; but I knew Isis too well. I could see the smile she was trying to hide. I could sense her elation.

'Lord Ra,' she said. 'I live to serve you.'

'Ha!' Ra said. 'You live for power, Isis. Don't try to deceive me. I know you created the snake that bit me! That's why no one else can find a cure. You desire my throne for your husband, the upstart Osiris.'

Isis started to protest, 'My lord –'

'Enough! If I were a younger god –' Ra made the mistake of moving his leg. He yelped in pain. The green venom spread further up his veins.

'Never mind.' He sighed miserably. 'I am weary of this world. Enough scheming and plotting. Just cure the poison.'

'Gladly, my king. But I will need –'

'My secret name,' Ra said. 'Yes, I know. Promise to heal me, and you will get all you desire...and more.'

I heard the warning in Ra's voice, but either Isis didn't notice, or she didn't care.

'I swear to heal you,' she said.

'Then approach, goddess.'

Isis leaned forward. I thought Ra would whisper his name in

her ear, but instead he grasped her hand and placed it against his withered brow. Her fingertips smouldered. She tried to pull away, but Ra held her wrist. The sun god's entire form glowed with fiery images of his long life: the first dawn; his sun boat shining on the newly risen land of Egypt; the creation of the other gods and mortal men; Ra's endless battles with Apophis as he passed through the Duat each night, keeping Chaos at bay. It was too much to take in – centuries passing with each heartbeat. His secret name was the sum of his experience, and even then, in those ancient times, Ra was unthinkably old. The fiery aura spread to Isis's hand, travelling up her arm until her whole body was wreathed in flames. She screamed once. Then the fires died. Isis collapsed, smoke curling from her dress.

'So,' Ra said. 'You survived.'

I couldn't tell if he felt disappointment or grudging respect.

Isis rose unsteadily to her feet. She looked shell-shocked, as if she'd just strolled through a war zone, but she raised her hand. A fiery hieroglyph burned on her palm – Ra's secret name, distilled into a single unbelievably powerful word.

She placed her hand on Ra's poisoned leg and spoke a spell. The green venom retreated from his veins. The swelling subsided. The bandages fell away, and the two fang marks closed.

Ra reclined on his throne and sighed with relief. 'At last. No pain.'

'My lord needs rest,' Isis suggested. 'A long, long rest.'

The sun god opened his eyes. There was no fire in them now. They looked like the milky eyes of a mortal old man.

'Bast!' he called.

The cat goddess materialized at his side. She was dressed in Egyptian armour of leather and iron, and she seemed younger, though perhaps that was just because she hadn't yet endured centuries in a prison abyss, fighting Apophis. I was tempted to shout to her and warn her about what was coming, but my voice wouldn't work.

Bast gave Isis a sideways look. 'My lord, is this... *woman* bothering you?' Ra shook his head. 'Nothing will bother me much longer, my faithful cat. Come with me now. We have important matters to discuss before I depart.'

'My lord? Where are you going?'

'Into forced retirement.' Ra glared at Isis. 'That *is* what you want, goddess of magic?'

Isis bowed.

'Never, my lord!' Bast drew her knives and stepped towards Isis, but Ra held out his arm.

'Enough, Bast,' he said. 'I have another fight in mind for you – one last, crucial fight. As for you, Isis, you may think you have won because you mastered my secret name. Do you realize what you've started? Osiris may become pharaoh, but his reign will be short and bitter. *His* royal seat will be a pale reflection of my throne of fire. This boat will no longer ride the Duat. The balance between Ma'at and Chaos will slowly degrade. Egypt itself will fall. The names of her gods will fade to a distant memory. Then one day the entire world will stand on the brink of destruction. You will cry out to Ra, and I will not be there. When that day comes, remember how your greed and ambition caused it to happen.'

'My lord.' Isis bowed respectfully, but I knew she wasn't thinking about some distant future. She was drunk with her victory. She thought Osiris would rule Egypt forever, and that Ra was just an old fool. She did not know that in a short time her victory would turn to tragedy. Osiris would be murdered by his brother, Set. And, some day, Ra's other predictions would come true as well.

'Let us go, Bast,' Ra said. 'We are no longer wanted.'

The throne erupted in a column of flames, burning away the blue-and-gold canopy. A ball of fire ascended into the heavens until it was lost in the glare of the sun.

When the smoke cleared, Isis stood alone and laughed with delight.

'I did it!' she exclaimed. 'Osiris, you will be king! I mastered the secret name of Ra!'

I wanted to tell her she had mastered nothing, but I could only watch as Isis danced across the boat. She was so pleased with her own success she paid no attention to the magical servant lights disappearing. The lines dropped. The sail went slack. Oars trailed in the water, and the sun boat drifted down the river, unmanned.

My vision faded, and I sank into darkness.

I woke in a soft bed. For a blissful moment, I thought I was back in my room at Brooklyn House. I could get up and have a lovely breakfast with my friends – Amos, Philip of Macedonia and Khufu – then spend the day teaching our initiates how to turn each other into reptiles. That sounded brilliant.

But of course I wasn't home. I sat up, and my head began

spinning. I was in a king-size bed with soft cotton sheets and a pile of feather pillows. The bedroom was quite posh, decorated in dazzling white, which did not help my dizziness. I felt as if I were back in the home of the sky goddess Nut. At any moment, the room might dissolve into clouds.

My legs felt stiff, but I managed to get out of bed. I was wearing one of those hotel robes so massive and plush that I looked like an albino Muppet. I staggered to the doorway and found a lovely living room, also bright white. Sliding glass doors led to a veranda that overlooked the sea from quite a height – possibly fifteen or twenty storeys. The sky and the water were gorgeous blue.

My eyes took a moment to adjust to the light. On a nearby table, Carter's and my few possessions were carefully laid out – our old rumpled clothes, our magic bags and the two scrolls from the Book of Ra, along with Bes's bag from the Chocolate Museum.

Carter was wrapped in a white robe like mine. He lay on the couch with his eyes closed. His whole body shivered. Bes sat next to him, dabbing Carter's forehead with a cool cloth.

'How – how is he?' I managed.

Bes glanced over. He looked like a miniature tourist in a loud Hawaiian shirt, khaki shorts and flip-flops. The ugly American – size extra-small.

'About time,' he said. 'I was beginning to think you'd never wake up.'

I took a step forward, but the room tilted back and forth.

'Careful.' Bes rushed over and took my arm. 'You got a nasty bump on the head.'

'Never mind that,' I muttered. 'I have to help Carter.'

'He's bad, Sadie. I don't know if –'

'I can help. My wand and the wax figurine –'

'Yeah. Yeah, okay. I'll get them.'

With Bes's assistance, I wobbled to Carter's side. Bes fetched my things while I checked Carter's forehead. His fever was worse than before. The veins in his neck had turned green from the poison, just like Ra's had in my vision.

I frowned at Bes. 'How long was I out?'

'It's almost noon on Tuesday.' He spread my magic supplies at Carter's feet. 'So, roughly twelve hours.'

'*Twelve hours?* Bes, that's the *maximum* time Set thought Carter could stay alive before the poison killed him! Why didn't you wake me sooner?'

His face turned as red as his Hawaiian shirt. 'I tried! I pulled you both out of the Mediterranean and got you to the hotel, didn't I? I used all the wake-up spells I know! You just kept muttering in your sleep about Walt, Anubis, secret names –'

'Fine!' I said. 'Just help me –'

The doorbell rang.

Bes gestured for me to stay calm. He called out in another language – possibly Arabic – and a hotel waiter opened the door. He bowed low to Bes, as if the dwarf were a sultan, then brought in a room service cart loaded with tropical fruit, fresh-baked breads and bottled sodas.

'Excellent,' Bes told me. 'Be right back.'

'You're wasting time!' I snapped.

Naturally, Bes ignored me. He retrieved his bag from the dining table and brought out the chocolate head of Vladimir

Lenin. The waiter's eyes widened. Bes put the head in the middle of the cart and nodded as if it made the perfect centrepiece.

Bes gave the waiter a few more orders in Arabic, then handed him some gold coins. The waiter grovelled and generally looked terrified. He exited backwards, still bowing.

'Where are we exactly?' I asked. 'And why are you a king here?'

'Alexandria, Egypt,' Bes said. 'Sorry about the rough arrival. It's a tricky place to teleport to. Cleopatra's old capital, you know, where the Egyptian Empire fell apart, so magic tends to get twisted around. The only working portals are in the old city, which is off the coast, under ten metres of water.'

'And this place? Obviously a luxury hotel, but how did you –'

'Penthouse Suite, Four Seasons Alexandria.' He sounded slightly embarrassed. 'People in Egypt still remember the old gods, even if they won't admit it. I was popular back in the day, so I can usually call in favours when I need them. Sorry I didn't have more time. I could've got us a private villa.'

'How dare you,' I said. 'Making us settle for a five-star hotel. Now, why don't you make sure we're not interrupted while I heal Carter?'

I grabbed the wax figurine Jaz had given me and knelt next to my brother. The statue was deformed from getting knocked around in my bag. Then again, Carter looked worse for wear, too. Hopefully the magic connection would still work.

'Carter,' I said. 'I'm going to heal you. But I need your help.'

I put my hand on his feverish forehead. Now I knew why

Jaz had appeared to me as a *ren*, the part of the soul that represented her name. I knew why she'd shown me the vision of Isis and Ra.

You're so close to understanding, Sadie, she'd said.

I'd never thought about it before, but the *ren* was the same as one's secret name. It was more than just special word. The secret name is your darkest thoughts, your most embarrassing moments, your biggest dreams, your worst fears, all wrapped together. It's the sum of your experiences, even those you'd never want to share. Your secret name makes you who you are.

That's why a secret name has power. It's also why you couldn't simply hear someone repeat a secret name and know how to use it. You had to *know* that person and understand their life. The more you understood the person, the more power their name could yield. You could only learn a secret name from the person himself – or from the person closest to his heart.

And, heaven help me, for me Carter was that person.

Carter, I thought. *What is your secret name?*

Even in sickness, his mind resisted me. You don't just hand over your secret name. Every human had one, just as each god did, but most humans spent their whole lives not knowing that, not ever putting in words their most private identity. Understandable, really. Try summing up your entire existence in five words or less. Not exactly easy, is it?

'You can do this,' I murmured. 'You're my brother. I love you. All the embarrassing bits, all the annoying bits, which I imagine is *most* of you – a thousand Zias might run away from you if they knew the truth. But I won't. I'll still be here. Now, tell me your name, you big idiot, so I can save your life.'

My hand tingled against his forehead. His life passed through my fingers – ghostly memories of when we were children, living with our parents in Los Angeles. I saw my birthday party when I turned six and the cake exploded. I saw our mother reading bedtime stories to us from a college science textbook; our dad playing jazz and dancing me around the room while Carter covered his ears and yelled, 'Dad!' I saw moments I hadn't shared with my brother, as well: Carter and Dad caught in a riot in Paris; Carter and Zia talking by candlelight in the First Nome; Carter by himself in the library at Brooklyn House, staring at his Eye of Horus amulet and struggling against the temptation to reclaim the power of a god. He'd never told me about that, but it made me feel relieved. I'd thought I was the only one who'd been so tempted.

Slowly, Carter relaxed. His worst fears passed through me, his most embarrassing secrets. His strength was failing as the poison gripped his heart. With his last bit of willpower, he told me his name.

[Of course, I won't tell you what it is. You couldn't use it anyway, hearing it from a recording, but I won't take chances.]

I raised the wax figurine and spoke Carter's secret name. Immediately, the poison receded from his veins. The wax figure turned green and melted in my hands. Carter's fever broke. He shuddered, took a deep breath and opened his eyes.

'Right,' I said sternly. 'Don't *ever* ride another snake monster again!'

'Sorry . . .' he croaked. 'Did you just –'

'Yeah.'

'With my secret name –'

'Yeah.'

'And all my secrets –'

'Yeah.'

He groaned and covered his face as if he wanted to fall back into a coma, but, honestly, I had no intention of teasing him. There's a difference between keeping your brother in his place and being cruel. I *wasn't* cruel. Besides, after seeing into the darkest recesses of Carter's mind, I was a bit ashamed, possibly even in awe. There really wasn't much there. Compared to my fears and embarrassing secrets – oh, dear. He was *tame*. I hoped our situations were never reversed and he had to heal *me*.

Bes came over with Lenin's head tucked in the crook of his arm. He'd obviously been having a nibble, as Lenin's forehead was missing – victim of a frontal choco-lobotomy.

'Good work, Sadie!' He broke off Lenin's nose and offered it to Carter. 'Here, boy. You've earned this.'

Carter frowned. 'Does chocolate have magic healing properties?'

Bes snorted. 'If it did, I'd be the healthiest dwarf in the world. Nah. It just tastes good.'

'And you'll need your strength,' I added. 'We have a lot to talk about.'

Despite our looming deadline – as of tomorrow, only two more days until the equinox and the end of the world – Bes insisted we rest until the following morning. He warned that if Carter exerted himself physically or magically any sooner after being poisoned, it might well kill him.

Losing the time made me quite agitated, but after going to so much trouble to revive my brother I rather wanted to keep him alive. And I'll admit I wasn't in much better shape. I was so drained magically myself I don't think I could have moved further than the veranda.

Bes called the front desk and ordered a personal shopper to buy us some new clothes and supplies in town. I'm not sure what the Arabic word is for *combat boots*, but the shopping lady managed to find a new pair. When she delivered our things, she tried to give the boots to Carter, then looked horrified when Bes pointed at me. I also got a supply of hair dye, a comfortable pair of jeans, a cotton top in desert camouflage colours and a headscarf that was probably all the rage with Egyptian women, but which I decided not to wear, as it would probably clash with the new purple highlights I wanted for my hair.

Carter got jeans, boots and a T-shirt that read *Property of Alexandria University* in English and Arabic. Clearly, even personal shoppers had him pegged as a complete geek.

The shopper also managed to find some supplies for our magic bags – blocks of wax, string, even some papyrus and ink – though I doubt Bes explained to her what they were for.

After she left, Bes, Carter and I ordered more food from room service. We sat on the deck and watched the afternoon go by. The breeze from the Mediterranean was cool and pleasant. Modern Alexandria stretched out to our left – an odd mix of gleaming high-rises, shabby, crumbling buildings and ancient ruins. The shoreline highway was dotted with palm trees and crowded with every sort of vehicle from BMWs to donkeys. From our penthouse suite, it all seemed a bit unreal – the raw energy of the city, the bustle and congestion below – while we sat on our veranda in the sky eating fresh fruit and the last melting bits of Lenin's head.

I wondered if this was how the gods felt, watching the mortal world from their throne room in the Duat.

As we talked, I set the two scrolls from the Book of Ra on the patio table. They looked so plain and harmless, yet we'd almost died retrieving them. Still one more to find, then the *real* fun would begin – figuring out how to use them to awaken Ra. It seemed impossible we could do so much in forty-eight hours, yet here we sat, sidelined and exhausted, forced to rest until the morning. Carter and his flash heroics, getting bitten by that Doctor Dolittle snake . . . and he calls *me* impulsive. Meanwhile, Amos and our rookie initiates were left alone at Brooklyn House, preparing to defend against Vlad Menshikov, a magician so ruthless, he was on a secret-name basis with the god of evil.

I told Carter what had happened in St Petersburg after he got poisoned – how I'd given up Set's name in exchange for the location of the last scroll: somewhere called Bahariya. I described my vision of Anubis and Walt, my chat with Jaz's spirit and my trip back in time to Ra's sun barge. The only thing I held back: what Set had said about Zia's village being named al-Hamrah Makan. And, yes, I know that was wrong – but I'd just been inside Carter's head. I now understood how important Zia was to him. I knew how badly *any* information about her would rattle him.

Carter sat in his lounge chair and listened intently. His

colour had returned to normal. His eyes were clear and alert. It was hard to believe he'd been at death's door only hours before. I wanted to credit my healing powers, but I had a feeling his recovery had just as much to do with rest, several ginger ales and a room-service cheeseburger with chips.

'Bahariya...' He looked at Bes. 'I know that name. Why do I know that name?'

Bes scratched his beard. He'd been glum and silent since I'd recounted our conversation with Set. The name Bahariya seemed especially to bother him.

'It's an oasis,' he said, 'way out in the desert. The mummies buried there were a secret until 1996. Then some fool donkey put its leg through a hole in the ground and broke open the top of a tomb.'

'Right!' Carter beamed at me, that *Gee, history is cool!* light in his eyes, so I knew he must be feeling better. 'It's called the Valley of the Golden Mummies.'

'I like gold,' I said. 'Mummies – not so much.'

'Oh, you just haven't met enough mummies,' Bes said.

I couldn't tell if he was joking, and I decided not to ask. 'So the last scroll is hidden there?'

Bes shrugged. 'It would make sense. The oasis is out of the way. Wasn't found until recently. There are also powerful curses in place to prevent portal travel. The mortal archaeologists have excavated some of the tombs, but there's still a huge network of tunnels and chambers no one's opened in thousands of years. *Lots* of mummies.'

I imagined horror-film mummies with their arms out and

their linen wraps coming undone, groaning as they chased screaming starlets and strangled archaeologists.

'When you say *lots* of mummies,' I ventured, 'how many is lots?'

'They've uncovered a few hundred,' Bes said, 'out of maybe ten thousand.'

'Ten thousand?' I looked at Carter, who didn't seem bothered by this at all.

'Sadie,' he said, 'it's not like they're going to come to life and kill you.'

'No,' Bes agreed. 'Probably not. Almost for sure not.'

'Thanks,' I muttered. 'I feel much better.'

(Yes, I know what I said earlier about dead people and cemeteries not bothering me. But ten thousand mummies? That was pushing it.)

'Anyway,' Bes said, 'most of the mummies are from Roman times. They're not even properly Egyptian. Bunch of Latin wannabes trying to get into *our* afterlife because it's cooler. But some of the older tombs...well, we'll just have to see. With two parts of the Book of Ra, you should be able to track down the third part once you get close enough.'

'How, exactly?' I asked.

Bes shrugged. 'When magic items get broken up, the pieces are like magnets. The closer they get, the more they attract each other.'

That didn't necessarily make me feel better. I imagined myself running through a tunnel with flaming scrolls stuck to both hands.

'Right,' I said. 'So all we have to do is creep through a network of tombs past ten thousand golden mummies, who probably, almost for sure, won't come to life and kill us.'

'Yeah,' Bes said. 'Well, they're not really solid gold. Most of them are just painted with gold. But, yeah.'

'That makes a huge difference.'

'Then it's decided.' Carter sounded positively thrilled. 'We can leave in the morning. How far is it?'

'About three hundred and twenty kilometres,' Bes said, 'but the roads are iffy. And portals... well, like I said, the oasis is cursed against them. And even if it wasn't, we're back in the First Nome. It would be wise to use as little magic as possible. If you're discovered in Desjardins's home territory...'

He didn't need to finish that sentence.

I gazed at the skyline of Alexandria curving along the shore of the glittering Mediterranean. I tried to picture it as it might've been in ancient times, before Cleopatra, Egypt's final pharaoh, chose the wrong side in a Roman civil war and lost her life and her kingdom. This was the city where Ancient Egypt had died. It didn't seem a very auspicious place to start a quest.

Unfortunately, I had no choice. I'd have to travel three hundred and twenty kilometres through the desert to some isolated oasis and find one needle of a scroll in a haystack of mummies. I didn't see how we could accomplish this in the time we had left.

Worse, I hadn't yet told Carter my last bit of information about Zia's village. I could just keep my mouth shut. That would be the selfish thing. It might even be the right thing, as I needed his help, and I couldn't afford to have him distracted. But I couldn't keep it from him. I'd invaded his mind and learned his secret name. The least I could do was be honest with him.

'Carter... there's something else. Set wanted you to know. Zia's village was named al-Hamrah Makan.'

Carter turned a bit green again. 'You just forgot to mention this?'

'Remember, Set is a liar,' I said. 'He wasn't being helpful. He volunteered the information because he wanted to cause chaos between us.'

I could already tell I was losing him. His mind was caught in a strong current that had been pulling him along since January – the idea that he could save Zia. Now that I'd been in his mind, I knew he wouldn't rest – he *couldn't* rest – until he'd found her. It went far beyond liking the girl. He'd convinced himself she was part of his destiny.

One of his darker secrets? Deep down, Carter still resented our father for failing to save our mum, even though she had died for a noble cause, and even though it was her choice to sacrifice herself. Carter simply could *not* fail Zia in the same way, no matter what the stakes. He needed someone to believe in him, someone to save – and he was convinced Zia was that person. Sorry, a little sister just wouldn't do.

It hurt me, especially since I didn't agree with him, but I knew better than to argue. It would only push him further away.

'Al-Hamrah Makan...' he said. 'My Arabic isn't very good. But Makan is red.'

'Yes,' Bes agreed. 'Al-Hamrah means "the sands".'

Carter's eyes widened. 'The Place of Red Sands! The voice at the Brooklyn Museum said Zia was asleep at the Place of Red Sands.' He looked at me pleadingly. 'Sadie, it's the ruins of her home village. *That's* where Iskandar hid her. We have to find her.'

Just like that: the fate of the world goes out of the window. We have to find Zia.

I could have pointed out several things: he was going on the word of an evil spirit that was probably speaking directly from Apophis. If Apophis knew where Zia was kept, why would he tell us, except to delay and distract us? And, if he wanted Zia dead, why hadn't he killed her already? Also, Set had given us the name al-Hamrah Makan. Set was *never* up to any good. He was clearly hoping to divide us. Finally, even if we had the name of the village, that didn't mean we could find it. The place had been wiped out almost a decade ago.

But, looking at Carter, I realized there was no reasoning with him. This wasn't a reasonable choice. He saw a chance to save Zia, and he was going to take it.

I simply said, 'It's a bad idea.' And, yes, it felt *quite* strange being forced to play the responsible sibling.

Carter turned to Bes. 'Could you find this village?'

The dwarf god tugged at his Hawaiian shirt. 'Maybe, but it would take time. You've got a little more than two days left. The equinox starts the day after tomorrow at sunset. Getting to the oasis of Bahariya is a full day of travel. Finding this ruined village – easily another day – and if it's on the Nile it's in the opposite direction. Once you've got the Book of Ra, you'll need to allow another day at least to figure out how to use it. I guarantee awakening Ra will mean a trip into the Duat, where time is always unpredictable. You'll have to be back with Ra at dawn on the equinox –'

'We don't have enough time,' I summed up. 'It's either the Book of Ra, or Zia.'

Why did I press Carter, when I knew what he was going to say?

'I can't leave her.' He looked at the sun, now dipping towards in the horizon. 'She's got a part to play, Sadie. I don't know what it is, but she's important. We can't lose her.'

I waited. It was obvious what had to happen, but Carter wasn't going to say it.

I took a deep breath. 'We'll have to separate. You and Bes go after Zia. I'll track down the scroll.'

Bes coughed. 'Speaking of bad ideas...'

Carter couldn't look me in the eyes. I knew he cared about me. He didn't want to be rid of me, but I could sense his relief. He wanted to be released from his responsibilities so he could hunt down Zia. 'You saved my life,' he said. 'I can't let you go alone into the desert.'

I unclasped my *shen* necklace. 'I won't go alone. Walt offered to help.'

'He can't,' Bes said.

'But you won't tell me why,' I said.

'I –' Bes faltered. 'Look, I promised Bast I'd watch you, keep you safe.'

'And I expect you to watch Carter very well. He'll need you to find this village. As for me, Walt and I can manage.'

'But –'

'Whatever Walt's secret is, whatever you're trying to protect him from, it's making him miserable. He wants to help. And I'm going to let him.'

The dwarf glared at me, possibly wondering if he could yell, '*BOO!*' and win the argument. I suppose he realized I was too stubborn.

He sighed in resignation. 'Two young people travelling alone through Egypt . . . a boy and a girl. It'll look strange.'

'I'll just say Walt's my brother.'

Carter winced. I hadn't meant to be harsh, but I suppose the comment was a bit hurtful. Looking back, I'm sorry for that, but at the time I was terrified and angry. Carter was putting me in an impossible position.

'Go,' I said firmly. 'Save Zia.'

Carter tried to read my expression, but I avoided looking at him. This was not the time for us to have one of our silent conversations. He didn't really want to know what I was thinking.

'How will we find each other?' he asked.

'Let's meet back here,' I suggested. 'We'll leave at dawn. Allow ourselves twenty-four hours, no longer, for me to find the scroll, you to find Zia's village and both of us to get back to Alexandria.'

Bes grunted. 'Not enough time. Even if everything goes perfectly, that'll leave you about twelve hours to put together the Book of Ra and use it before the eve of the equinox.'

He was right. It was impossible.

Yet Carter nodded. 'It's our only chance. We have to try.'

He looked at me hopefully, but I think I knew even then that we wouldn't meet in Alexandria. We were the Kanes, which meant *everything* would go wrong.

'Fine,' I muttered. 'Now, if you'll excuse me, I should go pack.'

I walked inside before I could start crying.

13. I Get a Demon Up My Nose

AT THIS POINT, I SHOULD CHANGE my secret name to *Embarrassed to Death by Sister*, because that pretty much sums up my existence.

I'm going skip over our travel preparations, how Sadie summoned Walt and explained the situation, how Bes and I said our farewells at dawn and rented a car from one of Bes's 'reliable friends', and how that car broke down halfway to Cairo.

Basically, I'm going to skip to the part where Bes and I were rumbling along a dusty road in the back of a pick-up truck driven by some Bedouins, looking for a village that no longer existed.

By this point it was late afternoon, and I was starting to think Bes's estimate of needing one day to find al-Hamrah Makan was way too optimistic. With each hour we wasted, my heart felt heavier. I'd risked everything to help Zia. I'd left Amos and our initiates alone at Brooklyn House to defend against the most evil magician in the world. I'd left my sister to continue the quest for the last scroll without me. If I failed to find Zia . . . well, I *couldn't* fail.

Travelling with professional nomads had some advantages. For one thing, the Bedouins knew every village, farm and dusty crossroads in Egypt. They were happy to stop and ask the locals about the vanished village we were seeking.

For another thing, the Bedouins revered Bes. They treated him as a living good-luck charm. When we stopped for lunch (which took two hours to make), the Bedouins even gave us the best part of the goat. As far as I could tell, the best part of the goat wasn't too different from the worst part of the goat, but I suppose it was a big honour.

The bad thing about travelling with Bedouins? They weren't in a hurry. It took us all day to wind our way south along the Nile Valley. The journey was hot and boring. In the back of the truck, I couldn't even talk to Bes without getting a mouthful of sand, so I had way too much time to think.

Sadie described my obsession pretty well. The moment she'd given me the name of Zia's village, I couldn't focus on anything else. Of course, I figured it was some sort of trick. Apophis was trying to divide us and keep us from succeeding on our quest. But I also believed he was telling the truth, if only because the truth is what would rattle me the most. He had destroyed Zia's village when she was a child – for what reason, I didn't know. Now she was hidden there in a magic sleep. Unless I saved her, Apophis would kill her.

Why hadn't he killed her already if he knew where she was? I wasn't sure – and that bothered me. Maybe he didn't have the power yet. Maybe he didn't want to. After all, if he was trying to lure me into a trap, she was the best bait. Whatever the case, Sadie was right: it wasn't a rational choice for me. I *had* to save Zia.

Despite that, I felt like a creep for leaving Sadie on her own yet again. First I'd let her go off to London even though I knew it was a bad idea. Now I'd sent her to track down a scroll in a catacomb full of mummies. Sure, Walt would help her, and she could usually take care of herself. But a good brother would have stayed with her. Sadie had just saved my life, and I was like, 'Great. See you later. Have fun with the mummies.'

I'll just say Walt is my brother.

Ouch.

If I'm honest with myself, Zia wasn't the only reason I was anxious to go off on my own. I was in shock that Sadie had discovered my secret name. Suddenly she knew me better than anyone in the world. I felt like she'd opened me up on the surgery table, examined me and sewn me back together. My first instinct was to run away, to put as much distance between us as possible.

I wondered if Ra had felt the same way when Isis learned his name – if that was the real reason he went into exile: complete humiliation.

Also, I needed time to process what Sadie had accomplished. For months we'd been trying to relearn the path of the gods. We'd struggled to figure out how the ancient magicians tapped the gods' powers without getting possessed or overwhelmed. Now I suspected Sadie had found the answer. It had something to do with a god's *ren*.

222

A secret name wasn't just a name, like a magic word. It was the sum of the god's experiences. The more you understood the god, the closer you got to knowing their secret name, and the more you could channel their power.

If that was true, then the path of the gods was basically sympathetic magic – finding a similarity between two things, like a regular corkscrew and a corkscrew-headed demon, and using that similarity to form a magic bond. Only here, the bond was between the magician and a god. If you could find a common trait or experience, you could tap the god's power.

That might explain how I'd blasted open the doors at the Hermitage with the Fist of Horus – a spell I'd never been able to do on my own. Without thinking about it, without needing to combine souls with Horus, I'd tapped into his emotions. We both hated feeling confined. I'd used that simple connection to invoke a spell and break the chains. Now, if I could just figure out how to do stuff like that more reliably, it might save us in the coming battles ...

We travelled for miles in the Bedouins' truck. The Nile snaked through green and brown fields to our left. We had nothing to drink but water from an old plastic jug that tasted like Vaseline. The goat meat wasn't sitting well in my stomach. Every once in a while I'd remember the poison that had coursed through my body, and my shoulder would start to ache where the *tjesu heru* had bitten me.

Around six in the evening we got our first lead. An old *fellahin*, a peasant farmer selling dates on the roadside, said he knew the village we were seeking. When he heard the name al-Hamrah Makan, he made a protective sign against the Evil

Eye, but since Bes was the one asking, the old man told us what he knew.

He said Red Sands was an evil place, very badly cursed. No one ever visited nowadays. But the old man remembered the village from before it had been destroyed. We would find it ten kilometres south, at a bend in the river where the sand turned bright red.

Well, duh, I thought, but I couldn't help being excited.

The Bedouins decided to make camp for the night. They wouldn't be going with us the rest of the way, but they said they'd be honoured if Bes and I borrowed their truck.

A few minutes later, Bes and I were cruising along in the pick-up. Bes wore a floppy hat almost as ugly as his Hawaiian shirt. It was pulled so low I wasn't sure he could see anything, especially since he was barely eye-level with the dashboard.

Every time we hit a bump, Bedouin trinkets jangled on the rearview mirror – a metal disc etched with Arabic calligraphy, a Christmas-tree-shaped pine air-freshener, some animal teeth on a leather strap, and a little icon of Elvis Presley for reasons I didn't understand. The truck had no suspension and hardly any padding on the seats. I felt like I was riding a mechanical bull. Even without the jostling, my stomach would've been upset. After months of searching and hoping, I couldn't believe I was so close to finding Zia.

'You look terrible,' Bes said.

'Thanks.'

'I mean magically speaking. You don't look ready for a fight. Whatever's waiting for us, you understand it isn't going to be friendly?'

Under the brim of his hat, his jaw jutted out like he was bracing for an argument.

'You think this is a mistake,' I said. 'You think I should've stayed with Sadie.'

He shrugged. 'I think if you were looking at it straight, you'd see this has *TRAP* written all over it. The old Chief Lector – Iskandar – he wouldn't have hidden your girlfriend –'

'She's not my girlfriend.'

' – without putting some protective spells around her. Set and Apophis apparently *both* want you to find this place, which means it *cannot* be good for you. You're leaving your sister and Walt on their own. On top of all that, we're traipsing through Desjardins's backyard, and after that stunt in St Petersburg, Menshikov won't rest until he finds you. So, yeah, I'd say this isn't your brightest idea.'

I stared out of the windshield. I wanted to be mad at Bes for calling me stupid, but I was afraid he might be right. I'd been hoping for a happy reunion with Zia. The chances were I'd never make it through tonight alive.

'Maybe Menshikov is still recovering from his head injuries,' I said hopefully.

Bes laughed. 'Take it from me, kid. Menshikov is already after you. He never forgets an insult.'

His voice smouldered with anger, like it had in St Petersburg when he'd told us about the dwarf wedding. I wondered what had really happened to Bes in that palace, and why he was still brooding over it three hundred years later.

'Was it Vlad?' I asked. 'Was he the one who captured you?'

It didn't seem so far-fetched. I'd met several magicians who were centuries old. But Bes shook his head.

'His grandfather, Prince Alexander Menshikov.' Bes said the name like it was a major insult. 'He was secretly the head of the Eighteenth Nome. Powerful. Cruel. A lot like his grandson. I'd never dealt with a magician like that. It was the first time I'd been captured.'

'But didn't the magicians lock all you gods in the Duat after Egypt fell?'

'Most of us,' Bes agreed. 'Some slept the entire two millennia until your dad unleashed us. Others broke out from time to time and the House of Life would track them down and put them back. Sekhmet broke out in 1918. Big influenza epidemic. But a few of the gods like me stayed in the mortal world the entire time. Back in the ancient days, I was just, you know, a friendly guy. I scared away spirits. The commoners liked me. So when Egypt fell, the Romans adopted me as one of their gods. Then, in the Middle Ages, the Christians modelled gargoyles after me, to protect their cathedrals and whatnot. They made up legends about gnomes, dwarves, helpful leprechauns – all based on me.'

'Helpful leprechauns?'

He scowled. 'You don't think I'm helpful? I look good in green tights.'

'I didn't need that image.'

Bes huffed. 'Anyway, the House of Life was never serious about tracking me down. I just kept a low profile and stayed out of trouble. I was never captured until Russia. Probably still be a prisoner there if it wasn't for –' He stopped himself, as if realizing he'd said too much.

He turned off the road. The truck rattled over hard-packed sand and rocks, heading for the river.

'Someone helped you escape?' I guessed. 'Bast?'

The dwarf's neck turned bright red. 'No . . . not Bast. She was stuck in the abyss fighting Apophis.'

'Then –'

'The point is I got free, and I got my revenge. I managed to get Alexander Menshikov convicted on corruption charges. He was disgraced, stripped of his wealth and titles. His whole family was shipped off to Siberia. Best day of my life. Unfortunately, his grandson Vladimir made a comeback. Eventually he moved back to St Petersburg, rebuilt his grandfather's fortune and took over the Eighteenth Nome. If Vlad had the chance to capture me . . .'

Bes shifted in the driver's seat like the springs were getting uncomfortable. 'I guess why I'm telling you this . . . You're okay, kid. The way you stood up for your sister on Waterloo Bridge, ready to take me on – that took guts. And trying to ride a *tjesu heru*? That was plenty brave. Stupid, but brave.'

'*Um*, thanks.'

'You remind me of myself,' Bes continued, 'back when I was a young dwarf. You got a stubborn streak. When it comes to girl problems, you're clueless.'

'Girl problems?' I thought nobody could embarrass me as much as Sadie had when she'd learned my secret name, but Bes was doing a pretty good job. 'This isn't just a girl problem.'

Bes regarded me like I was a poor lost puppy. 'You want to save Zia. I get that. You want her to like you. But when you rescue somebody...it complicates things. Don't get starry-eyed about somebody you can't have, especially if it blinds you to somebody who's really important. Don't...don't make my mistakes.'

I heard the pain in his voice. I knew he was trying to help, but it still felt weird getting guy advice from a four-foot-tall god in an ugly hat.

'The person who rescued you,' I said. 'It was a goddess, wasn't it? Someone besides Bast – somebody you were involved with?'

His knuckles turned white on the steering wheel. 'Kid.'

'Yeah?'

'I'm glad we had this talk. Now, if you value your teeth –'

'I'll shut up.'

'That's good.' Bes put his foot on the brake. 'Because I think we're here.'

The sun was going down at our backs. Everything in front of us was bathed in red light – the sand, the water of the Nile, the hills on the horizon. Even the fronds of the palm trees looked like they were tinged with blood.

Set would love this place, I thought.

There was no sign of civilization – just a few grey herons flying overhead and an occasional splash in the river: maybe fish or a crocodile. I imagined this part of the Nile hadn't looked too different in the time of the pharaohs.

'Come on,' Bes said. 'Bring your stuff.'

Bes didn't wait for me. When I caught up to him, he was standing on the riverbank, sifting sand through his fingers.

'It's not just the light,' I realized. 'That stuff is *really* red.'

Bes nodded. 'You know why?'

My mom would have said iron oxide or something like that. She'd had a scientific explanation for everything. But something told me Bes wasn't looking for that kind of answer.

'Red is the colour of evil,' I said. 'The desert. Chaos. Destruction.'

Bes dusted off his hands. 'This was a bad place to build a village.'

I looked around for any sign of a settlement. The red sand stretched in either direction for about a hundred yards. Thick grass and willow trees bordered the area, but the sand itself was completely barren. The way it glittered and shifted under my feet reminded me of the mounds of dried scarab shells in the Duat, holding back Apophis. I really wished I hadn't thought of that.

'There's nothing here,' I said. 'No ruins. Nothing.'

'Look again.' Bes pointed to the river. Old dead reeds stuck up here and there over an area the size of a soccer field. Then I realized the reeds weren't reeds – they were decaying boards and wooden poles, the remains of simple dwellings. I walked to the edge of the water. A few feet out, it was calm and shallow enough that I could make out a line of submerged mud bricks: the foundation of a wall slowly dissolving into silt.

'The whole village sank?'

'It was swallowed,' Bes said. 'The Nile is trying to wash away the evil that happened here.'

I shivered. The fang wounds on my shoulder started throbbing again. 'If it's such an evil place, why would Iskandar hide Zia here?'

'Good question,' Bes said. 'You want to find the answer, you'll have to wade out there.'

Part of me wanted to run back to the truck. The last time I'd waded into a river – the Rio Grande in El Paso – it hadn't gone so well. We'd battled the crocodile god Sobek and barely got away with our lives. *This* was the Nile. Gods and monsters would be much stronger here.

'You're coming too, aren't you?' I asked Bes.

The corner of his eye twitched. 'Running water's not good for gods. Loosens our connection to the Duat...'

He must have seen the look of desperation on my face.

'Yeah, okay,' he sighed. 'I'm right behind you.'

Before I could chicken out, I put one boot in the river and sank up to my ankle.

'Gross.' I waded out, my feet making sounds like a cow chewing gum.

A little too late, I realized how poorly prepared I was. I didn't have my sword, because I'd lost it in St Petersburg. I hadn't been able to summon it back. For all I knew, the Russian magicians had melted it down. I still had my wand, but that was mostly for defensive spells. If I had to go on the offence, I'd be at a serious disadvantage.

I pulled an old stick out of the mud and used it to poke around. Bes and I trudged through the shallows, trying to find anything useful. We kicked over some bricks, discovered a few intact sections of walls and brought up some pottery shards. I thought about the story Zia had told me – how her dad caused the destruction of the village by unearthing a demon trapped in a jar. For all I knew, these were shards of that same jar.

Nothing attacked us except mosquitoes. We didn't find any traps. But every splash in the river made me think of crocodiles (and not the nice albino kind like Philip back in Brooklyn) or the big toothy tiger fish Zia had shown me once in the First Nome. I imagined them swimming around my feet, trying to decide which leg looked the tastiest.

Out of the corner of my eye I kept seeing ripples and tiny whirlpools like something was following me. When I stabbed the water with my stick, there was nothing there.

After an hour of searching, the sun had almost set. We were supposed to make it back to Alexandria to meet up with Sadie by morning, which left us almost no time to find Zia. And twenty-four hours from now, the next time the sun went down, the equinox would begin.

We kept looking, but didn't find anything more interesting than a muddy deflated soccer ball and a set of dentures. [Yes, Sadie, they were even more disgusting than Gramps's.] I stopped to swat the mosquitoes off my neck. Bes snatched something out of the water – a wriggly fish or a frog – and stuck it in his mouth.

'Do you *have* to?' I asked.

'What?' he said, still chewing. 'It's dinnertime.'

I turned in disgust and poked my stick in the water.

Thunk.

I struck something harder than mud brick or wood. This was stone.

I traced my stick along the bottom. It wasn't a rock. It was a flat row of hewn blocks. The edge dropped off to another row of stones about a foot lower: like stairs, leading down.

'Bes,' I called.

He waded over. The water came up almost to his armpits. His form shimmered in the current like he might disappear any minute.

I showed him what I'd found.

'Huh.' He dunked his head underwater. When he came back up, his beard was covered in muck and weeds. 'Stairs, all right. Reminds me of the entrance to a tomb.'

'A tomb,' I said, 'in the middle of a village?'

Off to my left, there was another splash.

Bes frowned. 'Did you see that?'

'Yeah. Ever since we got into the water. You haven't noticed?'

Bes stuck his finger in the water as if testing the temperature. 'We should hurry.'

'Why?'

'Probably nothing.' He lied even worse than my dad. 'Let's get a look at this tomb. Part the river.'

He said that as if it were a perfectly normal request, like *Pass the salt.*

'I'm a combat magician,' I said. 'I don't know how to part a river.'

Bes looked offended. 'Oh, come on. That's standard stuff. Back in Khufu's day I knew a magician who parted the Nile just so he could climb to the bottom and retrieve a girl's necklace. Then there was that Israelite fellow, Mickey.'

'Moses?'

'Yeah, him,' Bes said. 'Anyway, you should totally be able to part the water. We gotta hurry.'

'If it's so easy, why don't you do it?'

'*Now* he gets an attitude. I told you, kid, running water interferes with godly power. Probably one of the reasons Iskandar hid your friend down there, if that's where she is. You can do this. Just –'

He suddenly tensed. 'Get to the shore.'

'But you said –'

'Now!'

Before we could move, the river erupted around us. Three separate waterspouts blasted upward, and Bes was pulled underwater.

I tried to run, but my feet stuck in the mud. The waterspouts surrounded me. They swirled into human shapes with heads, shoulders and arms made from ribbons of churning water, as if they were mummies created from the Nile.

Twenty feet downstream, Bes broke to the surface. 'Water demons!' he spluttered. 'Ward them off!'

'How?' I shouted.

Two of the water demons veered towards Bes. The dwarf god tried to keep his footing, but the river boiled into whitewater rapids, and he was already up to his armpits.

'Come on, kid!' he yelled. 'Every shepherd used to know charms against water demons!'

'Well, find me a shepherd, then!'

Bes yelled, 'BOO!' and the first water demon evaporated. He turned towards the second, but before he could scare it the water demon blasted him in the face.

Bes choked and stumbled, water shooting out his nostrils. The demon crashed over him, and Bes went under again.

'Bes!' I yelled.

The third demon surged towards me. I raised my wand and managed a weak shield of blue light. The demon slammed against it, knocking me backwards.

Its mouth and eyes spun like miniature whirlpools. Looking in its face was like using a scrying bowl. I could sense the thing's endless hunger, its hatred for humans. It wanted to break every dam, devour every city and drown the world in a sea of chaos. And it would start by killing me.

My concentration faltered. The thing rushed me, shattering my shield and pulling me underwater.

Ever get water up your nose? Imagine an entire wave up your nose – an *intelligent* wave that knows exactly how to drown you. I lost my wand. My lungs filled with liquid. All rational thought dissolved into panic.

I thrashed and kicked, knowing I was only in three or four feet of water, but I couldn't get up. I couldn't see anything through the murk. My head broke the surface, and I saw a fuzzy image of Bes getting tossed around atop a waterspout, screaming, 'Boo, already! Be more scared!'

Then I went under again, my hands clawing at the mud.

My heart pounded. My vision started to go dark. Even if I could have thought of a spell, I couldn't have spoken it. I wished I had sea-god powers, but they weren't exactly Horus's speciality.

I was losing consciousness when something gripped my arm. I punched at it wildly, and my fist connected with a bearded face.

I broke the surface again, gasping for breath. Bes was

half-drowning next to me, yelling: 'Stupid – *glub, glub* – trying to save your *glub glub*.'

The demon pulled me under again, but suddenly my thoughts were clearer. Maybe that last mouthful of oxygen had done the trick. Or maybe punching Bes had snapped me out of my panic.

I remembered Horus had been in a situation like this before. Set had once tried to drown him, pulling him into the Nile.

I latched on to that memory and made it my own.

I reached into the Duat and channelled the power of the war god into my body. Rage filled me. I would not be pinned down. I followed the Path of Horus. I would *not* let a stupid liquid mummy drown me in three feet of water.

My vision turned red. I screamed, expelling the water from my lungs in one huge blast.

WHOOOM! The Nile exploded. I collapsed on a field of mud.

At first I was too tired to do anything but cough. When I managed to stagger to my feet and wipe the silt out of my eyes, I saw that the river had changed its course. It now curved round the ruins of the village. Exposed in the glistening red mud were bricks and boards, trash, old clothes, the fender of a car and bones that might've been animal or human. A few fish flopped around, wondering where the river had gone. There was no sign of the water demons. About ten feet away, Bes was scowling at me in annoyance. He had a bloody nose and was buried up to his waist in mud.

'Usually when you part a river,' he grumbled, 'it doesn't involve punching a dwarf. Now, get me out of here!'

I managed to pry him free, which caused a sucking noise so impressive that I wished I had recorded it. [And, no, Sadie, I'm not going to try to make it for the microphone.]

'I'm s-sorry,' I stammered. 'I didn't mean to –'

He waved aside the apology. 'You handled the water demons. That's what matters. Now we gotta see if you can handle *that*.'

I turned and saw the tomb.

It was a rectangular pit about the size of a walk-in closet, lined with stone blocks. Steps led down to a closed stone door etched with hieroglyphs. The largest was the symbol for the House of Life:

'Those demons were guarding the entrance,' Bes said. 'There may be worse inside.'

Underneath the symbol, I recognized a row of phonetic hieroglyphs:

'Z – I – A,' I read. 'Zia's inside.'

'And that,' Bes muttered, 'is what we call in the magic business a *trap*. Last chance to change your mind, kid.'

But I wasn't really listening. Zia was down there. Even if I'd known what was about to happen, I don't think I could've stopped myself. I climbed down the steps and pushed open the door.

14. At the Tomb of Zia Rashid

THE SARCOPHAGUS WAS made of water.

It was an oversize human figure with rounded feet, wide shoulders, and a larger-than-life smiling face, like other Egyptian coffins I'd seen, but the whole thing was sculpted from pure glowing liquid. It sat on a stone dais in the middle of a square chamber. Egyptian art decorated the walls, but I didn't pay too much attention to that.

Inside the sarcophagus, Zia Rashid floated in white robes. Her arms were crossed over her chest. In her hands she gripped a shepherd's crook and a war flail, the symbols of a pharaoh. Her staff and wand floated at her side. Her short black hair drifted around her face, which was just as beautiful as I remembered. If you've ever seen the famous sculpture of Queen Nefertiti, Zia reminded me of her, with the raised eyebrows, high cheekbones, graceful nose and perfect red lips.

[Sadie says I'm overdoing it with the description, but it's

true. There's a reason Nefertiti was called the most beautiful woman in the world.]

As I approached the sarcophagus, the water began to shimmer. A current rippled down the sides, tracing the same symbol over and over:

Bes made a rumbling sound in his throat. 'You didn't tell me she was a godling.'

I hadn't thought to mention it, but of course that's why Iskandar had hidden Zia away. When our dad unleashed the gods at the British Museum, one of them – the river goddess Nephthys – had chosen Zia for a host.

'That's the symbol of Nephthys?' I guessed.

Bes nodded. 'Didn't you say this girl was a fire elementalist?'

'Yeah.'

'Hmph. Not a good combination. No wonder the Chief Lector put her in suspended animation. A fire magician hosting a water goddess – that could kill her, unless...huh, that's pretty clever.'

'What?'

'The combination of water over fire could also mask Zia's powers. If Iskandar was trying to hide her from Apophis...' His eyes widened. 'Holy Mother Nut. Is that the crook and flail?'

'Yeah, I think.' I wasn't sure why he acted so shocked. 'Didn't a lot of important people get buried with those?'

Bes gave me an incredulous look. 'You don't understand,

kid. Those are the *original* crook and flail, the royal instruments of Ra.'

Suddenly I felt like I'd swallowed a marble. I don't think I could've been more surprised if Bes had said, *By the way, you're leaning against a hydrogen bomb.* The crook and flail of Ra were the most powerful symbols of the most powerful Egyptian god. Yet in Zia's hands they didn't appear to be anything special. The crook looked like an oversize gold-and-blue candy cane. The flail was a wooden rod with three spiked chains at the end. They didn't glow or say PROPERTY OF RA.

'Why would they be here?' I asked.

'Dunno,' Bes said, 'but that's them. Last I heard they were locked in the First Nome's vaults. Only the Chief Lector had access. I guess Iskandar buried them with your friend here.'

'To protect her?'

Bes shrugged, clearly baffled. 'That'd be like wiring your home-security system to a nuclear missile. Complete overkill. No wonder Apophis hasn't been able to attack her. That's some *serious* protection against Chaos.'

'What happens if I wake her?'

'The spells shielding her will be broken. That could be why Apophis led you here. Once Zia's out of that sarcophagus, she's an easier target. As to why Apophis would want her dead, or why Iskandar would go to such trouble to guard her – your guess is as good as mine.'

I studied Zia's face. For three months, I'd dreamed of finding her. Now I was almost too scared to wake her. By breaking the sleep spell, I might accidentally hurt her, or leave her open to an attack from Apophis. Even if I succeeded, what if she woke up and decided that she hated me? I wanted to believe she possessed shared memories with her *shabti*, so that she would remember the times we'd had together. But if she hadn't I wasn't sure I could stand the rejection.

I touched the water coffin.

'Careful, kid,' Bes warned.

Magic energy rippled through me. It was subtle – like looking in the face of the water demon – but I could sense Zia's thoughts. She was trapped in a dream of drowning. She was trying to hold on to her last good memory: Iskandar's kindly face as he placed the crook and flail in her hands: *Keep these, my dear. You will need them. And do not fear. Dreams will not bother you.*

But Iskandar had been wrong. Nightmares had invaded her sleep. The voice of Apophis hissed in the darkness: *I destroyed your family. And I am coming for you.* Zia saw the demolition of her village over and over, while Apophis laughed, and the spirit of Nephthys churned uncomfortably inside her. Iskandar's magic had trapped the goddess, too, in an enchanted sleep, and she tried to protect Zia, calling on the Nile to cover this chamber and shield them both from the Serpent. Still, she couldn't stop the dreams. Zia had been having the same chaotic nightmare for three months, and her sanity was crumbling.

'I have to free her,' I said. 'She's partially conscious.'

Bes sucked air through his teeth. 'That shouldn't be possible, but if it's true –'

'She's in serious trouble.' I sank my hand deeper into the sarcophagus. I channelled the same kind of magic I'd used to part the river, only on a smaller scale. Slowly the water lost its shape, melting like an ice cube. Before Zia could spill off the dais, I caught her in my arms. She dropped the crook and flail. Her staff and wand clattered to the floor.

As the last of the sarcophagus trickled away, Zia's eyes flew open. She tried to breathe but couldn't seem to inhale.

'Bes, what's wrong with her?' I said. 'What do I do?'

'The goddess,' he said. 'Zia's body is rejecting the spirit of Nephthys. Get her to the river!'

Zia's face started to turn blue. I gathered her in my arms and raced up the slippery stairs, which wasn't easy with Zia kicking and hitting me all the way. I managed to make it across the mud without falling and eased her down next to the riverbank.

She clawed at her throat, her eyes full of fear; but as soon as her body touched the Nile, a blue aura flickered around her. Her face turned back to its normal colour. Water gushed from her mouth like she'd turned into a human fountain. Looking back on it, I suppose that was pretty gross, but at the time I was too relieved to care.

From the surface of the river rose the watery form of a woman in a blue dress. Most Egyptian gods grew weak in running water, but Nephthys was clearly an exception. She glowed with power. She wore a silver Egyptian crown on her long black hair. Her regal face reminded me of Isis, but this woman had a gentler smile and kinder eyes.

'Hello, Bes.' Her voice was soft and rustling, like a breeze through the river grass.

'Nephthys,' said the dwarf. 'Long time.'

The water goddess looked down at Zia, who was shivering in my arms, still gasping for breath.

'I am sorry for using her as a host,' Nephthys said. 'It was a poor choice, which almost destroyed us both. Guard her well, Carter Kane. She has a good heart, and an important destiny.'

'What destiny?' I asked. 'How do I protect her?'

Instead of answering, the spirit of Nephthys melted into the Nile.

Bes grunted with approval. 'The Nile's where she should be. That's her proper body.'

Zia sputtered and doubled over.

'She still can't breathe!' I did the only thing I could think of. I tried mouth-to-mouth resuscitation.

Yes, okay, I know how that sounds, but I wasn't thinking straight.

[Stop laughing, Sadie.]

Honestly, I wasn't trying to take advantage. I was just trying to help.

Zia didn't see it that way. She punched me in the chest so hard I made a sound like a squeaky toy. Then she turned to one side and retched.

I didn't think my breath was *that* bad.

When she focused on me again, her eyes blazed with anger – just like old times.

'Don't you *dare* kiss me!' she managed.

'I wasn't – I didn't –'

'Where's Iskandar?' she demanded. 'I thought...' Her eyes lost their focus. 'I had a dream that...' She started to tremble. 'Eternal Egypt, he's not... He *can't* be –'

'Zia –' I tried to put my hand on her shoulder, but she pushed me away. She turned towards the river and began to sob, her fingers clawing the mud.

I wanted to help her. I couldn't stand to see her in pain. But I looked at Bes, and he tapped his bloody nose, as if warning me: Go *slow, or she'll give you one of these.*

'Zia, we've got a lot to talk about,' I said, trying not to sound heartbroken. 'Let's get you away from the river.'

She sat on the steps of her own tomb and hugged her arms. Her clothes and hair were starting to dry, but in spite of the warm night and the dry wind from the desert, she still trembled.

At my request, Bes brought up her staff and wand from the tomb, along with the crook and flail, but he didn't look happy about it. He handled the items as if they were toxic.

I tried to explain things to Zia: about the *shabti*, Iskandar's death, Desjardins's becoming the Chief Lector and what had transpired in the last three months since the battle with Set, but I'm not sure how much she heard. She kept shaking her head, pressing her hands over her ears.

'Iskandar can't be dead.' Her voice quavered. 'He wouldn't have . . . he wouldn't have done this to me.'

'He was trying to protect you,' I said. 'He didn't know you'd have nightmares. I've been looking for you –'

'Why?' she demanded. 'What do you want from me? I remember you from London, but after that –'

'I met your *shabti* in New York. She – you – took Sadie and me to the First Nome. You started our training. We worked together in New Mexico, then at the Red Pyramid –'

'No.' She shut her eyes tight. 'No, that wasn't me.'

'But you can remember what the *shabti* did. Just try –'

'You're a Kane!' she cried. 'You're all outlaws. And you're here with – with *that*.' She gestured at Bes.

'*That* has a name,' Bes grumbled. 'I'm starting to wonder why I drove halfway across Egypt to wake you.'

'You're a god!' Zia said. Then she turned to me. 'And if *you* summoned him you'll be put to death!'

'Listen, girl,' Bes said. 'You were hosting the spirit of Nephthys. So if anyone gets put to death –'

Zia snatched up her staff. 'Be gone!'

Fortunately, she wasn't back to full strength. She managed to shoot a weak column of fire at Bes's face, but the dwarf god easily swatted the flames aside.

I grabbed the end of her staff. 'Zia, stop! He's not the enemy.'

'Can I punch her?' Bes asked. 'You punched me, kid. Seems only fair.'

'No punching,' I said. 'No blasting with flames. Zia, we're on the same side. The equinox starts tomorrow at sunset, and Apophis will break out of his prison. He means to destroy you. We're here to rescue you.'

The name *Apophis* hit her hard. She struggled to breathe, as if her lungs were filling with water again. 'No. No, it isn't possible. Why should I believe you?'

'Because...' I hesitated. What could I say? Because we'd fallen for each other three months ago? Because we've been through so much together and saved each other's lives? Those memories weren't hers. She remembered me – sort of. But our time together was like a movie she'd watched, with an actress playing her role, doing things she never would've done.

'You don't know me,' she said bitterly. 'Now, go, before I'm forced to fight you. I'll make my own way back to the First Nome.'

'Maybe she's right, kid,' Bes said. 'We should leave. We've worked enough magic here to send up all kinds of alarm bells.'

I clenched my fists. My worst fears had come true. Zia didn't like me. Everything we'd shared had crumbled with her ceramic replica. But, as I may have mentioned, I get stubborn when I'm told I can't do something.

'I'm not leaving you.' I gestured at the ruins of her village. 'Zia, this place was destroyed by Apophis. It wasn't an accident. It wasn't your dad's fault. The Serpent was targeting *you*. Iskandar raised you because he sensed you had an important destiny. He hid you with the pharaoh's crook and flail for the same reason – not just because you were hosting a goddess, but because he was dying and he was afraid he wouldn't be able to protect you any more. I don't know what your destiny is, exactly, but –'

'Stop!' She reignited the tip of her staff. It blazed more brightly this time. 'You're twisting my thoughts. You're just like the nightmares.'

'You know I'm not.' I probably should've shut up, but I couldn't believe Zia would actually incinerate me. 'Before he died, Iskandar realized the old ways had to be brought back. That's why he let Sadie and me live. Gods and the magicians have to work together. You – your *shabti* realized that, when we fought together at the Red Pyramid.'

'Kid,' Bes said more urgently. 'We really should go.'

'Come with us,' I told Zia. 'I know you've always felt alone. You never had anyone but Iskandar. I get that, but I'm your friend. We can protect you.'

'No one *protects* me!' She shot to her feet. 'I am a scribe in the House of Life!'

Flames shot from her staff. I grabbed for my wand, but of course I'd lost it in the river. Instinctively my hands closed round the symbols of the pharaoh – the shepherd's crook and the war flail. I held them up in a defensive X, and Zia's staff shattered instantly. The fire dissipated.

Zia stumbled backwards, smoke curling from her hands. She stared at me in absolute shock. 'You dare to use the symbols of Ra?'

I probably looked just as surprised. 'I – I didn't mean to! I just want to talk. You've got to be hungry. We've got food and water back at the pick-up truck –'

'Carter!' Bes tensed. 'Something's wrong...'

He turned too late. A blinding white light exploded around him. When the spots cleared from my eyes, Bes was frozen in a cage of bars glowing like fluorescent tubes. Standing next to him were the two people I least wanted to see:

Michel Desjardins and Vlad the Inhaler.

Desjardins looked even older than he had in my vision. His greying hair and forked beard were long and unkempt. His cream-coloured robes hung loosely on him. The leopard-skin cloak of the Chief Lector was slipping off his left shoulder.

Vlad Menshikov, on the other hand, looked well rested

and ready for a good game of Torture-the-Kane. He wore a fresh white linen suit and carried a new serpent staff. His silver snake necklace glinted against his tie. On his curly grey hair sat a white fedora, probably to cover the head injuries Set had given him. He smiled as if he were delighted to see me, which might've been convincing – except he didn't have his sunglasses any more. Through the wreckage of scar tissue and red welts, those horrible eyes gleamed with hatred.

'As I told you, Chief Lector,' Menshikov rasped, 'Kane's next move would be to find this poor girl and attempt to turn her.'

'Desjardins, listen,' I said. 'Menshikov's a traitor. He summoned Set. He's trying to free Apophis –'

'You see?' Menshikov cried. 'As I predicted, the boy tries to blame his illegal magic on me.'

'What?' I said. 'No!'

The Russian turned to examine Bes, who was still frozen in his glowing cage. 'Carter Kane, you claim to be innocent, and yet we find you here consorting with gods. Who have we here? Bes the dwarf! Fortunately, my grandfather taught me an excellent binding spell for this particular creature. Grandfather also taught me many spells of torment which were…quite effective on the dwarf god. I've always wanted to try them.'

Desjardins wrinkled his nose in distaste, but I couldn't tell whether it was because of me or of Menshikov.

'Carter Kane,' said the Chief Lector, 'I knew you desired the pharaoh's throne. I knew you were scheming with Horus. But now I find you holding the crook and flail of Ra, which were recently discovered to be missing from our vaults. Even for you, this is a brazen act of aggression.'

I looked down at the weapons in my hands. 'It's not like that. I just found them...'

I stopped. I couldn't tell him the symbols had been buried with Zia. Even if he believed me, it might get Zia in trouble.

Desjardins nodded as if I'd confessed. To my surprise, he looked a little sad about it. 'As I thought. Amos assured me you were an honourable servant of Ma'at. Instead, I find you are both a godling and thief.'

'Zia.' I turned towards her. 'You've got to listen. You're in danger. Menshikov is working for Apophis. He'll kill you.'

Menshikov did a good job of looking offended. 'Why would I wish to harm her? I sense she is free of Nephthys now. It's not her fault the goddess invaded her form.' He held out his hand to Zia. 'I am glad to see you safe, child. You are not to blame for Iskandar's odd decisions in his final days – hiding you here, softening his attitude towards these Kane criminals. Come away from the traitor. Come home with us.'

Zia hesitated. 'I had... I had strange dreams ...'

'You are confused,' Desjardins said gently. 'This is natural. Your *shabti* was relaying its memories to you. You *saw* Carter Kane and his sister make a pact with Set at the Red Pyramid. Rather than destroy the Red Lord, they let him go. Do you remember?'

Zia studied me warily.

'Remember why we did it,' I pleaded. 'Chaos is rising. Apophis will break free in less than twenty-four hours. Zia... I...'

The words stuck in my throat. I wanted to tell her how I felt about her, but her eyes hardened like amber.

'I don't know you,' she murmured. 'I'm sorry.'

Menshikov smiled. 'Of course you don't, child. You have no business with traitors. Now, with Lord Desjardins's permission, we will bring this young heretic back to the First Nome, where he will be given a fair trial –' Menshikov turned towards me, his ruined eyes burning with triumph – 'and then, executed.'

S
A
D
I
E

15. Camels Are Evil...

YES, CARTER, THE WHOLE BUSINESS with the water demons must've been horrible. But I feel *no* sympathy for you, as 1) you brought that trip entirely on yourself, and 2) while you were rescuing Zia, I was dealing with camels.

Camels are disgusting.

You may think, *But, Sadie, these were magical camels, summoned by one of Walt's amulets. Clever Walt! Surely magic camels are not as bad as normal camels.*

I can now attest that magic camels spit like, poo like, drool like, bite like, eat like, and, most disgustingly, smell like normal camels. If anything, their disgustingness is magically enhanced.

We didn't start with the camels, of course. We worked our way up to them in a series of progressively more horrible modes of transportation. First we took a bus to a small town west of Alexandria – a bus without air conditioning, packed with men who had not discovered the benefits of under-arm deodorant.

Then we hired a driver to take us to Bahariya – a driver who first had the nerve to play ABBA's greatest hits and eat raw onions, then drove us to the middle of nowhere and – surprise! – introduced us to his friends, the bandits, who were keen to rob defenceless American teenagers. I was delighted to show them how my staff turned into a large hungry lion. As far as I know, the bandits and driver are still running. However, the car had stopped, and no amount of magic would revive the engine.

At that point, we decided it was best to stay off the grid. I could deal with dirty looks from the locals. I could deal with attracting attention as an oddity – an American/British girl with purple-streaked hair, travelling alone with a boy who did not look like her brother. In fact, that fairly well described my life. But after the highway robbery incident, Walt and I realized just *how* much the locals were watching us, marking us as a target. I had no desire to be singled out by more bandits, or Egyptian police, or, even worse, any magicians who might be lurking undercover. So we summoned the magic camels, charmed a handful of sand to point the way to Bahariya and set out across the desert.

How was the desert, Sadie? you might wonder.

Thanks for asking. It was hot.

And another thing: why do deserts have to be so blinking huge? Why can't they be a few hundred metres wide, just enough to give you the idea of sandy, dry and miserable, then yield to some proper landscape, like a meadow with a river, or a high street with shops?

No such luck for us. The desert went on forever. I could

imagine Set, the god of the wastelands, laughing at us as we trudged over endless dunes. If this was his home, I didn't think much of the way he'd decorated.

I named my camel Katrina. She was a natural disaster. She slobbered everywhere and seemed to think the purple streak in my hair was some kind of exotic fruit. She was obsessed with trying to eat my head. I named Walt's camel Hindenburg. He was almost as large as a Zeppelin and definitely as full of gas.

As we rode side by side, Walt seemed lost in thought, peering at the horizon. He'd rushed to my aid in Alexandria without hesitation. As I'd suspected, our *shen* amulets were connected. With a little concentration, I'd been able to send him a mental message about our predicament. With a bit more effort, I'd been able to literally pull him through the Duat to my side. Quite a handy magic item: instant hot guy.

Once here, though, he'd grown increasingly quiet and uncomfortable. He was dressed like a normal American teen on an outdoor excursion – a black workout top that fitted him quite well, hiking pants and boots. But if you looked more closely, you could tell he'd come equipped with every magic item he'd ever made. Round his neck hung a veritable zoo of animal amulets. Three rings glinted on each hand. Round his waist was a corded belt I'd never seen before, so I assumed it had magic powers. He also carried a backpack, no doubt stuffed with more handy bits and bobs. Despite this personal arsenal, Walt seemed awfully nervous.

'Lovely weather,' I prompted.

He frowned, coming out of his daze. 'Sorry. I was… thinking.'

'You know, sometimes talking helps. For instance, oh, I don't know. If I had a major problem, something life-threatening, and I'd only confided to Jaz . . . and if Bes knew what was going on, but wasn't telling . . . and if I'd agreed to come on an adventure with a good friend, and had hours to chat as we crossed the desert, I might be tempted to tell her what was wrong.'

'Hypothetically,' he said.

'Yes. And if this girl were the last person on earth to know what was wrong with me, and really *cared* . . . well, I can imagine she'd get quite frustrated at being kept in the dark. And she might hypothetically strangle you – I mean me. Hypothetically.'

Walt managed a faint smile. Though I can't say his eyes melted me like Anubis's, he did have a gorgeous face. He looked nothing like my father, but he had the same sort of strength and rugged handsomeness – a kind of gentle gravity that made me feel safer and a bit more firmly planted on the earth.

'It's hard for me to talk about,' he said. 'I didn't mean to hide anything from you.'

'Fortunately, it's not too late.'

Our camels plodded along. Katrina tried to kiss, or possibly spit on Hindenburg, and Hindenburg farted in response. I found this a depressing commentary on boy-girl relationships.

At last Walt said, 'It has to do with the blood of the pharaohs. You guys – I mean the Kanes – you combine two powerful royal lines, Narmer and Ramesses the Great, right?'

'So I've been told. Sadie the Great does have a nice ring to it.'

Walt didn't respond to that. Perhaps he was imagining me as a pharaoh, which I'll admit is a rather frightening concept.

'My royal line...' He hesitated. 'How much do you know about Akhenaton?'

'Off the top of my head, I'd say he was a pharaoh. Probably of Egypt.'

Walt laughed, which was good. If I could keep his mood from getting too serious, it might be easier for him to open up.

'Top of the class,' he said. 'Akhenaton was the pharaoh who decided to do away with all the old gods and just worship Aten, the sun.'

'Oh...right.' The story vaguely rang a bell, which alarmed me, as it made me feel like almost as much of an Egyptian geek as Carter. 'He's the chap who moved the capital, eh?'

Walt nodded. 'He built an entirely new city at Amarna. He was kind of a weird dude, but he was the first one who had the idea that the old gods were bad. He tried to ban their worship, shut down their temples. He wanted to worship only one god, but he made a strange choice for the one god. He thought it was the sun. Not the sun god Ra – the *actual* sun disc, Aten. Anyway, the old priests and magicians, especially the priests of Amun-Ra –'

'Another name for Ra?' I guessed.

'More or less,' Walt said. 'So the priests of Amun-Ra's temple weren't too happy with Akhenaton. After he died, they defaced his statues, tried to wipe out his name from all the monuments and stuff. Amarna was completely abandoned. Egypt went back to the old ways.'

I let that sink in. Thousands of years before Iskandar had issued a rule exiling the gods, a pharaoh had had the same idea.

'And this was your great-great-whatever grandfather?' I asked.

Walt wrapped the camel's reins round his wrist. 'I'm one of Akhenaton's descendants. Yeah. We've got the same aptitude for magic as most royal lines, but...we've got problems, too. The gods weren't happy with Akhenaton, as you can imagine. His son Tutankhamen –'

'King Tut?' I asked. 'You're related to King Tut?'

'Unfortunately,' Walt said. 'Tutankhamen was the first to suffer the curse. He died at nineteen. And he was one of the luckier ones.'

'Hang on. What curse?'

That's when Katrina came to a screeching halt. You may protest that camels can't screech, but you're quite wrong. As she reached the top of a massive sand dune, Katrina made a wet screechy sound much worse than a car's brakes. Hindenburg came to more of a farting halt.

I looked down the other side of the dune. Below us, in the middle of the desert, a hazy valley of green fields and palm trees sprawled out, roughly the size of central London. Birds flew overhead. Small lakes sparkled in the afternoon sun. Smoke rose from cooking fires at a few dwellings dotted here and there. After so long in the desert, my eyes hurt from looking at all the colours, like when you come out of a dark cinema into a bright afternoon.

I understood how ancient travellers must've felt, discovering an oasis like this after days in the wilderness. It was the closest thing I'd ever seen to the Garden of Eden.

The camels hadn't stopped to admire the beautiful scenery, though. A trail of tiny footprints wound through the sand, all the way from the edge of the oasis to our dune. And coming up the hill was a very disgruntled-looking cat.

'It's about time,' said the cat.

I slid off Katrina's back and stared at the cat in amazement. Not because it spoke – I'd seen stranger things – but because I recognized the voice.

'Bast?' I said. 'What are you doing inside that – what *is* that, exactly?'

The cat stood on its hind legs and spread its front paws like: *Voilà!* 'An Egyptian mau, of course. Beautiful leopard spots, bluish fur –'

'It looks like it's been through a blender!'

I wasn't just being harsh. The cat was terribly beaten up. Large chunks of its fur were missing. It might once have been beautiful, but I was more inclined to think it had always been feral. Its remaining fur was dirty and matted, and its eyes were swollen and scarred almost as badly as Vlad Menshikov's.

Bast – or the cat – or *whatever* was in charge – dropped back on all fours and sniffed indignantly. 'Sadie, dear, I believe we've talked about battle scars on cats. This old tom is a warrior!'

A warrior who loses, I thought, but I decided not to say that.

Walt slid off Hindenburg's back. 'Bast, how – where are you?'

'Still deep in the Duat.' She sighed. 'It'll be another day at least before I can find my way out. Things down here are a bit...chaotic.'

'Are you all right?' I asked.

The cat nodded. 'I just have to be careful. The abyss is teeming with enemies. All the regular paths and river ways are guarded. I'll have to take a long detour to get back safely, and since the equinox starts tomorrow at sunset the timing is going to be tight. I thought I'd better send you a message.'

'So...' Walt knitted his eyebrows. 'That cat isn't real?'

'Of course it's real,' Bast said. 'Just controlled by a sliver of my *ba*. I can speak through cats easily, you know, at least for a few minutes at a time, but this is the first time you've been close to one. Did you realize that? Unbelievable! You really need to hang around more cats. By the way, this mau will need a reward when I'm gone. Some nice fish, perhaps, or some milk –'

'Bast,' I interrupted. 'You said you had a message?'

'Right. Apophis is waking.'

'We knew that!'

'But it's worse than we thought,' she said. 'He's got a legion of demons working on his cage, and he's timing his release to coincide with you waking Ra. In fact, he's *counting* on you freeing Ra. It's part of his plan.'

My head felt like it was turning to jelly, though that may have been because Katrina the camel was sucking on my hair. 'Apophis *wants* us to free his arch-enemy? That makes no sense.'

'I can't explain it,' Bast said, 'but as I got closer to his cage, I could glean his thoughts. I suppose because we fought so many centuries we have some sort of connection. At any rate, the equinox begins tomorrow at sunset, as I said. The following dawn, the morning of March twenty-first, Apophis intends to rise from the Duat. He plans to swallow the sun and destroy the world. And he believes your plan to awaken Ra will help him do that.'

Walt frowned. 'If Apophis wants us to succeed, why is he trying so hard to stop us?'

'Is he?' I asked.

A dozen small things that had bothered me over the past few days suddenly clicked together: why had Apophis only *scared* Carter in the Brooklyn Museum, when the Arrows of Sekhmet could have destroyed him? How had we escaped so easily from St Petersburg? Why had Set volunteered the location of the third scroll?

'Apophis wants chaos,' I said. 'He wants to divide his enemies. If Ra comes back, it could throw us into a civil war. The magicians are already divided. The gods would be fighting each other. There would be no clear ruler. And if Ra isn't reborn in a strong new form – if he's as old and feeble as I saw in my vision –'

'So we *shouldn't* awaken Ra?' Walt asked.

'That's not the answer either,' I said.

Bast tilted her head. 'I'm confused.'

My mind was racing. Katrina the camel was still chewing on my hair, turning it into a slimy mess, but I hardly noticed. 'We *have* to stick to the plan. We need Ra. Ma'at and Chaos have to balance, right? If Apophis rises, Ra has to as well.'

Walt twisted his rings. 'But if Apophis *wants* Ra awakened, if he thinks it will help him destroy the world –'

'We have to believe Apophis is wrong.' I remembered something Jaz's *ren* had told me: *We choose to believe in Ma'at.*

'Apophis can't imagine that anyone could unite the gods and magicians,' I said. 'He thinks the return of Ra will weaken us even further. We have to prove him wrong. We have to make order from chaos. That's what Egypt has always done. It's a risk – a *huge* risk – but, if we do nothing because we fear we'll fail, we play right into Apophis's hands.'

It's hard to give a rousing speech with a camel licking your head, but Walt nodded. The cat didn't look quite so enthusiastic. Then again, cats rarely do.

'Don't underestimate Apophis,' Bast said. 'You haven't fought him. I have.'

'Which is why we need you back quickly.' I told her about Vlad Menshikov's conversation with Set, and his plans to destroy Brooklyn House. 'Bast, our friends are in terrible danger. Menshikov is possibly even more insane than Amos realizes. As soon as you're able, go to Brooklyn. I have a feeling our last stand is going to be there. We'll get the third scroll and find Ra.'

'I don't like last stands,' the cat said. 'But you're right. It sounds bad. By the way, where are Bes and Carter?' She looked suspiciously at the camels. 'You didn't turn them into those, did you?'

'The idea is appealing,' I said. 'But, no.'

I told her briefly what Carter was up to.

Bast hissed with distaste. 'A foolish detour! I'll have words with that dwarf about letting you go off on your own.'

'What am I, invisible?' Walt protested.

'Sorry, dear, I didn't mean –' The cat's eyes twitched. It coughed like it had a hairball. 'My connection is failing. Good luck, Sadie. The best entrance to the tombs is on a small date farm just to the south-east. Look for a black water tower. And do watch out for the Romans. They're quite –'

The cat puffed up its tail. Then it blinked and looked around in confusion.

'What Romans?' I asked. 'They're quite what?'

'Mrow.' The cat stared at me with an expression that said: *Who are you and where is the food?*

I swatted the camel's nose away from my slimy hair.

'Come on, Walt,' I grumbled. 'Let's go find some mummies.'

We provided the cat with bits of beef jerky and some water from our supplies. It wasn't as good as fish and milk, but the cat seemed happy enough. As it was in sight of the oasis and obviously knew its way around better than we did, we left it to finish its meal. Walt turned the camels back into amulets, thank goodness, and we trudged into Bahariya on foot.

The date farm wasn't difficult to find. The black water tower sat at the edge of the property, and it was the tallest structure in sight. We made our way towards it, weaving through acres of palm trees, which provided some shade from the sun. An adobe farmhouse stood in the distance, but we didn't see any people. The Egyptians probably knew better than to be out in the afternoon heat.

When we reached the water tower, I didn't see any obvious tomb entrance. The tower looked quite old – four rusty steel posts holding a round tank the size of a garage about fifteen metres in the air. The tank had a slow leak. Every few seconds water dropped from the sky and smacked against the hard-packed sand underneath. There wasn't much else in sight except for more palm trees, a few tarnished farm tools and a weathered plywood sign lying on the ground. The sign was spray-painted in Arabic and English, probably from some attempt by the farmer to sell his wares in the market. The English read: *Dates – best price. Cold Bebsi.*

'Bebsi?' I asked.

'Pepsi,' Walt said. 'I read about that on the Internet. There's no "p" in Arabic. Everyone here calls soda Bebsi.'

'So you have to have Bebsi with your bizza?'

'Brobably.'

I snorted. 'If this is a famous dig site, shouldn't there be more activity? Archaeologists? Ticket booths? Souvenir merchants?'

'Maybe Bast sent us to a secret entrance,' Walt said. 'Better than sneaking past a bunch of guards and caretakers.'

A secret entrance sounded quite intriguing, but unless the water tower was a magic teleporter, or one of the date trees had a concealed door, I wasn't sure where this oh-so-helpful entrance might be. I kicked the Bebsi sign. There was nothing underneath except more sand, slowly turning to mud from the drip, drip, drip of the leaky tower.

Then I looked more closely at the wet spot on the ground.

'Hang on.' I knelt. The water was pooling in a little canal, as if the sand were seeping into a subterranean crack. The crevice was about a metre long and no wider than a pencil, but much too straight to be natural. I dug in the sand. Six centimetres down, my fingernails scraped stone.

'Help me clear this,' I told Walt.

A minute later we'd uncovered a flat paving stone about one metre square. I tried to work my fingers under the wet edges, but the stone was too thick and much too heavy to lift.

'We can use something as a lever,' Walt suggested. 'Pry it up.'

'Or,' I said, 'stand back.'

Walt looked ready to protest, but when I brought out my staff, he knew enough to get out of the way. With my new understanding of godly magic, I didn't so much *think* about what I needed as *feel* a connection to Isis. I remembered a time when she'd found her husband's coffin grown into the trunk of a cypress tree, and in her anger and desperation she blew the tree apart. I channelled those emotions and pointed at the stone. *'Ha-di!'*

Good news: the spell worked even better than in St Petersburg. The hieroglyph glowed at the end of my staff, and the stone was blasted to rubble, revealing a dark hole underneath.

Bad news: that's not all I destroyed. Around the hole, the ground began to crumble. Walt and I scrambled backwards as more stones fell into the pit, and I realized I'd just destabilized the entire roof of a subterranean room. The hole widened until it reached the support legs of the water tower. The water tower began to creak and sway.

'Run!' Walt yelled.

We didn't stop until we were hiding behind a palm tree thirty metres away. The water tower sprang a hundred different leaks, wobbled back and forth like a drunken man, then fell towards us and shattered, soaking us from head to toe and sending a flood through the rows of palm trees.

The noise was so deafening, it must've been heard throughout the oasis.

'*Oops*,' I said.

Walt looked at me like I was mad. I suppose I was guilty as charged. But it's just so very tempting to blow things up, isn't it?

We ran to the Sadie Kane Memorial Crater. It was now the size of a swimming pool. Five metres down, under a pile of sand and rocks, were rows of mummies, all wrapped in old cloth and laid out on stone slabs. The mummies were now flattened, I'm afraid, but I could tell they'd been brightly painted with red, blue and gold.

'Golden mummies.' Walt looked horrified. 'Part of the tomb system that hasn't been excavated yet. You just ruined –'

'I *did* say *Oops*. Now, help me down there, before the owner of this water tower shows up with a shotgun.'

16. ...But Not as Evil as Romans

TO BE FAIR, THE MUMMIES in that particular room were mostly ruined already, thanks to the moisture from the leaking tower above. Just add water to mummies for a truly horrible smell.

We climbed over the rubble and found a corridor leading deeper underground. I couldn't tell whether it was natural or man-made, but it snaked a good forty metres through solid rock before opening into another burial chamber. This room had not been damaged by water. Everything was remarkably well preserved. Walt had brought torches [flashlights, for you Americans], and in the dim light, on stone slabs and in niches carved along the walls, gold-painted mummies glittered. There were at least a hundred in this room alone, and more corridors led off in each direction.

Walt shone his light on three mummies lying together on a central dais. Their bodies were completely wrapped in linen, so they looked rather like bowling pins. Their likenesses were painted on the linen in meticulous detail – hands crossed

over their chests, jewellery adorning their necks, Egyptian
kilt and sandals, and a host of protective hieroglyphs and
images of the gods in a border on each side. All this was
typical Egyptian art, but their faces were done in a completely
different style – realistic portraits that looked cut-and-pasted
onto the mummies' heads. On the left was a man with a thin,
bearded face and sad dark eyes. On the right was a beautiful
woman with curly auburn hair. What really pulled at my heart,
though, was the mummy in the middle. Its body was tiny –
obviously a child. Its portrait showed a boy of about seven years
old. He had the man's eyes and the woman's hair.

'A family,' Walt guessed. 'Buried together.'

There was something tucked under the child's right elbow
– a small wooden horse, possibly his favourite toy. Even though
this family had been dead for thousands of years, I couldn't
help getting a bit teary-eyed. It was just so sad.

'How did they die?' I wondered.

From the corridor directly in front of us, a voice echoed,
'The wasting disease.'

My staff was instantly in my hand. Walt trained his torch
on the doorway, and a ghost stepped into the room. At least I
assumed he was a ghost, because he was see-through. He was a
heavy older man with short-cropped white hair, bulldog jowls
and a cross expression. He wore Roman-style robes and kohl
eyeliner, so he looked rather like Winston Churchill – if the
old prime minister had thrown a wild toga party and got his
face painted.

'Newly dead?' He eyed us warily. 'Haven't seen any new
arrivals in a long time. Where are your bodies?'

Walt and I glanced at each other.

'Actually,' I said, 'we're wearing them.'

The ghost's eyebrows shot up. '*Di immortales*! You're alive?'

'So far,' Walt said.

'Then you've brought offerings?' The man rubbed his hands. 'Oh, they *said* you would come, but we've waited ages! Where have you been?'

'*Um . . .*' I didn't want to disappoint a ghost, especially as he was beginning to glow more brightly, which in magic is often a prelude to exploding. 'Perhaps we should introduce ourselves. I'm Sadie Kane. This is Walt –'

'Of course! You need my name for the spells.' The ghost cleared his throat. 'I am Appius Claudius Iratus.'

I got the feeling I was supposed to be impressed. 'Right. That's not Egyptian, I gather?'

The ghost looked offended. 'Roman, of course. Following those cursed Egyptian customs is how we all ended up here to begin with! Bad enough I got stationed in this godforsaken oasis – as if Rome needs an entire legion to guard some date farms! Then I had the bad luck to fall ill. Told my wife on my deathbed: "Lobelia, an old-fashioned Roman burial. None of this local nonsense." But no! She never listened. *Had* to mummify me, so my *ba* is stuck here forever. Women! She probably moved back to Rome and died in the proper way.'

'Lobelia?' I asked, because really I hadn't heard much after that. What sort of parents name their child Lobelia?

The ghost huffed and crossed his arms. 'But you don't want to hear me ramble on, do you? You may call me Mad Claude. That's the translation in your tongue.'

I wondered how a Roman ghost could speak English – or if I simply understood him through some sort of telepathy. Either way, I was not relieved to find out his name was Mad Claude.

'Um . . .' Walt raised his hand. 'Are you mad as in angry? Or mad as in crazy?'

'Yes,' Claude said. 'Now, about those offerings. I see staffs, wands and amulets, so I assume you're priests with the local House of Life? Good, good. Then you'll know what to do.'

'What to do!' I agreed heartily. 'Yes, quite!'

Claude's eyes narrowed. 'Oh, Jupiter. You're novices, aren't you? Did the temple even *explain* the problem to you?'

'Um –'

He stormed over to the family of mummies we'd been looking at. 'This is Lucius, Flavia and little Purpens. They died of the wasting plague. I've been here so long, I could tell you practically *everyone's* story!'

'They talk to you?' I stepped away from the mummy family. Suddenly little Purpens didn't seem so cute.

Mad Claude waved his hand impatiently. 'Sometimes, yes. Not as much as in the old days. Their spirits sleep most of the time, now. The point is, no matter how bad a death these people had, their fate *after* death has been worse! All of us – all these Romans living in Egypt – got an Egyptian burial. Local customs, local priests, mummify the bodies for the next life, et cetera. We thought we were covering our bases – two religions, twice the insurance. Problem was, you foolish Egyptian priests didn't know what you were doing any more! By the time we Romans came along, most of your magic knowledge was lost.

267

But did you tell us that? No! You were happy to take our coins and do a shoddy job.'

'Ah.' I backed away a bit more from Mad Claude, who was now glowing quite dangerously. 'Well, I'm sure the House of Life has a customer service number for that –'

'You can't go halfway with these Egyptian rituals,' he grumbled. 'We ended up with mummified bodies and eternal souls tethered to them, and no one followed up! No one said the prayers to help us move to the next life. No one made offerings to nourish our *bas*. Do you know how hungry I am?'

'We've got some beef jerky,' Walt offered.

'We couldn't go to Pluto's realm like good Romans,' Mad Claude went on, 'because our bodies had been prepared for a different afterlife. We couldn't go to the Duat, because we weren't given the proper Egyptian rituals. Our souls were stuck here, attached to these bodies. Do you have any idea how *boring* it is down here?'

'So, if you're a *ba*,' I asked, 'why don't you have a bird's body?'

'I told you! We're all mixed up, not pure Roman ghost, not proper *ba*. If I had wings, believe me, I'd fly out of here! By the way, what year is it? Who's the emperor now?'

'Oh, his name is –' Walt coughed, then rushed on: 'You know, Claude, I'm sure we can help you.'

'We can?' I said. 'Oh, right! We can!'

Walt nodded encouragingly. 'The thing is, we have to find something first.'

'A scroll,' I put in. 'Part of the Book of Ra.'

Claude scratched his considerable jowls. 'And this will help you send our souls to the next life?'

'Well...' I said.

'Yes,' Walt said.

'Possibly,' I said. 'We don't really know until we find it. It's supposed to wake Ra, you see, which will help the Egyptian gods. I'd think that would improve your chances at getting into the afterlife. Besides, I'm on good terms with the Egyptian gods. They pop over for tea from time to time. If you helped us, I could put in a word.'

Honestly, I'd just been making up things to say. I'm sure this will surprise you, but I sometimes ramble when I get nervous.

[Oh, stop laughing, Carter.]

At any rate, Mad Claude's expression became shrewder. He studied us as if assessing our bank accounts. I wondered if the Roman Empire had used chariot salesmen, and if Mad Claude had been one. I imagined him on a Roman commercial in a cheap tartan toga: *I must be crazy to be giving away chariots at these prices!*

'On good terms with the Egyptian gods,' he mused. 'Put in a word, you say.'

Then he turned to Walt. Claude's expression was so calculating, so *eager*, it made my skin crawl. 'If the scroll you seek is ancient, it would be in the oldest section of the catacombs. Some natives were buried there, you know, long before we Romans came along. Their *bas* have all moved on now. No trouble getting into the Duat for *them*. But their burial sites are still intact, lots of relics and so on.'

'You'd be willing to show us?' Walt asked, with much more excitement than I could've managed.

'Oh, yes.' Mad Claude gave us his best 'used-chariot salesman' smile. 'And later we'll talk about an appropriate fee, eh? Come along, my friends. It's not far.'

Note to self: when a ghost offers to guide you deeper into a burial site and his name includes the word *Mad*, it's best to say no.

As we passed through tunnels and chambers, Mad Claude gave us a running commentary on the various mummies. Caligula the date merchant: 'Horrible name! But once you're named for an emperor, even a psychotic one, you can't do much about it. He died betting someone he could kiss a scorpion.' Varens the slaver: 'Disgusting man. Tried to go into the gladiator business. If you give a slave a sword, well... you can guess how he died!' Octavia the legion commander's wife: 'Went completely native! Had her cat mummified. She even believed she had the blood of the pharaohs and tried to channel the spirit of Isis. Her death, needless to say, was painful.'

He grinned at me like this was extremely funny. I tried not to look horrified.

What struck me most was the sheer number and variety of the mummies. Some were wrapped in real gold. Their portraits were so lifelike, their eyes seemed to follow me as we passed. They sat on ornately carved marble slabs surrounded by valuables: jewellery, vases, even some *shabti*. Other mummies looked as if nursery-school children had made them in art class.

They were crudely wrapped, painted with shaky hieroglyphs and little stick-figure gods. Their portraits were not much better than I could've done – which is to say, dreadful. Their bodies were stuffed three-deep in shallow niches, or simply piled in the corners of the room.

When I asked about them, Mad Claude was dismissive. 'Commoners. Wannabes. Didn't have money for artists and funeral rites, so they tried the do-it-yourself approach.'

I looked down at the portrait of the nearest mummy, her face a crude finger-painted image. I wondered if her grieving children had made it – one last gift for their mother. Despite the bad quality, I found it rather sweet. They had no money and no artistic skill, but they'd done their best to lovingly send her to the afterlife. Next time I saw Anubis, I would ask him about this. A woman like that deserved a chance at happiness in the next world, even if she couldn't pay. We had quite enough snobbery in this world without exporting it to the hereafter.

Walt trailed behind us, not speaking. He'd shine his light on this mummy or that, as if pondering each one's fate. I wondered if he was thinking of King Tut, his famous ancestor, whose tomb had been in a cavern not too different from this.

After several more long tunnels and crowded mummy rooms, we arrived in a burial chamber that was clearly much older. The wall paintings had faded, but they looked more authentically Egyptian, with the sideways-walking people and hieroglyphs that actually formed words, rather than simply providing decoration. Instead of realistic facial portraits, the mummies had the generic wide-eyed, smiling faces I'd seen on most Egyptian death masks. A few had crumbled to dust. Others were encased in stone sarcophagi.

'Natives,' Mad Claude confirmed. 'Egyptian nobles from before Rome took over. What you're looking for should be somewhere in this area.'

I scanned the room. The only other doorway was blocked with boulders and debris. While Walt began searching, I remembered what Bes had said – that the first two scrolls of Ra might help me find the third. I pulled them from my bag, hoping they would point the way like a dowsing rod, but nothing happened.

From the other side of the room, Walt called, 'What's this?'

He was standing in front of some sort of shrine – a niche set into the wall, with the statue of a man wrapped like a mummy. The figure was carved from wood, decorated with jewels and precious metals. His wrappings glistened like pearl in the light of the torch. He held a golden staff with a silver *djed* symbol on top. Around his feet stood several golden rodents – rats, perhaps. The skin of his face gleamed turquoise blue.

'It's my dad,' I guessed. 'Er...I mean Osiris, isn't it?'

Mad Claude arched his eyebrows. 'Your dad?'

Fortunately, Walt saved me from explaining. 'No,' he said. 'Look at his beard.'

The statue's beard was rather unusual. It was pencil thin from his sideburns around his jaw line, with a perfectly straight bit coming down for a goatee – as if someone had traced the beard with a grease pen, then stuck the pen on his chin.

'And the collar,' Walt continued. 'It's got a tassel thing hanging down in back. You don't see that with Osiris. And

those animals at his feet . . . are those rats? I remember some
story about rats –'

'I thought you were priests,' Mad Claude grumped.
'Obviously, the god is Ptah.'

'Ptah?' I'd heard quite a few odd Egyptian god names, but
this was a new one for me. 'Ptah, son of Pitooey? Is he the god
of spitting?'

Claude glared at me. 'Are you always so irreverent?'

'Usually, more.'

'A novice *and* a heretic,' he said. 'Just my luck. Well, girl,
I shouldn't have to teach *you* about your own gods, but, as I
understand it, Ptah was the god of craftsmen. We compared
him to our Roman god Vulcan.'

'Then what's he doing in a tomb?' Walt asked.

Claude scratched his non-existent head. 'I've never been
sure, actually. You don't see him in most Egyptian funeral
rites.'

Walt pointed to the statue's staff. When I looked more
closely, I realized the *djed* symbol was combined with something
else, a curved top that looked strangely familiar.

'That's the symbol *was*,' Walt said. 'It means power. Lots of
the gods had staffs like that, but I never realized it looks like –'

'Yes, yes,' Claude said impatiently. 'The priest's ceremonial
knife for opening the mouth of the dead. Honestly, you
Egyptian priests are hopeless. No wonder we conquered you
so easily.'

My hand acted quite on its own, reaching into my bag and bringing out the black *netjeri* blade Anubis had given me.

Mad Claude's eyes glinted. 'Ah, so you're *not* hopeless. That's perfect! With that knife and the proper spell, you should be able to touch my mummy and release me into the Duat.'

'No,' I said. 'No, there's more to it. The knife, the Book of Ra, this statue of the spit god. It all fits together somehow.'

Walt's face lit up. 'Sadie, Ptah was more than the craftsman god, right? Didn't they call him the God of Opening?'

'*Um* . . . possibly.'

'I thought you taught us that. Or maybe it was Carter.'

'Boring bit of information? Probably Carter.'

'But it's important,' Walt insisted. 'Ptah was a creation god. In some legends, he created the souls of mankind just by speaking a word. He could revive any soul, and open any door.'

My eyes drifted to the debris-filled doorway, the only other exit from the room. 'Open any door?'

I held up the two scrolls of Ra and walked towards the collapsed tunnel. The scrolls became uncomfortably warm.

'The last scroll is on the other side,' I said. 'We need to get past this rubble.'

I held the black knife in one hand and the scrolls in the other. I spoke the command for *open*. Nothing happened. I went back to the statue of Ptah and tried the same thing. No luck.

'Hullo, Ptah?' I called. 'Sorry about the spit comment. Look, we're trying to get the third scroll of Ra, which is on the other side, there. I suppose you were placed here to open a path. So would you mind terribly?'

Still nothing happened.

Mad Claude gripped the trim of his toga as if he wanted to strangle us with it. 'Look, I don't know why you need this scroll to free us if you've got the knife. But why don't you try an offering? All gods need offerings.'

Walt rummaged through his supplies. He placed a juice pouch and a bit of beef jerky at the foot of the statue. The statue did nothing. Even the gold rats at his feet apparently didn't want our beef jerky.

'Stupid spit god.' I threw myself down on the dusty ground. I had a mummy on either side of me, but I didn't care any more. I couldn't believe we were so close to the last scroll, after fighting demons, gods and Russian assassins, and now we'd been stopped by a pile of rocks.

'I hate to suggest it,' Walt said, 'but you could blast through with the *ha-di* spell.'

'And bring down the ceiling on top of us?' I said.

'You'd die,' Claude agreed. 'Which isn't an experience I'd recommend.'

Walt knelt next to me. 'There's got to be something...' He took stock of his amulets.

Mad Claude paced the room. 'I still don't understand. You're priests. You have the ceremonial knife. Why can't you release us?'

'The knife isn't for you!' I snapped. 'It's for Ra!'

Walt and Claude both stared at me. I hadn't realized it before, but as soon as I spoke, I knew it was the truth.

'Sorry,' I said. 'But the knife is used for the Opening of the Mouth ceremony, to free a soul. I'll need it to awaken Ra. That's why Anubis gave it to me.'

'You know Anubis!' Claude clapped with delight. 'He can free us all! And you –' He pointed at Walt. 'You're one of Anubis's chosen, aren't you? You can get us more knives if you need them! I sensed the presence of the god around you as soon as we met. Did you take his service when he realized you were dying?'

'Wait ... what?' I asked.

Walt wouldn't meet my eyes. 'I'm not a priest of Anubis.'

'But *dying?*' I choked up. 'How are you dying?'

Mad Claude looked incredulous. 'You mean you don't know? He's got the old pharaoh's curse. We didn't see it much in my day, but I recognize it, all right. Occasionally a person from one of the old Egyptian royal lines –'

'Claude, shut up,' I said. 'Walt, speak. How does this curse work?'

In the dim light, he looked thinner and older. On the wall behind him, his shadow loomed like a deformed monster.

'Akhenaton's curse runs in my family,' he said. 'Kind of a genetic disease. Not every generation, not every person, but when it strikes, it's bad. Tut died at nineteen. Most of the others ... twelve, thirteen. I'm sixteen now. My dad ... my dad was eighteen. I never knew him.'

'Eighteen?' That alone brought up a host of new questions, but I tried to stay focused. 'Can't it be cured ...?' Guilt washed over me, and I felt like a total imbecile. 'Oh, god. That's why you were talking to Jaz. She's a healer.'

Walt nodded grimly. 'I thought she might know spells that I hadn't been able to find. My dad's family – they spent years

276

searching. My mom has been looking for a cure since I was born. The doctors in Seattle couldn't do anything.'

'Doctors,' Mad Claude said with disgust. 'I had one in the legion, loved to put leeches on my legs. Only made me worse. Now, about this connection to Anubis, and using that knife...'

Walt shook his head. 'Claude, we'll try to help you, but not with the knife. I know magic items. I'm pretty sure it can be used only once, and we can't just make another. If Sadie needs it for Ra, she can't risk using it before that.'

'Excuses!' Claude roared.

'If you don't shut up,' I warned, 'I'm going to find your mummy and draw a moustache on your portrait!'

Claude turned as white as...well, a ghost. 'You wouldn't dare!'

'Walt,' I said, trying to ignore the Roman, 'was Jaz able to help?'

'She tried her best. But this curse has been defying healers for three thousand years. Modern doctors think it's related to sickle cell anaemia, but they don't know. They've been trying for decades to figure out how King Tut died, and they can't agree. Some say poison. Some say a genetic disease. It's the curse, but of course they can't say that.'

'Isn't there any way? I mean we know *gods*. Perhaps I could cure you like Isis did Ra. If I knew your secret name –'

'Sadie, I've thought of that,' he said. 'I've thought of everything. The curse can't be cured. It can only be slowed down if... if I avoid magic. That's why I got into talismans and amulets. They store magic in advance, so they don't require as much from the user. But it's only helped a little bit. I was *born* to do magic, so the curse progresses in me no matter what I do. Some days it's not so bad. Some days my whole body is in pain. When I do magic, it gets worse.'

'And the more you do –'

'The faster I die.'

I punched him in the chest. I couldn't help it. All my grief and guilt flipped right to anger. 'You idiot! Why are you here, then? You should've told me to shove off! Bes warned you to stay in Brooklyn. Why didn't you listen?'

What I told you earlier about Walt's eyes not melting me? I take it back. When he looked at me in that dusty tomb, his eyes were every bit as dark, tender and sad as Anubis's. 'I'm going to die anyway, Sadie. I want my life to mean something. And ... I want to spend as much time as I can with you.'

That hurt me worse than a punch in the chest. Much worse.

I think I might've kissed him. Or possibly slapped him.

Mad Claude, however, was not a sympathetic audience. 'Very sweet, I'm sure, but you promised me payment! Come back to the Roman tombs. Release my spirit from my mummy. Then release the others. After that, you can do as you like.'

'The others?' I asked. 'Are you mad?'

He stared at me.

'Silly question,' I conceded. 'But there are thousands of mummies. We have one knife.'

'You promised!'

'We did not,' I said. 'You said we'd discuss a fee *after* we found the scroll. We've found nothing but a dead end here.'

The ghost growled, more like a wolf than a human. 'If you won't come to us,' he said, 'we'll come to you.'

His spirit glowed, then disappeared in a flash.

I looked nervously at Walt. 'What did he mean by that?'

'I don't know,' he said. 'But we should figure out how to get through that rubble and get out of here – *quickly*.'

Despite our best efforts, nothing happened quickly. We couldn't move the debris. There were too many large boulders. We couldn't dig around, over, or under it. I didn't dare risk a *ha-di* spell or use the black knife's magic. Walt had no amulets that would help. I was frankly stumped. The statue of Ptah smiled at us but didn't offer any helpful suggestions, nor did he seem interested in the beef jerky and juice.

Finally, covered with dust, drenched with sweat, I plopped down on a stone sarcophagus and examined my blistered fingers.

Walt sat next to me. 'Don't give up. There has to be a way.'

'Does there?' I asked, feeling especially resentful. 'Like there has to be a cure for you? What if there *isn't*? What if...'

My voice broke. Walt turned his face so it was hidden in shadow.

'I'm sorry,' I said. 'That was terrible. But I just couldn't stand it if...'

I was so confused, I didn't know what to say, or how I felt. All I knew was that I didn't want to lose Walt.

'Did you mean it?' I asked. 'When you said you wanted to spend time...you know.'

Walt shrugged. 'Isn't it obvious?'

I didn't answer, but, please – *nothing* is obvious with boys. For such simple creatures, they are quite baffling.

I imagined I was blushing fiercely, so I decided to change the subject.

'Claude said he sensed the spirit of Anubis about you. You've been talking to Anubis a lot?'

Walt turned his rings. 'I thought maybe he could help me. Maybe grant me a little extra time before . . . before the end. I wanted to be around long enough to help you defeat Apophis. Then I'd feel as if I'd done something with my life. And . . . there were other reasons I wanted to talk to him. About some – some powers I've been developing.'

'What sort of powers?'

It was Walt's turn to change the subject. He looked at his hands like they'd become dangerous weapons. 'The thing is, I almost didn't come to Brooklyn. When I got the *djed* amulet – that calling card you guys sent – my mom didn't want me to leave. She knew that learning magic would make the curse accelerate. Part of me was afraid to go. Part of me was angry. It seemed like a cruel joke. You guys offered to train me for magic when I knew I wouldn't survive longer than a year or two.'

'A year or two?' I could hardly breathe. I'd always thought of a year as an incredibly long time. I'd waited *forever* to turn thirteen. And each school term seemed like an eternity. But suddenly two years seemed much too short. I'd only be fifteen, not even driving yet. I couldn't imagine what it would be like to know that I would die in two years – possibly sooner, if I continued doing what I was born to do, practicing magic. 'Why did you come to Brooklyn, then?'

'I had to,' Walt said. 'I've lived my whole life under the threat of death. My mom made everything so serious, so *huge*. But when I got to Brooklyn, I felt like I had a destiny, a purpose. Even if it made the curse more painful, it was worth it.'

'But it's so unfair.'

Walt looked at me, and I realized he was smiling. 'That's *my* line. I've been saying that for years. Sadie, I *want* to be here. The past two months I've felt as if I'm actually living for the first time. And getting to know you...' He cleared his throat. He was quite attractive when he got nervous. 'I started worrying about small things. My hair. My clothes. Whether I brushed my teeth. I mean, I'm *dying*, and I'm worrying about my teeth.'

'You have lovely teeth.'

He laughed. 'That's what I mean. A little comment like that, and I feel better. All these small things suddenly seem important. I don't feel like I'm dying. I feel happy.'

Personally, I felt miserable. For months I'd dreamed about Walt admitting he liked me, but not like this – not like, *I can be honest with you, because I'm dying anyway.*

Something he'd said was nagging at me, too. It reminded me of a lesson I'd taught at Brooklyn House, and an idea began to form in my mind.

'"Small things suddenly seem important",' I repeated. I looked down at a little mound of rubble we'd cleared from the blocked doorway. 'Oh, it couldn't be that easy.'

'What?' asked Walt.

'Rocks.'

'I just bared my soul, and you're thinking about rocks?'

'The doorway,' I said. 'Sympathetic magic. Do you think...'

He blinked. 'Sadie Kane, you're a genius.'

'Well, I *know* that. But can we make it work?'

Walt and I began gathering up more pebbles. We chipped some pieces from the larger boulders and added them to our pile. We tried our best to make a miniature replica of the rubble collection blocking the doorway.

My hope, of course, was to create a sympathetic bond, as I'd done with Carter and the wax figurine in Alexandria. The rocks in our replica pile came from the collapsed tunnel, so our pile and the original were already connected in substance, which should have made it easy to establish a link. But moving something very large with something very small is always tricky. If we didn't do it carefully, we could collapse the whole room. I didn't know how deep underground we were, but I imagined there was quite enough rock and earth over our heads to bury us forever.

'Ready?' I asked.

Walt nodded and pulled out his wand.

'Oh, no, cursed boy,' I said. 'You just watch my back. If the ceiling starts to fall and we need a shield, that's your job. But you'll do no magic unless absolutely necessary. I'll clear the doorway.'

'Sadie, I'm not fragile,' he complained. 'I don't need a protector.'

'Rubbish,' I said. 'That's macho bluster, and all boys like to be mothered.'

'What? God, you're annoying!'

I smiled sweetly. 'You did want to spend time with me.'

Before he could protest, I raised my wand and began the spell.

I imagined a bond between our small pile of rubble and the debris in the doorway. I imagined that, in the Duat, they were one and the same. I spoke the command for *join*:

'*Hi-nehm.*'

The symbol burned faintly over our miniature rubble pile.

Slowly and carefully, I brushed a few pebbles away from the pile. The debris in the corridor rumbled.

'It's working,' Walt said.

I didn't dare look. I stayed focused on my task – moving the pebbles a little at a time, dispersing the pile into smaller mounds. It was almost as hard as moving real boulders. I went into a daze. When Walt put his hand on my shoulder, I had no idea how much time had passed. I was so exhausted I couldn't see straight.

'It's done,' he said. 'You did great.'

The doorway was clear. The rubble had been pushed into the corners of our room, where it lay in smaller piles.

'Nice job, Sadie.' Walt leaned down and kissed me. He was probably just expressing appreciation or happiness, but the kiss didn't make me feel any less fuzzy-headed.

'*Um,*' I said – again with the incredible verbal skills.

Walt helped me to my feet. We headed down the corridor into the next room. For all the work we'd done to get there, the room wasn't very exciting, just a five-metre-square chamber with nothing inside except a red lacquered box on a sandstone pedestal. On top of the box was a carved wooden handle shaped like a demonic greyhound with tall ears – the Set animal.

'Oh, that can't be good,' Walt said.

But I walked straight up to the box, opened the lid and grabbed the scroll inside.

'Sadie!' Walt yelled.

'What?' I turned. 'It's Set's box. If he'd wanted to kill me, he could've done so in St Petersburg. He *wants* me to have this scroll. Probably thinks it'll be fun watching me kill myself trying to awaken Ra.' I looked up at the ceiling and shouted, 'Isn't that right, Set?'

My voice echoed through the catacombs. I no longer had the power to invoke Set's secret name, but I still felt as if I'd got his attention. The air turned sharper. The ground trembled as if something underneath it, something very large, was laughing.

Walt exhaled. 'I wish you wouldn't take chances like that.'

'This from a boy who's willing to die to spend time with me?'

Walt made an exaggerated bow. 'I take it back, Miss Kane. Please, go right ahead trying to kill yourself.'

'Thank you.'

I looked at the three scrolls in my hands – the entire Book of Ra, together for probably the first time since Mad Claude wore little Roman nappies. I had collected the scrolls, done the impossible, triumphed beyond all expectations. Yet it still wouldn't be enough unless we could find Ra and wake him before Apophis rose. 'No time to waste,' I said. 'Let's get –'

Deep moaning echoed through the corridors, as if something – or a whole *host* of somethings – had woken up in a very bad mood.

'Out of here,' Walt said. 'Great idea.'

As we ran through the previous chamber, I glanced at the statue of Ptah. I was tempted to take back the jerky and juice, just to be mean, but I decided against it.

I suppose it isn't your fault, I thought. *Can't be easy to have a name like Ptah. Enjoy the snack, but I do wish you'd helped us.*

We ran on. It wasn't easy to remember our path. Twice we had to double back before finding the room with the family of mummies where we'd met Mad Claude.

I was about to bolt blindly across the chamber and into the last tunnel, but Walt held me back and saved my life. He shone his light on the far exit, then on the corridors to either side.

'No,' I said. 'No, no, no.'

All three doorways were clogged with human figures wrapped in linen. They pressed together as far as I could see down each corridor. Some were still completely bound. They hopped and shuffled and waddled forward as if they were giant cocoons engaged in a sack race. Other mummies had partially broken free. They limped along on emaciated legs, hands like dried branches clawing at their wrappings. Most still wore their painted-face portraits, and the effect was gruesome – lifelike masks smiling serenely at the top of undead scarecrows of bones and painted linen.

'I hate mummies,' I whimpered.

'Maybe a fire spell,' Walt said. 'They've got to burn easily.'

'We'll burn ourselves, too! It's too close in here.'

'You have a better idea?'

I wanted to cry. Freedom so near – and, just as I'd feared, we were trapped by a crowd of mummies. But these were worse than movie mummies. They were silent and slow, pathetic ruined things that once were human.

One of the mummies on the floor grabbed my leg. Before I could even scream, Walt reached out and tapped the thing on the wrist. The mummy instantly turned to dust.

I stared at him in amazement. 'Is *that* the power you were worried about? That was brilliant! Do it again!'

Immediately I felt awful suggesting it. Walt's face was tight with pain.

'I can't do it a thousand more times,' he said sadly. 'Maybe if…'

Then, on the central dais, the mummy family began to stir.

I will not lie. When the child-size mummy of little Purpens sat up, I almost had an accident that would've ruined my new jeans. If my *ba* could've shed my skin and flown away, it would have.

I gripped Walt's arm.

At the far end of the room, the ghost of Mad Claude flickered into view. As he walked towards us, the rest of the mummies began to stir.

'You should be honoured, my friends.' He gave us a crazy grin. 'It takes a lot of excitement for *ba* to return to their withered old bodies. But we simply can't let you leave until you've freed us for the afterlife. Use the knife, do your spells and you can go.'

'We can't free you all!' I shouted.

'A shame,' Claude said. 'Then we'll take the knife and free ourselves. I suppose two more bodies in the catacombs won't make any difference.'

He said something in Latin, and all the mummies surged towards us, shuffling and tripping, falling and rolling. Some crumbled to pieces as they tried to walk. Others fell down and were trampled by their fellows. But more came forward.

We backed into the corridor. I had my staff in one hand. With my other, I held Walt's hand tightly. I'd never been good at summoning fire, but I managed to set the end of my staff ablaze.

'We'll try it your way,' I told Walt. 'Light them up and run.'

I knew it was a bad idea. In close quarters, a blaze would hurt us as much as the mummies. We'd die of smoke inhalation or suffocation or heat. Even if we managed to retreat into the catacombs, we'd just get lost and run into more mummies.

Walt lit his own staff.

'On three,' I suggested. I stared in horror at the child's mummy coming towards us, the portrait of a seven-year-old boy smiling at me from beyond the grave. 'One, two –'

I faltered. The mummies were only a metre away, but from behind me came a new sound – like water running. No – like skittering. A mass of living things charging towards us, thousands and thousands of tiny claws on stone, possibly insects or . . .

'Three comes next,' Walt said nervously. 'Are we torching them or not?'

'Hug the walls!' I shrieked. I didn't know exactly what was coming, but I knew I didn't want to be in their way. I pushed Walt against the stone and flattened myself next to him, our faces pressed against the wall, as a wave of claws and fur slammed into us and rolled over our backs: an army of rodents scuttling five-deep along the floor and racing horizontally across the walls, defying gravity.

Rats. Thousands of rats.

They ran straight over us, doing no damage except for the odd claw scratch. Not so bad, you might think, but have you ever been upright and trampled by an army of filthy rats? Do not pay money for the experience.

The rats flooded the burial chamber. They tore into the mummies, clawing and chewing and squealing their tiny battle cries. The mummies writhed under the assault, but they didn't stand a chance. The room was a hurricane of fur, teeth and shredded linen. It was like the old cartoons of termites swarming over wood and dissolving it to nothing.

'No!' yelled Mad Claude. 'No!'

But he was the only one screaming. The mummies withered silently under the fury of the rats.

'I'll get you!' Claude snarled as his spirit began to flicker. 'I'll have my revenge!'

And with one final evil glare, his image faded and was gone.

The rats divided their forces and scurried off down all three corridors, chewing through mummies as they went, until the room was silent and empty, the floor littered with dust, shreds of linen and a few bones.

Walt looked shaken. I fell against him and hugged him. I probably cried with relief. I was so glad to hold a warm living human being.

'It's okay.' He stroked my hair, which felt awfully good. 'That – that was the story about rats.'

'What?' I managed.

'They...they saved Memphis. An enemy army besieged the city, and the people prayed for help. Their patron god sent a horde of rats. They ate the enemy's bowstrings, their sandals, everything they could chew. The attackers had to withdraw.'

'The patron god – you mean –'

'Me.' From the exit corridor across the room, an Egyptian farmer stepped into view. He wore grubby robes, a head wrap, and sandals. He held a rifle at his side. He grinned at us, and as he got closer, I saw his eyes were blank white. His skin had a slightly bluish tint, as if he were suffocating and really enjoying the experience.

'Sorry I didn't answer sooner,' said the farmer. 'I am Ptah. And no, Sadie Kane, I am not the god of spit.'

'Please, have a seat,' the god said. 'Sorry about the mess, but what do expect from Romans? They never did clean up after themselves.'

Neither Walt nor I sat. A grinning god with a rifle was a bit off-putting.

'Ah, quite right.' Ptah blinked his blank white eyes. 'You're in a hurry.'

'Sorry,' I said. 'Are you a date farmer?'

Ptah looked down at his grubby robes. 'I'm just borrowing this poor fellow for a minute, you understand. I thought you wouldn't mind, as he was coming down here to shoot you for destroying his water tower.'

'No, carry on,' I said. 'But the mummies – what will happen to their *ba*?'

Ptah laughed. 'Don't worry about them. Now that their remains are destroyed, I imagine their *ba* will go on to whatever Roman afterlife awaits them. As it should be.'

He put his hand over his mouth and burped. A cloud of white gas billowed out, coalesced into a glowing *ba* and flew off down the corridor.

Walt pointed after the spirit bird. 'Did you just –'

'Yes.' Ptah sighed. 'I really try not to talk at all. That's how I create, you see, with words. They can get me into trouble. Once just for fun I made up the word "platypus" and –'

Instantly, a duckbilled, furry thing appeared on the floor, scrabbling around in a panic.

'Oh, dear,' Ptah said. 'Yes, that's exactly what happened. Slip of the tongue. Really the only way something like that could have been created.'

He waved his hand, and the platypus disappeared. 'At any rate, I have to be careful, so I can't talk long. I'm glad you found the Book of Ra! I always did like the old chap. I would have helped earlier, when you asked, but it took a while to get here from the Duat. Also, I can open only one door per customer. I thought you had that blocked corridor well in hand. But there's a much more important door that you need.'

'Sorry?' I asked.

'Your brother,' Ptah said. 'He's in a great deal of trouble.'

As exhausted, bedraggled and covered with rat scratches as I was, that news set my nerves tingling. Carter needed help. I had to save my brother's ridiculous hide.

'Can you send us there?' I asked.

Ptah smiled. 'Thought you'd never ask.'

He pointed to the nearest wall. The stones dissolved into a portal of swirling sand.

'And, my dear, some words of advice.' Ptah's milky eyes studied me. 'Courage. Hope. Sacrifice.'

I wasn't sure whether he was reading those qualities within me, or giving me a pep talk, or perhaps *creating* the traits I needed, the way he'd created the *ba* and the platypus. Whatever the case, I suddenly felt warmer inside, filled with new energy.

'You're beginning to understand,' he told me. 'Words are the source of all power. And names are more than just a collection of letters. Well done, Sadie. You may succeed yet.'

I stared at the funnel of sand. 'What will we face on the other side?'

'Enemies and friends,' Ptah said. 'But which are which I can't say. If you survive, go to the top of the Great Pyramid. That should do nicely for an entry point into the Duat. When you read the Book of Ra —'

He choked, doubling over and dropping his rifle.

'I must go,' he said, straightening with a great deal of effort.

'This host can't stand any more. But, Walt...' He smiled sadly. 'Thank you for the beef jerky and juice. There *is* an answer for you. It's not one you'll like, but it is the best way.'

'What do you mean?' Walt asked. 'What answer?'

The farmer blinked. Suddenly his eyes were normal. He looked at us in surprise, then yelled something in Arabic and raised his gun.

I grabbed Walt's hand, and together we jumped into the portal.

17. Menshikov Hires a Happy Death Squad

I GUESS WE'RE EVEN, SADIE. First, Walt and I rushed off to save you in London. Then, you and Walt rushed off to save me. The only one who got shafted on both deals was Walt. Poor guy gets hauled all over the world pulling us out of trouble. But I'll admit I needed the help.

Bes was locked in a glowing fluorescent cage. Zia was convinced we were enemies. My sword and wand were gone. I was holding a crook and flail that were apparently stolen property, and two of the most powerful magicians in the world, Michel Desjardins and Vlad the Inhaler, were ready to arrest me, try me and execute me – not necessarily in that order.

I backed up to the steps of Zia's tomb, but there was no place to go. Red mud stretched in all directions, dotted with wreckage and dead fish. I couldn't run or hide, which gave me two options: surrender or fight.

Menshikov's scarred eyes glittered. 'Feel free to resist, Kane. Using deadly force would make my job *so* much easier.'

'Vladimir, stop,' Desjardins said wearily, leaning on his staff. 'Carter, don't be foolish. Surrender now.'

Three months ago, Desjardins would've been thrilled to blast me to bits. Now he looked sad and tired, like my execution was an unpleasant necessity. Zia stood next to him. She glanced warily at Menshikov, as if she could sense something evil about the man.

If I could use that, possibly buy some time...

'What's your plan, Vlad?' I asked. 'You let us get away from St Petersburg too easily. Almost like you *want* us to awaken Ra.'

The Russian laughed. 'Is that why I followed you halfway across the world to stop you?'

He did his best to look scornful, but a smile tugged at his lips, as if we were sharing a private joke.

'You didn't come to stop me,' I guessed. 'You're counting on us to find the scrolls for you and put them together. Do you need Ra to wake up in order to free Apophis?'

'Enough, Carter.' Desjardins spoke in a monotone, like a surgery patient counting backwards waiting for anaesthesia to kick in. I didn't understand why he seemed so apathetic, but Menshikov looked angry enough for both of them. From the hatred in the Russian's eyes, I could tell I'd struck a nerve.

'That's it, isn't it?' I said. 'Ma'at and Chaos are connected. To free Apophis, you have to wake Ra, but you want to control the summoning, make sure Ra comes back old and weak.'

Menshikov's new oaken staff burst into green flames. 'Boy, you have no idea what you are saying.'

'Set teased you about a past mistake,' I remembered. 'You

tried to awaken Ra once before, didn't you? Using what – only the one scroll you had? Is that how you burned your face?'

'Carter!' Desjardins interrupted. 'Vlad Menshikov is a hero of the House of Life. He tried to *destroy* that scroll to keep anyone else from using it. *That's* how he was injured.'

For a moment I was too stunned to speak. 'That…can't be true.'

'You should do your homework, boy.' Menshikov fixed his ruined eyes on me. 'The Menshikovs are descended from the priests of Amun-Ra. You've heard of that temple?'

I tried to recall the stories my dad had told me. I knew Amun-Ra was another name for Ra, the sun god. And his temple…

'They pretty much controlled Egypt for centuries,' I remembered. 'They opposed Akhenaton when he outlawed the old gods, maybe even assassinated him.'

'Indeed,' Menshikov said. 'My ancestors were champions of the gods! They are the ones who *created* the Book of Ra and hid its three sections, hoping that some day a worthy magician would reawaken their sun god.'

I tried to wrap my mind around that. I could totally see Vlad Menshikov as an ancient bloodthirsty priest. 'But if you're descended from priests of Ra –'

'Why do I oppose the gods?' Menshikov glanced at the Chief Lector as if I'd asked a predictably stupid question. 'Because the gods destroyed our civilization! By the time Egypt fell and Lord Iskandar banned the path of the gods, even *my* family had come to realize the truth. The old ways must be forbidden. Yes, I tried to destroy the scroll, to make up for the sins of my ancestors. Those who summon the gods must be wiped out.'

I shook my head. 'I *saw* you summon Set. I heard you talk about freeing Apophis. Desjardins, Zia – this guy is lying. He's going to kill you both.'

Desjardins looked at me in a kind of daze. Amos had insisted the Chief Lector was smart, so how could he not understand the threat?

'No more,' Desjardins said. 'Come peacefully, Carter Kane, or be destroyed.'

I gave Zia one more pleading look. I could see the doubt in her eyes, but she wasn't in any shape to help me. She'd just woken up from a three-month-long nightmare. She wanted to believe the House of Life was still her home and Desjardins and Menshikov were the good guys. She didn't want to hear any more about Apophis.

I raised the crook and flail. 'I'm not going peacefully.'

Menshikov nodded. 'Then destruction it is.'

He pointed his staff at me, and my instincts took over. I lashed out with the crook.

I was much too far away to reach him, but some invisible force ripped the staff out of Menshikov's hand and sent it flying into the Nile. He held out his wand, but I slashed the air again, and Menshikov went flying. He landed on his back so hard he made a mud angel.

'Carter!' Desjardins pushed Zia behind him. His own staff lit with purple fire. 'You dare to use the weapons of Ra?'

I looked at my hands in amazement. I'd never felt so much

power come to me so easily – as if I were meant to be a king. In the back of my mind, I heard Horus's voice, urging me on: *This is your path. This is your birthright.*

'You're going to kill me anyway,' I told Desjardins.

My body began to glow. I rose off the ground. For the first time since New Year's, I was encased in the avatar of the hawk god – a falcon-headed warrior three times my normal size. In its hands were massive holographic replicas of the crook and flail. I hadn't paid much attention to the flail, but it was a wicked pain-bringer – a wooden handle with three barbed chains, each topped by a spiky metal asterisk – like a combination whip and meat tenderizer. I took a swipe at the ground, and the falcon warrior mirrored my action. The glowing flail pulverized the stone steps of Zia's tomb, sending blocks of limestone flying through the air.

Desjardins raised a shield to deflect the shards. Zia's eyes widened. I knew I was probably freaking her out and convincing her I was the bad guy, but I had to protect her. I couldn't let Menshikov take her away.

'Combat magic,' Desjardins said with disdain. 'This is what the House of Life was like when we followed the path of the gods, Carter Kane: magician fighting magician, backstabbing and duels between the different temples. Do you want those times to return?'

'It doesn't have to be that way,' I said. 'I don't want to fight you, Desjardins, but Menshikov is a traitor. Get out of here. Let me deal with him.'

Menshikov rose from the mud, smiling like he enjoyed

getting thrown around. 'Deal with me? How confident! By all means, Chief Lector, let the boy try. I'll be sure to pick up the pieces when I'm done.'

Desjardins started to say, 'Vladimir, no. It's not your place –'

But Menshikov didn't wait. He stomped the ground with his foot, and the mud turned dry and white all around him. Twin lines of hardening earth snaked towards me, crossing like a DNA helix. I wasn't sure what they would do, but I knew I didn't want them touching me. I smashed at them with my flail, taking out a section of mud large enough for a hot tub. The white lines just kept coming, bleaching their way down the pit and climbing the other side, racing towards me. I tried to move out of their way, but the warrior avatar wasn't exactly speedy.

The lines of magic reached my feet. They wove like vines up the avatar's legs until I was tangled to the waist. They squeezed against my shielding, draining my magic, and I heard Menshikov's voice forcing its way into my mind.

Snake, the voice whispered. *You are a slithering reptile.*

I fought back my terror. I'd been turned into an animal against my will once before, and it was one of the worst experiences of my life. This time, it was happening in slow motion. The combat avatar fought to maintain its form, but Menshikov's magic was strong. The glowing white vines kept rising, encircling my chest.

I swiped at Menshikov with my crook. The invisible force hooked him round the neck and lifted him off the ground.

'Do it!' he choked out. 'Show me – your power – godling!'

I raised my flail. One good hit, and I could smash Vlad Menshikov like a bug.

'Won't matter!' he gasped, clawing at his neck. 'Spell will – defeat you anyway. Show us you're – a murderer, Kane!'

I glanced at Zia's terrified face, and I hesitated too long. The white vines encircled my arms. The combat avatar crumpled to its knees, and I dropped Menshikov.

Pain wracked my body. My blood turned cold. The avatar's limbs shrank, the hawk's head slowly changing into the head of a serpent. I could feel my heart slowing, my vision darkening. The taste of venom filled my mouth.

Zia cried out. 'Stop it! This is too much!'

'On the contrary,' Menshikov said, rubbing his chafed neck. 'He deserves worse. Chief Lector, you saw how this boy threatened you. He wants the pharaoh's throne. He must be destroyed.'

Zia tried to run to me, but Desjardins held her back.

'Discontinue the spell, Vladimir,' he said. 'The boy can be contained in more humane ways.'

'Humane, my lord? He's barely human!'

The two magicians locked eyes. I don't know what would've happened – but just then a portal opened under Bes's cage.

I've seen plenty of portals, but none like this. The whirlpool opened level with the ground, sucking down a trampoline-size area of red sand, dead fish, old lumber, pottery shards and one glowing fluorescent cage containing a dwarf god. As the cage entered the vortex, the bars broke into splinters of light. Bes unfroze, found himself halfway submerged in sand and did some creative cursing. Then my sister and Walt shot straight up out of the portal, suspended horizontally, as if they were running towards the sky. When gravity took over, they waved their arms and fell back into the sand. They might've been pulled under except Bes grabbed them both and managed to haul them out of the whirlpool.

Bes dumped them on firm ground. Then he turned to Vlad Menshikov, planted his feet and ripped off his Hawaiian shirt and shorts like they were made of tissue. His eyes blazed with anger. His Speedo was embroidered with the words *Dwarf Pride*, which was something I really didn't need to see.

Menshikov only had time to say, 'How –'

'BOO!' yelled Bes.

The sound was like the blast of an H-bomb – or a U-bomb, for *Ugly*. The ground shook. The river rippled. My avatar collapsed, and Menshikov's spell dissolved with it – the venom taste in my mouth subsiding, the pressure lifting so I could breathe again. Sadie and Walt were already on the ground. Zia had quickly backed away. But Menshikov and Desjardins got a full blast of ugly right in their faces.

Their expressions turned to astonishment, and they disintegrated on the spot.

After a moment of shock, Zia gasped. 'You killed them!'

'Nah.' Bes dusted off his hands. 'Just scared 'em back home. They may be unconscious for a few hours while their brains try to process my magnificent physique, but they'll live. More important –' He scowled at Sadie and Walt. 'You two had the nerve to anchor a portal on *me*? Do I look like a relic?'

Sadie and Walt wisely didn't answer that. They got to their feet, brushing off the sand.

'It wasn't our idea!' Sadie protested. 'Ptah sent us here to help you.'

'Ptah?' I said. 'Ptah, the *god?*'

'No, Ptah the date farmer. I'll tell you later.'

'What's wrong with your hair?' I asked. 'It looks like a camel licked it.'

'Shut up.' Then she noticed Zia. 'My god, is that her? The real Zia?'

Zia stumbled back, trying to light up her staff. 'Get away!' The fire spluttered weakly.

'We're not going to hurt you,' Sadie promised.

Zia's legs shook. Her hands trembled. Then she did the only logical thing for someone who'd been through her kind of day after a three-month coma. Her eyes rolled back in her head, and she passed out.

Bes grunted. 'Strong girl. She held up under a full frontal 'BOO!' Still...we'd better pick her up and get out of here. Desjardins won't stay gone forever.'

'Sadie,' I said, 'did you get the scroll?'

She pulled all three scrolls out of her bag. Part of me was relieved. Part of me was frightened.

'We need to get to the Great Pyramid,' she said. 'Please tell me you have a car.'

Not only did we have a car, we had a whole bunch of Bedouins. We returned their truck well after dark, but the Bedouins seemed happy to see us, even though we'd brought three extra people, one of them unconscious. Somehow Bes made a deal with them to drive us to Cairo. After a few minutes' talking in their tent, he emerged wearing new robes. The Bedouins came out ripping the remains of his Hawaiian shirt into strips, which they carefully wrapped round their arms, their radio antenna and their rearview mirror as good-luck talismans.

We piled into the back of the truck. It was too crowded and noisy to talk much as we drove to Cairo. Bes told us to get some sleep while he kept watch. He promised he'd be nice to Zia if she woke up.

Sadie and Walt went straight to sleep, but I stared at the stars for a while. I was painfully aware of Zia – the *real* Zia – sleeping fitfully right next to me, and the magic weapons of Ra, the crook and the flail, now stashed in my bag. My body was still buzzing from the battle. Menshikov's spell had been broken, but I could still hear his voice in my head, trying to turn me into a cold-blooded reptile – sort of like him.

Finally, I managed to close my eyes. Without magical protection, my *ba* drifted as soon as I fell asleep.

I found myself in the Hall of Ages, in front of the pharaoh's throne. Between the columns on either side, holographic images shimmered. Just as Sadie had described, the edge of the magic curtain was turning from red to deep purple – indicating a new age. The images in purple were hard to make out, but I thought I saw two figures grappling in front of a burning chair.

'Yes,' said the voice of Horus. 'The battle approaches.'

He appeared in a ripple of light, standing on the steps

of the dais where the Chief Lector usually sat. He was in human form, a muscular young man with bronze skin and a shaved head. Jewels glinted on his leather battle armour, and his *khopesh* hung at his side. His eyes gleamed – one gold, one silver.

'How did you get here?' I asked. 'Isn't this place shielded against gods?'

'I'm not here, Carter. *You* are. But we were once joined. I am an echo in your mind – the part of Horus that never left you.'

'I don't understand.'

'Just listen. Your situation has changed. You stand on the threshold of greatness.'

He pointed at my chest. I looked down and realized I wasn't in my usual *ba* form. Instead of a bird, I was a human, dressed like Horus in Egyptian armour. In my hands were the crook and flail.

'These aren't mine,' I said. 'They were buried with Zia.'

'They could be yours,' Horus said. 'They are the symbols of the pharaoh – like staff and wand, only a hundred times more powerful. Even with no practice, you were able to channel their power. Imagine what we could do together.' He gestured to the empty throne. 'You could unite the House of Life as its leader. We could crush our enemies.'

I won't deny: part of me felt a thrill. Months ago, the idea of being a leader scared me to death. Now things had changed. My own understanding of magic had grown. I'd spent three months teaching and turning our initiates into a team. I understood the threat we were facing more clearly, and I was beginning to understand how to channel the power of Horus without being overwhelmed. What if Horus was right, and I could lead the gods and magicians against Apophis? I liked the idea of smashing our enemies, getting back at the forces of Chaos that had turned our lives upside down.

Then I remembered the way Zia had looked at me when I was about to kill Vlad Menshikov – like *I* was the monster. I remembered what Desjardins had said about the bad old days when magician fought magician. If Horus was an echo in my mind, maybe I was being affected by his desire to rule. I knew Horus well now. He was a good guy in many ways – brave, honourable, righteous. But he was also ambitious, greedy, jealous and single-minded when it came to his goals. And his biggest desire was to rule the gods.

'The crook and flail belong to Ra,' I said. 'We have to wake him.'

Horus tilted his head. 'Even though Apophis wants that to happen? Even though Ra is weak and old? I warned you about the divisions between the gods. You saw how Nekhbet and Babi tried to take matters into their own hands. The strife will only get worse. Chaos feeds on weak leaders, divided loyalties. That's what Vladimir Menshikov is after.'

The Hall of Ages trembled. Along either wall, the curtain of purple light expanded. As the holographic scene widened, I could tell that the chair was a fiery throne, like the one Sadie had described in her vision of Ra's boat. Two shadowy figures were locked in combat, grappling like wrestlers, but I couldn't tell if they were trying to push each other *into* the chair, or trying to keep each other out of it.

'Did Menshikov really try to destroy the Book of Ra?' I asked.

Horus's silver eye glinted. It always seemed a little brighter than his golden one, which made me feel disoriented, like the whole world was listing to one side. 'Like most things Menshikov says, it was a *partial* truth. He once believed as you do. He thought he could bring back Ra and restore Ma'at. He imagined himself as the high priest of a glorious new temple, even more powerful than his ancestors. In his pride, he thought he could reconstruct the Book of Ra from the one scroll in his possession. He was wrong. Ra had taken great pains not to be wakened. The curses on the scroll burned Menshikov's eyes. Sun fire seared his throat because he dared to read the words of the spell. After that, Menshikov turned bitter. At first he plotted to destroy the Book of Ra, but he did not have the power. Then he hit upon a new plan. He would awaken Ra, but for revenge. That's what he's been waiting for, all these years. That's why he wants you to collect the scrolls and reconstruct the Book of Ra. Menshikov wants to see the old god swallowed by Apophis. He wants to see the world plunged into darkness and chaos. He is quite insane.'

'Oh.'

[Great response, I know. But what do you say to a story like that?]

On the dais next to Horus, the empty throne of the pharaoh seemed to undulate in the purple light. That chair had always intimidated me. Long ago, the pharaoh had been the most powerful ruler in the world. He had controlled an empire that lasted twenty times longer than my own country, the US, had existed. How could I be worthy of sitting there?

'You can do it, Carter,' Horus urged. 'You can take control. Why take the risk of summoning Ra? Your sister will have to read the Book, you know. You saw what happened to Menshikov when just one scroll backfired. Can you imagine if three times that much power is unleashed on your sister?'

My mouth went dry. Bad enough I'd let Sadie go off to find the last scroll without me. How could I let her take a risk that might scar her like Vlad the Inhaler, or worse?

'You see the truth now,' Horus said. 'Claim the crook and flail for yourself. Take the throne. Together, we can defeat Apophis. We can return to Brooklyn and protect your friends and your home.'

Home. That sounded so tempting. And our friends were in terrible danger. I'd seen first-hand what Vlad Menshikov could do. I imagined little Felix or timid Cleo trying to fight against that kind of magic. I imagined Menshikov turning our young initiates into helpless snakes. I wasn't even sure Amos could stand against him. With the weapons of Ra, I could protect Brooklyn House.

Then I looked at the purple images flickering against the wall – two figures fighting before the fiery throne. That was our future. The key to success wasn't me, or even Horus – it was Ra, the original king of Egyptian gods. Next to the fiery throne of Ra, the pharaoh's seat seemed about as important as a La-Z-Boy recliner.

'We're not enough,' I told Horus. 'We need Ra.'

The god fixed me with his gold and silver eyes like I was

a small bit of prey miles below him, and he was considering whether or not I was worth diving for.

'You do not understand the threat,' he decided. 'Stay, Carter. And listen to your enemies plan your death.'

Horus disappeared.

I heard footsteps in the shadows behind the throne, then familiar raspy breathing. I hoped my *ba* was invisible. Vladimir Menshikov stepped into the light, half carrying his boss, Desjardins.

'Almost there, my lord,' Menshikov said.

The Russian looked well rested in a new white suit. The only sign of our recent fight was the bandage on his neck from where I'd crooked him. Desjardins, however, looked as if he'd aged a decade in a few hours. He stumbled along, leaning on Menshikov. His face was gaunt. His hair had turned stark white, and I didn't think it was all because he had seen Bes in a Speedo.

Menshikov tried to ease him onto the pharaoh's throne, but Desjardins protested. 'Never, Vladimir. The step. The step.'

'But surely, lord, in your condition –'

'Never!' Desjardins settled on the steps at the foot of the throne. I couldn't believe how much worse he looked.

'Ma'at is failing.' Desjardins held out his hand. A weak cloud of hieroglyphs drifted from his fingertips into the air. 'The power of Ma'at once sustained me, Vladimir. Now it seems to be sapping my life force. It is all I can do...' His voice trailed off.

'Fear not, my lord,' Menshikov said. 'Once the Kanes are dealt with, all will be well.'

'Will it?' Desjardins looked up, and for a moment his eyes flared with anger like they used to. 'Don't you ever have doubts, Vladimir?'

'No, my lord,' said the Russian. 'I have given my life to fighting the gods. I will continue to do so. If I may be so bold, Chief Lector, you should not have allowed Amos Kane into your presence. His words are like poison.'

Desjardins caught a hieroglyph from the air and studied it as it revolved in his palm. I didn't recognize the symbol, but it reminded me of a traffic light with a stick figure guy standing next to it.

'*Menhed*,' Desjardins said. 'The scribe's palette.'

I looked at the dimly flickering symbol, and I could see the resemblance to the writing tools in my supply bag. The rectangle was the palette, with places for black and red ink. The stick figure on one side was a writing stylus, attached with a string.

'Yes, my lord,' Menshikov said. 'How ... interesting.'

'It was my grandfather's favourite symbol,' Desjardins mused. 'Jean-François Champollion, you know. He broke the code of hieroglyphics using the Rosetta Stone – the first man outside the House of Life to do so.'

'Indeed, my lord. I have heard the story.' *A thousand times*, his expression seemed to say.

'He rose from nothing to become a great scientist,'

Desjardins continued, '*and* a great magician – respected by mortals and magicians alike.'

Menshikov smiled as if he were humouring a child who was becoming annoying. 'And now you are Chief Lector. He would be proud.'

'Would he?' Desjardins wondered. 'When Iskandar accepted my family into the House of Life, he said he welcomed the new blood and new ideas. He hoped we would reinvigorate the House. Yet what did we contribute? We changed nothing. We questioned nothing. The House has grown weak. We have fewer initiates every year.'

'Ah, my lord.' Menshikov bared his teeth. 'Let me show you we are *not* weak. Your attack force is assembled.'

He clapped his hands. At the far end of the hall, the huge bronze doors opened. At first I couldn't believe my eyes, but as the small army marched towards us I got more and more alarmed.

The dozen magicians were the *least* scary part of the group. They were mostly older men and women in traditional linen robes. Many had kohl round their eyes and hieroglyphic tattoos on their hands and faces. Some wore more amulets than Walt. The men had shaved heads; the women wore their hair short or tied back in ponytails. All of them had grim expressions, like an angry mob of peasants out to burn the Frankenstein monster, except instead of pitchforks they were armed with staffs and wands. Several had swords, too.

Marching on either side of them were demons – about twenty in all. I'd fought demons before, but something about these was different. They moved with more confidence, as if they shared a sense of purpose. They radiated evil so strongly my *ba* felt like it was getting a suntan. Their skin was every colour from green to black to violet. Some were dressed in armour, some in animal hides, some in flannel pyjamas. One had a chain saw for a head. Another had a guillotine. A third had a foot sprouting between his shoulders.

Even scarier than the demons were the winged snakes. Yeah, I know, you're thinking: 'Not more snakes!' Believe me, after getting bit by the *tjesu heru* in St Petersburg, I wasn't happy to see them either. These weren't three-headed, and they weren't any bigger than normal snakes, but just looking at them gave me the creeps. Imagine a cobra with the wings of an eagle. Now imagine it zipping through the air, exhaling long jets of fire like a flamethrower. Half a dozen of these monsters circled the attack squad, darting in and out and spitting fire. It was a miracle none of the magicians got torched.

As the group approached, Desjardins struggled to his feet. The magicians and demons knelt before him. One of the winged snakes flew in front of the Chief Lector, and Desjardins snatched it out of the air with surprising speed. The snake wriggled in his fist, but didn't try to strike.

'A *uraeus*?' Desjardins asked. 'This is dangerous, Vladimir. These are creatures of Ra.'

Menshikov inclined his head. 'They once served the temple of Amun-Ra, Chief Lector, but do not worry. Because of my ancestry, I can control them. I thought it fitting, using creatures of the sun god to destroy those who would wake him.'

Desjardins released the snake, which spouted fire and flew away.

'And the demons?' Desjardins asked. 'Since when do we use creatures of Chaos?'

'They are well controlled, my lord.' Menshikov's voice sounded strained, as if he were growing tired of humouring his boss. 'These mages know the proper binding spells. I handpicked them from nomes around the world. They have great skill.'

The Chief Lector focused on an Asian man in blue robes. 'Kwai, isn't it?'

The man nodded.

'As I recall,' Desjardins said, 'you were exiled to the Three-hundredth Nome in North Korea for murdering a fellow magician. And you, Sarah Jacobi –' he pointed to a woman with white robes and spiky black hair – 'you were sent to Antarctica for causing the tsunami in the Indian Ocean.'

Menshikov cleared his throat. 'My lord, many of these magicians have had issues in the past, but –'

'They are ruthless murderers and thieves,' Desjardins said. 'The worst of our House.'

'But they are anxious to prove their loyalty,' Menshikov assured him. 'They are happy to do it!'

He grinned at his minions, as if encouraging them to look happy. None of them did.

'Besides, my lord,' Menshikov continued quickly, 'if you want Brooklyn House destroyed, we must be ruthless. It is for the good of Ma'at.'

Desjardins frowned. 'And you, Vladimir? Will you lead them?'

'No, my lord. I have full confidence that this, ah, fine group can deal with Brooklyn on their own. They will attack at sunset. As for me, I will follow the Kanes into the Duat and deal with them personally. You, my lord, should stay here and rest. I will send a scryer to your quarters so you may observe our progress.'

'"Stay here,"' Desjardins quoted bitterly. '"And observe."'

Menshikov bowed. 'We will save the House of Life. I swear it. The Kanes will be destroyed, the gods put back into exile. Ma'at will be restored.'

I hoped Desjardins would come to his senses and call off the attack. Instead, his shoulders slumped. He turned his back on Menshikov and stared at the empty throne of the pharaoh.

'Go,' he said wearily. 'Get those creatures out of my sight.'

Menshikov smiled. 'My lord.'

He turned and marched down the Hall of Ages with his personal army in tow.

Once they were gone, Desjardins held up his hand. An orb of light fluttered from the ceiling and rested on his palm.

'Bring me the Book of Overcoming Apophis,' Desjardins told the light. 'I must consult it.'

The magic orb dipped as if bowing, then raced off.

Desjardins turned towards the purple curtain of light – the image of two figures fighting over a throne of fire.

'I will "observe", Vladimir,' he murmured to himself. 'But I will not "stay and rest".'

The scene faded, and my *ba* returned to my body.

18. Gambling on Doomsday Eve

FOR THE SECOND TIME THAT WEEK, I woke on a sofa in a hotel room with no idea how I'd got there.

The room wasn't nearly as nice as the Four Seasons Alexandria. The walls were cracked plaster. Exposed beams sagged along the ceiling. A portable fan hummed on the coffee table, but the air was as hot as a blast furnace. Afternoon light streamed through the open windows. From below came the sounds of cars honking and merchants hawking their wares in Arabic. The breeze smelled of exhaust, animal manure and apple *sisha* – the fruity molasses scent of water-pipe smoke. In other words, I knew we must be in Cairo.

At the window, Sadie, Bes, Walt and Zia were sitting round a table, playing a board game like old friends. The scene was so bizarre that I thought I must still be dreaming.

Then Sadie noticed I was awake. 'Well, well. Next time you take an extended *ba* trip, Carter, do let us know in advance. It's not fun carrying you up three flights of stairs.'

I rubbed my throbbing head. 'How long was I out?'

'Longer than me,' Zia said.

She looked amazing – calm and rested. Her freshly washed hair was swept behind her ears, and she wore a new white sleeveless dress that made her bronze skin glow.

I guess I was staring at her pretty hard, because she dropped her gaze. Her throat turned red.

'It's three in the afternoon,' she said. 'I've been up since ten this morning.'

'You look –'

'Better?' She raised her eyebrows, like she was challenging me to deny it. 'You missed the excitement. I tried to fight. I tried to escape. This is our third hotel room.'

'The first one caught fire,' Bes said.

'The second one exploded,' Walt said.

'I *said* I was sorry.' Zia frowned. 'At any rate, your sister finally calmed me down.'

'Which took several hours,' Sadie said, 'and all my diplomatic skill.'

'You have diplomatic skill?' I asked.

Sadie rolled her eyes. 'As if you'd notice, Carter!'

'Your sister is quite intelligent,' Zia said. 'She convinced me to reserve judgement on your plans until you woke up and we could talk. She's quite persuasive.'

'Thank you,' Sadie said smugly.

I stared at them both, and a feeling of terror set in. 'You're getting along? You *can't* get along! You and Sadie can't stand each other.'

'That was a *shabti*, Carter,' Zia said, though her neck was still bright red. 'I find Sadie...admirable.'

'You see?' Sadie said. 'I'm admirable!'

'This is a nightmare.' I sat up and the blankets fell away. I looked down and found I was wearing Pokémon pyjamas.

'Sadie,' I said, 'I'm going to kill you.'

She batted her eyes innocently. 'But the street merchant gave us a very good deal on those. Walt said they would fit you.'

Walt raised his hands. 'Don't blame me, man. I tried to stick up for you.'

Bes snorted, then did a pretty good imitation of Walt's voice: '"At least get the extra-large ones with Pikachu." Carter, your stuff's in the bathroom. Now, are we playing senet, or not?'

I stumbled into the bathroom and was relieved to find a set of normal clothes waiting for me – fresh underwear, jeans and a T-shirt that did not feature Pikachu. The shower made a sound like a dying elephant when I tried to turn it on, but I managed to run some rusty-smelling water in the sink and wash up as best I could.

When I came out again, I didn't exactly feel good as new, but at least I didn't smell like dead fish and goat meat.

My four companions were still playing senet. I'd heard of the game – supposedly one of the oldest in the world – but I'd never seen it played. The board was a rectangle with blue-and-white-chequered squares, three rows of ten spaces each. The game pieces were white and blue circles. Instead of dice, you threw four strips of ivory like Popsicle sticks, blank on one side and marked with hieroglyphs on the other.

'I thought the rules of this game were lost,' I said.

Bes raised an eyebrow. 'Maybe to you mortals. The gods never forgot.'

'It's quite easy,' Sadie said. 'You make an S around the board. First team to get all their pieces to the end wins.'

'Ha!' Bes said. 'There's much more to it than that. It takes years to master.'

'Is that so, dwarf god?' Zia tossed the four sticks, and all of them came up marked. 'Master that!'

Sadie and Zia gave each other a high five. Apparently, they were a team. Sadie moved a blue piece and bumped a white piece back to the start.

'Walt,' Bes grumbled, 'I told you not to move that piece!'

'It isn't my fault!'

Sadie smiled at me. 'It's girls versus boys. We're playing for Vlad Menshikov's sunglasses.'

She held up the broken white shades that Set had given her in St Petersburg.

'The world is about to end,' I said, 'and you're gambling over sunglasses?'

'Hey, man,' Walt said. 'We're totally multitasking. We've been talking for, like, six hours, but we had to wait for you to wake up to make any decisions, right?'

'Besides,' Sadie said, 'Bes assures us that you cannot play senet without gambling. It would shake the foundations of Ma'at.'

'That's true,' said the dwarf. 'Walt, roll, already.'

Walt threw the sticks and three came up blank.

Bes cursed. 'We need a two to move out of the House of Re-Atoum, kid. Did I not explain that?'

'Sorry!'

I wasn't sure what else to do, so I pulled up a chair.

The view out of the window was better than I'd realized. About a mile away, the Pyramids of Giza gleamed red in the afternoon light. We must've been in the south-west outskirts of the city – near El Mansoria. I'd been through this neighbourhood a dozen times with my dad on our way to various dig sites, but it was still disorienting to see the pyramids so close.

I had a million questions. I needed to tell my friends about my *ba* vision. But before I could get up the nerve Sadie launched into a long explanation of what they'd been up to while I was unconscious. Mostly she concentrated on how funny I looked when I slept, and the various whimpering noises I'd made as they pulled me out of the first two burning hotel rooms. She described the excellent fresh-baked flat bread, falafel and spiced beef they'd had for lunch ('Oh, sorry, we didn't save you any.') and the great deals they'd got shopping in the *souk*, the local open-air market.

'You went shopping?' I said.

'Well, of course,' she said. 'We can't do anything until sunset, anyway. Bes said so.'

'What do you mean?'

Bes tossed the sticks and moved one of his pieces to the home space. 'The equinox, kid. We're close enough now – all the portals in the world will shut down except for two times: sunset and sunrise, when night and day are perfectly balanced.'

'At any rate,' Sadie said, 'if we want to find Ra, we'll have to follow his journey, which means going into the Duat at sunset and coming back out at sunrise.'

'How do you know that?' I asked.

She pulled a scroll from her bag – a cylinder of papyrus much thicker than the ones we'd collected. The edges glowed like fire.

'The Book of Ra,' she said. 'I put it together. You may thank me now.'

My head started to spin. I remembered what Horus had said in my vision about the scroll burning Menshikov's face. 'You mean you read it without... without any trouble?'

She shrugged. 'Just the introduction: warnings, instructions, that sort of thing. I won't read the actual spell until we find Ra, but I know where we're going.'

'If we decide to go,' I said.

That got everyone's attention.

'*If?*' Zia asked. She was so close it was painful, but I could feel the distance she was putting between us: leaning away from me, tensing her shoulders, warning me to respect her space. 'Sadie told me you were quite determined.'

'I was,' I said, 'until I learned what Menshikov is planning.'

I told them what I'd seen in my vision – about Menshikov's strike force heading to Brooklyn at sunset and his plans to track us personally through the Duat. I explained what Horus said about the dangers of waking Ra, and how I could use the crook and flail instead to fight Apophis.

'But those symbols are sacred to Ra,' Zia said.

'They belong to any pharaoh who is strong enough to wield them,' I said. 'If we don't help Amos in Brooklyn –'

'Your uncle and all your friends will be destroyed,' Bes said. 'From what you've described, Menshikov has put together a nasty little army. *Uraei* – the flaming snakes – they're *very* bad news. Even if Bast gets back in time to help –'

'We need to let Amos know,' Walt said. 'At least warn him.'

'You have a scrying bowl?' I asked.

'Better.' He pulled out a cell phone. 'What do I tell him? Are we going back?'

I wavered. How could I leave Amos and my friends alone against an evil army? Part of me was itching to take up the pharaoh's weapons and smash our enemies. Horus's voice was still inside me, urging me to take charge.

'Carter, you can't go to Brooklyn.' Zia met my eyes, and I realized the fear and panic hadn't left her. She was holding those feelings back, but they were still bubbling under the surface. 'What I saw at Red Sands...that disturbed me too much.'

I felt like she'd just stomped on my heart. 'Look, I'm sorry about the avatar thing, the crook and flail. I didn't mean to freak you out, but –'

'Carter, *you* didn't disturb me. Vlad Menshikov did.'

'Oh...Right.'

She took a shaky breath. 'I never trusted that man. When I graduated from initiate training, Menshikov requested I be assigned to his nome. Thankfully, Iskandar declined.'

'So...why can't I go to Brooklyn?'

Zia examined the senet board as if it were a war map. 'I believe you're telling the truth. Menshikov is a traitor. What you described in your vision... I think Desjardins is being affected by evil magic. It's not Ma'at's failing that's draining his life force.'

'It's Menshikov,' Sadie guessed.

'I believe so....' Zia's voice became hoarse. 'And I believe my old mentor, Iskandar, *was* trying to protect me when he put me into that tomb. It was not a mistake that he let me hear the voice of Apophis in my dreams. It was some sort of warning – one last lesson. He hid the crook and flail with me for a reason. Perhaps he knew you would find me. At any rate, Menshikov must be stopped.'

'But you just said I couldn't go to Brooklyn,' I protested.

'I meant that you can't abandon your quest. I think Iskandar foresaw this path. He believed the gods must unite with the House of Life, and I trust his judgement. You *have* to awaken Ra.'

Hearing Zia say it, I felt for the first time like our quest was real. And crucial. And very, very crazy. But I also felt a little spark of hope. Maybe she didn't hate me completely.

Sadie picked up the senet sticks. 'Well, that's sorted, then. At sunset, we'll open a portal at the top of the Great Pyramid. We'll follow the sun boat's old course down the River of Night, find Ra, wake him and bring him out again at dawn. And possibly find somewhere for dinner along the way, because I'm hungry again.'

'It'll be dangerous,' Bes said. 'Reckless. Probably fatal.'

'So, an average day for us,' I summed up.

Walt frowned, still holding his phone. 'Then what should I tell Amos? He's on his own?'

'Not quite,' Zia said. 'I'll go to Brooklyn.'

I almost choked. '*You?*'

Zia gave me a cross look. 'I *am* good at magic, Carter.'

'That's not what I meant. It's just –'

'I want to speak with Amos myself,' she said. 'When the House of Life appears, perhaps I can intervene, stall for time. I have some influence with other magicians…at least I did when Iskandar was alive. Some of them might listen to reason, especially if Menshikov isn't there egging them on.'

I thought about the angry mob I'd seen in my vision. *Reasonable* wasn't the first word that came to mind.

Apparently Walt was thinking the same thing.

'If you teleport in at sunset,' he said, 'you'll arrive at the same time as the attackers. It's going to be chaos, not much time for talking. What if you have to fight?'

'Let's hope,' Zia said, 'it doesn't come to that.'

Not a very reassuring answer, but Walt nodded. 'I'll go with you.'

Sadie dropped her senet sticks on the floor. 'What? Walt, no! In your condition –'

She clamped her mouth shut, too late.

'What condition?' I asked.

If Walt had had an Evil Eye spell, I think he would've used it on my sister just then.

'My family history,' he said. 'Something I told Sadie…*in confidence.*'

He didn't sound happy about it, but he explained the curse

on his family, the bloodline of Akhenaton and what it meant for him.

I just sat there, stunned. Walt's secretive behaviour, his talks with Jaz, his moodiness – all of it made sense now. My own problems suddenly seemed a lot less significant.

'Oh, man,' I mumbled. 'Walt –'

'Look, Carter, whatever you're going to say, I appreciate the sentiment. But I'm through with sympathy. I've been living with this disease for years. I don't want people pitying me or treating me as though I'm special. I want to help you guys. I'll take Zia back to Brooklyn. That way, Amos will know she comes in peace. We'll try to stall the attack, hold them off until sunrise so you can come back with Ra. Besides…' He shrugged. 'If you fail, and we don't stop Apophis, we're all going to die tomorrow anyway.'

'That's looking on the bright side,' I said. Then something occurred to me: a thought so jarring it was like a tiny nuclear reaction in my head. 'Hold up. Menshikov said he was descended from the priests of Amun-Ra.'

Bes snorted disdainfully. 'Hated those guys. They were *so* full of themselves. But what does that have to do with anything?'

'Weren't those the same priests that fought Akhenaton and cursed Walt's ancestors?' I asked. 'What if Menshikov has the secret of the curse? What if he could cure –'

'Stop.' The anger in Walt's voice took me by surprise. His hands were shaking. 'Carter, I've come to terms with my fate. I *won't* get my hopes up for nothing. Menshikov is the enemy. Even if he could help, he wouldn't. If you cross paths with him, don't try to make any deals. Don't try to reason with him. Do what you need to. Take him down.'

I glanced at Sadie. Her eyes were gleaming, like I'd finally done something right.

'Okay, Walt,' I said. 'I won't mention it again.'

But Sadie and I had a very different silent conversation. For once, we were in total agreement. We were going to visit the Duat. And while we were there we'd turn the tables on Vlad Menshikov. We'd find him, beat the crud out of him and force him to tell us how to cure Walt. Suddenly, I felt a whole lot better about this quest.

'So we'll leave at sunset,' Zia said. 'Walt and I for Brooklyn. You and Sadie for the Duat. It's settled.'

'Except for one thing.' Bes glared at the senet sticks Sadie had dropped on the floor. 'You did *not* roll that. It's impossible!'

Sadie looked down. A grin spread across her face. She'd accidentally rolled a three, just what she needed to win.

She moved her last piece home, then picked up Menshikov's white glasses and tried them on. They looked creepy on her. I couldn't help thinking about Menshikov's burnt voice and his scarred eyes, and what might happen to my sister if she tried to read the Book of Ra.

'Impossible is my speciality,' she said. 'Come on, brother, dear. Let's get ready for the Great Pyramid.'

If you ever visit the pyramids, here's a tip: the best place to see them is from far away, like the horizon. The closer you get, the more disappointed you'll be.

That may sound harsh, but first of all, up close, the pyramids are going to seem smaller than you thought. Everybody who sees them says that. Sure, they were the tallest structures on the earth for thousands of years, but compared to modern buildings they don't seem so impressive. They've been stripped of the white casing stones and golden capstones that made them really cool in ancient times. They're still beautiful, especially when they're lit up at sunset, but you can appreciate them better from far away without getting caught in the tourist scene.

That's the second thing: the mobs of tourists and vendors. I don't care where you go on vacation: Times Square, Piccadilly Circus or the Roman Coliseum. It's always the same, with vendors selling cheap T-shirts and trinkets, and hordes of sweating tourists complaining and shuffling around trying to take pictures. The pyramids are no different, except the crowds are bigger and the vendors are really, really pushy. They know a lot of English words, but 'no' isn't one of them.

As we pressed through the crowds, the vendors tried to sell us three camel rides, a dozen T-shirts, more amulets than Walt was wearing (*Special price! Good magic!*) and eleven genuine mummy fingers, which I figured were probably made in China.

I asked Bes if he could scare away the mob, but he just laughed. 'Not worth it, kid. Tourists have been here almost as long as the pyramids. I'll make sure they don't notice us. Let's just get to the top.'

Security guards patrolled the base of the Great Pyramid, but no one tried to stop us. Maybe Bes made us invisible somehow, or maybe the guards just chose to ignore us because we were with the dwarf god. Either way, I soon found out why climbing the pyramids wasn't allowed: it's hard and dangerous. The

Great Pyramid is about four hundred and fifty feet tall. The stone sides were never meant for climbing. As we ascended, I almost fell twice. Walt twisted his ankle. Some of the blocks were loose and crumbling. Some of the 'steps' were five feet tall, and we had to hoist one another up. Finally, after twenty minutes of sweaty, difficult work, we reached the top. The smog over Cairo made everything to the east a big fuzzy smudge, but to the west we had a good view of the sun going down on the horizon, turning the desert crimson.

I tried to imagine what the view would've looked like from here roughly five thousand years ago, when the pyramid was newly built. Had the pharaoh Khufu stood up here at the top of his own tomb and admired his empire? Probably not. He'd probably been too smart to make that climb.

'Right.' Sadie plopped her bag on the nearest block of limestone. 'Bes, keep an eye out. Walt, help me with the portal, will you?'

Zia touched my arm, which made me jump.

'Can we talk?' she asked.

She climbed a little way down the pyramid. My pulse was racing, but I managed to follow without tripping and looking like an idiot.

Zia stared out over the desert. Her face was flushed in the light of the sunset. 'Carter, don't misunderstand. I appreciate you waking me. I know your heart was in the right place.'

My heart didn't feel in the right place. It felt like it was stuck in my oesophagus. 'But . . . ?' I asked.

She hugged her arms. 'I need time. This is very strange for me. Maybe we can be . . . closer some day, but for now –'

'You need time,' I said, my voice ragged. 'Assuming we don't all die tonight.'

Her eyes were luminous gold. I wondered if that was the last colour a bug saw when it was trapped in amber – and if the bug thought, *Wow, that's beautiful*, right before it was frozen forever.

'I'll do my best to protect your home,' she said. 'Promise me, if it comes to a choice, that you'll listen to your own heart, not the will of the gods.'

'I promise,' I said, though I doubted myself. I still heard Horus in my head, urging me to claim the weapons of the pharaoh. I wanted to say more, to tell her how I felt, but all I could get out was, '*Um* . . . yeah.'

Zia managed a dry smile. 'Sadie's right. You are . . . how did she put it? Endearingly clumsy.'

'Awesome. Thanks.'

A light flashed above us, and a portal opened at the tip of the pyramid. Unlike most portals, this wasn't swirling sand. It glowed with purple light – a doorway straight into the Duat.

Sadie turned towards me. 'This one's for us. Coming?'

'Be careful,' Zia said.

'Yeah,' I said. 'I'm not so good at that, but – yeah.'

As I trudged to the top, Sadie pulled Walt close and whispered something in his ear.

He nodded grimly. 'I will.'

Before I could ask what that was about, Sadie looked at Bes. 'Ready?'

'I'll follow you,' Bes promised. 'As soon as I get Walt and

Zia through their portal. I'll meet you on the River of Night, in the Fourth House.'

'The fourth what?' I asked.

'You'll see,' he promised. 'Now, go!'

I took one more look at Zia, wondering if this would be the last time I saw her. Then Sadie and I jumped into the churning purple doorway.

The Duat is a strange place.

[Sadie just called me Captain Obvious – but, hey, it's worth saying.]

The currents of the spirit world interact with your thoughts, pulling you here and there, shaping what you see to fit with what you know. So, even though we had stepped into another level of reality, it looked like the quayside of the River Thames below Gran and Gramps's flat.

'This is rude,' Sadie said.

I understood what she meant. It was hard for her to be back in London after her disastrous birthday trip. Also, last Christmas, we'd started our first journey to Brooklyn here. We'd walked down these steps to the docks with Amos and boarded his magic boat. At the time, I was grieving the loss of my dad, in shock that Gran and Gramps would give us up to an uncle I didn't even remember, and terrified of sailing into the unknown. Now, all those feelings welled up inside me, as sharp and painful as ever.

The river was shrouded with mist. There were no city lights, just an eerie glow in the sky. The skyline of London seemed fluid – buildings shifting around, rising and melting as if they couldn't find a comfortable place to settle.

Below us, the mist drifted away from the docks.

'Sadie,' I said, 'Look.'

At the bottom of the steps, a boat was moored, but it wasn't Amos's. It was the barque of the sun god, just as I'd seen in my vision – a once regal ship with a deckhouse and places for twenty oarsmen – but it was now barely able to stay afloat. The sail was tattered, the oars broken, the rigging covered with cobwebs.

Halfway down the steps, blocking our path, stood Gran and Gramps.

'Them again,' Sadie growled. 'Come on.'

She marched straight down the steps until we stood face to face with the glowing images of our grandparents.

'Shove off,' Sadie told them.

'My dear.' Gran's eyes glittered. 'Is that any way to address your grandmother?'

'Oh, pardon me,' said Sadie. 'This must be the part where I say "My, what big teeth you have." You're not my grandmother, Nekhbet! Now, get out of our way!'

The image of Gran shimmered. Her flowery housecoat turned into a cloak of greasy black feathers. Her face shrivelled into a saggy wrinkled mask, and most of her hair fell out, which put her at a 9.5 on the Ugly meter, right up there with Bes.

'Show more respect, love,' the goddess cooed. 'We're only here to give you a friendly warning. You're about to pass the Point of No Return. If you step on that boat, there will be no turning back – no stopping until you've passed through all Twelve Houses of the Night, or until you die.'

Gramps barked, '*Aghh!*'

He scratched his armpits, which might've meant he was possessed by the baboon god Babi – or not, since this behaviour wasn't too strange for Gramps.

'Listen to Babi,' Nekhbet urged. 'You have no idea what awaits you on the river. You could barely fend off the two of us in London, girl. The armies of Chaos are much worse!'

'She's not alone this time.' I stepped forward with the crook and flail. 'Now, get lost.'

Gramps snarled and backed away.

Nekhbet's eyes narrowed. 'You would wield the pharaoh's weapons?' Her tone held a hint of grudging admiration. 'A bold move, child, but that will not save you.'

'You don't get it,' I said. 'We're saving *you*, too. We're saving *all* of us from Apophis. When we come back with Ra, you're going to help. You're going to follow our orders, and you're going to convince the other gods to do the same.'

'Ridiculous,' Nekhbet hissed.

I raised the crook, and power flowed through me – the power of a king. The crook was the tool of a shepherd. A king leads his people like a shepherd leads his flock. I exerted my will, and the two gods crumpled to their knees.

The images of Nekhbet and Gramps evaporated, revealing the gods' true forms. Nekhbet was a massive vulture with a golden crown on her head and an elaborate jewelled collar round her neck. Her wings were still black and greasy, but they glistened as if she'd been rolling in gold dust. Babi was a giant grey baboon with fiery red eyes, scimitar fangs and arms as thick as tree trunks.

They both glared at me with pure hatred. I knew if I wavered even for a moment, if I let the power of the crook falter, they would tear me apart.

'Swear loyalty,' I commanded. 'When we return with Ra, you will obey him.'

'You'll never succeed,' Nekhbet said.

'Then it won't do any harm to pledge your loyalty,' I said. 'Swear it!'

I raised the war flail, and the gods cringed.

'*Agh*,' Babi muttered.

'We swear,' Nekhbet said. 'But it is an empty promise. You sail to your death.'

I slashed my crook through the air, and the gods vanished into the mist.

Sadie took a deep breath. 'Well done. You sounded confident.'

'A complete act.'

'I know,' she said. 'Now the hard part: finding Ra and waking him up. And having a nice dinner along the way, preferably. Without dying.'

I looked down at the boat. Thoth, the god of knowledge, had once told us that we'd always have the power to summon a boat when we needed one, because we were the blood of the pharaohs. But I'd never thought it would be *this* boat, and in such bad shape. Two kids in a broken-down leaky barge, alone against the forces of Chaos.

'All aboard,' I told Sadie.

19. The Revenge of Bullwinkle the Moose God

I SHOULD MENTION THAT Carter was wearing a skirt.

[Ha! You are *not* grabbing the microphone. It's my turn.]

He neglected to tell you that as soon as we entered the Duat our appearances changed, and we found ourselves wearing Ancient Egyptian clothes.

They looked quite good on me. My white silk gown shimmered. My arms were bedecked with gold rings and bracelets. True, the jewelled neck collar was a bit heavy, like one of those lead aprons you might wear for an X-ray at the dentist's, and my hair was plaited with enough hairspray to petrify a major god. But otherwise I'm sure I looked rather alluring.

Carter, on the other hand, was dressed in a man-skirt – a simple linen wrap, with his crook and flail hanging from a utility-belt sort of thing round his waist. His chest was bare except for a golden neck collar, like mine. His eyes were lined with kohl, and he wore no shoes.

To Ancient Egyptians, I'm sure he would've looked regal and warlike, a fine specimen of manhood. [You see? I managed to say that without laughing.] And I suppose Carter wasn't the worst-looking guy with his shirt off, but that didn't mean I wanted to adventure through the underworld with a brother who was wearing nothing but jewellery and a beach towel.

As we stepped onto the sun god's boat, Carter immediately got a splinter in his foot.

'Why are you barefooted?' I demanded.

'It wasn't *my* idea!' He winced as he plucked a toothpick-size piece of deck from between his toes. 'I guess because ancient warriors fought barefoot. Sandals got too slippery from sweat and blood, and all.'

'And the skirt?'

'Let's just go, all right?'

That proved easier said than done.

The boat drifted away from the docks, then got stuck in a backwater a few metres downstream. We began turning in circles.

'Tiny question,' I said. 'Do you know anything about boats?'

'Nothing,' Carter admitted.

Our tattered sail was about as useful as a ripped tissue. The oars were either broken or trailing uselessly in the water, and they looked quite heavy. I didn't see how the two of us could row a boat meant for a crew of twenty, even *if* the river stayed calm. On our last trip through the Duat, the ride had been more like a roller coaster.

'What about those glowing balls of light?' I asked. 'Like the crew we had on the *Egyptian Queen?*'

'Can you summon some?'

'Right,' I grumbled. 'Throw the hard questions back to me.'

I looked around the boat, hoping to spot a button that read: PUSH HERE FOR GLOWING SAILORS! I saw nothing so helpful. I knew the sun god's barque had once had a crew of lights. I'd seen them in my vision. But how to summon them?

The tent pavilion was empty. The throne of fire was gone. The boat was silent except for water gurgling through the cracks in the hull. The spinning of the ship was starting to make me sick.

Then a horrible feeling crept over me. A dozen tiny voices whispered at the base of my skull: *Isis. Schemer. Poisoner. Traitor.*

I realized my nausea wasn't just from the spiralling current. The entire ship was sending malicious thoughts my way. The boards under my feet, the railing, the oars and rigging – every part of the sun god's barque hated my presence.

'Carter, the boat doesn't like me,' I announced.

'You're saying the boat has good taste?'

'Ha-ha. I mean, it senses Isis. She poisoned Ra and forced him into exile, after all. This boat remembers.'

'Well…apologize, or something.'

'Hullo, boat,' I said, feeling quite foolish. 'Sorry about the poisoning business. But you see – I'm not Isis. I'm Sadie Kane.'

Traitor, the voices whispered.

'I can see why you'd think so,' I admitted. 'I probably have that "Isis magic" smell to me, don't I? But, honestly, I sent Isis packing. She doesn't live here any more. My brother and I are going to bring back Ra.'

The boat shuddered. The dozen little voices fell silent, as if for the first time in their immortal lives they were truly and properly stunned. (Well, they hadn't met *me* yet, had they?)

'That would be good, yes?' I ventured. 'Ra back, just like old times, rolling on the river, and so on? We're here to make things right, but to do that we need to journey through the Houses of the Night. If you could just cooperate –'

A dozen glowing orbs blazed to life. They circled me like an angry swarm of flaming tennis balls, their heat so intense I thought they'd combust my new dress.

'Sadie,' Carter warned. 'They don't look happy.'

And he wonders why I called him Captain Obvious.

I tried to remain calm.

'Behave,' I told the lights sternly. 'This isn't for me. It's for Ra. If you want your pharaoh back, you'll man your stations.'

I thought I'd be roasted like a tandoori chicken, but I stood my ground. Since I was surrounded, I really I had no choice. I exerted my magic and tried to bend the lights to my will – the way I might have done to turn someone into a rat or a lizard.

You will be helpful, I ordered. *You will do your work obediently.*

There was a collective hiss inside my head, which either meant I'd blown a brain gasket, or the lights were relenting.

The crew scattered. They took up their stations, hauling lines, mending the sail, manning the unbroken oars, and guiding the tiller.

The leaky hull groaned as the boat turned its nose downstream.

Carter exhaled. 'Good job. You okay?'

I nodded, but my head felt like it was still spinning in

circles. I wasn't sure if I'd convinced the orbs, or if they were simply biding their time, waiting for revenge. Either way, I wasn't thrilled to have put our fate in their hands.

We sailed into the dark. The cityscape of London melted away. My stomach got that familiar free-fall sensation as we passed deeper into the Duat.

'We're entering the Second House,' I guessed.

Carter grabbed the mast to steady himself. 'You mean the Houses of the Night, like Bes mentioned? What are they, anyway?'

It felt strange to be explaining Egyptian myths to Carter. I thought he might be teasing me, but he seemed genuinely perplexed.

'Something I read in the Book of Ra,' I said. 'Each hour of the night is a "House". We have to pass through the twelve stages of the river, representing twelve hours of the night.'

Carter peered into the darkness ahead of us. 'So if we're in the Second House, you mean an hour has already passed? It didn't feel that long.'

He was right. It didn't. Then again, I had no idea how time flowed in the Duat. One House of the Night might not correspond exactly to one mortal hour in the world above.

Anubis once told me he'd been in the Land of the Dead for five thousand years, but he still felt like a teenager, as if no time had passed.

I shuddered. What if we popped out on the other side of the River of Night and found that several aeons had passed? I'd just turned thirteen. I wasn't ready to be thirteen hundred.

I also wished I hadn't thought of Anubis. I touched the

shen amulet on my necklace. After all that had happened with Walt, the idea of seeing Anubis made me feel strangely guilty, but also a bit excited. Perhaps Anubis would help us on our journey. Perhaps he'd whisk me away to some private spot for a chat as he had last time we'd visited the Duat – a romantic little graveyard, dinner for two at the Coffin Café...

Snap out of it, Sadie, I thought. *Concentrate.*

I pulled the Book of Ra from my bag and scanned the instructions again. I'd read them several times already, but they were cryptic and confusing – much like a maths textbook. The scroll was chock-full of terms like 'first from Chaos', 'breath into clay', 'the night's flock', 'reborn in fire', 'the acres of the sun', 'the kiss of the knife', 'the gambler of light' and 'the last scarab' – most of which made no sense to me.

I gathered that as we passed through the twelve stages of the river, I'd have to read the three sections of the Book of Ra at three separate locations, probably to revive the different aspects of the sun god, and each of three aspects would present us with some sort of challenge. I knew that if I failed – if I so much as stumbled over one word while reading the spells – I would end up worse than Vlad Menshikov. The idea terrified me, but I couldn't dwell on the possibility of failure. I simply had to hope that when the time came the scroll's gibberish would make sense.

The current accelerated. So did the leaking of the boat. Carter demonstrated his combat magic skill by summoning a bucket and bailing out water, while I concentrated on keeping the crew in line. The deeper we sailed into the Duat, the more rebellious the glowing orbs became. They chafed against my will, remembering how much they wanted to incinerate me.

It's unnerving to float down a magic river with voices whispering in your head: *Die, traitor, die*. Every so often I'd get the feeling we were being followed. I'd turn and think I could see a whitish smudge against the black, like the after-image of a flash, but I decided it must be my imagination. Even more unnerving was the darkness ahead – no shoreline, no landmarks, no visibility at all. The crew could've steered us straight into a boulder or the mouth of a monster, and we would've had absolutely no warning. We just kept sailing through the dark empty void.

'Why is it so...nothing?' I murmured.

Carter emptied his bucket. He made an odd sight – a boy dressed as a pharaoh with the royal crook and flail, bailing water from a leaky boat.

'Maybe the Houses of the Night follow human sleep patterns,' he suggested.

'Human what?'

'Sleep patterns. Mom used to tell us about them before bedtime. Remember?'

I didn't. Then again, I'd only been six when our mum died. She'd been a scientist as well as a magician, and had thought nothing of reading us Newton's laws or the periodic table as bedtime stories. Most of it had gone over my head, but I *wanted* to remember. I'd always been irritated that Carter remembered Mum so much better than I did.

'Sleep has different stages,' Carter said. 'Like, the first few hours, the brain is almost in a coma – a really deep sleep with hardly any dreams. Maybe that's why this part of the river is so dark and formless. Then, later in the night, the brain goes through REM – rapid eye movement. That's when dreams happen. The cycles get more rapid and more vivid. Maybe the Houses of the Night follow a pattern like that.'

It seemed a bit far-fetched to me. Then again, Mum had always told us science and magic weren't mutually exclusive. She'd called them two dialects of the same language. Bast had once told us there were millions of different channels and tributaries to the Duat's river. The geography could change with each journey, responding to the traveller's thoughts. If the river was shaped by *all* the sleeping minds in the world, if its course got more vivid and crazy as the night went along, then we were in for a rough ride.

The river eventually narrowed. A shoreline appeared on either side – black volcanic sand sparkling in the lights of our magic crew. The air turned colder. The underside of the boat scraped against rocks and sandbars, which made the leaks worse. Carter gave up on the bucket and pulled wax from his supply bag. Together we tried to plug the leaks, speaking binding spells to hold the boat together. If I'd had any chewing-gum, I would've used that as well.

We didn't pass any signposts – NOW ENTERING THE THIRD HOUSE, SERVICES NEXT EXIT – but we'd clearly entered a different section of the river. Time was slipping away at an alarming rate, and still we hadn't *done* anything.

'Perhaps the first challenge is boredom,' I said. 'When will something happen?'

I should've known better than to say that aloud. Right in

front of us, a shape loomed out of the darkness. A sandalled foot the size of a water bed planted itself on the prow of our ship and stopped us dead in the water.

It wasn't an attractive foot, either. Definitely male. Its toes were splattered with mud, and its toenails were yellow, cracked and overgrown. The leather sandal straps were covered in lichen and barnacles. In short, the foot looked and smelled very much like it had been standing on the same rock in the middle of the river, wearing the same sandal, for several thousand years.

Unfortunately, it was attached to a leg, which was attached to a body. The giant leaned down to look at us.

'You are bored?' his voice boomed, not in an unfriendly way. 'I could kill you, if that would help.'

He wore a kilt like Carter's, except that the giant's skirt could have supplied enough fabric to make ten ship sails. His body was humanoid and muscular, covered with man-fur – the sort of gross body hair that makes me want to start a charity waxing foundation for overly fuzzy men. He had the head of a ram: a white snout with a brass ring in his nose and long curly horns hung with dozens of bronze bells. His eyes were set far apart, with luminous red irises and vertical slits for pupils. I suppose that all sounds rather frightening, but the ram man didn't strike me as devilish. In fact he looked quite familiar, for some reason. He seemed more melancholy than threatening, as if he'd been standing on his little rock island in the middle of the river for so long he'd forgotten why he was there.

[Carter asks when I became a ram whisperer. Do shut up, Carter.]

I honestly felt sorry for the ram man. His eyes were full of loneliness. I couldn't believe he would hurt us – until he drew from his belt two very large knives with curly blades like his horns.

'You're silent,' he noted. 'Is that a yes for the killing?'

'No, thanks!' I said, trying to sound grateful for the offer. 'One word and one question, please. The word is *pedicure*. The question is: who are you?'

'Ahhh-ha-ha-ha,' he said, bleating like a sheep. 'If you knew my name, we wouldn't need introductions, and I could let you pass. Unfortunately, no one ever knows my name. A shame, too. I see you've found the Book of Ra. You've revived his crew and managed to sail his boat to the gates of the Fourth House. No one's ever got this far before. I'm terribly sorry I have to slice you to pieces.'

He hefted his knives, one in each hand. Our glowing orbs swarmed in a frenzy, whispering, *Yes! Slice her! Yes!*

'Just a mo,' I called up to the giant. 'If we name you, we can pass?'

'Naturally.' He sighed. 'But no one ever can.'

I glanced at Carter. This wasn't the first time we'd been stopped on the River of Night and challenged to name a guardian on pain of death. Apparently, it was quite a common experience for Egyptian souls and magicians passing through the Duat. But I couldn't believe we'd get such an easy test. I was sure now that I recognized the ram man. We'd seen his statue in the Brooklyn Museum.

'It's him, isn't it?' I asked Carter. 'The chap who looks like Bullwinkle?'

'Don't call him Bullwinkle!' Carter hissed. He looked up at the giant ram man and said, 'You're Khnum, aren't you?'

The ram man made a rumbling sound deep in his throat. He scraped one of his knives against the ship's rail. 'Is that a question? Or is that your final answer?'

Carter blinked. '*Um* –'

'Not our final answer!' I yelped, realizing that we'd almost stepped into a trap. 'Not even close. Khnum is your common name, isn't it? You want us to say your true name, your *ren*.'

Khnum tilted his head, the bells on his horns jingling. 'That would be nice. But, alas, no one knows it. Even I have forgotten it.'

'How can you forget your own name?' Carter asked. 'And, yes, that's a question.'

'I am part of Ra,' said the ram god. 'I am his aspect in the underworld – a third of his personality. But when Ra stopped making his nightly journey he no longer needed me. He left me here at the gates of the Fourth House, discarded like an old coat. Now I guard the gates ... I have no other purpose. If I could recover my name, I could yield my spirit to whoever frees me. They could reunite me with Ra, but until then I cannot leave this place.'

He sounded horribly depressed, like a little lost sheep, or rather a ten-metre-tall lost sheep with very large knives. I wanted to help him. Even more than that, I wanted to find a way not to get myself sliced to bits.

'If you don't remember your name,' I said, 'why couldn't we just tell you any old name? How would you know whether it was the right answer or not?'

Khnum let his knives trail in the water. 'I hadn't thought of that.'

Carter glared at me as if to say *Why did you tell him?*

The ram god bleated. 'I think I will know my *ren* when I hear it,' he decided, 'though I cannot be sure. Being only part of Ra, I am not sure of much. I've lost most of my memories, most of my power and identity. I am no more than a husk of my former self.'

'Your former self must've been enormous,' I muttered.

The god might have smiled, though it was hard to tell with the ram face. 'I'm sorry you don't have my *ren*. You're a bright girl. You're the first to make it this far. The first and the best.' He sighed forlornly. 'Ah, well. I suppose we should get to the killing.'

The first and the best. My mind started racing.

'Wait,' I said. 'I know your name.'

Carter yelped. 'You do? Tell him!'

I thought of a line from the Book of Ra – *first from Chaos.* I drew on the memories of Isis, the only goddess who had ever known Ra's secret name, and I began to understand the nature of the sun god.

'Ra was the first god to rise out of Chaos,' I said.

Khnum frowned. 'That's my name?'

'No, just listen,' I said. 'You said you're not complete without Ra, just a husk of your former self. But that's true of *all* the other Egyptian gods as well. Ra is older, more powerful. He's the *original* source of Ma'at, like –'

'Like the taproot of the gods,' Carter volunteered.

'Right,' I said. 'I have no idea what a taproot is, but – right.

All these aeons, the other gods have been slowly fading, losing power, because Ra is missing. They might not admit it, but he's their *heart*. They're dependent on him. All this time, we've been wondering if it was worth it, to bring back Ra. We didn't know why it was so important, but now I understand.'

Carter nodded, slowly warming to the idea. 'Ra's the centre of Ma'at. He has to come back if the gods are going to win.'

'And that's why Apophis wants to bring back Ra,' I guessed. 'The two are connected – Ma'at and Chaos. If Apophis can swallow Ra while the sun god is old and weak –'

'All the gods die,' Carter said. 'The world crumbles into Chaos.'

Khnum turned his head so he could study me with one glowing red eye. 'That's all quite interesting,' he said. 'But I'm not hearing my secret name. To wake Ra, you must first name me.'

I opened the Book of Ra and took a deep breath. I began to read the first part of the spell. Now, you may be thinking, *Gosh, Sadie. Your big test was to read some words off a scroll? What's so hard about that?*

If you think that, you've clearly never read a spell. Imagine reading aloud onstage in front of a thousand hostile teachers who are waiting to give you bad marks. Imagine you can only read by looking at the backwards reflection in a mirror. Imagine all the words are mixed around, and you have to put the sentences together in the right order as you go. Imagine if you make one mistake, one stumble, one mispronunciation, you'll die. Imagine doing all that at once, and you'll have some idea what it's like to cast a spell from a scroll.

Despite that, I felt strangely confident. The spell suddenly made sense.

"'I name you First from Chaos'," I said. "'Khnum, who is Ra, the evening sun. I summon your *ba* to awaken the Great One, for I am –'"

My first near-fatal mistake: the scroll said something like *insert your name here*. And I almost read it aloud that way: 'For I am insert your name here!'

Well? It would've been an honest mistake. Instead, I managed to say, "'I am Sadie Kane, restorer of the throne of fire. I name you Breath into Clay, the Ram of Night's Flock, the Divine –'"

I almost lost it again. I was sure the Egyptian title said *the Divine Pooter*. But that made no sense, unless Khnum had magic powers I didn't want to know about. Thankfully, I remembered something from the Brooklyn Museum. Khnum had been depicted as a potter sculpting a human from clay.

"'– the Divine Potter'," I corrected myself. "'I name you Khnum, protector of the fourth gate. I return your name. I return your essence to Ra.'"

The god's huge eyes dilated. His nostrils flared. 'Yes.' He sheathed his knives. 'Well done, my lady. You may pass into the Fourth House. But beware the fires, and be prepared for the second form of Ra. He will not be so grateful for your help.'

'What do you mean?' I asked.

But the ram god's body dissolved into mist. The Book of Ra sucked in the wisps of smoke, and it rolled shut. Khnum and his island were gone. The boat drifted on into a narrower tunnel.

'Sadie,' Carter said, 'that was amazing.'

Normally, I would've been happy to astonish him with my brilliance. But my heart was racing. My hands were sweating, and I thought I might throw up. On top of that, I could feel the glowing orb crew coming out of their shock, beginning to fight me again.

No slice, they complained. *No slice!*

Mind your own business, I thought back at them. *And keep the boat going.*

'*Um*, Sadie?' Carter asked. 'Why is your face turning red?'

I thought he was accusing me of blushing. Then I realized he, too, was red. The whole boat was awash in ruby light. I turned to look ahead of us, and I made a sound in my throat not too different from Khnum's bleating.

'Oh, no,' I said. 'Not this place again.'

Roughly a hundred metres ahead of us, the tunnel opened into a huge cavern. I recognized the massive boiling Lake of Fire, but the last time I hadn't seen it from this angle.

We were picking up speed, heading down a series of rapids like a water slide. At the end of the rapids, the water turned into a fiery waterfall and dropped straight down into the lake about half a mile below. We were hurtling towards the precipice with absolutely no way to stop.

Keep the boat going, the crew whispered with glee. *Keep the boat going!*

We probably had less than a minute, but it seemed longer. I suppose, if time flies when you're having fun, it really creeps when you're hurtling towards your death.

'We've got to turn around!' Carter said. 'Even if that *wasn't* fire, we'll never survive the drop!'

He began yelling at the orbs of light, 'Turn around! Paddle! Mayday!'

They happily ignored him.

I stared at the flaming drop to oblivion and the Lake of Fire below. Despite the waves of heat rolling over us like dragon breath, I felt cold. I realized what needed to happen.

'"Reborn in fire",' I said.

'What?' Carter asked.

'It's a line from the Book of Ra. We can't turn round. We have to go over – straight into the lake.'

'Are you crazy? We'll burn up!'

I ripped open my magic bag and rummaged through my supplies. 'We have to take the ship through the fire. That was part of the sun's nightly rebirth, right? Ra would have done it.'

'Ra wasn't flammable!'

The waterfall was only twenty metres away now. My hands trembled as I poured ink into my writing palette. If you've never tried to use a calligraphy set while standing up on a boat, it isn't easy.

'What are you doing?' Carter asked. 'Writing your will?'

I took a deep breath and dipped my stylus in black ink. I visualized the hieroglyphs I needed. I wished Zia were with us. Not just because we had hit it off rather well in Cairo – [oh, stop pouting, Carter – it's not *my* fault she realized I'm the brilliant one in the family] – but because Zia was an expert with fire glyphs, and that's just what we needed.

'Push up your hair,' I told Carter. 'I need to paint your forehead.'

'I'm not plunging to my death with LOSER painted on my head!'

'I'm trying to save you. Hurry!'

He pushed his hair out of the way. I painted the glyphs for *fire* and *shield* on his forehead, and immediately my brother burst into flame.

I know – it was like a dream come true and a nightmare, all at once. He danced around, spewing some very creative curse words before realizing that the fire wasn't hurting him. He was simply encased in a protective sheet of flames.

'What, exactly –' His eyes widened. 'Hold on to something!'

The boat tipped sickeningly over the edge of the falls. I dashed the hieroglyphs onto the back of my hand, but it wasn't a good copy. The flames spluttered weakly around me. Alas, I didn't have time for anything better. I wrapped my arms round the rail, and we plummeted straight down.

Strange how many things can go through your mind as you fall to certain doom. From up high, the Lake of Fire looked quite beautiful, like the surface of the sun. I wondered if I would feel any pain on impact, or if we would simply evaporate. It was hard to see anything as we plummeted through the ash and smoke, but I thought I spotted a familiar island about a mile away – the black temple where I'd first met Anubis. I wondered if he could see me from there, and if he would rush to my rescue. I wondered if my chances of survival would be better if I pushed away from the boat and fell like a cliff diver, but I couldn't make myself do it. I held on to the rail with all my might. I wasn't sure if the magical fire shield was protecting me, but I was sweating fiercely, and I was fairly certain I'd left my throat and most of my internal organs at the top of the waterfall.

Finally we hit bottom with an understated *whooooom*.

How to describe the sensation of plunging into a lake of liquid fire? Well... it burned. And yet it was somehow wet, too. I didn't dare breathe. After a moment's hesitation, I opened my eyes. All I could see were swirling red and yellow flames. We were still underwater... or under fire? I realized two things: I was not burning to death, and the boat was moving forward.

I couldn't believe my crazy protection glyphs had actually worked. As the boat slid through the swirling currents of heat, the voices of the crew whispered in my mind – more joyful than angry now.

Renew, they said. *New life. New light.*

That sounded promising until I grasped some less pleasant facts. I still couldn't breathe. My body liked breathing. Also, it was getting much hotter. I could feel my protection glyph failing, the ink burning against my hand. I reached out blindly and grabbed an arm – Carter's, I assumed. We held hands, and even though I couldn't see him, it was comforting to know he was there. Perhaps it was my imagination, but the heat seemed to lessen.

Long ago, Amos had told us that we were more powerful together. We increased each other's magic just by being in proximity. I hoped that was true now. I tried to send my thoughts to Carter, urging him to help me maintain the fire shield.

The ship sailed on through the flames. I thought we were starting to ascend, but it might have been wishful thinking. My vision began to go dark. My lungs were screaming. If I inhaled fire, I wondered if I would end up like Vlad Menshikov.

Just when I knew I would pass out, the boat surged upward, and we broke the surface.

I gasped – and not just because I needed the air. We had docked at the shoreline of the boiling lake, in front of a large limestone gateway, like the entrance to the ancient temple I'd seen at Luxor. I was still holding Carter's hand. As far as I could tell, we were both fine.

The sun boat was better than fine. It had been renewed. Its sail gleamed white, the symbol of the sun shining gold in its centre. The oars were repaired and newly polished. The paint was freshly lacquered black and gold and green. The hull no longer leaked, and the tent house was once more a beautiful pavilion. There was no throne, and no Ra, but the crew glowed brightly and cheerfully as they tied off the lines to the dock.

I couldn't help it. I threw my arms round Carter and let out a sob. 'Are you all right?'

He pulled away awkwardly and nodded. The glyph on his forehead had burned off.

'Thanks to you,' he said. 'Where –'

'Sunny Acres,' said a familiar voice.

Bes came down the steps to the dock. He wore a new, even louder Hawaiian shirt and only his Speedo for pants, so I can't say he was a sight for sore eyes. Now that he was in the Duat, he fairly glowed with power. His hair had turned darker and curlier, and his face looked decades younger.

'Bes!' I said. 'What took you so long? Are Walt and Zia –'

'They're fine,' he said. 'And I told you I'd meet you at the Fourth House.' He jabbed his thumb at a sign carved into the limestone archway. 'Used to be called the House of Rest. Apparently they've changed the name.'

The sign was in hieroglyphs, but I had no trouble reading it.

'"Sunny Acres Assisted-Living Community",' I read. '"Formerly the House of Rest. Under New Management." What exactly –'

'We should get going,' Bes said. 'Before your stalker arrives.'

'Stalker?' Carter asked.

Bes pointed to the top of the fiery waterfall, now a good half mile away. At first I didn't see anything. Then there was a streak of white against the red flames – as if a man in an ice-cream suit had plunged into the lake. Apparently I hadn't imagined that white smudge in the darkness. We *were* being followed.

'Menshikov?' I said. 'That's – that's –'

'Bad news,' Bes said. 'Now, come on. We have to find the sun god.'

20. We Visit the House of the Helpful Hippo

HOSPITALS. CLASSROOMS. Now I'll add to my list of least-favourite places: old people's homes.

That may sound odd, as I lived with my grandparents. I suppose their flat counts as an old people's home. But I mean *institutions*. Nursing homes. Those are the worst. They smell like an unholy mixture of canteen food, cleaning supplies and pensioners. The inmates (sorry, patients) always look so miserable. And the homes have absurdly happy names, like Sunny Acres. Please.

We stepped through the limestone gateway into a large open hall – the Egyptian version of assisted living. Rows of colourfully painted columns were studded with iron sconces holding blazing torches. Potted palms and flowering hibiscus plants were placed here and there in a failed attempt to make the place feel cheerful. Large windows looked out on the Lake of Fire, which I suppose was a nice view if you enjoyed brimstone. The walls were painted with scenes of the Egyptian

351

afterlife, along with jolly hieroglyphic mottos like IMMORTALITY WITH SECURITY and LIFE STARTS AT 3,000!

Glowing servant lights and clay *shabti* in white medical uniforms bustled about, carrying trays of medication and pushing wheelchairs. The patients, however, didn't bustle much. A dozen withered figures in linen hospital gowns sat around the room, staring vacantly into space. A few wandered the room, pushing wheelie poles with IV bags. All wore bracelets with their names in hieroglyphs.

Some looked human, but many had animal heads. An old man with the head of a crane rocked back and forth in a metal folding chair, pecking at a game of senet on the coffee table. An old woman with a grizzled lioness's head scooted herself around in a wheelchair, mumbling, 'Meow, meow.' A shrivelled blue-skinned man not much taller than Bes hugged one of the limestone columns and cried softly, as if he were afraid the column might try to leave him.

In other words, the scene was thoroughly depressing.

'What *is* this place?' I asked. 'Are those all gods?'

Carter seemed just as mystified as I was. Bes looked like he was about to crawl out of his skin.

'Never actually been here,' he admitted. 'Heard rumours, but...' He swallowed as if he'd just eaten a spoonful of peanut butter. 'Come on. Let's ask at the nurses' station.'

The desk was a crescent of granite with a row of telephones (though I couldn't imagine who they'd call from the Duat), a computer, lots of clipboards and a platter-size stone disc with a triangular fin – a sundial, which seemed strange, as there was no sun.

Behind the counter, a short, heavy woman stood with her back to us, checking a whiteboard with names and medication times. Her glossy black hair was plaited down her back like an extra-large beaver's tail, and her nurse's cap barely fitted on her wide head.

We were halfway to the desk when Bes froze. 'It's her.'

'Who?' Carter asked.

'This is bad.' Bes turned pale. 'I should've known. . . . Curse it! You'll have to go without me.'

I looked more closely at the nurse, who still had her back to us. She did seem a bit imposing, with massive beefy arms, a neck thicker than my waist and oddly tinted purplish skin. But I couldn't understand why she bothered Bes so much.

I turned to ask him, but Bes had ducked behind the nearest potted plant. It wasn't big enough to hide him and certainly didn't camouflage his Hawaiian shirt.

'Bes, stop it,' I said.

'Shhh! I'm invisible!'

Carter sighed. 'We don't have time for this. Come on, Sadie.'

He led the way to the nurses' station.

'Excuse us,' he called across the desk.

The nurse turned and I yelped. I tried to contain my shock, but it was difficult, as the woman was a hippopotamus.

I don't mean that as an unflattering comparison. She was *actually* a hippo. Her long snout was shaped like an upside-down valentine heart, with bristly whiskers, tiny nostrils and a mouth with two large bottom teeth. Her eyes were small and beady. Her face looked quite odd framed with luxurious black hair, but it wasn't nearly as peculiar as her body. She wore her nurse's blouse open like a jacket, revealing a bikini top that – how to put this delicately – was trying to cover a very great deal of top with very little fabric. Her purple-pink belly was incredibly swollen, as if she were nine months pregnant.

'May I help you?' she asked. Her voice was pleasant and kindly – not what one would expect from a hippopotamus. Come to think of it, I wouldn't expect *any* voice from a hippopotamus.

'*Um*, hippo – I mean, h-hullo!' I stammered. 'My brother and I are looking for...' I glanced at Carter and found he was *not* staring at the nurse's face. 'Carter!'

'What?' He shook himself out of his trance. 'Right. Sorry. *Uh*, aren't you a goddess? Tawaret, or something?'

The hippo woman bared her two enormous teeth in what I hoped was a smile. 'Why, how nice to be recognized! Yes, dear. I'm Tawaret. You said you were looking for someone? A relative? Are you gods?'

Behind us, the potted hibiscus rustled as Bes picked it up and tried to move it behind a column. Tawaret's eyes widened.

'Is that Bes?' she called. 'Bes!'

The dwarf stood abruptly and brushed off his shirt. His face was redder than Set's. 'Plant looks like it's getting enough water,' he muttered. 'I should check the ones over there.'

He started to walk away, but Tawaret called again, 'Bes! It's me, Tawaret! Over here!'

Bes stiffened like she'd shot him in the back. He turned with a tortured smile.

'Well...hey. Tawaret. Wow!'

She scrambled out from behind the desk, wearing high heels that seemed inadvisable for a pregnant water mammal. She spread her chubby arms for a hug and Bes thrust out his hand to shake. They ended up doing an awkward sort of dance, half hug, half shake, which made one thing perfectly obvious to me.

'So, you two used to date?' I asked.

Bes shot eye-daggers at me. Tawaret blushed, which made it the first time I'd ever embarrassed a hippo.

'A long time ago...' Tawaret turned to the dwarf god. 'Bes, how are you? After that horrible time at the palace, I was afraid –'

'Good!' he shouted. 'Yes, thanks. Good. You're good? Good! We're here on important business, as Sadie was about to tell you.'

He kicked me in the shin, which I thought quite unnecessary.

'Yes, right,' I said. 'We're looking for Ra, to awaken him.'

If Bes had been hoping to redirect Tawaret's train of thought, the plan worked. Tawaret opened her mouth in a silent gasp and as if I'd just suggested something horrible, like a hippo hunt.

'Awaken Ra?' she said. 'Oh, dear...oh, that is unfortunate. Bes, you're helping them with this?'

'Uh-hum,' he stuttered. 'Just, you know –'

'Bes is doing us a favour,' I said. 'Our friend Bast asked him to look after us.'

I could tell right away I'd made matters worse. The temperature in the air seemed to drop ten degrees.

'I see,' Tawaret said. 'A favour for Bast.'

I wasn't sure what I'd said wrong, but I tried my best to backtrack. 'Please. Look, the fate of the world is at stake It's very important we find Ra.'

Tawaret crossed her arms sceptically. 'Dear, he's been missing for millennia. And trying to awaken him would be terribly dangerous. Why now?'

'Tell her, Sadie.' Bes inched backwards as if preparing to dive into the hibiscus. 'No secrets here. Tawaret can be trusted completely.'

'Bes!' She perked up immediately and fluttered her eyelashes. 'Do you mean that?'

'Sadie, talk!' Bes pleaded.

And so I did. I showed Tawaret the Book of Ra. I explained why we needed to wake the sun god – the threat of Apophis's ascension, mass chaos and destruction, the world about to end at sunrise, et cetera. It was difficult to judge her hippoish expressions [yes, Carter, I'm *sure* that's a word], but, as I spoke, Tawaret twirled her long black hair nervously.

'That's not good,' she said. 'Not good at all.'

She glanced behind her at the sundial. Despite the lack of sun, the needle cast a clear shadow over the hieroglyphic number five:

'You're running out of time,' she said.

Carter frowned at the sundial. 'Isn't this place the Fourth House of the Night?'

'Yes, dear,' Tawaret agreed. 'It goes by different names

– Sunny Acres, the House of Rest – but it's also the Fourth House.'

'So how can the sundial be on five?' he asked. 'Shouldn't we be, like, frozen at the fourth hour?'

'Doesn't work that way, kid,' Bes put in. 'Time in the mortal world doesn't stop passing just because you're in the Fourth House. If you want to follow the sun god's voyage, you have to keep in sync with his timing.'

I felt a head-splitting explanation coming on. I was ready to accept blissful ignorance and get on with finding Ra, but Carter, naturally, wouldn't let it drop.

'So what happens if we get too far behind?' he asked.

Tawaret checked the sundial again, which was slowly creeping past five. 'The houses are connected to their times of night. You can stay in each one as long as you want, but you can only enter or exit them close to the hours they represent.'

'Uh-huh.' I rubbed my temples. 'Do you have any headache medicine behind that nurses' station?'

'It's not that confusing,' said Carter, just to be annoying. 'It's like a revolving door. You have to wait for an opening and jump in.'

'More or less,' Tawaret agreed. 'There *is* a little wiggle room with most of the Houses. You can leave the Fourth House, for instance, pretty much whenever you want. But certain gates are impossible to pass unless you time it exactly right. You can only enter the First House at sunset. You can only exit the Twelfth House at dawn. And the gates of the Eighth House, the House of Challenges…can only be entered during the eighth hour.'

'House of Challenges?' I said. 'I hate it already.'

'Oh, you have Bes with you.' Tawaret stared at him dreamily. 'The challenges won't be a problem.'

Bes shot me a panicked look, like, *Save me!*

'But if you take too long,' Tawaret continued, 'the gates will close before you can get there. You'll be locked in the Duat until tomorrow night.'

'And if we don't stop Apophis,' I said, 'there won't *be* a tomorrow night. *That* part I understand.'

'So can you help us?' Carter asked Tawaret. 'Where is Ra?'

The goddess fidgeted with her hair. Her hands were a cross between human and hippo, with short stubby fingers and thick nails.

'That's the problem, dear,' she said. 'I don't know. The Fourth House is enormous. Ra is probably here somewhere, but the hallways and doors go on forever. We have *so* many patients.'

'Don't you keep track of them?' Carter asked. 'Isn't there a map or something?'

Tawaret shook her head sadly. 'I do my best, but it's just me, the *shabti* and the servant lights ... And there are thousands of old gods.'

My heart sank. I could barely keep track of the ten or so major gods I'd met, but *thousands*? In this room alone, I counted a dozen patients, six hallways leading off in different directions, two staircases and three lifts. Perhaps it was my imagination, but it seemed as if some of the hallways had appeared since we'd entered the room.

'*All* these old folks are gods?' I asked.

Tawaret nodded. 'Most were minor deities even in ancient

times. The magicians didn't consider them worth imprisoning. Over the centuries, they've wasted away, lonely and forgotten. Eventually they made their way here. They simply wait.'

'To die?' I asked.

Tawaret got a faraway look in her eyes. 'I wish I knew. Sometimes they disappear, but I don't know if they simply get lost wandering the halls, or find a new room to hide in, or truly fade to nothing. The sad truth is it amounts to the same thing. Their names have been forgotten by the world above. Once your name is no longer spoken, what good is life?'

She glanced at Bes, as if trying to tell him something.

The dwarf god looked away quickly. 'That's Mekhit, isn't it?' He pointed to the old lion woman who was making her way around in a wheelchair. 'She had a temple near Abydos, I think. Minor lion goddess. Always got confused with Sekhmet.'

The lioness snarled weakly when Bes said the name Sekhmet. Then she went back to rolling her chair, muttering, 'Meow, meow.'

'Sad story,' Tawaret said. 'She came here with her husband, the god Onuris. They were a celebrity couple in the old days, so romantic. He once travelled all the way to Nubia to rescue her. They got married. Happy ending, we all thought. But they were both forgotten. They came here together. Then Onuris disappeared. Mekhit's mind began to go quickly after that. Now she rolls her chair around the room aimlessly all day. She can't remember her own name, though we keep reminding her.'

I thought about Khnum, whom we'd met on the river, and how sad he'd seemed, not knowing his secret name. I looked at the old goddess Mekhit, meowing and snarling and scooting along with no memory of her former glory. I imagined trying to care for a thousand gods like that – senior citizens who never got better and never died.

'Tawaret, how can you stand it?' I said in awe. 'Why do you work here?'

She touched her nurse's cap self-consciously. 'A long story, dear. And we have very little time. I wasn't always here. I was once a protector goddess. I scared away demons, though not as well as Bes.'

'You were plenty scary,' Bes said.

The hippo goddess sighed with adoration. 'That's *so* sweet. I also protected mothers giving birth –'

'Because you're pregnant?' Carter asked, nodding at her enormous belly.

Tawaret looked mystified. 'No. Why would you think that?'

'Um –'

'So!' I broke in. 'You were explaining why you take care of ageing gods.'

Tawaret checked the sundial and I was alarmed to see how fast the shadow was creeping towards six. 'I've always liked to help people, but in the world above, well ... it became clear I wasn't needed any more.'

She was careful not to look at Bes, but the dwarf god blushed even more.

'Someone *was* needed to look after the ageing gods,' Tawaret continued. 'I suppose I understand their sadness. I understand about waiting forever –'

Bes coughed into his fist. 'Look at the time! Yes, about Ra. Have you seen him since you've been working here?'

Tawaret considered. 'It's possible. I saw a falcon-headed god in a room in the south-east wing, oh, ages ago. I thought it was Nemty, but it's possible it could have been Ra. He sometimes liked to go about in falcon form.'

'Which way?' I pleaded. 'If we can get close, the Book of Ra may be able to guide us.'

Tawaret turned to Bes. 'Are *you* asking me for this, Bes? Do you truly believe it's important, or are you just doing it because Bast told you to?'

'No! Yes!' He puffed out his cheeks in exasperation. 'I mean, yes, it's important. Yes, I'm asking. I need your help.'

Tawaret pulled a torch from the nearest sconce. 'In that case, right this way.'

We wandered the halls of an infinite magic nursing home, led by a hippo nurse with a torch. Really, just an ordinary night for the Kanes.

We passed so many bedrooms I lost count. Most of the doors were closed, but a few were open, showing frail old gods in their beds, staring at the flickering blue light of televisions or simply lying in the dark crying. After twenty or thirty such rooms, I stopped looking. It was too depressing.

I held the Book of Ra, hoping it would get warmer as we approached the sun god, but no such luck. Tawaret hesitated at each intersection. I could tell she felt uncertain about where she was leading us.

After a few more hallways and still no change in the scroll, I began to feel frantic. Carter must've noticed.

'It's okay,' he promised. 'We'll find him.'

I remembered how fast the sundial had been moving at the nurses' station. And I thought about Vlad Menshikov. I wanted to believe he'd been turned into a deep-fried Russian when he fell into the Lake of Fire, but that was probably too much to hope for. If he was still hunting us, he couldn't be far behind.

We turned down another corridor and Tawaret froze. 'Oh, dear.'

In front of us, an old woman with the head of a frog was jumping around – and when I say jumping, I mean she leaped about five metres, croaked a few times, then leaped against the wall and stuck there before leaping to the opposite wall. Her body and limbs looked human, dressed in a green hospital gown, but her head was all amphibian – brown, moist and warty. Her bulbous eyes turned in every direction, and by the distressed sound of her croaking I guessed she was lost.

'Heket's got out again,' Tawaret said. 'Excuse me a moment.'

She hurried over to the frog woman.

Bes pulled a handkerchief from the pocket of his Hawaiian shirt. He dabbed his forehead nervously. 'I wondered what had ever happened to Heket. She's the frog goddess, you know.'

'I never would've guessed,' Carter said.

I watched as Tawaret tried to calm down the old goddess. She spoke in soothing tones, promising to help Heket find her room if she'd just stop bouncing off the walls.

'She's brilliant,' I said. 'Tawaret, I mean.'

'Yeah,' Bes said. 'Yeah, she's fine.'

'*Fine?*' I said. 'Clearly, she likes you. Why are you so...'

Suddenly the truth smacked me in the face. I felt almost as thick as Carter.

'Oh, I see. She mentioned a horrible time at a palace, didn't she? She's the one who freed you in Russia.'

Bes mopped his neck with the handkerchief. He really was sweating quite a lot. 'Wh-what makes you say that?'

'Because you're so embarrassed around her! Like...' I was about to say 'like she's seen you in your underpants', but I doubted that would mean much to the God of Speedos. 'Like she's seen you at your worst and you want to forget it.'

Bes stared at Tawaret with a pained expression, the way he had stared at Prince Menshikov's palace in St Petersburg.

'She's *always* saving me,' he said bitterly. 'She's always wonderful, nice, kind. Back in ancient times, everyone assumed we were dating. They always said we were a cute couple – the two demon-scaring gods, the two misfits, whatever. We did go out a few times, but Tawaret was just too – too *nice*. And I was kind of obsessed with somebody else.'

'Bast,' Carter guessed.

The dwarf god's shoulders slumped. 'That obvious, huh? Yeah, Bast. She was the most popular goddess with the common folk. I was the most popular god. So, you know, we'd see each other at festivals and such. She was...well, beautiful.'

Typical man, I thought. *Only seeing the surface.* But I kept my mouth shut.

'Anyway,' Bes sighed, 'Bast treated me like a little brother.

She still does. Has no interest in me at all, but it took me a long time to realize that. I was so obsessed that I wasn't very good to Tawaret over the years.'

'But she came to get you in Russia,' I said.

He nodded. 'I sent out distress calls. I thought Bast would come to my aid. Or Horus. Or somebody. I didn't know where they all were, you understand, but I had a lot of friends back in the old days. I figured somebody would show up. The only one who did was Tawaret. She risked her life sneaking into the palace during the dwarf wedding. She saw the whole thing – saw me humiliated in front of the big folk. During the night, she broke my cage and freed me. I owe her everything. But once I was free... I just fled. I was so ashamed I couldn't look at her. Every time I think of her, I think about that night and I hear the laughing.'

The pain in his voice was raw, as if he were describing something that had happened yesterday, not three centuries ago.

'Bes, it isn't her fault,' I said gently. 'She cares about you. It's obvious.'

'It's too late,' he said. 'I've hurt her too much. I wish I could turn back the clock, but...'

He faltered. Tawaret was walking towards us, leading the frog goddess by the arm.

'Now, dear,' Tawaret said, 'just come with us and we'll find your room. No need for leaping.'

'But it's a leap of faith,' Heket croaked. (I mean she made that sound; she didn't die in front of us, thankfully.) 'My temple is around here somewhere. It was in Qus. Lovely city.'

'Yes, dear,' Tawaret said. 'But your temple is gone now. All our temples are gone. You have a nice bedroom, though –'

'No,' Heket murmured. 'The priests will have sacrifices for me. I have to...'

She fixed her large yellow eyes on me, and I understood how a fly must feel right before it's zapped by a frog tongue.

'That's my priestess!' Heket said. 'She's come to visit me.'

'No, dear,' Tawaret said. 'That's Sadie Kane.'

'My priestess.' Heket patted my shoulder with her moist webbed hand, and I did my best not to cringe. 'Tell the temple to start without me, will you? I'll be along later. Will you tell them?'

'*Um*, yeah,' I said. 'Of course, Lady Heket.'

'Good, good.' Her eyes became unfocused. 'Very sleepy now. Hard work, remembering...'

'Yes, dear,' Tawaret said. 'Why don't you lie down in one of these rooms for now?'

She shepherded Heket into the nearest vacant room.

Bes followed her with sad eyes. 'I'm a terrible dwarf.'

Perhaps I should've reassured him, but my mind was racing on to other matters. *Start without me*, Heket had said. A *leap of faith*.

Suddenly I found it hard to breathe.

'Sadie?' Carter asked. 'What's wrong?'

'I know why the scroll isn't guiding us,' I said. 'I have to start the second part of the spell.'

'But we're not there yet,' Carter said.

'And we won't be unless I start the spell. It's part of finding Ra.'

'What is?' Tawaret appeared at Bes's side and almost scared the dwarf out of his Hawaiian shirt.

'The spell,' I said. 'I have to take a leap of faith.'

'I think the frog goddess infected her,' Carter fretted.

'No, you dolt!' I said. 'This is the only way to find Ra. I'm sure of it.'

'Hey, kid,' Bes said, 'if you start that spell, and we don't find Ra by the time you're finished reading it –'

'I know. The spell will backfire.' When I said *backfire*, I meant it quite literally. If the spell didn't find its proper target, the power of the Book of Ra might blow up in my face.

'It's the only way,' I insisted. 'We don't have time to wander the halls forever, and Ra will only appear if we invoke him. We have to prove ourselves by taking the risk. You'll have to lead me. I can't stumble on the words.'

'You have courage, dear.' Tawaret held up her torch. 'Don't worry, I'll guide you. Just do your reading.'

I opened the scroll to the second section. The rows of hieroglyphs, which had once seemed like disconnected phrases of rubbish, now made perfect sense.

'"I invoke the name of Ra",' I read aloud, '"the sleeping king, lord of the noonday sun, who sits upon the throne of fire..."'

Well, you get the idea. I described how Ra rose from the sea of Chaos. I recalled his light shining on the primordial land of Egypt, bringing life to the Nile Valley. As I read, I felt warmer.

'Sadie,' Carter said, 'you're smoking.'

Hard not to panic when someone makes a comment like

that, but I realized Carter was right. Smoke was curling off my body, forming a column of grey that drifted down the hallway.

'Is it my imagination,' Carter asked, 'or is the smoke showing us the way? Ow!'

He said that last part because I stomped his foot, which I could do quite well without breaking my concentration. He got the message: *Shut up and start walking.*

Tawaret took my arm and guided me forward. Bes and Carter flanked us like security guards. We followed the trail of smoke down two more corridors and up a flight of stairs. The Book of Ra became uncomfortably warm in my hands. The smoke from my body began obscuring the letters.

'You're doing well, Sadie,' Tawaret said. 'This hallway looks familiar.'

I don't know how she could tell, but I stayed focused on the scroll. I described Ra's sun boat sailing across the sky. I spoke of his kingly wisdom and the battles he'd won against Apophis.

A bead of sweat trickled down my face. My eyes began to burn. I hoped they weren't literally on fire.

When I came to the line, 'Ra, the sun's zenith . . .' I realized we'd stopped in front of a door.

It didn't look any different from any other door, but I pushed it open and stepped inside. I kept reading, though I was quickly approaching the end of the spell.

Inside, the room was dark. In the sputtering light of Tawaret's torch, I saw the oldest man in the world sleeping in bed – his face shrivelled, his arms like sticks, his skin so translucent I could see every vein. Some of the mummies in Baharia had looked more alive than this old husk.

"'The light of Ra returns", I read. I nodded at the heavily curtained windows, and fortunately Bes and Carter got my meaning. They yanked back the curtains, and red light from the Lake of Fire flooded the room. The old man didn't move. His mouth was pursed like his lips had been sewn together.

I moved to his bedside and kept reading. I described Ra awakening at dawn, sitting in his throne as his boat climbed the sky, the plants turning towards the warmth of the sun.

'It's not working,' Bes muttered.

I began to panic. There were only two lines left. I could feel the power of the spell backing up, beginning to overheat my body. I was still smoking, and I didn't like the smell of flame-broiled Sadie. I had to awaken Ra or I'd burn alive.

The god's mouth . . . Of course.

I set the scroll on Ra's bed and did my best to hold it open with one hand. "'I sing the praises of the sun god."'

I stretched out my free hand to Carter and snapped my fingers.

Thank goodness, Carter understood.

He rummaged through my bag and passed me the obsidian *netjeri* blade from Anubis. If ever there was a moment for Opening the Mouth, this was it.

I touched the knife to the old man's lips and spoke the last line of the spell: "'Awake, my king, with the new day."'

The old man gasped. Smoke spiralled into his mouth like he'd become a vacuum cleaner, and the magic of the spell funnelled into him. My temperature dropped to normal. I almost collapsed with relief.

Ra's eyes fluttered open. With horrified fascination, I watched as blood began to flow through his veins again, slowly inflating him like a hot-air balloon.

He turned towards me, his eyes unfocused and milky with cataracts. '*Uh?*'

'He still looks old,' Carter said nervously. 'Isn't he supposed to look young?'

Tawaret curtsied to the sun god (which you should not try at home if you are a pregnant hippo in heels) and felt Ra's forehead. 'He isn't whole yet,' she said. 'You'll need to complete the night's journey.'

'And the third part of the spell,' Carter guessed. 'He's got one more aspect, right? The scarab?'

Bes nodded, though he didn't look terribly optimistic. 'Khepri, the beetle. Maybe if we find the last part of his soul, he'll be reborn properly.'

Ra broke into a toothless grin. 'I like zebras!'

I was so tired, I wondered if I'd heard him correctly. 'Sorry, did you say zebras?'

He beamed at us like a child who'd just discovered something wonderful. 'Weasels are sick.'

'O-h-h-kay,' Carter said. 'Maybe he needs these...'

Carter took the crook and flail from his belt. He offered them to Ra. The old god pulled the crook to his mouth and began gumming it like a pacifier.

I started to feel uneasy, and not just because of Ra's condition. How much time had passed, and where was Vlad Menshikov?

'Let's get him to the boat,' I said. 'Bes, can you –'

'Yep. Excuse me, Lord Ra. I'll have to carry you.' He scooped the sun god out of bed and we bolted from the room. Ra couldn't have weighed very much, and Bes didn't have any difficulty keeping up despite his short legs. We ran down the corridor, retracing our steps, as Ra warbled, '*Wheeee! Wheeee! Wheeee!*'

Perhaps *he* was having a good time, but I was mortified. We'd been through so much trouble, and *this* was the sort of god we'd woken? Carter looked as grim as I felt.

We raced past other decrepit gods, who all got quite excited. Some pointed and made gurgling noises. One old jackal-headed god rattled his IV pole and yelled, 'Here comes the sun! There goes the sun!'

We burst into the lobby, and Ra said, '*Uh-oh. Uh-oh* on the floor.'

His head lolled. I thought he wanted to get down. Then I realized he was looking at something. On the floor next to my foot lay a glittering silver necklace: a familiar amulet shaped like a snake.

For someone who'd been smoking hot only a few minutes before, I suddenly felt terribly chilly. 'Menshikov,' I said. 'He was here.'

Carter drew his wand and scanned the room. 'But where is he? Why would he just drop that and walk away?'

'He left it on purpose,' I guessed. 'He wants to taunt us.'

As soon as I said it, I knew it was true. I could almost hear Menshikov laughing as he continued his journey downriver, leaving us behind.

'We have to get to the boat!' I said. 'Hurry, before –'

'Sadie.' Bes pointed to the nurses' station. His expression was grim.

'Oh, no,' Tawaret said. 'No, no, no…'

On the sundial, the needle's shadow was pointing to eight. That meant even if we could still leave the Fourth House, even if we could get through the Fifth, Sixth, and Seventh Houses, it wouldn't matter. According to what Tawaret had told us, the gates of the Eighth House would already be closed.

No wonder Menshikov had left us here without bothering to fight us.

We'd already lost.

C
A
R
T
E
R

21. We Buy Some Time

AFTER SAYING GOODBYE TO ZIA at the Great Pyramid, I didn't think I could possibly get more depressed. I was wrong.

Standing on the docks of the Lake of Fire, I felt like I might as well do a cannonball into the lava.

It wasn't fair. We'd come all this way and risked so much just to be beaten by a time limit. Game over. How was *anyone* supposed to succeed in bringing back Ra? It was impossible.

Carter, this isn't a game, the voice of Horus said inside my head. *It isn't supposed to be possible. You must keep going.*

I didn't see why. The gates of the Eighth House were already closed. Menshikov had sailed on and left us behind.

Maybe that had been his plan all along. He'd let us wake Ra only partially so the sun god remained old and feeble. Then Menshikov would leave us trapped in the Duat while he used whatever evil magic he'd planned to free Apophis. When the dawn came, there would be no sunrise, no return of Ra. Instead Apophis would rise and destroy civilization.

Our friends would have fought all night at Brooklyn House for nothing. Twenty-four hours from now, when we finally managed to leave the Duat, we'd find the world a dark, frozen wasteland, ruled by Chaos. Everything we cared about would be gone. Then Apophis could swallow Ra and complete his victory.

Why should we keep charging forward when the battle was lost?

A general never shows despair, Horus said. *He instils confidence in his troops. He leads them forward, even into the mouth of death.*

You're Mr Cheerful, I thought. *Who invited you back into my head?*

But, as irritating as Horus was, he had a point. Sadie had talked about hope – about believing that we could make Ma'at out of Chaos, even if it seemed impossible. Maybe that was all we could do: keep on trying, keep on believing we could salvage something from the disaster.

Amos, Zia, Walt, Jaz, Bast and our young trainees...all of them were counting on us. If our friends were still alive, I couldn't give up. I owed them better than that.

Tawaret escorted us to the sun boat while a couple of her *shabti* carried Ra aboard.

'Bes, I'm so sorry,' she said. 'I wish there was more I could do.'

'It's not your fault.' Bes held out his hand like he wanted to shake, but when their fingers touched, he clasped hers. 'Tawaret, it was never your fault.'

She sniffled. 'Oh, Bes...'

'*Wheee!*' Ra interrupted as the *shabti* set him in the boat. 'See zebras! *Wheee!*'

Bes cleared his throat.

Tawaret let go of his hands. 'You – you should go. Perhaps Aaru will provide an answer.'

'Aaru?' I asked. 'Who's that?'

Tawaret didn't exactly smile, but her eyes softened with kindness. 'Not who, my dear. *Where*. It's the Seventh House. Tell your father hello.'

My spirits lifted just a little. 'Dad will be there?'

'Good luck, Carter and Sadie.' Tawaret kissed us both on the cheek, which felt sort of like getting sideswiped by a friendly, bristly, slightly moist blimp.

The goddess looked at Bes, and I was sure she was going to cry. Then she turned and hurried up the steps, her *shabti* behind her.

'Weasels are sick,' Ra said thoughtfully.

On that bit of godly wisdom, we boarded the ship. The glowing crew lights manned the oars, and the sun boat pulled away from the docks.

'Eat.' Ra began gumming a piece of rope.

'No, you can't eat that, you silly old man,' Sadie chided.

'*Uh*, kid?' Bes said. 'Maybe you shouldn't call the king of the gods a silly old man.'

'Well, he *is*,' Sadie said. 'Come on, Ra. Come into the tent. I want to see something.'

'No tent,' he muttered. 'Zebras.'

Sadie tried to grab his arm, but he crawled away from her and stuck out his tongue. Finally she took the pharaoh's crook from my belt (without asking, of course) and waved it like a dog bone. 'Want the crook, Ra? Nice tasty crook?'

Ra grabbed for it weakly. Sadie backed up and eventually managed to coax Ra into the pavilion. As soon as he reached the empty dais, a brilliant light exploded around him, completely blinding me.

'Carter, look!' Sadie cried.

'I wish I could.' I blinked the yellow spots out of my eyes.

On the dais stood a chair of molten gold, a fiery throne carved with glowing white hieroglyphs. It looked just like Sadie had described from her vision, but in real life it was the most beautiful and terrifying piece of furniture I'd ever seen. The crew lights buzzed around it in excitement, brighter than ever.

Ra didn't seem to notice the chair, or he didn't care. His hospital gown had changed into regal robes with a collar of gold, but he still looked like the same withered old man.

'Have a seat,' Sadie told him.

'Don't wanna chair,' he muttered.

'That was almost a complete sentence,' I said. 'Maybe it's a good sign?'

'Zebras!' Ra grabbed the crook from Sadie and hobbled across the deck, yelling, 'Wheee! Wheee!'

'Lord Ra!' Bes called. 'Careful!'

I considered tackling the sun god before he could fall out of the boat, but I didn't know how the crew would react to that. Then Ra solved our problem for us. He smacked into the mast and crumpled to the deck.

We all rushed forward, but the old god seemed only dazed. He drooled and muttered as we dragged him back into the pavilion and set him on his throne. It was tricky, because the throne gave off heat of about a thousand degrees and I didn't want to catch fire (again); but the heat didn't seem to bother Ra.

We stepped back and looked at the king of the gods, slumped in his chair snoring and cradling his crook like a teddy bear. I placed the war flail across his lap, hoping it might make a difference – maybe complete his powers or something. No such luck.

'Sick weasels,' Ra muttered.

'Behold,' Sadie said bitterly. 'The glorious Ra.'

Bes shot her an irritated look. 'That's right, kid. Make fun. We gods just love to have mortals laughing at us.'

Sadie's expression softened. 'I'm sorry, Bes. I didn't mean –'

'Whatever.' He stormed to the prow of the boat.

Sadie gave me a pleading look. 'Honestly, I didn't –'

'He's just stressed,' I told her. 'Like all of us. It'll be okay.'

Sadie brushed a tear from her cheek. 'The world is about to end, we're stuck in the Duat and you think it'll be okay?'

'We're going to see Dad.' I tried to sound confident, even though I didn't feel it. *A general never shows despair.* 'He'll help us.'

We sailed through the Lake of Fire until the shores narrowed and the flaming current turned back into water. The glow of the lake faded behind us. The river got swifter and I knew we'd entered the Fifth House.

I thought about Dad and whether or not he'd really be able to help us. The last few months he'd been strangely silent. I guess that shouldn't have surprised me, since he was the Lord of the Underworld now. He probably didn't get good cell-phone reception down here. Still, the idea of seeing him at the moment of my biggest failure made me nervous.

Even though the river was dark, the throne of fire was almost too bright to look at. Our boat cast a warm glow over the shores.

On either side of the river, ghostly villages appeared out of the gloom. Lost souls ran to the riverbank to watch us pass. After so many millennia in the darkness, they looked stunned to see the sun god. Many tried to shout for joy, but their mouths made no sound. Others stretched out their arms towards Ra. They smiled as they basked in his warm light. Their forms seemed to solidify. Colour returned to their faces and their clothes. As they faded behind us in the darkness, I was left with the image of their grateful faces and outstretched hands.

Somehow that made me feel better. At least we'd shown them the sun one last time before Chaos destroyed the world.

I wondered if Amos and our friends were still alive, defending Brooklyn House against Vlad Menshikov's attack squad and waiting for us to show up. I wished I could see Zia again, if only to apologize for failing her.

The Fifth and Sixth houses passed quickly, though I couldn't be sure how much time actually went by. We saw more ghost villages, beaches made of bones, entire caverns where winged *ba* flew around in confusion, bonking into walls and swarming the sun boat like moths around a porch light. We navigated some scary rapids, though the glowing crew lights made it look easy. A few times dragon-like monsters rose out of the river, but Bes yelled, 'Boo!' and the monsters whimpered and sank beneath the water. Ra slept through it all, snoring fitfully on his burning throne.

Finally the river slowed and widened. The water turned as smooth as melted chocolate. The sun boat entered a new cavern and the ceiling overhead blazed with blue crystals, reflecting Ra's light so it looked like the regular sun was crossing a brilliant blue sky. Marsh grass and palm trees lined the shore. Farther away, rolling green hills were dotted with cosy-looking white adobe cottages. A flock of geese flew overhead. The air smelled like jasmine and fresh-baked bread. My whole body relaxed – the way you might feel after a long trip, when you walk into your house and finally get to collapse on your bed.

'Aaru,' Bes announced. He didn't sound as grumpy now. The worry lines on his face faded. 'The Egyptian afterlife. The Seventh House. I suppose you'd call it Paradise.'

'Not that I'm complaining,' Sadie said. 'It's much nicer than Sunny Acres and I smell decent food at last. But does this mean we're dead?'

Bes shook his head. 'This was a regular part of Ra's nightly route – his pit stop, I guess you'd say. He would hang out for a while with his host, eat, drink and rest up before the last stretch of his journey, which was the most dangerous.'

'His host?' I asked, though I was pretty sure whom Bes meant.

Our boat turned towards a dock, where a man and a woman stood waiting for us. Dad wore his usual brown suit. His skin glowed with a bluish tint. Mom shimmered in ghostly white, her feet not quite touching the boards.

'Of course,' Bes said. 'This is the House of Osiris.'

'Sadie, Carter.' Dad pulled us into a hug like we were still little kids, but neither of us protested.

He felt solid and human, so much like his old self that it took all my willpower not to break down in tears. His goatee was neatly trimmed. His bald head gleamed. Even his cologne smelled the same: the faint scent of amber.

He held us at arm's length to examine us, his eyes shining. I could almost believe he was still a regular mortal, but if I looked closely, I could see another layer to his appearance, like a fuzzy superimposed image: a blue-skinned man in white robes and the crown of a pharaoh. Round his neck was a *djed* amulet, the symbol of Osiris.

'Dad,' I said. 'We failed.'

'Shhh,' he said. 'None of that. This is a time to rest and renew.'

Mom smiled. 'We've been watching your progress. You've both been so brave.'

Seeing her was even harder than seeing Dad. I couldn't hug her because she had no physical substance, and when she touched my face it felt like nothing more than a warm breeze. She looked exactly as I remembered – her blonde hair loose around her shoulders, her blue eyes full of life – but she was only a spirit now. Her white dress seemed to be woven from mist. If I looked directly at her, she seemed to dissolve in the light of the sun boat.

'I'm so proud of you both,' she said. 'Come, we've prepared a feast.'

I was in a daze as they led us ashore. Bes took charge of carrying the sun god, who seemed in a good mood after head-butting the mast and taking a nap. Ra gave everyone a toothless grin and said, 'Oh, pretty. Feast? Zebras?'

Ghostly servants in Ancient Egyptian clothes ushered us towards an outdoor pavilion lined with life-size statues of the gods. We crossed a footbridge over a moat full of albino crocodiles, which made me think about Philip of Macedonia and what might be happening back at Brooklyn House.

Then I stepped inside the pavilion and my jaw dropped.

A feast was spread out on a long mahogany table – *our* old dining table from the house in LA. I could even see the notch I'd carved in the wood with my first Swiss Army knife – the only time I recall my dad getting really mad at me. The chairs were stainless steel with leather seats, just like I remembered; and when I looked outside the view shimmered back and forth – now the grassy hills and glittering blue sky of the afterlife, now the white walls and huge glass windows of our old house.

'Oh...' Sadie said in a small voice. Her eyes were fixed on the centre of the table. Among platters of pizza, bowls of sugar-coated strawberries and every other kind of food you could imagine was a white-and-blue ice-cream cake, the exact same cake that we'd exploded on Sadie's sixth birthday.

'I hope you don't mind,' Mom said. 'I thought it was a shame you never got to taste it. Happy birthday, Sadie.'

'Please, sit.' Dad spread his arms. 'Bes, old friend, would you put Lord Ra at the head of the table?'

I started to sit in the chair farthest from Ra, since I didn't want him slobbering all over me while he gummed his food, but Mom said, 'Oh, not there, dear. Sit by me. That chair is for . . . another guest.'

She said the last two words like they left a bitter taste in her mouth.

I looked around the table. There were seven chairs and only six of us. 'Who else is coming?'

'Anubis?' Sadie asked hopefully.

Dad chuckled. 'Not Anubis, though I'm sure he'd be here if he could.'

Sadie slumped as if someone had let the air out of her. [Yes, Sadie, you *were* that obvious.]

'Where is he, then?' she asked.

Dad hesitated just long enough for me to sense his discomfort. 'Away. Let's eat, shall we?'

I sat down and accepted a slice of birthday cake from a ghostly waiter. You wouldn't think I'd be hungry, with the world ending and our mission failed, sitting in the Land of the Dead at a dinner table from my past with my mom's ghost next to me and my dad the colour of a blueberry. But my stomach didn't care about that. It let me know that I was still alive and I needed food. The cake was chocolate with vanilla ice cream. It tasted perfect. Before I knew it, I'd polished off my slice and was loading my plate with pepperoni pizza. The statues of the gods stood behind us – Horus, Isis, Thoth, Sobek – all keeping silent watch as we ate. Outside the pavilion, the lands of Aaru spread out as if the cavern were endless – green hills and meadows, herds of fat cattle, fields of grain, orchards full of date trees. Streams cut the marshes into a patchwork of islands, just like the Nile Delta, with picture-perfect villages for the blessed dead. Sailboats cruised the river.

'This is what it looks like to the Ancient Egyptians,' Dad said, as if reading my thoughts. 'But each soul sees Aaru slightly differently.'

'Like our house in LA?' I asked. 'Our family back together around a dining table? Is this even real?'

Dad's eyes turned sad, the way they used to whenever I'd ask about Mom's death.

'The birthday cake is good, eh?' he asked. 'My little girl, thirteen. I can't believe –'

Sadie swept her plate off the table. It shattered against the stone floor. 'What does it matter?' she shouted. 'The cruddy sundial – the stupid gates – we failed!'

She buried her face in her arms and began to sob.

'Sadie.' Mom hovered next to her like a friendly fog bank. 'It's all right.'

'Moon pie,' Ra said helpfully, a beard of cake frosting smeared around his mouth. He started to fall out of his chair and Bes pushed him back into place.

'Sadie's right,' I said. 'Ra's in worse shape than we imagined. Even if we could get him back to the mortal world, he could never defeat Apophis – unless Apophis laughs to death.'

Dad frowned. 'Carter, he is still Ra, pharaoh of the gods. Show some respect.'

'Don't like bubbles!' Ra swatted at a glowing servant light that was trying to wipe his mouth.

'Lord Ra,' Dad said, 'do you remember me? I'm Osiris. You

dined here at my table every night, resting before your journey towards the dawn. Do you recall?'

'Want a weasel,' Ra said.

Sadie slapped the table. 'What does that even *mean*?'

Bes scooped up a fistful of chocolate-covered things – I was afraid they might be grasshoppers – and tossed them into his mouth. 'We haven't finished the Book of Ra. We'd need to find Khepri.'

Dad stroked his goatee. 'Yes, the scarab god, Ra's form as the rising sun. Perhaps if you found Khepri, Ra could be fully reborn. But you would need to pass through the gates of the Eighth House.'

'Which are closed,' I said. 'We'd have to, like, reverse time.'

Bes stopped munching grasshoppers. His eyes widened like he'd just had a revelation. He looked at my dad incredulously. 'Him? You invited him?'

'Who?' I asked. 'What do you mean?'

I stared at my dad, but he wouldn't meet my eyes.

'Dad, what is it?' I demanded. 'There's a way through the gates? Can you teleport us to the other side or something?'

'I wish I could, Carter. But the journey must be followed. It is part of Ra's rebirth. I can't interfere with that. However, you're right: you need extra time. There might be a way, though I'd never suggest it if the stakes weren't so high –'

'It's dangerous,' our mom warned. 'I think it's *too* dangerous.'

'What's too dangerous?' Sadie asked.

'Me, I suppose,' said a voice behind me.

I turned and found a man standing with his hands on the

back of my chair. Either he'd approached so silently I hadn't heard him, or he'd materialized out of thin air.

He looked about twenty, thin and tall and kind of glamorous. His face was totally human, but his irises were silver. His head was shaven except for a glossy black ponytail on one side of his head, like Ancient Egyptian youth used to wear. His silvery suit looked to have been tailored in Italy (I only know that because Amos and my dad both paid a *lot* of attention to suits). The fabric shimmered like some bizarre mix of silk and aluminium foil. His shirt was black and collarless, and several pounds of platinum chains hung round his neck. The biggest piece of bling was a silver crescent amulet. When his fingers drummed on the back of my chair, his rings and platinum Rolex flashed. If I'd seen him in the mortal world, I might've guessed he was a young Native American billionaire casino owner. But here in the Duat, with that crescent-shaped amulet round his neck...

'Moon pie!' Ra cackled with delight.

'You're Khonsu,' I guessed. 'The moon god.'

He gave me a wolfish grin, looking at me as if I were an appetizer.

'At your service,' he said. 'Care to play a game?'

'Not you,' Bes growled.

Khonsu spread his arms in a big air hug. 'Bes, old buddy! How've you been?'

'Don't "old buddy" me, you scam artist.'

'I'm hurt!' Khonsu sat down on my right and leaned towards me conspiratorially. 'Poor Bes gambled with me ages ago, you see. He wanted more time with Bast. He wagered a few feet of his height. I'm afraid he lost.'

'That's not what happened!' Bes roared.

'Gentlemen,' my father said in his sternest Dad tone. 'You are both guests at my table. I won't have any fighting.'

'Absolutely, Osiris.' Khonsu beamed at him. 'I'm honoured to be here. And these are your famous children? Wonderful! Are you ready to play, kids?'

'Julius, they don't understand the risks,' our mother protested. 'We can't let them do this.'

'Hang on,' Sadie said. 'Do *what*, exactly?'

Khonsu snapped his fingers and all the food on the table disappeared, replaced by a glowing silver senet board. 'Haven't you heard about me, Sadie? Didn't Isis tell you some stories? Or Nut? Now, there was a gambler! The sky goddess wouldn't stop playing until she'd won five whole days from me. Do you know the odds against winning that much time? Astronomical! Of course, she's covered with stars, so I suppose she *is* astronomical.'

Khonsu laughed at his own joke. He didn't seem bothered that no one joined him.

'I remember,' I said. 'You gambled with Nut and she won enough moonlight to create five extra days, the Demon Days. That let her get around Ra's commandment that her five children couldn't be born on any day of the year.'

'Nuts,' Ra muttered. 'Bad nuts.'

The moon god raised an eyebrow. 'Dear me, Ra *is* in bad shape, isn't he? But yes, Carter Kane. You're absolutely right. I'm the moon god, but I also have some influence over time.

I can lengthen or shorten the lives of mortals. Even gods can be affected by my powers. The moon is changeable, you see. Its light waxes and wanes. In my hands, time can also wax and wane. You need – what, about three extra hours? I can weave that for you out of moonlight, if you and your sister are willing to gamble for it. I can make it so that the gates of the Eighth House have not yet closed.'

I didn't understand how he could possibly do that – back up time, insert three extra hours into the night – but for the first time since Sunny Acres I felt a small spark of hope. 'If you can help, why not just *give* us the extra time? The fate of the world is at stake.'

Khonsu laughed. 'Good one! *Give* you time! No, seriously. If I started giving away something that valuable, Ma'at would crumble. Besides, you can't play senet without gambling. Bes can tell you that.'

Bes spat a chocolate grasshopper leg out of his mouth. 'Don't do it, Carter. You know what they said about Khonsu in the old days? Some of the pyramids have a poem about him carved into the stones. It's called the "Cannibal Hymn". For a price, Khonsu would help the pharaoh slay any gods who were bothering him. Khonsu would devour their souls and gain their strength.'

The moon god rolled his eyes. 'Ancient history, Bes! I haven't devoured a soul in... what month is this? March? At any rate, I've completely adapted to this modern world. I'm quite civilized now. You should see my penthouse at the Luxor in Las Vegas. I mean, *Thank you!* America has a proper civilization!'

He smiled at me, his silver eyes flashing like a shark's. 'So what do you say, Carter? Sadie? Play me at senet. Three pieces for me, three for you. You'll need three hours of moonlight, so you two will need one additional person to stake a wager. For every piece your team manages to move off the board, I'll grant you an extra hour. If you win, that's three extra hours – just enough time to make it past the gates of the Eighth House.'

'And if we lose?' I asked.

'Oh . . . you know.' Khonsu waved his hand as if this were an annoying technicality. 'For each piece *I* move off the board, I'll take a *ren* from one of you.'

Sadie sat forward. 'You'll take our secret names – as in, we have to share them with you?'

'Share . . .' Khonsu stroked his ponytail, as if trying to remember the meaning of that word. 'No, no sharing. I'll *devour* your *ren*, you see.'

'Erase part of our souls,' Sadie said. 'Take our memories, our identity.'

The moon god shrugged. 'On the bright side, you wouldn't die. You'd just –'

'Turn into a vegetable,' Sadie guessed. 'Like Ra, there.'

'Don't want vegetables,' Ra muttered irritably. He tried to chew on Bes's shirt, but the dwarf god scooted away.

'Three hours,' I said. 'Wagered against three souls.'

'Carter, Sadie, you don't have to do this,' my mother said. 'We don't expect you to take this risk.'

I'd seen her so many times in pictures and in my memories, but for the first time it really struck me how much she looked like Sadie – or how much Sadie was starting to look like her.

They both had the same fiery determination in their eyes. They both tilted their chins up when they were expecting a fight. And they both weren't very good at hiding their feelings. I could tell from Mom's shaky voice that she realized what had to happen. She was telling us we had options, but she knew very well that we didn't.

I looked at Sadie and we came to a silent agreement.

'Mom, it's okay,' I said. 'You gave your life to close Apophis's prison. How can we back out?'

Khonsu rubbed his hands. 'Ah, yes, Apophis's prison! Your friend Menshikov is there right now, loosening the Serpent's bonds. I have so many bets on what will happen! Will you get there in time to stop him? Will you return Ra to the world? Will you defeat Menshikov? I'm giving a hundred to one on that!'

Mom turned desperately to my father. 'Julius, tell them! It's too dangerous.'

My dad was still holding a plate of half-eaten birthday cake. He stared at the melting ice cream as if it were the saddest thing in the world.

'Carter and Sadie,' he said at last, 'I brought Khonsu here so that you'd have the choice. But, whatever you do, I'm still proud of you both. If the world ends tonight, that won't change.'

He met my eyes and I could see how much it hurt him to think about losing us. Last Christmas at the British Museum, he'd sacrificed his life to release Osiris and restore balance to the Duat. He'd left Sadie and me alone, and I'd resented him a long time for that. Now I realized what it was like to be in his position. He'd been willing to give up everything, even his life, for a bigger purpose.

'I understand, Dad,' I told him. 'We're Kanes. We don't run from hard choices.'

He didn't answer, but he nodded slowly. His eyes burned with fierce pride.

'For once,' Sadie said, 'Carter's right. Khonsu, we'll play your stupid game.'

'Excellent!' Khonsu said. 'That's two souls. Two hours to win. Ah, but you'll need three hours to get through the gates on time, won't you? Hmm. I'm afraid you can't use Ra. He's not in his right mind. Your mother is already dead. Your father is the judge of the underworld, so he's disqualified from soul wagering ...'

'I'll do it,' Bes said. His face was grim but determined.

'Old buddy!' Khonsu cried. 'I'm delighted.'

'Stuff it, moon god,' Bes said. 'I don't like it, but I'll do it.'

'Bes,' I said, 'you've done enough for us. Bast would never expect you –'

'I'm not doing it for Bast!' he grumbled. Then he took a deep breath. 'Look, you kids are the real deal. Last couple of days – for the first time in ages – I've felt wanted again. Important. Not like a sideshow attraction. If things go wrong, just tell Tawaret...' He cleared his throat and gave Sadie a meaningful look. 'Tell her I tried to turn back the clock.'

'Oh, Bes.' Sadie got up and ran around the table. She hugged the dwarf god and kissed his cheek.

'All right, all right,' he muttered. 'Don't go sappy on me. Let's play this game.'

'Time is money,' Khonsu agreed.

Our parents stood.

'We cannot stay for this,' Dad said. 'But, children . . .'

He didn't seem to know how to complete the thought. *Good luck* probably wouldn't have cut it. I could see the guilt and worry in his eyes, but he was trying hard not to show it. A *good general*, Horus would have said.

'We love you,' our mother finished. 'You will prevail.'

With that, our parents turned to mist and vanished. Everything outside the pavilion darkened like a stage set. The senet game began to glow brighter.

'Shiny,' Ra said.

'Three blue pieces for you,' Khonsu said. 'Three silver pieces for me. Now, who's feeling lucky?'

The game started well enough. Sadie had skill at tossing the sticks. Bes had several thousand years of gaming experience. And I got the job of moving the pieces and making sure Ra didn't eat them.

At first it wasn't obvious who was winning. We just rolled and moved, and it was hard to believe we were playing for our souls, or true names, or whatever you want to call them.

We bumped one of Khonsu's pieces back to start, but he didn't seem upset. He seemed delighted by just about everything.

'Doesn't it bother you?' I asked at one point. 'Devouring innocent souls?'

'Not really.' He polished his crescent amulet. 'Why should it?'

'But we're trying to save the world,' Sadie said, 'Ma'at, the gods – everything. Don't you care if the world crumbles into Chaos?'

'Oh, it wouldn't be so bad,' Khonsu said. 'Change comes in phases, Ma'at and Chaos, Chaos and Ma'at. Being the moon god, I appreciate variation. Now, Ra, poor guy – he always stuck to a schedule. Same path every night. So predictable and boring. Retiring was the most interesting thing he ever did. If Apophis takes over and swallows the sun, well – I suppose the moon will still be there.'

'You're insane,' Sadie said.

'Ha! I'll bet you five extra minutes of moonlight that I'm perfectly sane.'

'Forget it,' Sadie said. 'Just roll.'

Khonsu tossed the sticks. The bad news: he made alarming progress. He rolled a five and got one of his pieces almost to the end of the board. The good news: the piece got stuck at the House of Three Truths, which meant he could only roll a three to get it out.

Bes studied the board intently. He didn't seem to like what he saw. We had one piece way back at the start and two pieces on the last row of the board.

'Careful now,' Khonsu warned. 'This is where it gets interesting.'

Sadie rolled a four, which gave us two options. Our lead piece could go out. Or our second piece could bump Khonsu's piece from the House of Three Truths and send it back to Start.

'Bump him,' I said. 'It's safer.'

391

Bes shook his head. 'Then *we're* stuck in the House of Three Truths. The chances of him rolling a three are slim. Take your first piece out. That way you'll be assured of at least one extra hour.'

'But one extra hour won't do it,' Sadie said.

Khonsu seemed to be enjoying our indecision. He sipped wine from a silvery goblet and smiled. Meanwhile Ra entertained himself by trying to pick the spikes off his war flail. 'Ow, ow, ow.'

My forehead beaded with sweat. How was I sweating in a *board* game? 'Bes, are you sure?'

'It's your best bet,' he said.

'*Bes* best?' Khonsu chuckled. 'Nice!'

I wanted to smack the moon god, but I kept my mouth shut. I moved our first piece out of play.

'Congratulations!' Khonsu said. 'I owe you one hour of moonlight. Now it's my turn.'

He tossed the sticks. They clattered on the dining table, and I felt like someone had snipped an elevator cable in my chest, plunging my heart straight down a shaft. Khonsu had rolled a three.

'Whoopsie!' Ra dropped his flail.

Khonsu moved his piece out of play. 'Oh, what a shame. Now, whose *ren* do I collect first?'

'No, please!' Sadie said. 'Trade back. Take the hour you owe us instead.'

'Those aren't the rules,' Khonsu chided.

I looked down at the gouge I'd made in the table when I was eight. I knew that memory was about to disappear, like all

392

my others. If I gave my *ren* to Khonsu, at least Sadie could still cast the final part of the spell. She would need Bes to protect her and advise her. I was the only expendable one.

I started to say, 'I –'

'Me,' said Bes. 'The move was my idea.'

'Bes, no!' Sadie cried.

The dwarf stood. He planted his feet and balled his fists, like he was getting ready to let loose with a 'BOO'. I wished he'd do that and scare away Khonsu, but instead he looked at us with resignation. 'It was part of the strategy, kids.'

'What?' I asked. 'You *planned* this?'

He slipped off his Hawaiian shirt and folded it carefully, setting it on the table. 'Most important thing is getting all three of your pieces off the board and losing no more than one. This was the only way to do it. You'll beat him easily now. Sometimes you have to lose a piece to win a game.'

'So true,' Khonsu said. 'What a delight! A god's *ren*. Are you ready, Bes?'

'Bes, don't,' I pleaded. 'This isn't right.'

He scowled at me. 'Hey, kid, *you* were willing to sacrifice. Are you saying I'm not as brave as some pipsqueak magician? Besides, I'm a god. Who knows? Sometimes we come back. Now, win the game and get out of here. Kick Menshikov in the knee for me.'

I tried to think of something to say, something that would stop this, but Bes said, 'I'm ready.'

Khonsu closed his eyes and inhaled deeply, like he was enjoying some fresh mountain air. Bes's form flickered. He dissolved into a montage of lightning-fast images – a troupe

393

of dwarves dancing at a temple in the firelight; a crowd of Egyptians partying at a festival, carrying Bes and Bast on their shoulders; Bes and Tawaret in togas at some Roman villa, eating grapes and laughing together on a sofa; Bes dressed like George Washington in a powdered wig and silk suit, doing cartwheels in front of some British redcoats; Bes in the olive fatigues of a US Marine, scaring away a demon in a World War II Nazi uniform.

As his silhouette melted, more recent images flickered past: Bes in a chauffeur's uniform with a placard that read KANE; Bes pulling us out of our sinking limo in the Mediterranean; Bes casting spells on me in Alexandria when I was poisoned, trying desperately to heal me; Bes and me in the back of the Bedouins' pick-up truck, sharing goat meat and Vaseline-flavoured water as we travelled along the bank of the Nile. His last memory: two kids, Sadie and me, looking at him with love and concern. Then the image faded, and Bes was gone. Even his Hawaiian shirt had disappeared.

'You took all of him!' I yelled. 'His body – everything. That wasn't the deal!'

Khonsu opened his eyes and sighed deeply. 'That was lovely.' He smiled at us as if nothing had happened. 'I believe it's your turn.'

His silver eyes were cold and luminous, and I had a feeling that for the rest of my life I would hate looking at the moon.

Maybe it was rage, or Bes's strategy, or maybe we just got lucky, but the rest of the game Sadie and I destroyed Khonsu easily. We bumped his pieces at every opportunity. Within five minutes, our last piece was off the board.

Khonsu spread his hands. 'Well done! Three hours are yours. If you hurry, you can make the gates of the Eighth House.'

'I hate you,' Sadie said. It was the first she'd spoken since Bes disappeared. 'You're cold, calculating, horrible –'

'And I'm just what you needed.' Khonsu took off his platinum Rolex and wound back the time – one, two, three hours. All around us, the statues of the gods flickered and jumped like the world was being slammed into reverse.

'Now,' Khonsu said, 'would you like to spend your hard-earned time complaining? Or do you want to save this poor old fool of a king?'

'Zebras?' Ra muttered hopefully.

'Where are our parents?' I asked. 'At least let us say goodbye.'

Khonsu shook his head. 'Time is precious, Carter Kane. You should've learned that lesson. It's best that I send you on your way, but if you ever want to gamble with me again – for seconds, hours, even days – just let me know. Your credit is good.'

I couldn't stand it. I lunged at Khonsu, but the moon god vanished. The whole pavilion faded, and Sadie and I were standing on the deck of the sun boat again, sailing down the dark river. The glowing crew lights buzzed around us, manning the oars and trimming the sail. Ra sat on his fiery throne, playing with his crook and flail like they were puppets having an imaginary conversation.

In front of us, a pair of enormous stone gates loomed out of the darkness. Eight massive snakes were carved into the rock, four on each side. The gates were slowly closing, but the sun boat slipped through just in time and we passed into the Eighth House.

I have to say, the House of Challenges didn't seem very challenging. We fought monsters, yes. Serpents loomed out of the river. Demons arose. Ships full of ghosts tried to board the sun boat. We destroyed them all. I was so angry, so devastated at losing Bes, that I imagined every threat was the moon god Khonsu. Our enemies didn't stand a chance.

Sadie cast spells I'd never seen her use. She summoned sheets of ice that probably matched her emotions, leaving several demon icebergs in our wake. She turned an entire shipful of pirate ghosts into Khonsu bobble-heads, then vaporized them in a miniature nuclear explosion. Meanwhile, Ra played happily with his toys while the light servants flittered around the deck in agitation, apparently sensing that our journey was reaching a critical phase. The Ninth, Tenth and Eleventh Houses passed in a blur. From time to time I heard a splash in the water behind us, like the oar of another boat. I looked back, wondering if Menshikov had somehow got on our tail again, but I didn't see anything. If something *was* following us, it knew better than to show itself.

At last I heard a roar up ahead, like another waterfall or a stretch of rapids. The light orbs worked furiously, taking down the sail, pushing on the oars, but we kept gaining speed.

We passed under a low archway carved like the goddess Nut, her starry limbs stretched out protectively and her face smiling in welcome. I got the feeling we were entering the Twelfth House, the last part of the Duat before we emerged into a new dawn.

I hoped to see light at the end of the tunnel, literally, but instead our path had been sabotaged. I could see where the river was *supposed* to go. The tunnel continued ahead, slowly winding out of the Duat. I could even smell fresh air – the scent of the mortal world. But the far end of the tunnel had been drained to a field of mud. In front of us, the river plunged into a massive pit, as if an asteroid had punched a hole in the earth and diverted the water straight down. We were racing towards the drop.

'We could jump,' Sadie said. 'Abandon ship...'

But I think we came to the same conclusion. We needed the sun boat. We needed Ra. We had to follow the course of the river wherever it led.

'It's a trap,' Sadie said. 'The work of Apophis.'

'I know,' I said. 'Let's go tell him we don't like his work.'

We both grabbed the mast as the ship plunged into the maelstrom.

It seemed as if we fell forever. You know the feeling when you dive to the bottom of a deep pool, like your nose and ears are going to explode, and your eyes are going to pop out of your head? Imagine that feeling a hundred times worse. We were sinking into the Duat deeper than we'd ever been – deeper than any mortal was supposed to go. The molecules of my body felt like they were heating up, buzzing so fast they might fly apart.

We didn't crash. We didn't hit bottom. The boat simply flipped direction, like down had become sideways, and we sailed into a cavern that glowed with harsh red light. The magical pressure was so intense that my ears rang. I was nauseated and I could barely think straight, but I recognized the shoreline up ahead: a beach made of millions of dead scarab shells, shifting and surging as a force underneath – a massive serpentine shape – struggled to break free. Dozens of demons were digging through the scarab shells with shovels. And standing on the shore, waiting for us patiently, was Vlad Menshikov, his clothes charred and smoking, his staff glowing with green fire.

'Welcome, children,' he called across the water. 'Come. Join me for the end of the world.'

22. Friends in the Strangest Places

MENSHIKOV LOOKED LIKE HE'D SWUM through the Lake of Fire without a magic shield. His curly grey hair had been reduced to black stubble. His white suit was shredded and peppered with burn holes. His whole face was blistered, so his ruined eyes didn't seem out of place. As Bes might've said, Menshikov was wearing his ugly outfit.

The memory of Bes made me angry. Everything we'd gone through, everything we'd lost, was all Vlad Menshikov's fault.

The sun boat ground to a halt on the scarab-shell beach.

Ra warbled, 'Hel-lo-o-o-o-o!' and stumbled to his feet. He began chasing a blue servant orb around the deck as if it were a pretty butterfly.

The demons dropped their shovels and assembled on the shore. They looked at each other uncertainly, no doubt wondering if this were some sort of clever trick. Surely this doddering old fool could not be the sun god.

'Wonderful,' Menshikov said. 'You brought Ra, after all.'

It took me a moment to realize what was different about his voice. The gravelly breathing was gone. His tone was a deep, smooth baritone.

'I was worried,' he continued. 'You took so long in the Fourth House that I thought you'd be trapped for the night. We could have freed Lord Apophis without you, of course, but it would've been so inconvenient to hunt you down later. This is much better. Lord Apophis will be hungry when he wakes. He'll be most pleased that you brought him a snack.'

'Wheee, snack,' Ra giggled. He hobbled around the boat, trying to smash the servant light with his flail.

The demons began to laugh. Menshikov gave them an indulgent smile.

'Yes, quite amusing,' he said. 'My grandfather entertained Peter the Great with a dwarf wedding. I will do even better. I will entertain the Lord of Chaos himself with a senile sun god!'

The voice of Horus spoke urgently in my mind: *Take back the weapons of the pharaoh. This is your last chance!*

Deep inside, I knew it was a bad idea. If I claimed the weapons of the pharaoh now, I'd never return them. And the powers I'd gain wouldn't be enough to defeat Apophis. Still, I was tempted. It would feel so good to grab the crook and flail from that stupid old god Ra and smash Menshikov into the ground.

The Russian's eyes glittered with malice. 'A rematch, Carter Kane? By all means. I notice you don't have your dwarf babysitter this time. Let's see what you can do on your own.'

My vision turned red, and it had nothing to do with the light in the cavern. I stepped off the boat and summoned the hawk god's avatar. I'd never tried the spell so deep in the Duat before. I got more than I asked for. Instead of being encased in a glowing holograph, I felt myself growing taller and stronger. My eyesight grew sharper.

Sadie made a strangled sound. 'Carter?'

'Large bird!' Ra said.

I looked down and found I was a flesh-and-blood giant, fifteen feet tall, dressed in the battle armour of Horus. I brought my enormous hands to my head and patted feathers instead of hair. My mouth was a razor-sharp beak. I shouted with elation and it came out as a screech, echoing through the cavern. The demons scrambled back nervously. I looked down at Menshikov, who now seemed as insignificant as a mouse. I was ready to pulverize him, but Menshikov sneered and pointed his staff.

Whatever he was planning, Sadie was faster. She threw down her own staff and it transformed into a kite (the bird-of-prey kind) as large as a pterodactyl.

Typical. I pull something really cool like morphing into a hawk warrior, and Sadie has to show me up. Her kite buffeted the air with its massive wings. Menshikov and his demons went somersaulting backwards across the beach.

'Two large birds!' Ra started to clap.

'Carter, guard me!' Sadie pulled out the Book of Ra. 'I need to start the spell.'

I thought the giant kite was doing a pretty good job with guard duty, but I stepped forward and got ready to fight.

Menshikov rose to his feet. 'By all means, Sadie Kane, start your little spell. Don't you understand? The spirit of Khepri *created* this prison. Ra gave part of his own soul, his ability to be reborn, to keep Apophis chained.'

Sadie looked like he'd slapped her in the face. '"The last scarab –"'

'Exactly,' Menshikov agreed. 'All these scarabs were multiplied from one – Khepri, the third soul of Ra. My demons will find it eventually, digging through the shells. It's one of the only scarabs still alive now, and once we crush it Apophis will be free. Even if you summon it back to Ra, Apophis will still be freed! Either way, Ra is too weak to fight. Apophis will devour him, as the ancient prophecies predicted, and Chaos will destroy Ma'at once and for all. You can't win.'

'You're insane,' I said, my voice much deeper than usual. 'You'll be destroyed, too.'

I saw the fractured light in his eyes, and I realized something that shocked me to the core. Menshikov didn't want this any more than we did. He'd lived with grief and despair so long that Apophis had twisted his soul, made him a prisoner of his own hateful feelings. Vladimir Menshikov pretended to gloat, but he didn't feel any sense of triumph. Inside he was terrified, defeated, miserable. He was enslaved by Apophis. I almost felt sorry for him.

'We're already dead, Carter Kane,' he said. 'This place was never meant for humans. Don't you feel it? The power of Chaos is seeping into our bodies, withering our souls. But I have bigger plans. A *host* can live indefinitely, no matter what sickness he may have, no matter how injured he may be.

Apophis has already healed my voice. Soon I will be whole again. I will live forever!'

'A host...' When I realized what he meant, I almost lost control of my new giant form. 'You're not serious. Menshikov, stop this before it's too late.'

'And die?' he asked.

Behind me, a new voice said, 'There are worse things than death, Vladimir.'

I turned and saw a second boat gliding towards the shore – a small grey skiff with a single magic oar that rowed itself. The eye of Horus was painted on the boat's prow, and its lone passenger was Michel Desjardins. The Chief Lector's hair and beard were now white as snow. Glowing hieroglyphs floated from his cream-coloured robes, making a trail of divine words behind him.

Desjardins stepped ashore. 'You toy with something *much* worse than death, my old friend. Pray that I kill you before you succeed.'

Of all the weird things I'd experienced that night, Desjardins stepping up to fight on *our* side was definitely the weirdest.

He walked between my giant hawk warrior and Sadie's mega-kite like they were no big deal, and planted his staff in the dead scarabs.

'Surrender, Vladimir.'

Menshikov laughed. 'Have you looked at yourself lately, my lord? My curses have been sapping your strength for months, and you didn't even realize it. You're nearly dead now. *I* am the most powerful magician in the world.'

It was true that Desjardins didn't look good. His face was almost as gaunt and wrinkled as the sun god's. But the cloud of hieroglyphs seemed stronger around him. His eyes blazed with intensity, just as they had months ago in New Mexico, when he'd battled us in the streets of Las Cruces and vowed to destroy us. He took another step forward and the mob of demons edged away. I suppose they recognized the leopard-skin cape around his shoulders as a mark of power.

'I have failed in many things,' Desjardins admitted. 'But I will not fail in this. I will *not* let you destroy the House of Life.'

'The House?' Menshikov's voice turned shrill. 'It died centuries ago! It should've been disbanded when Egypt fell.' He kicked at the dried scarab shells. 'The House has as much life as these hollow bug husks. Wake up, Michel! Egypt is gone, meaningless, ancient history. It's time to destroy the world and start anew. Chaos always wins.'

'Not always.' Desjardins turned to Sadie. 'Begin your spell. I will deal with this wretch.'

The ground surged under us, trembling, as Apophis tried to rise.

'Think first, children,' Menshikov warned. 'The world will end no matter what you do. Mortals can't leave this cavern alive, but the two of you have been godlings. Combine with Horus and Isis again, pledge to serve Apophis and you could survive this night. Desjardins has always been your enemy. Slay him for me now and present his body as a gift to Apophis! I will assure you both positions of honour in a new world ruled by Chaos, unrestricted by any rules. I can even give you the secret of curing Walt Stone.'

He smiled at Sadie's stunned expression. 'Yes, my girl. I *do* know how. The remedy was passed down for generations among the priests of Amun-Ra. Kill Desjardins, join Apophis and the boy you love will be spared.'

I'll be honest. His words were persuasive. I could imagine a new world where anything was possible, where no laws applied, not even the laws of physics, and we could be anything we wanted.

Chaos is impatient. It's random. And above all it's selfish. It tears down everything just for the sake of change, feeding on itself in constant hunger. But Chaos can also be appealing. It tempts you to believe that nothing matters except what *you* want. And there was *so* much that I wanted. Menshikov's restored voice was smooth and confident, like Amos's tone whenever he used magic to persuade mortals.

That was the problem. Menshikov's promise was a trick. His words weren't even his own. They were being forced out of him. His eyes moved like they were reading a teleprompter. He spoke the will of Apophis, but when he finished he locked eyes with me, and just briefly I saw his real thoughts – a tortured plea he would've screamed if he had control of his own mouth: *Kill me now. Please.*

'I'm sorry, Menshikov,' I said, and I sincerely meant it. 'Magicians and gods have to stand together. The world may need fixing, but it's worth preserving. We won't let Chaos win.'

Then a lot of things happened at once. Sadie opened her scroll and began to read. Menshikov screamed, 'Attack!' and the demons rushed forward. The giant kite spread its wings, deflecting a blast of green fire from Menshikov's staff that probably would've incinerated Sadie on the spot. I charged to protect her, while Desjardins summoned a whirlwind around his body and flew towards Vlad Menshikov.

I waded through demons. I knocked over one with a razor-blade head, grabbed his ankles and swung him around like a weapon, slicing his allies into piles of sand. Sadie's giant kite picked up two more in its claws and tossed them into the river.

Meanwhile Desjardins and Menshikov rose into the air, locked inside a tornado. They whirled around each other, firing blasts of fire, poison and acid. Demons who got too close melted instantly.

In the midst of all this, Sadie read from the Book of Ra. I didn't know how she could concentrate, but her words rang out clear and loud. She invoked the dawn and the rise of a new day. Golden mist began to spread around her feet, weaving through the dried shells as if searching for life. The entire beach shuddered, and far underground Apophis roared in outrage.

'Oh, noes!' Ra yelled behind me. 'Vegetables!'

I turned and saw one of the largest demons boarding the sun boat, wicked knives in all four of his hands. Ra gave him the raspberry and scampered away, hiding behind his fiery throne.

I threw Razor-blade Head into a crowd of his friends, grabbed a spear from another demon and threw it towards the boat.

If it had just been *me* throwing, my complete lack of long-shot skills might have caused me to impale the sun god, which would have been pretty embarrassing. Fortunately, my new giant form had aim worthy of Horus. The spear hit the four-armed demon square in the back. He dropped his knives, staggered to the edge of the boat and fell into the River of Night.

Ra leaned over the side and gave him one last raspberry for good measure.

Desjardins's tornado still spun him around, locked in combat with Menshikov. I couldn't tell which magician had the upper hand. Sadie's kite was doing its best to protect her, impaling demons with its beak and crushing them in its huge claws. Somehow Sadie kept her concentration. The golden mist thickened as it spread over the beach.

The remaining demons began to pull back as Sadie spoke the last words of her spell: "'Khepri, the scarab who rises from death, the rebirth of Ra!'"

The Book of Ra vanished in a flash. The ground rumbled, and from the mass of dead shells, a single scarab rose into the air, a living golden beetle that floated towards Sadie and came to rest in her hands.

Sadie smiled triumphantly. I almost dared to hope we'd won. Then hissing laughter filled the cavern. Desjardins lost control of his whirlwind, and the Chief Lector went flying towards the sun boat, slamming into the prow so hard he broke the rail and lay absolutely still.

Vladimir Menshikov dropped to the ground, landing in a crouch. Around his feet, the dead scarab shells dissolved, turning into blood-red sand.

'Brilliant,' he said. 'Brilliant, Sadie Kane!'

He stood, and all the magical energy in the cavern seemed to race towards his body – golden mist, red light, glowing hieroglyphs – all of it collapsing into Menshikov as if he'd taken on the gravity of a black hole.

His ruined eyes healed. His blistered face became smooth, young and handsome. His white suit mended itself, then the fabric turned dark red. His skin rippled and I realized with a chill that he was growing snake scales.

On the sun boat, Ra muttered, 'Oh, noes. Need zebras.'

The entire beach turned to red sand.

Menshikov held out his hand to my sister. 'Give me the scarab, Sadie. I will have mercy on you. You and your brother will live. Walt will live.'

Sadie clutched the scarab. I got ready to charge. Even in the body of a giant hawk warrior, I could feel the Chaos energy getting stronger and stronger, sapping my strength. Menshikov had warned us that no mortal could survive this cavern, and I believed him. We didn't have much time, but we had to stop Apophis. In the back of my mind, I accepted the fact that I would die. I was acting now for the sake of our friends, for the Kane family, for the whole mortal world.

'You want the scarab, Apophis?' Sadie's voice was full of loathing. 'Then come and get it, you disgusting –' She called Apophis some words so bad that Gran would've washed her mouth out with soap for a year. [And no, Sadie, I'm not going to say them into the microphone.]

Menshikov stepped towards her. I picked up a shovel one of the demons had dropped. Sadie's giant kite flew at Menshikov, its talons poised to strike, but Menshikov flicked his hand like he was shooing away a fly. The monster dissolved into cloud of feathers.

'Do you take me for a god?' Menshikov roared.

As he focused on Sadie, I skirted behind him, doing my best to sneak closer – which is not easy when you're a fifteen-foot-tall birdman.

'I am Chaos itself!' Menshikov bellowed. 'I will unknit your bones, dissolve your soul and send you back to the primordial ooze you came from. Now, give me the scarab!'

'Tempting,' Sadie said. 'What do you think, Carter?'

Menshikov realized the trap too late. I lunged forward and hit him upside the head with the shovel. Menshikov crumpled. I body-slammed him into the sand, then stood up and stomped him in a little deeper. I buried him as best I could, then Sadie pointed at his burial site and spoke the glyph for fire. The sand melted, hardening into a coffin-size block of solid glass.

I would've spat on it, too, but I wasn't sure I could do that with a falcon beak.

The surviving demons did the sensible thing. They fled in panic. A few jumped into the river and let themselves dissolve, which was a real time-saver for us.

'That wasn't so hard,' Sadie said, though I could tell the Chaos energy was starting to wear her down, too. Even when she was five and had pneumonia, I don't think she looked this bad.

'Hurry,' I said. My adrenalin was fading quickly. My avatar form was starting to feel like an extra five hundred pounds of dead weight. 'Get the scarab to Ra.'

She nodded and ran towards the sun boat, but she'd only made it halfway when Menshikov's glass grave blew up.

The most powerful explosive magic I'd ever seen was Sadie's *ha-di* spell. This blast was about fifty times more powerful.

A high-powered wave of sand and glass shards knocked me off my feet and shredded my avatar. Back in my regular body, blind and in pain, I crawled away from the laughing voice of Apophis.

'Where did you go, Sadie Kane?' Apophis called, his voice now as deep as a cannon shot. 'Where is that bad little girl with my scarab?'

I blinked the sand out of my eyes. Vlad Menshikov – no, he might look like Vlad, but he was Apophis now – was about fifty feet away, stalking around the rim of the crater he'd made in the beach. He either didn't see me, or he assumed I was dead. He was looking for Sadie, but she was nowhere. The blast must've buried her in the sand, or worse.

My throat closed up. I wanted to get to my feet and tackle Apophis, but my body wouldn't work. My magic was depleted. The power of Chaos was sapping my life force. Just from being near Apophis I felt like I was coming undone – my brain synapses, my DNA, everything that made me Carter Kane was slowly dissolving.

Finally, Apophis spread his arms. 'No matter. I'll dig your body up later. First, I'll deal with the old man.'

For a second I thought he meant Desjardins, who was still crumpled lifelessly over the broken railing, but Apophis climbed into the boat, ignoring the Chief Lector, and approached the throne of fire.

'Hello, Ra,' he said in a kindly voice. 'It's been a long time.'

A feeble voice from behind the chair said, 'Can't play. Go away.'

'Would you like a treat?' Apophis asked. 'We used to play so nicely together. Every night, trying to kill each other. Don't you remember?'

Ra poked his bald head above the throne. 'Treat?'

'How about a stuffed date?' Apophis pulled one out of the air. 'You used to love stuffed dates, didn't you? All you have to do is come out and let me devour – I mean, entertain you.'

'Want a cookie,' Ra said.

'What kind?'

'Weasel cookie.'

I'm here to tell you, that comment about weasel cookies probably saved the known universe.

Apophis stepped back, obviously confused by a comment that was even more chaotic than *he* was. And, in that moment, Michel Desjardins struck.

The Chief Lector must have been playing dead, or maybe he just recovered quickly. He rose up and launched himself at Apophis, slamming him against the burning throne.

Menshikov screamed in his old raspy voice. Steam hissed like water on a barbecue. Desjardins's robes caught fire. Ra scrambled to the back of the boat and poked his crook in the air as if that would make the bad men go away.

I struggled to my feet, but I still felt like I was carrying a few hundred extra pounds. Menshikov and Desjardins grappled with each other in front of the throne. This was the scene I'd witnessed in the Hall of Ages: the first moment in a new age.

I knew I should help, but I scrambled along the beach,

trying to gauge the spot where I'd last seen Sadie. I fell to my knees and started to dig.

Desjardins and Menshikov struggled back and forth, shouting out words of power. I glanced over and saw a cloud of hieroglyphs and red light swirling around them as the Chief Lector summoned Ma'at, and Apophis just as quickly dissolved his spells with Chaos. As for Ra, the almighty sun god, he had scrambled to the stern of the boat and was cowering under the tiller.

I kept digging.

'Sadie,' I muttered. 'Come on. Where are you?'

Think, I told myself.

I closed my eyes. I thought about Sadie – every memory we'd shared since Christmas. We'd lived apart for years, but over the last three months I'd become closer to her than to anyone else in the world. If she could figure out my secret name while I was unconscious, surely I could find her in a pile of sand.

I scrambled a few feet to the left and began to dig again. Immediately I scratched Sadie's nose. She groaned, which at least meant she was alive. I brushed off her face and she coughed. Then she raised her arms and I pulled her out of the sand. I was so relieved I almost sobbed, but being a macho guy and all, I didn't.

[Shut up, Sadie. I'm telling this part.]

Apophis and Desjardins were still fighting back and forth on the sun boat.

Desjardins yelled, '*Heh-sieh!*' and a hieroglyph blazed between them:

Apophis went flying off the boat like he'd been hooked by a moving train. He sailed right over us and landed in the sand about forty feet away.

'Nice one,' Sadie muttered in a daze. 'Glyph for "*Turn back*."'

Desjardins staggered off the sun boat. His robes were still smouldering, but from his sleeve he pulled a ceramic statuette – a red snake carved with hieroglyphs.

Sadie gasped. 'A *shabti* of Apophis? The penalty for making those is death!'

I could understand why. Images had power. In the wrong hands, they could strengthen or even summon the being they represented, and a statue of Apophis was way too dangerous to play with. But it was also a necessary ingredient for certain spells . . .

'An execration,' I said. 'He's trying to erase Apophis.'

'That's impossible!' Sadie said. 'He'll be destroyed!'

Desjardins began to chant. Hieroglyphs glowed in the air around him, swirling into a cone of protective power. Sadie tried to get to her feet, but she wasn't in much better shape than I was.

Apophis sat up. His face was a nightmare of burns from the throne of fire. He looked like a half-cooked hamburger patty someone had dropped in the sand. [Sadie says that's too gross. Well, I'm sorry. It's accurate.]

When he saw the statue in the Chief Lector's hands,

he roared in outrage. 'Are you insane, Michel? You can't execrate me!'

'Apophis,' Desjardins chanted, 'I name you Lord of Chaos, Serpent in the Dark, Fear of the Twelve Houses, the Hated One –'

'Stop it!' Apophis bellowed. 'I cannot be contained!'

He shot a blast of fire at Desjardins, but the energy simply joined the swirling cloud around the Chief Lector, turning into the hieroglyph for *heat*. Desjardins stumbled forward, ageing before our eyes, becoming more stooped and frail, but his voice remained strong. 'I speak for the gods. I speak for the House of Life. I am a servant of Ma'at. I cast you underfoot.'

Desjardins threw down the red snake and Apophis fell to his side.

The Lord of Chaos hurled everything he had at Desjardins – ice, poison, lightning, boulders – but nothing connected. They all simply turned into hieroglyphs in the Chief Lector's shield, Chaos forced into patterns of words – into the divine language of creation.

Desjardins smashed the ceramic snake under his foot. Apophis writhed in agony. The thing that used to be Vladimir Menshikov crumbled like a wax shell and a creature rose out of it – a red snake, covered in slime like a new hatchling. It began to grow, its red scales glistening and its eyes glowing.

Its voice hissed in my mind: *I cannot be contained!*

But it was having trouble rising. The sand churned around it. A portal was opening, anchored on Apophis himself.

'I erase your name,' Desjardins said. 'I remove you from the memory of Egypt.'

Apophis screamed. The beach imploded around him, swallowing the serpent and sucking the red sand into the vortex.

I grabbed Sadie and ran for the boat. Desjardins had collapsed to his knees in exhaustion, but somehow I managed to hook his arm and drag him to the shore. Together Sadie and I hauled him aboard the sun boat. Ra finally scrambled out from his hiding place under the tiller. The glowing servant lights manned the oars and we pulled away as the entire beach sank into the dark waters, flashes of red lightning rippling under the surface.

Desjardins was dying.

The hieroglyphs had faded around him. His forehead was burning hot. His skin was as dry and thin as rice paper, and his voice was a ragged whisper.

'Execration w-won't last,' he warned. 'Only bought you some time.'

I gripped his hand like he was an old friend, not a former enemy. After playing senet with the moon god, buying time wasn't something I took lightly. 'Why did you do it?' I asked. 'You used all your life force to banish him.'

Desjardins smiled faintly. 'Don't like you much. But you were right. The old ways...our only chance. Tell Amos... tell Amos what happened.' He clawed feebly at his leopard-skin cape and I realized he wanted to remove it. I helped him and he pressed the cape into my hands. 'Show this to...the others....Tell Amos...'

His eyes rolled into his head and the Chief Lector passed.

His body disintegrated into hieroglyphs – too many to read, the story of his entire life. Then the words floated away down the River of Night.

'Bye-bye,' Ra muttered. 'Weasels are sick.'

I'd almost forgotten about the old god. He slumped in his throne again, resting his head on the loop of his crook and swatting his flail half-heartedly at the servant lights.

Sadie took a shaky breath. 'Desjardins *saved* us. I – I didn't like him either, but –'

'I know,' I said. 'But we have to keep going. Do you still have the scarab?'

Sadie pulled the wriggling golden scarab from her pocket. Together we approached Ra.

'Take it,' I told him.

Ra wrinkled his already wrinkled nose. 'Don't want a bug.'

'It's your soul!' Sadie snapped. 'You'll take it and you'll like it!'

Ra looked cowed. He took the beetle and, to my horror, popped it in his mouth.

'No!' Sadie yelped.

Too late. Ra had swallowed.

'Oh, god,' Sadie said. 'Was he supposed to do that? Maybe he was supposed to do that.'

'Don't like bugs,' Ra muttered.

We waited for him to change into a powerful youthful king. Instead, he burped. He stayed old, and weird, and disgusting.

In a daze, I walked with Sadie back to the front of the ship. We'd done everything we could, and yet I felt like we'd lost. As we sailed on, the magic pressure seemed to ease. The river appeared level, but I could sense we were rising rapidly through the Duat. Despite that, I still felt like my insides were melting. Sadie didn't look any better.

Menshikov's words echoed in my head: *Mortals can't leave this cavern alive.*

'It's Chaos sickness,' Sadie said. 'We're not going to make it, are we?'

'We have to hold on,' I said. 'At least until dawn.'

'All that,' Sadie said, 'and what happened? We retrieved a senile god. We lost Bes and the Chief Lector. And we're dying.'

I took Sadie's hand. 'Maybe not. Look.'

Ahead of us, the tunnel was getting brighter. The cavern walls dissolved and the river widened. Two pillars rose from the water – two giant golden scarab statues. Beyond them gleamed the morning skyline of Manhattan. The River of Night was emptying out into New York Harbor.

'Each new dawn is a new world,' I remembered our dad saying. 'Maybe we'll be healed.'

'Ra, too?' Sadie asked.

I didn't have an answer, but I was starting to feel better, stronger, like I'd had a good night's sleep. As we passed between the golden scarab statues, I looked to our right. Across the water, smoke was rising from Brooklyn – flashes of multicoloured light and streaks of fire as winged creatures engaged in aerial combat.

'They're still alive,' Sadie said. 'They need help!'

We turned the sun boat towards home – and sailed straight into battle.

S
A
D
I
E

23. We Throw a Wild House Party

[FATAL MISTAKE, CARTER. Giving me the microphone at the most important part? You'll never get it back now. The end of the story is mine. Ha-ha-ha!]

Oh, that felt good. I'd be excellent at world domination.

But I digress.

You might've seen news reports about the strange double sunrise over Brooklyn on the morning of March twenty-first. There were many theories: haze in the air from pollution, a temperature drop in the lower atmosphere, aliens, or perhaps another sewer-gas leak causing mass hysteria. We love sewer gas in Brooklyn!

I can confirm, however, that there briefly *were* two suns in the sky. I know this because I was in one of them. The normal sun rose as usual. But there was also the boat of Ra, blazing as it rose from the Duat, out of New York Harbor and into the sky of the mortal world.

To observers below, the second sun appeared to merge with the light of the first. What actually happened? The sun boat dimmed as it descended towards Brooklyn House, where the mansion's anti-mortal camouflage shielding enveloped it and made it seem to disappear.

The shielding was already working overtime, as a full-fledged war was in progress. Freak the Griffin was diving through the air, engaging the winged flaming snakes, the *uraei*, in aerial combat.

[I know that's a horrible word to pronounce, *uraei*, but Carter insists it's the plural for *uraeus* and there's no arguing with him. Just say *you're right* and leave off the *t*, and you've got it.]

Freak yelled, 'Freeeeek!' and gobbled up a *uraeus*, but he was sorely outnumbered. His fur was singed and his buzzing wings must've been damaged, as he kept spinning in circles like a broken helicopter.

His rooftop nest was on fire. Our portal sphinx was broken, and the chimney was stained with a massive black starburst where something or someone had exploded. A squad of enemy magicians and demons had taken cover behind the air-conditioning unit and were pinned in combat against Zia and Walt, who were guarding the stairwell. Both sides threw fire, *shabti* and glowing hieroglyphic bombs across the no-man's-land of the roof.

As we descended over the enemy, old Ra (yes, he was still just as senile and withered as ever) leaned over the side and waved at everyone with his crook. 'Hel-lo-o-o-o! Zebras!'

Both sides looked up in amazement. 'Ra!' one demon screamed. Then everyone took up the cry: 'Ra?' 'Ra!' 'Ra!'

They sounded like the world's most terrified pep squad.

The *uraei* stopped spitting fire, much to Freak's surprise, and immediately flew to the sun boat. They began circling us like an honour guard, and I remembered what Menshikov had said about them originally being creatures of Ra. Apparently they recognized their old master (emphasis on *old*).

Most of the enemies below us scattered as the boat came down, but the slowest of the demons said, 'Ra?' and looked up just as our sun boat landed on top of him with a satisfying *crunch*.

Carter and I jumped into battle. In spite of all we'd be through, I felt wonderful. The Chaos sickness had disappeared as soon as we'd risen from the Duat. My magic was strong. My spirits were high. If I'd just had a shower, some fresh clothes and a proper cup of tea, I would've been in paradise. (Strike that; now that I'd seen Paradise, I didn't much like it. I'd settle for my own room.)

I zapped one demon into a tiger and unleashed him on his brethren. Carter popped into avatar form – the glowing golden kind, thank goodness; the three-metre-tall birdman had been a bit too scary for me. He smashed his way through the terrified enemy magicians, and with a sweep of his hand sent them sailing into the East River. Zia and Walt came out from the stairwell and helped us mop up the stragglers. Then they ran to us with big grins on their faces. They looked battered and bruised but still very much alive.

'FREEEEEK!' said the griffin. He swooped down and landed next to Carter, head-butting his combat avatar, which I hoped was a sign of affection.

'Hey, buddy.' Carter rubbed his head, careful to avoid the monster's chain-saw wings. 'What's happening, guys?'

'Talking didn't work,' Zia said drily.

'The enemy's been trying to break in all night,' Walt said. 'Amos and Bast have held them off, but –' He glanced at the sun boat and his voice faltered. 'Is that – that isn't –'

'Zebra!' Ra called, tottering towards us with a big toothless grin.

He walked straight up to Zia and pulled something out of his mouth – the glowing gold scarab, now quite wet but undigested. He offered it to her. 'I like zebras.'

Zia backed up. 'This is – this is Ra, the Lord of the Sun? Why is he offering me a bug?'

'And what does he mean about zebras?' Walt asked.

Ra looked at Walt and clucked disapprovingly. 'Weasels are sick.'

Suddenly a chill went through me. My head spun as if the Chaos sickness was returning. In the back of mind, an idea started to form – something *very* important.

Zebras . . . Zia. Weasels . . . Walt.

Before I could think about this further, a large BOOM! shook the building. Chunks of limestone flew from the side of the mansion and rained down on the warehouse yard.

'They've breached the walls again!' Walt said. 'Hurry!'

I consider myself fairly scattered and hyper, but the rest of the battle happened too fast even for *me* to keep track of it. Ra absolutely refused to be parted from Zebra and Weasel (sorry, Zia and Walt), so we left him in their care at the sun boat while Freak lowered Carter and me to the deck below. We dropped from his claws onto the buffet table and found Bast whirling around with her knives in hand, slicing demons to sand and kicking magicians into the swimming pool, where our albino crocodile, Philip of Macedonia, was only too happy to entertain them.

'Sadie!' she cried with relief. [Yes, Carter, she called *my* name instead of yours, but she's known me longer, after all.] She seemed to be having a great deal of fun, but her tone was urgent. 'They've breached the east wall. Get inside!'

We ran through the doorway, dodging a random wombat that went flying over our heads – possibly someone's spell gone awry – and stepped into complete pandemonium.

'Holy Horus,' Carter said.

In fact, Horus was about the only thing *not* doing battle in the Great Room. Khufu, our intrepid baboon, was riding an old magician around the room, choking him with his own wand and steering him into walls as the mage turned blue. Felix had unleashed a squad of penguins on another magician, who cowered in a magic circle with some sort of post-traumatic stress, screaming, 'Not Antarctica again! Anything but that!' Alyssa was summoning the powers of Geb to repair a massive hole the enemy had blasted in the far wall. Julian had summoned a combat avatar for the first time and was slicing demons with his glowing sword. Even bookish Cleo was dashing about the room, pulling scrolls from her pouch and reading random words of power like 'Blind!' 'Horizontal!' and 'Gassy!' (which, by the way, work wonders to incapacitate an enemy). Everywhere I looked, our initiates were ruling the day. They fought as if they'd been waiting all night for the chance to strike, which I suppose was exactly the case. And there was Jaz – Jaz! Up and looking quite healthy! – knocking an enemy *shabti* straight into the fireplace, where it broke into a thousand pieces.

I felt an overwhelming sense of pride and not a small amount of amazement. I'd been so worried about our young trainees' surviving, yet they were quite simply *dominating* a much more seasoned group of magicians.

Most impressive, though, was Amos. I'd seen him do magic, but never like this. He stood at the base of Thoth's statue, swirling his staff and summoning lightning and thunder, blasting enemy magicians and flinging them away in miniature storm clouds. A woman magician charged at him, her staff glowing with red flames, but Amos simply tapped the floor. The marble tiles turned to sand at her feet, and the woman sank up to her neck.

Carter and I looked at each other, grinned and joined the fight.

It was a complete rout. Soon the demons had been reduced to sand piles, and the enemy magicians began scattering in panic. No doubt they'd been expecting to fight a band of untrained children. They hadn't counted on the full Kane treatment.

One of the women managed to open a portal in the far wall.

Stop them, the voice of Isis spoke in my mind, which was quite a shock after such a long silence. *They must hear the truth.*

I don't know where I got the idea, but I raised my arms and

shimmering rainbow wings appeared on either side of me – the wings of Isis.

I swept my arms. A blast of wind and multicoloured light knocked our enemies off their feet, leaving our friends perfectly unharmed.

'Listen!' I bellowed.

Everyone fell silent. My voice normally sounds bossy, but now it seemed magnified by a factor of ten. The wings probably commanded attention as well.

'We're not your enemies!' I said. 'I don't care if you like us, but the world has changed. You need to hear what's happened.'

My magic wings faded as I told everyone about our trip through the Duat, Ra's rebirth, Menshikov's betrayal, the rising of Apophis and Desjardins's sacrifice to banish the Serpent.

'Lies!' An Asian man in charred blue robes stepped forward. From the vision Carter had described, I supposed that he was Kwai.

'It's true,' Carter said. His avatar no longer surrounded him. His clothes had reverted to the normal mortal ones we'd bought him in Cairo, but somehow he still looked quite imposing, quite confident. He held up the leopard-skin cape of the Chief Lector, and I could feel a ripple of shock spread through the room.

'Desjardins fought at our side,' Carter said. 'He defeated Menshikov and execrated Apophis. He sacrificed his life to buy us a little time. But Apophis will be back. Desjardins wanted you to know. With his last words, he told me to show you this cape and explain the truth. Especially you,

Amos. He wanted you to know – the path of gods has to be restored.'

The enemy's escape portal was still swirling. No one had stepped through yet.

The woman who'd summoned it spat on our floor. She had white robes and spiky black hair. She shouted to her comrades, 'What are you waiting for? They bring us the Chief Lector's cape and tell us this crazy story. They're Kanes! Traitors! They probably killed Desjardins and Menshikov themselves.'

Amos's voice boomed across the Great Room: 'Sarah Jacobi! You of all people know that isn't true. You've devoted your life to studying the ways of Chaos. You can *sense* the unleashing of Apophis, can't you? And the return of Ra.'

Amos pointed out through the glass doors leading to the deck. I don't know how he sensed it without looking, but the sun boat was just floating down, coming to rest in Philip's swimming pool. It was quite an impressive landing. Zia and Walt stood on either side of the throne of fire. They'd managed to prop up Ra so that he looked a bit more regal with his crook and flail in his hands, though he still had a goofy grin on his face.

Bast, who'd been standing on the deck frozen in shock, fell to her knees. 'My king!'

'Hel-llo-o-o-o-o,' Ra warbled. 'Goooodbye!'

I wasn't sure what he meant, but Bast shot to her feet, suddenly alarmed.

'He's going to rise into the heavens!' she said. 'Walt, Zia, jump off!'

They did, just in time. The sun boat began to glow. Bast

turned to me and called, 'I'll escort him to the other gods! Don't worry. Back soon!' She jumped on board, and the sun boat floated into the sky, turning into a ball of fire. Then it blended with the sunlight and was gone.

'There is your proof,' Amos announced. 'The gods and the House of Life must work together. Sadie and Carter are right. The Serpent will not stay down for long, now that he has broken his chains. Who will join us?'

Several enemy magicians threw down their staffs and wands.

The woman in white, Sarah Jacobi, snarled, 'The other nomes will never recognize your claim, Kane. You are tainted with the power of Set! We'll spread the word. We'll let them know you murdered Desjardins. They'll never follow you!'

She leaped through the portal. The man in blue, Kwai, studied us with contempt, then followed Jacobi. Three others did as well, but we let them leave in peace.

Reverently, Amos took the leopard-skin cape from Carter's hands. 'Poor Michel.'

Everyone gathered around the statue of Thoth. For the first time, I realized how badly the Great Room had been damaged. Walls had been cracked, windows broken, relics smashed and Amos's musical instruments half melted. For the second time in three months, we'd almost destroyed Brooklyn House. That had to be a record. And yet I wanted to give everyone in the room a huge hug.

'You all were brilliant,' I said. 'You destroyed the enemy in seconds! If you can fight so well, how were they able to keep you pinned down all night?'

'But we could barely keep them out!' Felix said. He looked mystified by his own success. 'By dawn, I was, like, completely out of energy.'

The others nodded grimly.

'And I was in a coma,' said a familiar voice. Jaz pushed through the crowd and embraced Carter and me. It was so good to see her that I felt ridiculous I'd ever been jealous of her and Walt.

'You're all right now?' I held her shoulders and studied her face for any sign of sickness, but she looked her usual bubbly self.

'I'm fine!' she said. 'Right at dawn, I woke up feeling great. I guess as soon as you arrived...I don't know. Something happened.'

'The power of Ra,' Amos said. 'When he rose, he brought new life, new energy to all of us. He revitalized our spirit. Without that, we would've failed.'

I turned to Walt, not daring to ask. Was it possible he'd been cured as well? But the look in his eyes told me *that* prayer had not been answered. I suppose he could feel the pain in his limbs after doing so much magic.

Weasels are sick, Ra had often repeated. I wasn't sure why Ra was so interested in Walt's condition, but apparently it was beyond even the sun god's power to fix.

'Amos,' Carter said, interrupting my thoughts, 'what did

Jacobi mean about the other nomes not recognizing your claim?'

I couldn't help it. I sighed and rolled my eyes at him. My brother can be quite thick sometimes.

'What?' he demanded.

'Carter,' I said, 'do you remember our talking about the most powerful magicians in the world? Desjardins was the first. Menshikov was the third. And you were worried about who the second might be?'

'Yeah,' he admitted. 'But –'

'And now that Desjardins is dead, the *second* most powerful magician is the *most* powerful magician. And who do you think that is?'

Slowly, his brain cells must've fired, which is proof that miracles can happen. He turned to stare at Amos.

Our uncle nodded solemnly.

'I'm afraid so, children.' Amos draped the leopard-skin cape around his shoulders. 'Like it or not, the responsibility of leadership falls to me. I am the new Chief Lector.'

24. I Make an Impossible Promise

I DON'T LIKE GOODBYES, and yet I have to tell you about so many of them.

[No, Carter. That wasn't an invitation to take the microphone. Push off!]

By sunset, Brooklyn House was back in order. Alyssa took care of the masonry almost single-handedly with the power of the earth god. Our initiates knew the *hi-nehm* spell well enough to fix most of the other broken things. Khufu showed as much dexterity with rags and cleaning fluid as he did with a basketball, and it's truly amazing how much polishing, dusting and scrubbing one can accomplish by attaching large dusting cloths to the wings of a griffin.

We had several meetings during the day. Philip of Macedonia kept guard in the pool, and our *shabti* army patrolled the grounds, but no one tried to attack – neither the forces of Apophis nor our fellow magicians. I could almost feel the collective shock spreading throughout the three hundred and sixty nomes as they learned the news: Desjardins was dead, Apophis had risen, Ra was back and Amos Kane was the new Chief Lector. Which fact was most alarming to them, I didn't know, but I thought we'd have at least a little breathing space while the other nomes processed the turn of events and decided what to do.

Just before sunset, Carter and I were back on the roof as Zia opened a portal to Cairo for herself and Amos.

With her black hair freshly cut and a new set of beige robes, Zia looked like she hadn't changed a bit since we first spoke with her at the Metropolitan Museum, even though so much had happened since then. And I suppose, technically speaking, that hadn't been her at the museum at all, since it was her *shabti*.

[Yes, I know. Horribly confusing to keep track of all that. You should learn the spell for summoning headache medicine. It works wonders.]

The swirling gate appeared and Zia turned to say her goodbyes.

'I'll accompany Amos – I mean the Chief Lector – to the First Nome,' she promised. 'I'll make sure he is recognized as the leader of the House.'

'They'll oppose you,' I said. 'Be careful.'

Amos smiled. 'We'll be fine. Don't worry.'

He was dressed in his usual dapper style: a gold silk suit that matched his new leopard-skin cape, a porkpie hat and gold beads in his braided hair. At his side sat a leather duffel bag and a saxophone case. I imagined him sitting on the steps of the pharaoh's throne, playing tenor sax – John Coltrane, perhaps – as a new age unfolded in purple light and glowing hieroglyphs popped out of his horn.

'I'll keep in touch,' he promised. 'Besides, you have things well in hand here at Brooklyn House. You don't need a mentor any more.'

I tried to look brave, though I hated his leaving. Just because I was thirteen didn't mean I wanted adult responsibilities. Certainly I didn't want to run the Twenty-first Nome or lead armies into war. But I suppose no one who's put in such a position ever feels ready.

Zia put her hand on Carter's arm. He jumped as if she'd touched him with a defibrillator paddle.

'We'll talk soon,' she said, 'after ... after things have settled. But thank you.'

Carter nodded, though he looked crestfallen. We all knew things wouldn't settle any time soon. There was no guarantee we'd even live long enough to see Zia again.

'Take care of yourself,' Carter said. 'You've got an important role to play.'

Zia glanced at me. A strange sort of understanding passed between us. I think she'd begun to have a suspicion, a deep-seated dread, about what her role might be. I can't say I understood it yet myself, but I shared her disquiet. *Zebras*, Ra had said. He'd woken up talking about zebras.

'If you need us,' I said, 'don't hesitate. I'll pop over and give those First Nome magicians a proper thrashing.'

Amos kissed my forehead. He patted Carter on the shoulder. 'You've both made me proud. You've given me hope for the first time in years.'

I wanted them to stay longer. I wanted to talk with them a bit more. But my experience with Khonsu had taught me not to be greedy about time. It was best to appreciate what you had and not yearn for more.

Amos and Zia stepped through the portal and disappeared.

Just as the sun was setting, an exhausted-looking Bast appeared in the Great Room. Instead of her usual bodysuit, she wore a formal Egyptian dress and heavy jewellery that looked quite uncomfortable.

'I'd forgotten how hard it is riding the sun boat through the sky,' she said, wiping her brow. 'And *hot*. Next time, I'll bring a saucer and a cooler full of milk.'

'Is Ra okay?' I asked.

The cat goddess pursed her lips. 'Well...he's the same. I steered the boat to the throne room of the gods. They're getting a fresh crew ready for tonight's journey. But you should come see him before he leaves.'

'Tonight's journey?' Carter asked. 'Through the Duat? We just brought him back!'

Bast spread her hands. 'What did you expect? You've restarted the ancient cycle. Ra will spend the days in the heavens and the nights on the river. The gods will have to guard him as they used to. Come on; we only have a few minutes.'

I was about to ask how she planned on getting us to the gods' throne room. Bast had repeatedly told us she's no good at summoning portals. Then a door of pure shadow opened in the middle of the air. Anubis stepped through, looking annoyingly gorgeous as usual in his black jeans and leather jacket, with a white cotton shirt that hugged his chest so well I wondered if he was showing off on purpose. I suspected not. He probably rolled out of bed in the morning looking that perfect.

Right… that image did *not* help improve my concentration.

'Hello, Sadie,' he said. [Yes, Carter. He addressed me first, too. What can I say? I'm just *that* important.]

I tried to look cross with him. 'So it's you. Missed you in the underworld while we were gambling our *souls* away.'

'Yes, I'm glad you survived,' he said. 'Your eulogy would've been hard to write.'

'Oh, ha-ha. Where were you?'

Extra sadness crept into his brown eyes. 'A side project,' he said. 'But right now we should hurry.'

He gestured towards the door of darkness. Just to show him I wasn't afraid, I marched through first.

On the other side, we found ourselves in the throne room of the gods. A crowd of assembled deities turned to face us. The palace seemed even grander than the last time we'd been there. The columns were taller, more intricately painted. The polished marble floor swirled with constellation designs, as if we were stepping across the galaxy. The ceiling blazed like one giant fluorescent panel. The dais and throne of Horus had been moved to one side, so it looked more like an observer's chair now, rather than the main event.

In the centre of the room, the sun boat glowed in dry dock scaffolding. Its light-orb crew fluttered about, cleaning the hull and checking the rigging. *Uraei* circled the throne of fire, where Ra sat dressed in the raiment of an Egyptian king, his flail and crook in his lap. His chin was on his chest and he snored loudly.

A muscular young man in leather armour stepped towards us. He had a shaven head and two different-coloured eyes – one silver, one gold.

'Welcome, Carter and Sadie,' Horus said. 'We are honoured.'

His words didn't match his tone, which was stiff and formal. The other gods bowed respectfully to us, but I could feel their hostility simmering just below the surface. They were all dressed in their finest armour and looked quite imposing. Sobek the crocodile god (not my favourite) wore glittering green chain mail and carried a massive staff that flowed with water. Nekhbet looked about as cleaned-up as a vulture can, her feathered black cloak silky and plush. She inclined her head to me, but her eyes told me she still wanted to tear me apart. Babi the baboon god had had his teeth brushed and his fur combed. He was holding a rugby ball – possibly because Gramps had infected him with the obsession.

Khonsu stood in his glittery silver suit, tossing a coin in the air and smiling. I wanted to punch him, but he nodded as if we were old friends. Even Set was there, in his devilish red disco suit, leaning against a column at the back of the crowd, holding his black iron staff. I remembered that he'd promised not to kill me only until we freed Ra, but at the moment he seemed relaxed. He tipped his hat and grinned at me as if enjoying my discomfort.

Thoth the knowledge god was the only one who hadn't dressed up. He wore his usual jeans and lab coat covered with scribbles. He studied me with his strange kaleidoscope eyes and I got the feeling he was the only one in the room who actually pitied my discomfort.

Isis stepped forward. Her long black hair was braided down behind the shoulders of her gossamer dress. Her rainbow wings shimmered behind her. She bowed to me formally, but I could feel the waves of cold coming off her.

Horus turned to the assembled gods. I realized he was no longer wearing the pharaoh's crown.

'Behold!' he told the crowd. 'Carter and Sadie Kane, who awakened our king! Let there be no doubt: Apophis the enemy has risen. We must unite behind Ra.'

Ra muttered in his sleep, 'Fish, cookie, weasel,' then went back to snoring.

Horus cleared his throat. 'I pledge my loyalty! I expect you all to do the same. I will protect Ra's boat as we pass through the Duat tonight. Each of you shall take turns with this duty until the sun god is...fully recovered.'

He sounded absolutely unconvinced this would ever happen.

'We will find a way to defeat Apophis!' he said. 'Now, celebrate the return of Ra! I embrace Carter Kane as a brother.'

Music began to play, echoing through the halls. Ra, still on his throne on his boat, woke up and started clapping. He grinned as gods swirled around him, some in human form, some dissolving into wisps of cloud, flame, or light.

Isis took my hands. 'I hope you know what you're doing, Sadie,' she said in a frigid voice. 'Our greatest enemy rises and you have dethroned my son and made a senile god our leader.'

'Give it a chance,' I said, though my ankles felt like they were turning to butter.

Horus clasped Carter's shoulders. His words weren't any friendlier.

'I *am* your ally, Carter,' Horus promised. 'I will lend you my strength whenever you ask. You will revive the path of my magic in the House of Life and we will fight together to destroy the Serpent. But make no mistake: you have cost me a throne. If your choice costs us the war, I swear my last act before Apophis swallows me will be to crush you like a gnat. And if it comes to pass that we win this war without Ra's help, if you have disgraced me for nothing, I swear that the death of Cleopatra and the curse of Akhenaton will look like nothing compared to the wrath I will visit on you and your family for all time. Do you understand?'

To Carter's credit, he held up under the gaze of the war god.

'Just do your part,' Carter said.

Horus laughed for the audience as if he and Carter had just shared a good joke. 'Go now, Carter. See what your victory has cost. Let us hope all your allies do not share such a fate.'

Horus turned his back on us and joined the celebration. Isis smiled at me one last time and dissolved into a sparkling rainbow.

Bast stood at my side, holding her tongue, but she looked as if she wanted to shred Horus like a scratching post.

Anubis looked embarrassed. 'I'm sorry, Sadie. The gods can be –'

'Ungrateful?' I asked. 'Infuriating?'

His face flushed. I supposed he thought I was referring to him.

'We can be slow to realize what is important,' he said at last. 'Sometimes, it takes us a while to appreciate something new, something that might change us for the better.'

He fixed me with those warm eyes and I wanted to melt into a puddle.

'We should go,' Bast interrupted. 'One more stop, if you're up for it.'

'The cost of victory,' Carter remembered. 'Bes? Is he alive?'

Bast sighed. 'Difficult question. This way.'

The last place I wanted to see again was Sunny Acres.

Nothing much had changed in the nursing home. No renewing sunlight had helped the senile gods. They were still wheeling their IV poles around, banging into walls, singing ancient hymns as they searched in vain for temples that no longer existed.

A new patient had joined them. Bes sat in a hospital gown in a wicker chair, gazing out of the window at the Lake of Fire.

Tawaret knelt at his side, her tiny hippo eyes red from crying. She was trying to get him to drink from a glass.

Water dribbled down his chin. He gazed blankly at the fiery waterfall in the distance, his craggy face awash in red light. His curly hair was newly combed and he wore a fresh blue Hawaiian shirt and shorts, so he looked quite comfortable. But his brow was furrowed. His fingers gripped the armrests, as if he knew he should remember something, but couldn't.

437

'That's all right, Bes.' Tawaret's voice quivered as she dabbed a napkin under his chin. 'We'll work on it. I'll take care of you.'

Then she noticed us. Her expression hardened. For a kindly goddess of childbirth, Tawaret could look quite scary when she wanted to.

She patted the dwarf god's knee. 'I'll be right back, dear Bes.'

She stood, which was quite an accomplishment with her swollen belly and steered us away from his chair. 'How dare you come here! As if you haven't done enough!'

I was about to break into tears and apologize when I realized her anger wasn't aimed at Carter or me. She was glaring at Bast.

'Tawaret…' Bast turned up her palms. 'I didn't want this. He was my friend.'

'He was one of your cat toys!' Tawaret shouted so loudly, a few of the patients started crying. 'You're as selfish as *all* your kind, Bast. You used him and discarded him. You *knew* he loved you and took advantage of it. You played with him like a mouse under your paw.'

'That's not fair,' Bast murmured, but her hair started to puff up as it does when she's scared. I couldn't blame her. There's almost nothing more frightening than an enraged hippo.

Tawaret stomped her foot so hard, her high heel broke. 'Bes deserved better than this. He deserved better than *you*. He had a good heart. I – I never forgot him!'

I sensed a very violent, one-sided cat–hippo fight about to begin. I don't know if I spoke up to save Bast, or to spare the traumatized patients, or to assuage my own guilt, but I stepped between the goddesses. 'We'll fix this,' I blurted out. 'Tawaret, I swear on my life. We will find a way to heal Bes.'

She looked at me and the anger drained from her eyes until there was nothing left but pity. 'Child, oh child . . . I know you mean well. But don't give me false hope. I've lived with false hopes too long. Go – see him if you must. See what's happened to the best dwarf in the world. Then leave us alone. Don't promise me what can't happen.'

She turned and hobbled on her broken shoe to the nurses' desk. Bast lowered her head. She wore a very uncatlike expression: shame.

'I'll wait here,' she announced.

I could tell that was her final answer, so Carter and I approached Bes by ourselves.

The dwarf god hadn't moved. He sat in his wicker chair, his mouth slightly open, his eyes fixed on the Lake of Fire.

'Bes.' I put my hand on his arm. 'Can you hear me?'

He didn't answer, of course. He wore a bracelet on his wrist with his name written in hieroglyphs, lovingly decorated, probably by Tawaret herself.

'I'm so sorry,' I said. 'We'll get your *ren* back. We'll find a way to heal you. Won't we, Carter?'

'Yeah.' He cleared his throat and I can assure you he was *not* acting very macho at that moment. 'Yeah, I swear it, Bes. If it's . . .'

He was probably going to say *if it's the last thing we do,* but he wisely decided against it. Given the impending war with Apophis, it was best not to think about how soon our lives might end.

I leaned down and kissed Bes's forehead. I remembered how we'd met at Waterloo Station, when he'd chauffeured Liz and Emma and me to safety. I remembered how he'd scared away Nekhbet and Babi in his ridiculous Speedo. I thought about the silly chocolate Lenin head he'd bought in St Petersburg and how he'd pulled Walt and me to safety from the portal at Red Sands. I couldn't think of him as *small*. He had an enormous, colourful, ludicrous, wonderful personality – and it seemed impossible that it was gone forever. He'd given his immortal life to buy us one extra hour.

I couldn't help sobbing. Finally Carter had to pull me away. I don't remember how we got back home, but I remember feeling as if we were falling rather than ascending – as if the mortal world had become a deeper and sadder place than anywhere in the Duat.

That evening I sat alone on my bed with the windows open. The first night of spring had turned surprisingly warm and pleasant. Lights glittered along the riverfront. The neighbourhood bagel factory filled the air with the scent of baking bread. I was listening to my SAD playlist and wondering how it was possible that my birthday had been only a few days ago.

The world had changed. The sun god had returned. Apophis was free from his cage and, although he'd been banished to some deep part of the abyss, he'd be working his way back very quickly. War was coming. We had so much work to do. Yet I was sitting here, listening to the same songs as before, staring at my poster of Anubis and feeling helplessly conflicted about something as trivial and infuriating as . . . yes, you guessed it. *Boys.*

There was a knock at the door.

'Come in,' I said without much enthusiasm. I assumed it was Carter. We often chatted at the end of the day, just to debrief. Instead, it was Walt, and suddenly I was very aware that I was wearing a ratty old T-shirt and pyjama bottoms. My hair no doubt looked as horrible as Nekhbet's. Carter seeing me this way wouldn't be a problem. But Walt? Bad.

'What are you doing here?' I yelped, a bit too loudly.

He blinked, obviously surprised by my lack of hospitality. 'Sorry, I'll go.'

'No! I mean . . . that's all right. You just surprised me. And – you know . . . we have rules about boys being in the girls' rooms without, *um*, supervision.'

I realize that sounded terribly stodgy of me, almost Carteresque. But I was nervous.

Walt folded his arms. They were very nice arms. He was wearing his basketball jersey and running shorts, his usual collection of amulets round his neck. He looked so healthy, so athletic, it was difficult to believe he was dying of an ancient curse.

'Well, you're the instructor,' he said. 'Can you supervise me?'

No doubt I was blushing horribly. 'Right. I suppose if you leave the door ajar . . . *Er*, what brings you here?'

He leaned against the closet door. With some horror, I realized it was still open, revealing my poster of Anubis.

'There's so much going on,' Walt said. 'You've got enough to worry about. I don't want you worrying about me as well.'

'Too late,' I admitted.

He nodded, as if he shared my frustration. 'That day in the desert, at Bahariya... would you think I'm crazy if I tell you that was the best day of my life?'

My heart fluttered, but I tried to stay calm. 'Well, Egyptian public transportation, roadside bandits, smelly camels, psychotic Roman mummies and possessed date farmers... Gosh, it was quite a day.'

'And you,' he said.

'Yes, well... I suppose I belong in that list of catastrophes.'

'That's not what I meant.'

I was feeling like quite a bad supervisor – nervous and confused, and having very un-supervisory thoughts. My eyes strayed to the closet door. Walt noticed.

'Oh.' He pointed to Anubis. 'You want me to close this?'

'Yes,' I said. 'No. Possibly. I mean, it doesn't matter. Well, not that it *doesn't* matter, but –'

Walt laughed as if my discomfort didn't bother him at all. 'Sadie, look. I just wanted to say, whatever happens, I'm glad I met you. I'm glad I came to Brooklyn. Jaz is working on a cure for me. Maybe she'll find something, but either way... it's okay.'

'It's *not* okay!' I think my anger surprised me more than it did him. 'Walt, you're dying of a cruddy curse. And – and I had Menshikov *right there*, ready to tell me the cure, and... I failed you. Like I failed Bes. I didn't even bring back Ra properly.'

I was furious with myself for crying, but I couldn't help it. Walt came over and sat next to me. He didn't try to put his arm round me, which was just as well. I was already confused enough.

'You didn't fail me,' he said. 'You didn't fail anybody. You did what was right, and that takes sacrifice.'

'Not you,' I said. 'I don't want you to die.'

His smile made me feel as if the world had been reduced to just two people.

'Ra's return may not have cured me,' he said, 'but it still gave me new hope. You're amazing, Sadie. One way or another, we're going to make this work. I'm not leaving you.'

That sounded so good, so excellent and so impossible. 'How can you promise that?'

He eyes drifted to the picture of Anubis, then back to me. 'Just try not to worry about me. We have to concentrate on defeating Apophis.'

'Any idea how?'

He gestured towards my bedside table, where my beaten-up old tape recorder sat – a gift from my grandparents ages ago.

'Tell people what really happened,' he said. 'Don't let Jacobi and the others spread lies about your family. I came to Brooklyn because I got your first message – the recording about the Red Pyramid, the *djed* amulet. You asked for help and we answered. It's time to ask for help again.'

'But how many magicians did we really reach the first time – twenty?'

'Hey, we did pretty well last night.' Walt held my eyes. I thought he might kiss me, but something made us both hesitate – a sense that it would only make things more uncertain, more fragile. 'Send out another tape, Sadie. Just tell the truth. When you talk...' He shrugged and then stood to leave. 'Well, you're pretty hard to ignore.'

A few moments after he left, Carter came in, a book tucked under his arm. He found me listening to my sad music, staring at the tape recorder on the dresser.

'Was that Walt coming out of your room?' he asked. A little brotherly protectiveness crept into his voice. 'What's up?'

'Oh, just...' My eyes fixed on the book he was carrying. It was a tattered old textbook and I wondered if he meant to assign me some sort of homework. But the cover looked *so* familiar: the diamond design, the multicoloured foil letters. 'What is that?'

Carter sat next to me. Nervously, he offered me the book. 'It's, *um*...not a gold necklace. Or even a magic knife. But I told you I had a birthday present for you. This – this is it.'

I ran my fingers over the title: *Blackley's Survey of the Sciences for First-Year College, Twelfth Edition*. Then I opened the book. On the inside cover, a name was written in lovely cursive: *Ruby Kane.*

It was Mum's college textbook – the same one she used to read to us from at bedtime. The very same copy.

I blinked back tears. 'How did you –'

'The retrieval *shabti* in the library,' Carter said. 'They can find any book. I know it's...kind of a lame present. It didn't cost me anything and I didn't make it, but –'

'Shut up, you idiot!' I flung my arms around him. 'It's an amazing birthday present. And you're an amazing brother!'

[Fine, Carter. There it is, recorded for all time. Just don't get a big head. I spoke in a moment of weakness.]

We turned the pages, smiling at the crayon moustache Carter had drawn on Isaac Newton and the outdated diagrams of the solar system. We found an old food stain that was probably my apple sauce. I *loved* apple sauce. We ran our hands over the margin notes done in Mum's beautiful cursive.

I felt closer to my mother just holding the book and amazed by Carter's thoughtfulness. Even though I'd learned his secret name and supposed I knew everything about him, the boy had still managed to surprise me.

'So, what were saying about Walt?' he asked. 'What's going on?'

Reluctantly, I closed *Blackley's Survey of the Sciences*. And yes, that's probably the only time in my life I'd ever closed a textbook with reluctance. I rose and set the book on my dresser. Then I picked up my old cassette recorder.

'We have work to do,' I told Carter. I tossed him the microphone.

So now you know what really happened on the equinox, how the old Chief Lector died and how Amos took his place. Desjardins sacrificed his life to buy us time, but Apophis is quickly working his way out of the abyss. We may have weeks, if we're lucky. Days, if we're not.

Amos is trying to assert himself as the leader of the House of Life, but it's not going to be easy. Some nomes are in rebellion. Many believe the Kanes have taken over by force.

We're sending out this tape to set the record straight.

We don't have all the answers yet. We don't know when or where Apophis will strike. We don't know how to heal Ra, or Bes, or even Walt. We don't know what role Zia will play, or if the gods can be trusted to help us. Most important, I am completely torn between two amazing guys – one who's dying and another who's the god of death. What sort of choice is that, I ask you?

[Right, sorry...getting off track again.]

The point is, wherever you are, whatever type of magic you practise, we need your help. Unless we unite and learn the path of the gods quickly, we don't stand a chance.

I hope Walt is right and you'll find me hard to ignore, because the clock is ticking. We'll keep a room ready for you at Brooklyn House.

AUTHOR'S NOTE

Before publishing such an alarming transcript, I felt compelled to do some fact-checking on Sadie and Carter's story. I wish I could tell you they had made all this up. Unfortunately, it appears that much of what they have reported is based on fact.

The Egyptian relics and locations they mention in America, England, Russia and Egypt do exist. Prince Menshikov's Palace in St Petersburg is real, and the story of the dwarf wedding is true, though I can find no mention that one of the dwarves might have been a god, or that the prince had a grandson named Vladimir.

All the Egyptian gods and monsters Carter and Sadie met are attested to in ancient sources. Many different accounts survive of Ra's nightly journey through the Duat and, while the stories vary greatly, Carter and Sadie's account closely fits what we know from Egyptian mythology.

In short, I believe they might be telling the truth. Their call for help is genuine. Should further audio recordings fall into my hands, I will relay the information, but, if Apophis truly is rising, there may no opportunity. For the sake of the entire world, I hope I'm wrong.

GLOSSARY

Commands used by Carter and Sadie

A'max 'Burn'

Ha-di 'Destroy'

Ha-tep 'Be at peace'

Heh-sieh 'Turn back'

Heqat Summons a staff

Hi-nehm 'Join'

L'mun 'Hide'

N'dah 'Protect'

Sa-per 'Miss'

W'peh 'Open'

Other Egyptian Terms

Aaru the Egyptian afterlife, paradise

Aten the sun (the physical object, not the god)

Ba soul

Barque the pharaoh's boat

Bau an evil spirit

Duat magical realm

Hieroglyphics the writing system of Ancient Egypt, which used symbols or pictures to denote objects, concepts or sounds

Khopesh a sword with a hook-shaped blade

Ma'at order of the universe

Menhed the scribe's palette

Netjeri blade a knife made from meteoric iron for the opening of the mouth in a ceremony

Pharaoh a ruler of Ancient Egypt

Ren name, identity

Sarcophagus a stone coffin, often decorated with sculpture and inscriptions

Sau a charm maker

Scarab beetle

Shabti a magical figurine made out of clay

Shen eternal

Souk open air market

Stele limestone grave marker

Tjesu heru a snake with two heads – one on its tail – and dragon legs

Tyet the symbol of Isis

Was power

EGYPTIAN GODS AND GODDESSES MENTIONED IN *THE THRONE OF FIRE*

Anubis the god of funerals and death
Apophis the god of chaos
Babi the baboon god
Bast the cat goddess
Bes the dwarf god
Geb the earth god
Heket the frog goddess
Horus the war god, son of Isis and Osiris
Isis the goddess of magic, wife of her brother Osiris and
    mother of Horus
Khepri the scarab god, Ra's aspect in the morning
Khnum the ram-headed god, Ra's aspect at sunset in the
    underworld
Khonsu the moon god
Mekhit minor lion goddess, married to Onuris
Nekhbet the vulture goddess
Nephthys the river goddess
Nut the sky goddess
Osiris the god of the underworld, husband of his sister Isis
    and father of Horus

Ptah the god of craftsmen

Ra the sun god, the god of order. Also known as Amun-Ra.

Sekhmet the lion goddess

Set the god of evil

Shu the air god

Sobek the crocodile god

Tawaret the hippo goddess

Thoth the god of knowledge